William Tooke, Jean-Henri Castéra

The Life of Catharine II, Empress of Russia - An Enlarged Translation

from the French

Vol. II

William Tooke, Jean-Henri Castéra

The Life of Catharine II, Empress of Russia - An Enlarged Translation from the French
Vol. II

ISBN/EAN: 9783337273927

Printed in Europe, USA, Canada, Australia, Japan

Cover: Foto ©Raphael Reischuk / pixelio.de

More available books at **www.hansebooks.com**

THE

L I F E

OF

CATHARINE II.

EMPRESS OF RUSSIA,

AN ENLARGED TRANSLATION FROM
THE FRENCH.

WITH SEVEN PORTRAITS ELEGANTLY ENGRAVED,
AND A CORRECT MAP OF THE RUSSIAN EMPIRE.

Nihil compositum miraculi causâ, verùm audita scriptaque
senioribus tradam. TACIT. Ann. lib. xi.

IN THREE VOLUMES.

VOL. II.

LONDON:

PRINTED FOR T. N. LONGMAN, PATERNOSTER-ROW;
AND J. DEBRETT, PICCADILLY.

1798.

CONTENTS

OF THE

SECOND VOLUME.

CHAP.

CHAP. VIII.

APPENDIX to the SECOND VOLUME.

15

LIFE

LIFE

OF THE

EMPRESS CATHARINE II.

CHAP. IV.

State of Poland from the time of the kings of the firſt race to the death of Auguſtus III. —Election of prince Poniatofsky.—Freſh conſpiracy at St. Peterſburg.—Journey of the empreſs into Livonia.—Aſſaſſination of prince Ivan in the caſtle of Schluſſelburg.—Puniſhment of Mirovitch, and other events of 1763, 1764, &c.

POLAND, which had ſometimes acted ſo conſpicuous a part in the politics of Europe, and which, from the extent of its territory, the fertility of its ſoil, the high ſpirit and courage of its inhabitants, ſeemed formed for acquiring a ſtill greater preponderance, has loſt, by the defects

of its government, a part of the advantages it
had received from nature.

This kingdom had long been under the influence of Ruffia; and that influence had become
the more powerful under Catharine, as, independently of the army of Romantzoff, encamped
on the banks of the Viftula, 50,000 men had
taken up their quarters in Livonia, Efthonia,
and Courland. Auguftus III. declining in his
health, as well from the irregularities of his life
as from the vexation occafioned him by the in-
vafion of Saxony, was now verging faft to
the grave.   All fuch as had formed pretenfions
to the fucceffion, accordingly began to examine
their ftrength; and the court of Peterfburg was
the centre of their intrigues.   The afpiring
mind of Catharine was flattered at feeing herfelf
the arbiter of thefe ambitious rivals.   But, while
fhe thought proper to foment their divifions and
to encourage their hopes, fhe was fecretly decided in her choice.   She was in want of a king,
whofe weaknefs and fervility fhe knew: fhe
made choice of Poniatofsky.

It will not be ufelefs here to caft an eye upon
the ftate of that rich and unhappy country,
which we fhall fee more than once exciting the
ambition of Catharine, and which fhe long continued

tinued to harafs, the better to prepare it for being ufurped.

The hiftory of Poland, like that of almoft all the other countries of Europe, reaches back to an æra extremely remote, and filled with uncertainty. All that we know with tolerable precifion is, that Poland at firft was governed by a race of kings *, whofe power was nearly abfolute. To this race fucceeded the Piafts, who are thought to have been elective, but who, for feveral generations, preferved the crown in their family. The kingdom was frequently difturbed by the pretenfions of the magnats, who combined againft the monarch, and oppofed to him a power which balanced that of the crown.

One of the laft kings of the race of the Piafts, Cafimir III. furnamed the great, or the father of the peafantry, repreffed the dangerous and always turbulent authority of the grandees, by conferring a variety of privileges on the inferior nobleffe, and by that means alarming them with a dangerous rivalfhip. But that prince, however addicted to juftice, and how great foever his concern in behalf of the unhappy peafants, was never able to mitigate the barbarous lot to which they are doomed in Poland.

---

* The race of Lefko.

Lewis

Lewis of Hungary, nephew and fucceffor of Cafimir, was not in a capacity to benefit by the advantages that monarch had acquired, becaufe, on beftowing on him the crown, the nobility obliged him to fubfcribe to burdenfome conditions. On the death of Lewis, without leaving a male heir, that turbulent nobility made an offer of the throne to Ladiflaus Yagellon, duke of Lithuania, and impofed on him the fame conditions as had been accepted by Lewis. One of thefe conditions was, not to raife fubfidies without the confent of the diets. His fucceffors were, equally with him, forced to be continually making new facrifices for obtaining the impofts that were neceffary to their government; and Sigifmond Auguftus was at length induced to confent *, that at his death the crown fhould become abfolutely elective. This prince, who had no fon, was without difficulty brought to agree to make a declaration, by which he purchafed his repofe. In a fhort time afterwards a charter was framed †, which became the bafis and guarantee of that privilege. The four principal articles of the charter were :

* In the year 1550.

† Known under the name of *Paßa conventa*.

1. That

1. That the crown fhould be elective; and that the king fhould never appoint a fucceffor during his lifetime.

2. That general diets fhould be affembled every two years.

3. That every nobleman of Poland fhould have the right of voting at the election of a king.

4. That if the king fhall prefume to infringe the laws, and to difavow the privileges of the nation*, the fubjects fhall be abfolved from their oath of allegiance.

The privileges fecured by this charter were ftill farther extended; and all the fucceffors of Sigifmond Auguftus down to Staniflaus Poniatofsky inclufively, were only elected upon their fwearing to maintain them. Could lefs then be expected from princes who received the crown as a matter of favour, and who, if they had not accepted it on thefe conditions, would have been obliged to forego it in favour of a lefs fcrupulous competitor? The nobles, the more they increafed their power, abufed it the more. Not contented with freely granting their fuffrages, they fold them. Henry de Valois was the firft who purchafed, by means of promifes and gold,

---

* That is to fay, of the nobles; for the reft is counted for nothing.

the

the throne of the Yagellons; means which have fince only yielded to the terror of arms.

On every acceffion to the throne the nobility ufurped fome additional privilege. During the reign of John Cafimir, the *liberum veto* was treated. This was a right given to each nobleman fingly to put a ftop to the deliberation of a whole diet, and to diffolve it by the fole act of his will; a right which has been one of the principal fources of the troubles, the anarchy, and the total deftruction of Poland.

But by fuch an extent of power as every nobleman had, we may form a judgment of that enjoyed by the palatines*, the great officers, and, in general, all the wealthy Poles. Some-

---

* In Poland are 32 palatines, who are properly governors of provinces, 3 caftellans, and 1 ftaroft. Though the quality of the two latter be inferior to that of a palatine, yet there are four of them who poffefs the firft ranks amongft the temporal nobles, the caftellan of Cracow being the firft of all. The office of a palatine is to lead the troops of his palatinate to the army; to prefide in the affemblies of the nobility in his province; to fet a price upon merchandizes and commodities; to take care that the weights and meafures be not altered; and to judge and defend the jews. He has a vice-palatine under him, who muft take an oath to him, and who ought to have an eftate in land, which they call *poffeffionatus*. To thefe follow the order of nobility, who are alone capable of poffeffing all the offices and lands in the duchy and kingdom.

times

times they raifed regiments independent on the authority of the king; at other times they formed confederacies, which, under pretence of defending the laws, fowed fedition and revolt, and in the facred name of liberty exercifed the abfurdeft tyranny.

It is the blind ambition of the polifh nobles that has been for 300 years gradually confummating the ruin of their country. That nation, naturally brave, which has often conquered the Ottomans, and which has given law to Pruffia and to Ruffia, has not been able, fince thefe diffentions, to refift any of the armies by which it has been attacked. The forces of the kings of Sweden, Charles Guftavus and Charles XII. alternately found it an eafy prey; and from the moment that the Ruffians were able to oppofe difciplined troops to its brilliant and licentious pofpolite, they have found themfelves in a capacity to dictate laws to the nation.

Under fuch circumftances the Poles called themfelves free. But what fort of a freedom was that they enjoyed, even while they were exercifing the boafted right of electing their kings? The age in which we live has produced examples to the contrary; and one * of the men

* Sarnifky.

who

who beſt underſtood their hiſtory, has defied
them to ſhew but two inſtances of a free election.

There is ſcarcely a great potentate in Europe
that has not had more or leſs influence in theſe
elections : but for upwards of fifty years Ruſſia
has been the only power by which they have been
actually directed.

Such was the ſituation of Poland when the
death of Auguſtus III. * revived the cabals of
the pretenders to the throne, and furniſhed Catharine the means of diſplaying her political
talents with the utmoſt effect.　That ſovereign,
whom the courts of Vienna and Verſailles were
in hopes of detaching from Pruſſia, began their
operations by artfully obtaining from thoſe
courts an aſſurance that they would not interfere
in the affairs of Poland.　In 1764, the marquis
de Paulmy, ambaſſador from France at Warſaw,
declared † at the diet, that Lewis XV. would
have nothing to do in the election of the new
king ; and ſhortly after the count de Mercy
held the ſame language on the part of Maria
Thereſa.

The promiſe of theſe two courts, however,
was not ſufficient for Catharine.　She was deſi-

* The 5th of October, 1763.　　† The 16th of March.

rous

rous of fome, affurance that fhe fhould not be
thwarted by that of Berlin : in this fhe fucceeded.
Frederic had long been foliciting her to fign a
treaty of defenfive alliance ; and fhe coveted it
the more as fhe had employed fo much art in
inducing him to defire it. Imagining that the
delays which fhe made to the conclufion of this
bufinefs, arofe only from the repugnance fhe
had to a minifter * who had been the friend of
her hufband, the pruffian monarch made choice
of a plenipotentiary who fhould neceffarily be
more agreeable to that princefs : he fent to
St. Peterfburg the count of Solms, who had
married a princefs of Anhalt-Bernburg, coufin-
german to Catharine. The count de Solms
was extremely well received by the emprefs,
with whom he fhortly after, in the name of the
king of Pruffia, concluded a treaty, fubjoined
to which was the fecret article as follows :

" It being for the intereft of his majefty the king of
" Pruffia and of her majefty the emprefs of all the Ruffias,
" to exert their utmoft care and all their efforts for main-
" taining the republic of Poland in its ftate of free election,
" and that it fhould not be permitted to any one to render
" the faid kingdom hereditary in his family, or to make
" himfelf abfolute therein ; his majefty the king of Pruffia
" and her imperial majefty have promifed and mutually en-
" gage themfelves, in the moft folemn manner, by this

* The baron de Goltz.

" fecret

" secret article, not only not to permit any one, whoever
" he be, to attempt to divest the republic of its right of
" free election, to render the kingdom hereditary, or to
" make himself absolute therein, in all cases whenever such
" attempt should be made; but also to prevent and to frus-
" trate, by all possible means, and in common consent, the
" views and designs that have a tendency to that end, as
" soon as they shall be discovered, and even, in case of ne-
" cessity, to recur to the force of arms, to defend the re-
" public from the overthrow of its constitution and its
" fundamental laws.

" The present secret article shall have the same force and
" vigour as if it had been inserted word for word in the
" principal treaty of defensive alliance signed this day, and
" shall be ratified at the same time.

" In virtue whereof two similar copies of it have been
" made, which we, the ministers plenipotentiary of his
" majesty the king of Prussia, and of her majesty the em-
" press of all the Russias, authorized to that purpose, have
" signed and sealed with the seal of our arms.

" Done at St. Petersburg, the 11th of April (the
" 31st of March O. S.) 1764.

" C. DE SOLMS. PANIN. GALLITZIN."

The new sovereign of Saxony, who flattered
himself with the prospect of inheriting the throne
of Augustus III. as he had inherited his elector-
ate, addressed himself to the empress, to prevail
upon her to approve his pretensions: but she
made no hesitation to deprive him of all hope.
She wrote to him, " That she advised him, as
" a true friend, not to expose his interests in
                                                " an

" an affair which in the issue could not answer
" his expectations."

Conscious of her power in Poland, Catharine
dismissed, one after another, the candidates who
were not agreeable to her, without, however,
giving any intimation as yet concerning the
person whom she intended to favour. The
greater number of the Poles were for electing
a Piast, a descendant of their ancient kings.
Catharine also for some time appeared to be of
the same sentiment. But all at once it was heard
with amazement at Warsaw, that it was count
Poniatofsky whom that monarch had destined
to the throne. This choice excited an almost
universal discontent and violent murmurs. The
polish magnats, incensed at the prospect of
being governed by a young man* of a birth not
very illustrious, and whose elevation was neither
justified by shining actions nor extraordinary
virtues, reciprocally interrogated one another,
what services count Poniatofsky had rendered
the republic, for obtaining so glorious a reward?

Count Poniatofsky was endowed with those
qualities which are more adapted to conciliate
the friendship of particular persons, than to fit
him for swaying a sceptre. Tall, well-made, of
a figure at once commanding and agreeable, he

---

* He was at that time 32 years of age.

spoke

ſpoke and wrote with fluency the ſeven principal
languages of Europe, and in a graceful diction :
but he poſſeſſed only a ſlight knowledge of
affairs.   His eloquence was vague and deſultory,
his preſumption too apparent.   Rather weak
than gentle, rather prodigal than generous, he
might eaſily miſlead women, and dazzle a thought-
leſs multitude, but not perſuade men of cultivated
minds.   He was doubtleſs fitter to ſubmit to
be governed than to govern himſelf.   Nevertheleſs, ſupported by the influence and arms
of Ruſſia, and having no obſtacle to fear on
the part of other powers, his triumph was not
long in ſuſpenſe.   The conſequence of Catharine
was involved in this triumph.   That princeſs
ſet ſo great a value on ſeeing the crown of
the Sarmates on the brow of her former favourite, that ſhe wrote without delay to count
Kayſerling, her ambaſſador at Warſaw, to employ every means in behalf of Poniatofsky.
One of her letters was intercepted, and contained
the following words :—" Mon cher comte, ſou-
" venez-vous de mon candidat. Je vous écris
" ceci deux heures après minuit : jugez ſi la
" choſe m'eſt indifférente * !"

* " My dear count, remember my candidate.   I write
" this to you at two o'clock in the morning ; judge whether
" I am indifferent about the affair !"

Count

Count Kayſerling was careful not to diſobey. Neither he nor the ruſſian generals neglected any thing for ſecuring the choice which their ſovereign deſired. The dyetines were already convoked. That of Warſaw elected Poniatoſsky by an unanimous ſuffrage: but whatever pains had been taken for bringing thoſe of the provinces to the ſame favourable diſpoſition, his ſuccefs was not the ſame. His competitors obtained a majority of voices in ſome, and at leaſt an equal number with his in the others.

At the aſſembling of the diet of convocation, the ruſſian troops entered Warſaw, under pretence of preſerving liberty and order.

Crowds of foreigners at the ſame time poured into that city, all ready to unite at the very firſt ſignal. Count Branichky, grand general of the crown, and prince Radzivil, took arms in order to prevent the Ruſſians from extorting the ſuffrages: but what could they do againſt foreign armies who were maſters of the country; and againſt a part of their countrymen diſpoſed to join thoſe armies? It is a difficult matter to form an adequate idea of the tumult that began to prevail in the diet of Warſaw. Count Malakoſsky, venerable for his great age and his virtues, had been appointed its marſhal. He endeavoured in vain to reduce it to order, and

to

to clear it of ftrangers. He was anfwered by furious vociferations, and fabres were drawn. The eloquent Mokranofsky, nuntio of Cracow, ran the rifk of his life under the fwords of the ruffian officers, who endeavoured to pierce him from the galleries of the fpeakers. He at firft thought of ftanding on his defence; but, prefently returning his fabre into the fheath, and expofing his breaft:—" If you muft needs have " a victim," faid he to the Ruffians, " I ftand " here before you. But at leaft I fhall die " free, as I have hitherto lived."—It is not improbable that he would have fallen a prey to their fury, had not prince Adam Chartorinfky had the generous courage to throw himfelf in the way, and to fhield him with his body. Thus, in the firft fittings of the diet nothing paffed but injurious fpeeches and tumultuous quarrels.

Some one at Peterfburg who knew what dif-pleafure the election of Poniatofsky would oc-cafion to the Poles, and, wanting to vilify him in the eyes of Catharine, had the boldnefs to tell that monarch, that he whofe intereft fhe efpoufed feemed the lefs proper to fill the throne of Poland, as his grandfather had been intendant of a little eftate belonging to the princes Lubo-mirfky.—" Though he had been fo himfelf," re-

turned

turned she, somewhat nettled, " I will have him " to be king, and he shall be."

Holding this language, Catharine was under no apprehensions of being deceived. Independently of the troops which she had already in Poland, she caused a body of 12,000 men to enter Lithuania, and fresh reinforcements were advancing towards Kief. Her ambassador ruled at Warsaw, and her armies, if the expression may be allowed, compressed the republic.

Several of the provinces now heavily accused their nuncios of having badly corresponded with their desires in submitting to the influence of the court of Petersburg. They did not confine themselves to murmurs. They had recourse to arms; they formed into different confederacies; but these movements were attended by no consequences. The Russians threatened: the malcontents were presently silenced.

At length the diet of election was opened; held, according to custom, in the plain of Vola, at the distance of about three miles from Warsaw. This diet began by a solemn mass, and a sermon*. Count Kayserling, ambassador from

---

* The preacher took his text from these words: Eligite ex vobis meliorem, qui vobis placuerit, et posuite eum super solium. 2 Kings, x. 3.

Russia,

Ruſſia, being at that time indiſpoſed, could not repair to Vola, but ſent to the diet a letter, addreſſed to him by the empreſs, recommending to him count Poniatoſsky in the moſt preſſing terms.

The other party, however, had not been idle, either during the election of the nuncios or repreſentatives, who, in the name of the body of the nobility, were to chuſe a king, nor at the firſt aſſembling of the ſtates *. In the former caſe great tumults were raiſed, but they ſubſiſted not long. In the latter 22 ſenators entered a proteſt againſt the proceedings of the diet, the principal reaſons of which were grounded on the preſence and interference of the foreign troops. Forty-five nuncios ſigned an act of adheſion to this proteſt.

Count Branichky, who was at the head of theſe proteſters, retired from the diet. But that aſſembly, ſoon after its opening, took its revenge. An order was made for diveſting him of the poſt of crown general. Branichky denied their power; drew together. into one body a great part of that army of which they had attempted to deprive him, but which ſtill faithfully adhered to him; augmented it by levies; and prepared

* May 7, 1764.

to maintain himfelf by force; poffeffed, as it fhould feem, by a fpirit of defpair and fury, having no power in the leaft adequate to the height of his attempt. Prince Radzivil, on his part, was alfo up in arms, and with the fame obftinacy, and no greater ftrength, ftruggled againft the election.

The ambaffadors of France, Spain, and the empire, finding their political intrigues of no more avail towards obftructing the election, than the hoftile attempts of prince Radzivil and count Branichky were likely to be, retired from the diet and left Poland, declaring that they had not been fent to a party, but to the whole republic*.

An action at length happened † between prince Radzivil and the ruffian troops, wherein the Poles, having fought a long time with their ufual irregular bravery, were as ufual defeated by the Ruffians.

The fpirit of Poland appeared ftrongly in all the circumftances of this action. The princefs Radzivil, but newly married, and a fifter of that prince, both of them young and beautiful, fought on horfeback with fabres, and encouraged the foldiery both by their words and their example.

* June the 7th, 1764.   † On the 3d of July.

Branichky was alfo defeated by a body of Ruffians; and thefe two nobles, the only very confiderable perfons who oppofed the ruffian nomination, were obliged to fly out of their country, and to take, fhelter in the turkifh domi- nions, where they particularly value themfelves on protecting the unfortunate; and thefe noble fugitives found refuge where Charles XII. had found it.

During all this time Poniatofsky, accompanied with a great number of his friends, was vifiting each nuncio in particular, and endeavouring to gain them by teftimonies of benevolence and flattering promifes. The palatines being all affembled and ranged in order round the fhopa*,

* The general diet for the election of a king is always held in the open field, about two miles from Warfaw, near the village of Vola, where a fort of booth is erected, covered with boards, at the public charge, which in the polifh language is called *fhopa*, or a fhelter from bad weather. This place is built and prepared by the treafurer of the crown: it is furrounded with a ditch, and has three doors. The day appointed for the diet being come, the fenate and the nobility proceed to St. John's church at Warfaw, to hear the mafs of the holy ghoft, to implore its influence in the election of a new king who may have all the qualities ne- ceffary to defend the interefts of the church and of the republic: after which they go to the fhopa and proceed to bufinefs.

a large

a large building, open on all fides occupied by the fenate and the equeftrian order. The primate afked with a loud voice, at three diftinct times, who they would have for king? All anfwered unanimoufly :—" Count Poniatofsky!" —The next day * he was proclaimed king of Poland, and grand duke of Lithuania, under the name of Staniflaus Auguftus. Thus the diet and the kingdom being freed, in the manner we have feen, from all thofe who were the declared oppofers of Poniatofsky, the election was foon concluded in favour of that prince with an unanimity unknown in the annals of Poland.

The new monarch, on his return to Warfaw, paffed along the ftreets of that capital amidft the acclamations of all the people, and from that fame day he took poffeffion of the palace of the republic. Some nuncios had abftained from appearing at the diet; the greater part of the prime nobility took umbrage at the appointment of Poniatofsky : but, no fooner was he on the throne than they came almoft all to do him homage; and he began to reign in as much tranquillity as if his election had not been effected by. violence †.

Some

* The 7th of September.

† Staniflaus Poniatofsky behaved at firft with great judgment and circumfpection. He received with kindnefs thofe

ζ 2   who

Some time previous to this election, Catharine
had declared her intention of visiting the scene
of

---

who had acted seemingly in the most direct opposition to his
interest. The son of count Bruhl exerted himself to his pre-
judice, and yet that prince left him in possession of the post
of grand master of the artillery which he had promised
to count Branichky, palatin of Belsh, and of which indeed
the latter had the generosity not to wish to deprive him.—
Soon after his election, he received letters of congratulation
from many of the courts of Europe. The most remarkable
is that from the king of Prussia, written with his majesty's
own hand. From the matter and the occasion, as well as the
character of the writer, it is extremely worthy of being
inserted at length. Nothing can be more glorious than
a communication of such sentiments in the intercourse between sovereigns. " Your majesty must reflect, that, as
" you enjoy a crown by election and not by descent, the
" world will be more observant of your majesty's actions than
" of any other potentate in Europe : and it is but reasonable.
" The latter being the mere effect of consanguinity, no more
" is looked for (though much more is to be wished) from
" him, than what men are endowed with in common : but,
" from a man exalted, by the voice of his equals, from
" a subject to a king, from a man voluntarily elected to
" reign over those by whom he was chosen, every thing is
" expected that can possibly deserve and adorn a crown.
" Gratitude to his people is the first great duty of such
" a monarch : for to them alone (under Providence) he
" is indebted that he is one. A king who is so by birth, if
" he acts derogatory to his station, is a satire only on him-
" self ;

of her fucceffes, and to make the tour of Livonia. But whilft this monarch was employed abroad in difpofing of crowns, at home her throne feemed to be tottering under her; and that vaft power, which extended to the remoteft part of Afia, which awed all Europe, and abfolutely governed fo many of its neighbours, was not fecure of its own duration for a moment. Every breath of a confpiracy feemed to fhake it: and fuch was the critical ftate of that empire, that the defigns of the obfcureft perfon in it were not unattended by danger.

In the courfe of this fummer an event of that nature happened in Ruffia which is highly deferving of a place in hiftory, from the extraordinary circumflances by which it was accompanied, though fo extremely myfterious and unaccountable in many particulars, that we defpair of affording any clear fatisfaction to the reader concerning them.

" felf; but an elected one, who behaves inconfiftent with
" his dignity, reflects difhonour alfo on his fubjects. Your
" majefty, I am fure, will pardon this warmth. It is the
" effufion of the fincereft regard. The amiable part of the
" picture is not fo much a leffon of what you ought to be,
" as a prophecy of what your majefty will be."

The

The emprefs, in the fummer of 1764, in purfuance of her intentions already mentioned, fet
out on her journey through Efthonia, Livonia,
and Courland. On her way, fhe paffed over
from Oranienbaum to Cronftadt; and thinking
to give the foreign minifters an advantageous
idea of her marine, fhe invited them to follow
her to that port. They did fo : but the opinion
they formed of her naval forces fell far fhort
of that which fhe entertained of them herfelf.
There was but a fmall number of fhips, which
they judged but little adapted to keep the fea:
and the englifh ambaffador, with that franknefs
peculiar to his nation, did not diffemble that her
navy was far from appearing to him to be very
formidable. She afterwards proved that it was
poffible for it to become fo.

On quitting Cronftadt, her majefty, having
left the government of Peterfburg to count
Panin, took the road of Livonia, accompanied
by count Gregory Orloff and a fmall retinue of
nobility of both fexes. During her abfence on
this expedition, in the prifon of the dethroned
Ivan an infurrection broke out under the conduct
of a certain Mirovitch, which coft that unfortunate prince his life.

Ivan

Ivan Antonovitch, ftyled Ivan the third in the manifeftoes that were publifhed in his name while emperor, was born in 1740; great grand-fon of tzar Ivan Alexèyevitch, the elder half-brother of Peter the great *. On running over the feries of ruffian monarchs from Alexèy Michailovitch downwards, our feelings are at every moment hurt by the inteftine difturbances that have happened from different pretenders, of

---

* See the genealogical tables in the former volume, tab. iii.

Ivan III. if we reckon by the line of the tzars, or VI. if from the firft fovereign of Ruffia, was proclaimed emperor on the death of cmprefs Anne, and Biren regent; but this high elevation was foon to be followed by a dreadful fall. The father and the mother of the young emperor were dif-contented at feeing themfelves excluded from the regency; and the infolence with which they were treated by Biren in-creafed their difpleafure. Munich, on his part, not having obtained from the regent what he thought due to his fer-vices, joined himfelf to thofe princes, and, in the night be-tween the 20th and 21ft of November, Manftein, aid-de-camp to Munich, arrefted the regent. The princefs Anne caufed herfelf to be proclaimed regent during the minority of her fon. The whole nation rejoiced at being freed from an abominable tyrant: he was conducted to Schluffelburg, tried, and condemned to death: but his punifhment was mitigated to an exile for life in Siberia. This exile was again moderated, by transferring him to Yaroflauf, where he remained till 1762, when Peter III. as we have already feen, recalled him to court; and he was fhortly after reftored to his dukedom by Catharine.

c 4   which

which so many within so short a space of time, and in general attended with such shocks, no princely house in Europe has experienced, especially in modern times. But a cruel fatality seems, in a particular manner, to have propagated the seeds of discord between the families of the two imperial brothers.

We have seen him seized and confined with his parents and relations; at first conveyed to the citadel of Riga, then in the fortress of Dunamund; from thence removed to Oranienburg, at the south-eastern extremity of european Russia. At all these places the being together alleviated the miseries of imprisonment, and especially the humane behaviour of captain Korf, which first awakened the gratitude of the infant emperor, and was all his life after recollected with emotion; solely on account of this lenity, the suspicion of the court fell upon Korf*, and he was removed from his office. About the latter end of 1745, or the beginning of the year 1746, the family was separated; all the rest being brought more northward to Kolmogori, Ivan was left behind in Oranienburg. To his great misfortune it came into the mind of a monk to carry him off; in their flight they had reached Smo-

* Afterwards promoted to the rank of general by Peter III.

lensk,

lenſk, where the affair was diſcovered, and they were detained. From thence the wretched captive, lately the envied emperor of a quarter of the globe, was now brought, for greater ſecurity, to Schluſſelburg, and there lodged in a caſematt of the fortreſs, the very loop-hole of which was immediately bricked up. He was never brought out into the open air, and no ray of heaven ever viſited his eyes. In this ſubterranean vault it was neceſſary to keep a lamp always burning; and as no clock was either to be ſeen or heard, Ivan knew no difference between day and night. His interior guard, a captain and a lieutenant, were ſhut up with him; and there was a time when they did not dare to ſpeak to him, not ſo much as to anſwer him the ſimpleſt queſtion. What wonder if his ignorance ſhould at length border on ſtupidity? This dreadful abode was however afterwards changed for that preſently to be deſcribed, in the corridor under the covered way, in the caſtle. Elizabeth cauſed him once to be brought in a covered cart to Peterſburg, and ſaw and converſed with him. Peter III. alſo viſited him incognito; and what paſſed on this occaſion has been already related. Catharine too had a converſation with him ſoon after the commencement of her reign, as ſhe relates in her manifeſto of

the

the 28th of Auguſt 1764*, in order, as is there ſaid, to form a judgment of his under-ſtanding and talents. To her great ſurpriſe ſhe found him to the laſt degree deficient in both. She obſerved in him a total privation of ſenſe and reaſon, with a defect in his utter-ance, that even had he any thing rational to utter, would have rendered him entirely unin-telligible.

All perſons, however, were not ſo thoroughly convinced of the incapacity of this prince. He was now arrived at the age of twenty-four years, and he might evidently be made an inſtrument, or at leaſt a pretence, for exciting dangerous commotions. His juſt title to the crown, of which he had been formerly in poſſeſſion, his long ſufferings, without any other guilt than that poſſeſſion and that title, his youth, and even the obſcurity which attended his life, and which therefore gave latitude for conjecture and inven-tion, formed very proper materials for working on the minds of the populace. At the moment when Catharine was taking her departure from the reſidence, ſhe had intelligence of freſh con-ſpiracies among the guards. Several of them were taken up; but experience having ſhewn that the detection of one conſpiracy always en-

* Which ſee at the end of this volume.

couraged

couraged the hatching of fome other; and, willing to avoid irritating the multitude by the frequency of punifhments, the confpirators were proceeded againft in private, and many of them were fuffered to pine out their lives in prifon.

From the depth of his dungeon prince Ivan afforded hopes to thofe who held in abhorrence the prefent ufurpation. It was for reftoring the throne to this unfortunate captive that almoft all thefe plots were formed. It was for his fake that men who had never feen him, and whofe very exiftence was utterly unknown to him, were continually braving the fcaffold. Faithful to the fyftem of calumny that had been of fuch fervice to the deftruction of Peter III. the court of Ruffia inceffantly employed it againft Ivan. One while it was given out that he was ftupid, and incapable of uttering articulate founds; at another, that he was a drunkard, and as ferocious as a favage. Sometimes it was even pretended, that he was fubject to fits of madnefs, and be-lieved himfelf a prophet. But many there were to whom thefe reports feemed no better than tales invented by the blackeft malignity, and afterwards innocently propagated by perfons who did not reflect on the numberlefs interefts that might concur in their invention. Doubtlefs, Ivan, to whom all kinds of inftruction were

refufed,

refufed *, and who was kept fhut up in a loath-
fome prifon, denied the converfe of any human
being from whom he could derive information,
muft neceffarily have been of a very confined
underftanding : but there is ftill a great diftance
between ignorance and imbecility or madnefs.
What evidently proves that Ivan was neither
mad nor ftupid is, in the firft place, the converfation he had † at count Schuvaloff's with the
emprefs Elizabeth.   Not only the graces of his
figure and the accents of his voice, but the
moving complaints he uttered, awakened the
fenfibility of all that were prefent, and even
drew from the emprefs abundance of tears.   If
that young prince had committed fome act of
lunacy, would it have failed of publication ?
Again, afterwards we find a frefh proof of his
good fenfe and his fenfibility in the difcourfe
which he held to Peter III. when he faw him, for
the firft time, at Schluffelburg.   Baron Korf
has faithfully tranfmitted it to us, as we have
related it in the firft volume of this work ‡.
Peter III. talked with him feveral times afterwards, and perfifted in his intention of declaring

* It however has been affirmed, that a german officer,
who for fome time had the cuftody of him, clandeftinely
taught him to read.

† In 1756.   ‡ See vol. i. p. 258, 259.

him

him his heir. Now it may well be imagined, that Volkoff, Goudovitch, and his other confidants, would have diffuaded him from it, if they could have brought themfelves to imagine Ivan likely to be for ever unfit to wear the crown. But, to conclude, whatever might be the character of that prince, the daring attempts that were repeatedly made in his favour did not render him lefs formidable to Catharine and to the tranquillity of the empire.

Chance foon furnifhed an inftrument to put him out of the way of being any difturbance to either. The regiment of Smolenfk was in garrifon in the town of Schluffelburg; and a company of about 100 men guarded the fortrefs in which prince Ivan was confined. In this regiment was an officer named Vaffily Mirovitch, whofe grandfather had been implicated in the rebellion of the kozac Mazeppa, and had fought under Charles XII. againft Peter the great. The eftates of the family of Mirovitch had accordingly been forfeited to the crown. This young man, who had a good fhare of ambition, preferred with warmth his pretenfions to have them reftored; and this it was that made him known at court. The family-eftates were not given up; but he was continually flattered with the hopes of their recovery, if he would fhew

himfelf

himſelf active in ſecuring the tranquillity of the empire.

The inner guard placed over the imperial priſoner conſiſted of two officers, captain Vlaſ-ſieff and lieutenant Tſchekin, who ſlept with him in his cell. Theſe had a diſcretionary order, ſigned by the empreſs, by which they were enjoined to put the unhappy prince to death, on any inſurrection that might be made in his favour, on the preſumption that it could not otherwiſe be quelled.

The door of Ivan's priſon opened under a ſort of low arcades, which, together with it, form the thickneſs of the caſtle-wall within the ramparts; in this arcade or corridor eight ſol-diers uſually kept guard, as well on his account, as becauſe the ſeveral vaults on a line with his contain ſtores of various kinds for the uſe of the fortreſs. The other ſoldiers were in the guard-houſe, at the gate of the caſtle, and at their proper ſtations. The detachment had for its commander an officer, who himſelf was under the orders of the governor.

It has been affirmed that, ſome time before the execution of his project, Mirovitch had opened himſelf to a lieutenant of the regiment of Veliki Luki, named Uſchakoff; and that Uſchakoff bound himſelf by an oath, which he

took

took at the altar of the church of St. Mary of Kafan in St. Peterſburg, to aid him in the enter-prife to the beſt of his power. But as this latter was drowned, a few days after this is faid to have happened, as he was aſſiſting in the launch of a veſſel, it is impoſſible to afcertain the fact.

It is more apparent that he talked in vague terms of the confpiracy with one of the valets of the court, and that he mentioned it afterwards to Simeon Tſchevarideff, lieutenant of artillery, and ſpoke of the advantages that would accrue from the reſcue of Ivan, and the delivering of him to the regiments of the guards. While he thought to raiſe his confequence by putting on the air of a confpirator without accomplices, he however faid nothing to Tſchevarideff pofitively either of the time or the manner of executing his plot.

He had already performed his week's duty in the fortrefs, without venturing an attempt. But, tormented by the anxieties arifing from fufpenfe, and condemning his own irrefolution, he afked permiſſion to be continued on guard for one week longer. This was granted him without hefitation.

After having admitted into his confidence a man of the name of Jacob Piſhkoff, he began

at

at about ten o'clock on a fine fummer's night*,
to fall into conversation with three corporals
and two common foldiers; and after tampering
with them fome time, and obviating fuch difficulties as were fuggefted by their fears, they were
foon gained over to his plan, and they promifed
to follow his orders. Neverthelefs, whether from
timidity or from precaution, they refolved with
one confent to wait till the night was farther advanced. Between the hours of one and two in
the morning, they came together again. Mirovitch and the corporals then made about fifty †
of the foldiers who were on guard to put themfelves under arms, and thus marched towards
the prifon of Ivan. On the way they met Berednikoff, the governor of the fortrefs, whom
they thought faft locked in the arms of fleep;
but who, rouzed by fome noife, whether made
by them or accidentally occafioned, had come
out to fee what was the matter. The governor,
authoritatively demanded of Mirovitch the reafon of his appearance in arms at the head of the
foldiers? Without returning any anfwer, Mirovitch knocked him down with the butt end of
his firelock, and, ordering fome of his people to
fecure him, continued his march. Being arrived

---

* The $\frac{4}{15}$th of July.

† It is probable that 38 was the exact number.

at

at the corridor into which the door of Ivan's chamber opened, the centinels put themfelves in a pofture to oppofe his paffage. He immediately ordered his men to fire upon them, which they did. The centinels returned their fire; but none were hurt either on the one fide or the other.

The foldiers of Mirovitch, furprifed at the refiftance they met, fhewed figns of an inclination to retreat. Their chief withheld them; but they infifted on his fhewing them the order which he faid he had received from Peterfburg. He directly drew from his pocket and read to them a forged decree of the fenate, recalling prince Ivan to the throne, and excluding Catharine from it, becaufe fhe was gone into Livonia to marry count Poniatofsky. The ignorant and credulous foldiers implicitly gave credit to the decree, and again put themfelves in order to obey him. A piece of artillery was now brought to Mirovitch, who himfelf pointed it at the door of the dungeon; but at that inftant the door opened, and he entered, unmolefted, with all his fuite.

The officers Vlaffieff and Tfchekin, fet over the prince as his guard, were fhut up with him, and had called out to the centinels to fire. But, on hearing Mirovitch give orders to beat in the door, and judging that they had not the means of making any resistance to the assailants, they fell sword in hand on the wretched victim now attempted to be carried off.

At the noise of the firing Ivan had awoke; and, hearing the cries and the threats of his guards, he conjured them to spare his miserable life. But, on seeing that these barbarians had no regard to his prayers, he found new force in his despair, and, though naked, defended himself for a considerable time. Having his right hand pierced through and his body covered with wounds, he seized the sword from one of the monsters and broke it; but while he was struggling to get the piece out of his hand, the other stabbed him from behind, and threw him down. He who had his sword broke now plunged his bayonet into his body, and several times repeating his blow, under these strokes the unhappy prince expired.

They then opened the door, and shewed Mirovitch at once the bleeding body of the murdered prince, and the order by which they were authorised to put him to death, if any attempt should be made to convey him away.

Mirovitch, struck with horror, at first started back some paces; then threw himself on the body of Ivan, and cried out:—" I have missed

" my

" my aim; I have now nothing to do but to
" die."—But he prefently rofe up. So far
from attempting to flee from the punifhment
which he muft now forefee, or to take his revenge
on the two affaffins by fhooting them on the fpot,
he returned to the place where he had left
the governor in the hands of his foldiers; and,
furrendering to him his fword, coldly faid:—
" It is I that am now your prifoner."

The next day the body of the poor unfortunate Ivan was expofed before the church *
in the caftle of Schluffelburg, cloathed in the
habit of a failor. As foon as it was known
immenſe crowds of people flocked thither from
the neighbouring towns and from St. Peterſburg;
and it is impoffible to defcribe the grief and
indignation that were excited at the view of an
unfortunate being, who, after having been cruelly

---

* An old lutheran church built of timber for the ufe of
the garrifon while Nœteburg was in poffeffion of the Swedes,
long before it was taken from them by Peter the great.
The church is in a very decayed ftate, full of rubbifh, and not
employed in any religious purpofes. The painted altar is removed from its proper place at the eaft end, and ftands againſt
the north fide wall, and in its place, filling the enclofure
where the altar rails have been, is a large pile of deal planks,
in a ftate of rottennefs: under this ftack of wood the body
of Ivan was thrown, where it lay for fome time.

precipitated

precipitated from the throne while yet in his cradle, paffed his days in a dark and doleful dungeon, where he was inhumanly put to death by affaffins. Ivan was full fix feet high, with a fine blond head of hair, a red beard, regular features, and of a complection extremely fair: accordingly, the beauty of his perfon and his youth * heightened the fenfibility that was univerfally difcovered at the unhappinefs of his lot, and the cruelty of his murderers. His body was wrapt up in a fheep-fkin, put into a coffin, and inhumed without ceremony.

The concourfe and the murmurs increafed to fuch a degree that a tumult was now apprehended. To avoid any fatal confequences to themfelves the two affaffins Vlaffieff and Tfchekin, as foon as they had perpetrated their crime, put themfelves on board of a veffel which they found on the point of failing for Denmark, where, on their arrival, the ruffian minifter took them under his protection†.

The governor of Schluffelburg difpatched to Peterfburg a full relation of the horrid outrage of Mirovitch, and of the tragical end of Ivan.

* He had not yet completed his 24th year.

† They fhortly after returned to Ruffia, and were advanced in the fervice.

He

He accompanied this account with a manifefto that had been found in the pocket of Mirovitch, and which, it was faid, had been long fabricated in concert with lieutenant Ufchakoff. This manifefto, which contained many fcurrilous invectives and imprecations againft Catharine, and reprefented prince Ivan as the fole legitimate emperor, it was obferved, was to have been publifhed at the moment the prince. was fet at liberty and was making his entry into St. Peterfburg. Panin immediately fent off a courier to the emprefs with an exact account of thefe particulars.

Her majefty was then at Riga; and, under a vifible impatience of mind, was frequently inquiring after news from the refidence: a circumftance by no means unaccountable, if we confider the frequent caufes of alarm from plots and cabals with which fhe had been inceffantly haraffed fince the beginning of her reign. Her inquietude increafed from day to day, and fhe would often rife in the night to afk whether no courier was arrived*. Some perfons afterwards recollected thefe circumftances to her

---

* Thefe facts have often been confirmed by general Brown; who, being a good roman catholic, honeftly attributed thefe perturbations of Catharine to fupernatural prefentiments.

difad-

difadvantage, as if fhe was anxioufly counting the days fince the period when Mirovitch was ftationed on guard *. At length, after three days had elapfed, the difpatches of Panin were brought to her hand.

The fenate paffed fentence alone upon Mirovitch, condemning him to be beheaded. The two officers were rewarded.

The public was much divided in opinion concerning the whole of this tranfaction. It was thought inconceivable that an infignificant private individual fhould hazard an enterprife, that, if even at firft all things fhould go well, yet could never be profecuted to final fuccefs by him. That in the attack no one fhould be hurt; that upon Ivan's death all fhould be immediately as quiet as if nothing had happened; that no enquiry was fet on foot about any accomplices in Peterfburg, of which there had been fome talk at firft; feemed to give room to furmife that fimply this death was the object in view, and to this fole end the whole machinery was directed. None of the court party could have done this fervice to the abfent emprefs,

---

* The circumftance that Mirovitch had fuffered his week's duty on guard to expire before he could fummon up courage enough to attempt the execution of his project, was not, on this occafion, forgotten.

without

without her knowledge and confent. But, on the other hand, the flanderous manifefto found upon Mirovitch was produced, which he intended to have publifhed immediately upon his having Ivan in his poffeffion, and which count Panin, it was faid, had actually read and fent to the fovereign; but particularly the execution of the rebel: if perhaps it was he, and not fome unknown malefactor, who underwent that punifhment.—Let it fuffice, the public emotions of pity and difpleafure at the fad cataftrophe of the imperial progeny, and himfelf once emperor, were plainly manifefted by every kind of expreffion. The multitudes of people who, notwithftanding all that could be done to check their impetuofity, ftill flocked to the caftle, infifting on feeing the body, were fo great, that the government was obliged to give orders to remove it from the caftle-church, and convey it in the filence of the night with the utmoft fecrecy, to the monaftery of Tichfina, 200 verfts from Peterfburg. Among the regiments of guards in that city, who thought they had the exclufive right to depofe and to murder emperors, violent commotions arofe; that efpecially in the night of the 24th of July, caufed the greateft alarm: it was only by the prudent meafure of prince Galitzin, who caufed powder and ball to be publicly diftributed among

the

the marching regiments that were encamped in the vicinity of Peterſburg, that tranquillity was reſtored.   When the two officers by whom the prince was aſſaſſinated appeared at court, every one beheld them with looks of undiſſembled contempt and abhorrence.

Catharine's throne was now firmly eſtabliſhed. Even the angry ſpirit that perſecuted the family of Ivan ſeemed at length appeaſed.   As her majeſty afterwards ſet at liberty the other members of it, it may be neceſſary to make ſome brief mention of them here.   The parents and relations of the unfortunate young emperor had been brought to Kolmogori, a village-like town in the government of Archangel, on an iſland of the Dwina.   Here they dwelt poor and melancholy, in cloſe confine-ment.   The mother, Anna Carlovna, died in child-bed, while Elizabeth was yet reigning, in March 1746, and was taken from hence, and buried in the ſame monaſtery where afterwards Peter III. at laſt found reſt.   The father, An-thony Ulric, died in 1776.   He left behind him two princes, Peter and Alexey, two princeſſes, Catharine and Elizabeth, and ſeveral natural children : all, except the elder of the princeſſes, born in priſon.   For a ſeries of 17 years they were very ſeverely treated by Golovtzin, the laſt viceroy of Archangel.   After his death, which

which happened in 1779, Catharine appointed
in his place a man of more generous fentiments,
the general-governor Melgunef, who vifited the
unfortunate captives, adminiftered to them every
confolation in his power, took with him a letter
from the princefs Elizabeth to the emprefs; and,
on delivering it, defcribed their fituation in fuch
affecting terms, that her majefty immediately
refolved to open a negotiation with the court of
Denmark. The dowager-queen of that kingdom, Juliana Maria, was a fifter of duke Anthony Ulric. In the following year, 1780, the
bufinefs was brought to a conclufion : the accommodation was eafy, as Catharine acted with her
wonted magnanimity. If, as is probable, a deed
of renunciation of all pretenfions to the ruffian
throne was required of the ftate-prifoners in behalf of themfelves and their pofterity, neither
could this occafion any difficulty. The emprefs
directly fent them 200,000 rubles, to provide
the family with clothes, plate, porcelaine, &c.
befitting their rank. This fhe accompanied
with a prefent of rich furs and jewels from the
imperial cabinet ; and appointed perfons of
quality to attend the princes and princeffes on
their voyage. At Archangel Melgunef firft
difcovered to them their liberation, and the intended voyage to Denmark. They heard the
news

news with forrow, and earneftly intreated to be fent back to their old prifon ; till the perfuafions of the generous Melgunef raifed their fpirits, and infpired them with courage *. In July a frigate brought the whole family to Bergen in Norway, where the princes and princeffes were taken on board a danifh fhip, leaving the illegitimate children to return with the imperial frigate. The parting with thefe half-relatives excited the moft painful emotions in the breafts of the family. The moft fenfible of them, Elizabeth, furvived not long her grief and the fhock her frame had received at this fudden change of fortune. The four brothers and fifters of Ivan were, at the time when they obtained their liberty, between 30 and 40 years of age. The danifh court affigned them the city of Horfens in Jutland, as the place of their refidence. Towards their eftablifhment there Ca-

* The dowager queen of Denmark, in the letter of thanks which fhe wrote to the emprefs in terms of the tendereft fenfibility, highly extolled, as fhe had reafon to do, the behaviour of this worthy man in the whole of his conduct. This teftimony faved him, on occafion of an unmerited accufation that was brought againft him concerning his behaviour in this bufinefs, and which threatened him with imminent danger : and, on his having juftified himfelf, to the fatisfaction of all impartial judges, Catharine rewarded him with the order of St. Andrew, and made him many prefents befides.

tharine

tharine prefented them with 20,000 rubles, and paid annually to the maintenance of their dignity, 30,000 rubles. In October 1782, the princefs Elizabeth died at Horfens; and her death was followed by that of her brother Alexèy in October 1787. The natural children of the duke of Brunfwic received in Ruffia an annual penfion: one of them, a daughter named Amelia, after her return, married lieutenant Karikin, who, for twelve years, had the guard of the family at Kolmogori, and with whom fhe had long been intimately acquainted.

To return to our hiftory. Catharine, foon after the fhocking event that had happened at Schluffelburg, arrived from off her journey through the conquered provinces. On her entry into Peterfburg, fhe was furrounded by an im- menfe concourfe of people, who endeavoured to find out by her countenance what was pafling in her heart; but, always miftrefs of herfelf, the face of that princefs was ever covered with fmiles. Her ftep was as firm, her front as ferene, as thofe who feel no inward reproaches ufually are.

Lieutenant-general Weymar had already been charged to repair to Schluffelburg. After hav- ing privately examined Mirovitch and his ac- complices, they were brought to Peterfburg, where

where their trial was opened before a commiffion compofed of five prelates, of an equal number of fenators, and feveral general officers. Mirovitch appeared before the judges with all that tranquillity which only the hope of pardon can communicate to a criminal like him. He replied with a frivolous and often infolent air, to the interrogatories that were put to him. It is true that the judges themfelves feemed not to make it a matter of great importance, and rather appeared as if they dreaded to fathom this execrable myftery. One alone * had fo much fenfe of propriety as to declare againft fuch an extraordinary mode of procedure. But he was blamed for his indifcreet zeal, and advifed to keep filence, if he would not lofe his office, and be degraded from his rank of nobleffe. In fine, after fome days fpent in the trial, Mirovitch was condemned to lofe his head †, not as guilty of high treafon, but only as a difturber of the public peace. Unmoved at this fentence, he walked to the fcaffold like a man who had nothing to fear, and who thought himfelf fure of obtaining a pardon, as indeed, according to a report, it had been promifed him. But if he really reckoned on a pardon, he was cruelly

* He was a fenator.   † On the 26th of September.

deceived.

deceived. The time for his execution was accelerated; and the unhappy wretch, if he had before been the inftrument, was now the victim of a barbarous policy. Thofe who confidered him in the former point of view were aftonifhed that the emprefs fhould fuffer him to fall under the axe. But how could fhe have fcreened him from punifhment without manifeftly drawing upon herfelf the charge of having prompted his crime ? and if fhe were really concerned in it, can it be thought that fhe would hefitate a moment in getting rid of a witnefs who would have expofed her to everlafting vexation ?

Mirovitch was the only perfon condemned to death. The foldiers whom he had engaged to join him in the intended refcue were punifhed with various degrees of feverity. Pifhkoff, who was confidered as the moft guilty, was fentenced to run the gantlet twelve times through a line of a thoufand men. The three corporals and the two fuziliers, feduced after Pifhkoff, were flogged ten times along the fame line; after which they were put to the public works, with a log chained to their leg. The other foldiers who acted under the orders of Mirovitch were likewife whipped through the ranks; and after being incorporated in other regiments, were fent into diftant garrifons. Tfchevarideff was degraded

degraded from his rank of officer, for having heard without revealing the vague confidential communications of Mirovitch.   Fifty-eight perfons were punifhed.   A great appearance of feverity was exercifed againft them ; and this, among other circumftances, was calculated to obviate any fufpicions that might arife con-cerning any more eminent inftigators of their crime.

CHAP. V.

*Discontents at Petersburg.—Misunderstanding be-
tween the counts Gregory Orloff and Panin.—Vis-
sensky becomes favourite of the empress.—Resignation of the chancellor Vorontzoff.—Prince Radzivil at the head of the confederates.—The bishop
of Cracow carried off.—The duke de Choiseul in-
cites the Turks to declare war against Russia.—
Treaty entered into by the empress with England.—Tournament at Petersburg.—Reform of
the courts of justice.—Convocation of deputies
from all the provinces of the empire.—Wise
reply of the Samoyèdes.—Wicked attempt of
Tschoglokoff.—Travels of several learned men
in the interior of Russia.—Academical institutions.—Inoculation of the empress and the grand
duke, with other events from 1764 to 1768.*

THE beneficial effects of Catharine's regulations and establishments for the internal administration of government were every day becoming more apparent in all parts of Russia.
That vast empire, rendered more compact,
better regulated, more simply organised, animated with a new spirit, must naturally have a

powerful

powerful influence on the commerce, on the finances, the politics, nay even on the exiſtence of the other nations of the earth: and it certainly had. The time was paſt when foreign cabinets, with a ſort of aſſurance of effect, could direct affairs, give birth to reſolutions, and put a ſtop to proceedings at Peterſburg; the government diſplayed that ſpirit of independence which became ſo great a monarchy: on the contrary, the queſtion was now, how Catharine was acting, and what ſhe was purpoſing in regard to all that the princes and republics, from the Memel to the Tagus, were meditating and transacting. A ſagacious hiſtorian, who is certainly no flatterer of deſpots, ſays of the late empreſs of Ruſſia, to which every one muſt ſubſcribe, " The volumes of modern hiſtory can " produce no reign like this: for no monarch " has ever yet ſucceeded in the attainment of " ſuch a dictature in the grand republic of " Europe, as Catharine II. now holds; and " none of all the kings who have heretofore " given cauſe to dread the erection of an uni- " verſal monarchy, ſeem to have had any " knowledge of her art; to preſent herſelf " with the pride of a conqueror in the moſt " perilous ſituations, and with an unuſual, a " totally new dignity in the moſt common

" transf-

" tranfactions. And it is manifeftly not alone
" the fupreme authority which here gives law,
" but the judgment which knows when to
" fhew that authority, and when to employ
" it *."

Theoretical politicians, indeed, and ftatiftical calculators, have pretended to affirm, that this complaifance of the reft of Europe has been fhewn without reafon; and that the affumption that the power of Ruffia is fo formidable is one of thofe that are only admitted upon truft. But the confequence feems here demonftrable, if any where in a cafe like this : whoever undertakes many things, and performs all that he undertakes, is probably ftill able to undertake and to perform more. Whoever, juft at the time when the politician has calculated that he is reduced to his laft foldier and his laft ruble, appears with a formidable army, and difpofes of millions with magnanimous prodigality, cannot be yet at the extremity of his forces or his wealth. And (what is completely decifive) whoever, in the grand european republic, at the time when a Frederic and a Jofeph, when the intriguing

* M. Spittler, in his " Sketch of the Hiftory of the " Governments of Europe," part ii. p. 420.

French

French and the enterprifing Britons compofe the
fenate of that republic, can hold the dictature,
is furely born to be dictator, is endowed with
all the qualities requifite to that end : the power,
the art, and the judgment.   This will apply to
Catharine.   In her were united what the world
has feldom feen together.   From merely phyfical
power many things may afford fecurity ; but the
fuperiority of mind, the refinement of policy, is
capable of reaching lengths, of which the former
will fall fhort.——Whom fhe favoured with her
efteem and friendfhip, never advanced farther to
confidence, but remained in a refpectful, almoft
dependent fituation.   Whoever incurred her
wrath, fhe could fo place before all Europe, that
the effects of it were no longer beheld as a hoftile
contention between two equal potentates, but as
the chaftifement of a felon.——When fhe iffued
her commands, it was in the fweet accents of
righteoufnefs and peace.   However her paffions
were excited, fhe yet remained tranquil, till the
proper maturity enfured the event ; and thus her
actions acquired the diftinctive marks of irre-
fiftible majefty.   But never yet has a monarch
underftood, like her, how to be bountiful exactly
at the fitteft time, and to make prefents with
fuch fignificance as to fix the gratitude of the receiver,

ceiver, and to acquire the veneration that is due to a beneficent deity *.

While Catharine was giving law to Poland, amusing Austria, conciliating the friendship of Prussia, and treating with England, she was also tampering with the other courts of Europe, and labouring efficaciously towards very soon making herself dreaded by them. She exerted herself to the utmost in giving new spirit to the commerce of her country, in augmenting her navy, and above all in softening the manners of her people, as yet not far advanced in civilization. But, badly seconded by the great personages of the empire, and even by such as were about her, the progress of her institutions was at

* We will take the liberty of making here one other extract from Spittler's work, concerning the interference of Russia in the affairs of Poland : — " It was an ingenious contrivance, " formed in a truly roman style, and completed accordingly. " Not only a numerous and free nation was to be deprived of " its liberty and national subsistence, but all Europe was to " be lulled asleep. The annexations of Lewis XIV. were a " trifling business in comparison of what Catharine II. per- " formed in Poland and against that country. But what " loud and violent cries were raised against the former ; and " in what soft murmurs did the voice of truth repeat the " ancient law of nations, when there seemed to be no longer " any law between Russia and Poland ? &c." See Spittler's work on the governments of Europe, p. 423.

first

firſt but ſlow. The ſpirit of diviſion continued
to reign in Peterſburg. The outrages that
were to be prevented or puniſhed, always made
it neceſſary for Catharine to keep well with the
conſpirators to whom ſhe was indebted for the
throne : but the favours ſhe was inceſſantly
heaping on that greedy and inſolent crew, were
ſo many additional ſources of hatred and diſcontent. Some new plot or conſpiracy was forming
every day ; and every day the good fortune of
the empreſs, or rather her prudence, delivered
her from danger. Puniſhments were ſecret and
terrible. The authors of one plot could but
rarely undertake a ſecond.

What moſt afflicted the empreſs was the miſ-
underſtanding that prevailed between her favourite and her chief miniſter, becauſe the de-
votedneſs and audacity of the one were not leſs
uſeful to her than the name and abilities of the
other. Panin had certainly conſiderable imper-,
fections ; but he was the only one who had a
true notion of buſineſs. His cold imagination,
his melancholy, his pride, his obſtinacy, and
above all his indolence, were highly diſpleaſing
to Catharine : but ſhe did ample juſtice to his
talents, and continued to give him her confidence. Beſides, though the empreſs was not
satisfied

fatisfied with him, he had the art of revifing his opinions, when he found them difagreeable to her.

The influence of Orloff was founded on a different bafis: but he ufed it without difcretion, and was continually leffening its ftability. No longer employing thofe affiduities which were the only means in his power of fecuring the favour he enjoyed, and even negligent of his ufual attendance at court, abfenting himfelf for feveral weeks together for purfuing the chace of the bear, and indifferent to the amufements of the palace, if ever any warmth of attachment fubfifted, it muft naturally now fubfide, and decline into perfect indifference.

Panin, remarking this conduct, thought he might improve it to bring on the difmiffion of the arrogant favourite. Perceiving that the emprefs frequently beheld with complacency a' young officer, named Viffenfky, thenceforward he put in practice every thing he could devife to encourage the inclination. Viffenfky was foon admitted into favour; and, directed by the artful minifter, behaved in fuch a manner as to give reafon to believe that Orloff would foon be difcarded. But the latter, who was not willing to lofe his confequence, made a fudden alter-ation in his conduct, and by that means pre-

ferved his ftation. The new favourite was difmiffed with brilliant prefents, and an employment that fixed him in one of the remoter
provinces.

Though Panin enjoyed great intereft and a
high refpect, with the advantages accruing from
his poft of governor to the grand duke and his
title of minifter, the return of the chancellor
Vorontzoff, whofe functions he performed *ad
interim*, gave him uneafinefs. Jealous to preferve his authority entire, and the fplendor of a
reprefentation which was of great value to him,
he humbled himfelf fo far as to flatter the favourite, whofe downfal he had been endeavouring to
procure. Orloff was not of an impracticable
temper. Always recollecting with bitternefs
the fteps which the chancellor had taken to
prevent him from fharing in the throne, he
requefted the emprefs to keep him away from
the management of affairs; and he became the
apologift for an enemy lefs bold, but more artful. Catharine accofted the chancellor with
extreme coldnefs. Inftead of replacing him in
the functions of minifter, as at his departure fhe
had given him reafon to hope, fhe caufed it to
be fuggefted to him that it would not be taken
amifs if he were to refign a place which he
could no longer fill to the fatisfaction of his
                                        fovereign.

sovereign. The chancellor hesitated for some time: but at length the advice of his friends prevailed. He seemed voluntarily to resign what was actually taken from him. His resignation was accepted with expressions of regret, which were not more sincere than his wishes for retirement; and, in order to convince him of the secret joy his compliance gave, he was presented with a gratuity of 50,000 rubles and a pension of 7000.

Among the numberless means employed by Catharine for detecting the authors of the plots that were perpetually disturbing her repose, she did not neglect the interception of the correspondence of the foreign ministers. That of the agent* of France was sold to her. She even succeeded in procuring a duplicate of his cypher; and she thought she perceived in his letters, if not the adherence to the machinations of the conspirators, at least the knowledge of all the mysterious affairs that were carrying on among the people about her. Her pride was hurt at this discovery; her resentment against the court of Versailles increased; and the cold reception she gave to the agent of that court

---

* Berenger, who had the title of chargé d'affaires.

reduced

reduced him to the neceſſity of making his
retreat *.

Lewis XV. then ſent to Peterſburg the marquis
de Beauſſet †, a man of great vanity and but
ſmall capacity, to whom the miniſters of Catharine complained heavily of the chargé d'affaires
his predeceſſor. But, as Beauſſet was unac-

---

* That princeſs, ſurmiſing afterwards that Voltaire
might have learnt ſome of the facts contained in the corre-
ſpondence of the agents of his nation, wrote to that celebrated genius in ſuch a manner as to diſſuade him from
giving credit to them, if he were acquainted with the buſineſs, and to inform him of nothing if he were not. " All
" your countrymen," ſhe writes to him, " do not entertain
" the ſame ſentiments of me as you do. I know ſome who
" wiſh to perſuade themſelves that it is impoſſible for me to
" do any thing that is good; who put their invention to
" the rack to perſuade others to think ſo likewiſe; and
" woe to their emiſſaries if they dare to think otherwiſe
" than as they are taught. I have candour enough to be-
" lieve it an advantage which they give me over them,
" becauſe whoever only knows facts from the mouth of his
" flatterers, knows them but badly, ſees them in a falſe
" light, and acts in conſequence. Since, however, my
" fame does not depend on them, but entirely on my
" principles, on my actions, I comfort myſelf, as well as I
" can, in not obtaining their approbation. As a good
" chriſtian, I forgive them; and I pity thoſe who envy
" me."

† He was preſented to the empreſs the 1ſt of May
1765.

quainted

quainted with the true caufe of thefe complaints, he paid them but little attention, and took no precautions to prevent their being renewed againſt him. He even thought they were only to be aſcribed to the blind jealoufy which the glory of the french nation excited in the emprefs; fo far from it, that her ambition was ftriving to ufurp the efteem and draw upon her the praifes of that nation. She correfponded with Voltaire and d'Alembert. She made an offer to the latter of the place of governor to the grand duke, with a falary of 24,000 livres, and all conveniencies for finiſhing the Encyclopédie at Peterfburg; advantages which the philofopher thought proper to refufe *. Being informed that Diderot was not in good circumftances, and was defirous of felling his library to enable him to portion out his daughter; fhe bought that library, left it in his own poffeffion, and fettled on him a handfome appointment as the librarian of it. Some time previous to this, fhe had fent to Morand, the famous furgeon, a collection of gold and filver medals which had been ftruck in Ruffia, as a teftimony of her fatisfaction with the anatomical fubjects and chirurgical inftruments which he had procured for her. Almoft

* See the appendix to the former volume, No. IV. p. 470.

all

all the men of letters and the moſt diſtinguiſhed
artiſts of Paris received ſome proofs of her munificence, and admiring her bounties, forgetting
or unacquainted with her frailties,

They ſwelled with lies the hundred trumps of Fame.

In the mean time the ſecret deſign propoſed
by that princeſs in crowning count Ciolek Poniatofsky began to unfold. Thinking herſelf ſecure
of the entire ſubmiſſion of that monarch, ſhe
put off all conſtraint, and openly avowed the
deſigns which even policy had made it a crime in
the Poles to have imputed to her. Her pretenſions were, doubtleſs, extravagant: but, as ſhe
was deſirous that they ſhould not be uſeleſs, ſhe
only declared them when on the point of marching the troops that were deſtined to ſupport
them, and propoſed nothing but in an imperious
tone. After having traced out on the map the
lines of demarcation, by which Ruſſia pur-
loined a great part of the territory of Poland,
Catharine inſiſted on the recognition of the
validity of theſe lines, and that the limits of the
two countries ſhould thus be fixed. She exacted,
farther, that the king and the republic ſhould
contract with her a treaty of alliance offenſive
and defenſive, and that they ſhould allow the
diſſidents to enjoy all the ſame rights with

9   the

the catholics, not excepting that of a capacity for being members of the senate. The last of these demands, the only one that was equitable, raised the indignation of an intolerant and despotic nobility. Murmurs were now heard on all sides: mention was made of having recourse to arms. Whether he was really ashamed of the sacrifices that were prescribed to his recognition, or rather afraid of putting the nation in a ferment, the king himself declared that he could not consent to these sacrifices. But in order to be the better able to form a judgment of the pretexts with which Catharine covered her ambition, it will be necessary to understand what the polish dissidents were.

Poland was originally circumscribed within very narrow bounds. The inhabitants, between the 9th and 10th centuries, adopted the christian religion as it was then professed by the church of Rome. About the same time many of the neighbouring provinces, which were then independent states, at different periods embraced that worship according to the ritual of the Greeks. In process of time, many of these neighbouring states, either by conquest, by right of succession, by marriage, or by compact, became united to the kingdom of Poland; upon all which accessions the new provinces were upon

an

an exact equality with the old in every refpect, and each obferved their own peculiar modes of worfhip.

Of all thefe acceffions, that which fell to it by the marriage of Yagellon, grand duke of Lithu-ania, with the daughter and heirefs of Lewis king of Poland, in 1386, was the largeft and moft confiderable. By this event the grand duchy of Lithuania, together with the provinces of White-Ruffia, Podlachia, Volhinia, Podolia, and fhortly afterwards Red-Ruffia, became an-nexed to the kingdom of Poland; with this diftinction, that the union between the kingdom and the grand duchy depended only on the con-tinuance of the line of the Yagellons, that family being the natural fovereigns of Lithuania. The inhabitants of all thefe provinces were of the greek religion, as well as thofe of Moldavia, Vallachia, and the Ukraine, which were added to the kingdom by the fucceffors of Yagellon: fo that by thefe great acceffions, the members of the greek church became at that time far fuperior, both in numbers and power, to thofe of the roman catholic perfuafion. It was thought a happinefs peculiar to Poland, that, while other countries have at different times been a prey to inteftine feuds and rancour on the fcore of the religion of Chrift, the great variety of opinions

on

on that fubject never produced any ftrife or animofity among the people of this nation.

The reformation made very early progrefs in Poland, and the majority of the fenators and nobility became members either of the lutheran or calviniftic communions. To prevent therefore any mifchiefs that might arife from thefe differences of religion, Sigifmund Auguftus paffed a law at the diet of Vilna, on the 16th of June 1563, declaring that all thofe of the equeftrian and noble orders, whether of lithuanian or ruffian extraction, fhould enjoy equal rights, provided they profefs the chriftian religion. This he afterwards confirmed at the diet of Grodno, in 1568, adding, to prevent all mifconftructions in favour of any party, that it was to be underftood of every fuch perfon, of whatever chriftian communion or confeffion he be.

Under favour of this toleration proteftantifm made rapid advances in Poland. By this wife act of Sigifmund Auguftus, all fects, whether proteftant, greek or arian, enjoyed the full liberty of exercifing their worfhip, and the right of voting in the diets and of holding the fame offices as the catholics. None were at the time offended by this act of juftice: on the contrary, all were glad to fee that the difference of religion produced

duced none in the political and civil rights
of the several members of the community. As
a diftinction among themfelves, the followers of
the different modes of worfhip were called diffidents: but that name, which has fince been
made a fignal for profcription, had nothing then
injurious in it; and the fucceffors of Sigifmund
Auguftus, when they fwore to obferve the
pacta conventa, fwore alfo to preferve peace
among the diffidents *. When Henry de
Valois

---

* It appears, from the very beginning of the republic,
that the term *diffidents* equally comprehended the greeks,
catholics, reformed, and lutherans. The words of that
famous conftitution which was paffed by the diet, which
formed the republic in the year 1573, are, *Nos qui fumus*
diffidentes in religione, i. e. We who differ in religious matters.
In-the fame conftitution it is declared, that they will
acknowledge no man for king or fovereign, " who fhall not
" confirm by oath all the rights, privileges, and liberties,
" which they now enjoy, and which are to be laid before
" him after the election. Particularly, he fhall be bound
" to fwear, that he will maintain the peace among the diffi-
" dents in points of religion." In the conftitutions of the
fame diet are the following remarkable ftipulations : " We
" will engage, in our own names, and in the names of our
" fucceffors for ever, by the obligations of our oath, of our
" faith, of our honour, and of our confciences, to preferve
" peace among us who are diffidents in religion ; to fhed
" no blood, nor to inflict on any one the penalties of con-
" fifcation of goods, defamation, imprifonment, or exile, or
" account

Valois * was elected king of Poland, he wanted
to difpenfe himfelf from an oath that wounded
his intolerant fuperftition: but his attempts
were in vain. He muft relinquifh the crown
or fwear to protect the diffidents: he took
the oath.

However, when the roman catholics, after the
death of Sigifmund III. had gained an evident
fuperiority, they gave full fcope to that fiery
zeal by which they are made to believe that their
religion is the only one that is good, and will not
permit them to endure any other. They began
by perfecuting the arians, whofe opinions had
already made great progrefs; they proceeded to
diveft them of all their rights, and even to drive
them out of Poland. The greek and proteftant
chriftians, who had affifted in perfecuting the
arians, were very foon punifhed for their imprudence. The catholics attacked them in their

------

" account of the difference of our faith, and rites in our
" churches. More than that, if any one fhould undertake,
" for the above reafon, to fhed the blood of his fellow-
" citizens, we fhould be all obliged to oppofe him, even
" though he fhould fhelter himfelf under the pretext of a
" decree, or any other judicial act."

* The bigoted and vicious Henry III. of France.

turn,

turn, and fucceeded, in 1733, in entirely excluding them from the diets *.

The

* Upon the death of Sigifmund Auguftus, in 1574, the
polifh conftitution was entirely changed, and the nation
affumed the form of a republic. His grandfather Cafimir III. was the firft who convened the nobility, in order
to oblige them to accept the new impofitions. Sigifmund
and his father ufed the fame method ; but after his death
the whole legiflative authority fell into the hands of the
nobility. At this period, we are told by their hiftorians,
the roman catholics in the kingdom did not bear a proportion in number to the greeks and reformed, of more than
one to feven. The grand-marfhal Firley, who convened the
firft diet of the republic, that diet which formed its prefent
model, and made the crown elective, was a proteftant. A
perpetual peace betwixt the Greeks, the roman catholics,
and the proteftants, was therein eftablifhed as a fundamental
law of the republic. The wars in Germany under Charles V.
and in France under Catharine de Medicis, made them fenfible of the neceffity they were under of tolerating each
other. They therefore entered into an engagement of mutual defence and affection, and that a difference of religion
fhould never prove the caufe of civil diffenfion, unanimoufly
refolving to make an example of that perfon who, under
fuch a pretext, fhould excite difturbance. As this law has
been repeated in all the public acts, conftitutions, and pacta
conventa, from that time to the prefent, it cannot but be
allowed to be a fundamental law : nor can any other law be
produced, whofe fanction has been more folemnly, more
conftantly, and more frequently repeated. However, when
the roman catholics, after the death of Sigifmund III. had
acquired

The humiliation they felt on being deprived of the right of suffrage, converted many of the Poles to catholicifm. But if the diffidents diminifhed in numbers, thofe who remained were only fo much the more attached to their fects. Againft thefe proceedings they urged the treaty of Oliva, concluded in 1660, by which their privileges were fecured, and of which fo many potentates were the guarantees. The catholics, who ruled alone in the diets, and confequently might give ample range to their intolerance, without moleftation or obftacle, procured a decree attaching the guilt of high treafon to fuch diffidents as fhould have recourfe to foreign powers for obtaining the execution of the treaty thus atrocioufly infringed, and the re-eftablifhment of the laws fo defpotically repealed. This decree was the finifhing ftroke to the patience of the diffidents. Ruffia obferved their indignation, and fanned it in fecret. The greek diffidents

---

acquired a manifeft fuperiority, though they did not think proper openly to controvert it, yet they fhewed a difpofition, when opportunity was favourable, to infringe it, by placing under their fignatures, *falvis juribus ecclefiæ romanæ catholicæ*, with a faving to the rights of the roman catholic church. Whereupon the diffidents, by way of reprifal, wrote under their fignatures, *falva pace inter diffidentes*, with a faving to the peace amongft the diffidents.

then

then addreſſed themſelves to the court of Peterſburg.   The proteſtants implored the interceſſion
of thoſe of London, Copenhagen, and Berlin.
Theſe courts promiſed to ſupport them; and
this was the moſt ſpecious pretext for the military
interference of Ruſſia.   This was the ſtate of
affairs at the cloſe of the year 1765.

On the aſſembling of the diet on the 1ſt
of September 1766, the miniſters of the protecting courts preſented their memorials in behalf
of the diſſidents, which excited a violent murmur.
Soltyk, biſhop of Cracow, a haughty and fanatical
prelate, maintained that the diſſidents had no
right of appeal to privileges that were aboliſhed,
and that they had violated the conſtitution of the
republic in having recourſe to the intervention of
foreign powers.   Not ſatisfied with the iniquitous
laws that had been paſſed againſt the diſſidents,
he moved for the enacting of new ones ſtill more
ſevere.   His opinion was adopted by Maſſalſky,
biſhop of Vilna, and a great majority of the
nobles, who blindly confounded religious prejudices with political rights; and the oppoſition
of ſome perſons, more enlightened or more
equitable, occaſioned violent debates.   The diſorder roſe to its height.   The king attempted
to deliver himſelf in favour of more moderate
ſentiments: he was abruptly reproached with
being

being an abettor of the enemies of the flate. He took the refolution to retire *. Several other fittings followed, not lefs fcandalous than the former; and the terrible laws enacted againft the diffidents were imprudently confirmed. The ruffian troops now advanced to the gates of Warfaw. Prince Repnin demanded in the name of the emprefs, not only a toleration fecured by law in behalf of the diffidents, but a complete political equality with the catholic party. This was rejected with a furious triumph. Nothing was now left for the diffidents, but; what the conflitution allowed, to confederate: this courfe they immediately adopted under the ruffian protection. Fear feemed for a moment to open the eyes of the diet. It thought to fatisfy the emprefs by granting the diffidents fomewhat more liberty in the exercife of their

* The bifhop of Kief had already taken the liberty to fay in an affemby, " that if they would take his advice, " they would have the king hanged; as there were " ftill furely fome men to be found among the Poles, cha- " ritable enough to do the ftate that fervice." The fame prelate afterwards proceeded from infolence to fury, fo far as to tell the king to his face, in prefence of all the court:—" I formerly ufed to pray to God for your profpe- " rity; my prayer to him at prefent is, that he would fend " you to the devil."

F 2 religion.

religion.   But this palliative was not fufficient
for Catharine.   The diffidents, continuing to
infift on an entire equality of rights, formed into
divers confederations, which were prefently joined
by numbers of catholics, won over by Ruffia.

This was a lamentable time for Poland;
parties and counter-parties, uniting and fplitting
again into others in the moft unexampled manner.
From grievances in religion political feuds arofe;
feveral of the difcontented went over to the
diffidents, without otherwife agreeing with them
in opinion.   A civil war raged now with all
its horrors, and ruffian troops were every day
entering the territories of the republic in greater
numbers.   A general confederation fprung up,
compofed of the moft heterogeneous parts,
united neither by a common underftanding nor
by the cement of affection: prince Charles
Radzivil, who had been abfent from the country,
was their marfhal.   This prince had been one
of the foremoft of the opponents to the election
of Poniatofsky; for which he had been obliged
to quit the country, and fuffer the confifcation of
his property.   He even affected more contempt
than hatred towards him.   He no fooner faw
him abandoned by the Ruffians, than he united
his confederation with thofe of the diffidents, and
                                        convened

convened the principal leaders of them in his palace in Warfaw, under the very eyes of the monarch.

1767. In this extremity Staniſlaus Auguſtus, who felt the neceſſity of regaining the protection of Ruſſia, aſſembled a diet extraordinary. This diet, however, but ill correſponded with his views. Notwithſtanding the preſence of the ruſſian army, and the haughty behaviour of prince Repnin, who lorded in Warfaw far more than the king himſelf, the biſhop of Cracow and his adherents, as raſh and fanatical as ever, had the preſumption to make ſpeeches againſt the diſſidents, which common prudence, if not ſound reaſon, ſhould have adviſed them againſt. It was not long before they ſuffered for their folly. That very evening *, while the biſhop was at table at count Miniſheck's, the ruſſian colonel Igelſtrom, followed by a detachment of ſoldiers, entered the room, in the name of the empreſs, and ſeized on the prelate, without meeting the ſmalleſt reſiſtance from any that were preſent. Prince Repnin dictated to the diet the act of confirmation of the rights of the diſſidents; and, to the utter aſtoniſhment of the Poles, who always boaſted of their freedom, cauſed the

* The 13th of October.

furious

furious oppoſers of that act in the diet, the biſhop
of Kief, the vayvode of Cracow, count Rjeurſky,.
vayvode of Dolin, his eldeſt ſon *, and ſome
other nobles, to be ſeparately arreſted in Warſaw, and, together with the biſhop of Cracow,
conducted to Siberia.

The day following this outrage, prince Repnin addreſſed to the confederates a note, in
which he pretended that he had only violated
the liberty of the Poles for the benefit of
Poland †.

The

* The ſecond ſon of count Rjeurſky requeſted permiſſion
to accompany his father in bondage. He was anſwered,
that they had no orders to arreſt him.

† The declaration of prince Repnin delivered to the con-
federated eſtates was as follows : " The troops of her impe-
" rial majeſty, my ſovereign, friends and allies of the confe-
" derated republic, have arreſted the biſhop of Cracow, the
" biſhop of Kief, the vayvode of Dolin, &c. for having
" failed, by their conduct, in the reſpect that is due
" to the dignity of her imperial majeſty, by attacking
" the purity of her ſalutary, diſintereſted, and amicable
" intentions in favour of the republic. The illuſtrious gene-
" ral confederation of the republic, of the crown, and of
" Lithuania, being under the protection of her imperial
" majeſty, the underſigned notifies this to it, with poſitive
" and ſolemn aſſurances of the continuation of that high
" protection and of the aſſiſtance and ſupport of her impe-
" rial majeſty to the general confederation united for the
" preſervation of the poliſh laws and liberties, with redreſs
" of

The members of the diet fent up an addrefs to the king, requefting him to demand the prifoners. The king immediately prayed prince Repnin to releafe them : but Repnin rejected it with difdain; and they did not return from the defarts of Siberia till after an exile of fix years *.

In the mean time the deliberations of the diet were carried on under the impulfes of fear ; and after feveral ufelefs fittings, a committee was nominated for fettling the rights of the diffidents, in concert with the minifters of the patronifing courts. They regularly applied for orders to prince Repnin, whofe anti-chamber was the

---

" of all the abufes that have crept into the government " contrary to the fundamental laws of the country. Her " majefty is only defirous of the welfare of the republic, and " will not difcontinue to grant it her affiftance to the attain- " ment of that end, without any intereft or pecuniary con- " fideration ; wifhing for no other than the fafety, the hap- " pinefs, and the liberty of the polifh nation, as that has " been already clearly expreffed in the declarations of her " imperial majefty, which guarantee to the republic its " actual poffeffions, as well as its laws, its form of govern- " ment, and the prerogatives of each individual. Done at " Warfaw, the 14th of October 1767.

(Signed)   " NICHOLAS prince REPNIN."

* In the beginning of the year 1773.

F 4   refort

refort of the plenipotentiaries from Pruffia, England, Denmark, and Sweden; and when the
committee had received thefe orders, it made a
report of them to the diet, who were careful not
to contradict them. The diffidents therefore
obtained whatever the ruffian ambaffador was
pleafed to demand in their behalf. The ancient
laws to which they appealed were once more put
in force; and others were enacted which were
ftill more favourable to them. It was, however,
nothing more than an act of juftice, which had
nothing againft it but the manner in which it
was performed. They had been arbitrarily
abolifhed; it was therefore but right to reftore
them. The fole caufe of affliction to the true
friends of the liberty of Poland was a heap of
regulations admitted by the orders of Catharine,
tending to prolong the troubles and anarchy of
that unhappy country, and to leave it for ever
without defence againft the ufurpations which
fhe had in contemplation.

A fervile obedience had fuddenly fucceeded
in Warfaw to the exceffes of a proud independence. But this forced fituation could not long
continue. Murmurs were on all lips, and vengeance was in every heart. No fooner had the
diet broke up, but the catholic nobles were
clamorous in their complaints on account of the

laws

laws promulgated in favour of the diffidents, and formed new confederations for the defence of the romifh religion. The confederates had ftandards, on which were painted the virgin Mary and the infant Jefus: they, like the crufaders of the fifteenth century, wore croffes embroidered on their clothes; and, what was more ridiculous ftill, they put themfelves under the protection of the Turks; and the difciples of Mohammed were preparing to fight in the caufe that was called by the name of Chrift.

Staniflaus Auguftus, unable either to infpire confidence into his fubjects, or to recover the friendfhip of the Ruffians, was the fubject of accufation to all parties, and lived in his capital more like a prifoner than a king. Catharine might perhaps have pardoned him fome moments of defection, but the influence of Orloff oppofed it. Prince Repnin commanded like a defpot in Warfaw; and, to flatter the favourite of his fovereign, he let no opportunity efcape of humiliating a feeble and unfortunate king. We fhall juft cite one fingle fact to prove what little refpect the ruffian ambaffador had for the polifh monarch. One evening that the king was at the theatre, the ambaffador made it late before he came. As he did not appear, the curtain drew up, and the piece began. The performers were

in

in the second act, when a sort of bustle being made in the ambassador's box, the king sent a page to know what was the matter. Answer was brought that prince Repnin was come, and was surprised to find that they had not waited for his arrival before the curtain was drawn up. The king ordered the curtain to be dropped, and the piece to begin again.

All Europe beheld with astonishment the conduct of the court of Russia. It was thought scarcely conceivable that Catharine should become, all at once, the enemy of a king whom she herself had put upon the throne. But what could the faint remembrance of an extinguished attachment prevail upon the heart of a princess, who was aiming, by imposing shackles on Poland, to domineer over the powers of the north, and to make herself formidable to those of the south?

She was sure that the king of Prussia desired nothing better than to share the polish provinces with her. She managed at her pleasure both Sweden and Denmark, the one by her intrigues, and the other by the hope she held out to it of the cession of Holstein. She flattered England by a treaty of alliance and commerce. All seemed to concur to favour her ambition.

The

The duke de Choifeul, who, under the appearance of levity, concealed a deep and penetrating genius, and who perhaps was deficient in nothing, for being a great minifter, but more conftancy in his defigns, and lefs propenfity to diffipate the treafures of France, was the firft who difcovered the fecret views of Catharine. He faw that the augmentation of power which fhe was about to acquire muft have a natural tendency to diminifh the confideration and influence of the court of Verfailles. He refolved to attack the evil in its fource, and, to defeat the projects of Ruffia by diffipating its means, he fell upon the defign of involving it in a war with the ottoman porte.

That minifter then made application to count de Vergennes, ambaffador from France to Conftantinople; and after having ftated to him the particulars of his apprehenfions, exhorted him to fecond his projects. The duke de Choifeul was not ignorant either of the weaknefs and decline of the ottoman empire, nor the vices of a government which were the fole caufe of that weaknefs: but he ftill thought it fit to give Ruffia employment for a good while to come; and that, whatever might be the fuccefs of the war, he wifhed him to undertake it.

Vergennes

Vergennes adminiftered with no lefs ability than zeal to the views of his court. A long refidence in Turkey had fupplied him with an intimate knowledge of the principal members of the divan, and the means of fucceeding with it. He employed thofe means. He reprefented to the ottoman minifters how unjuft and dangerous it was that Ruffia fhould dare to violate the rights of the Poles, and invade their territory. He convinced them that the demarcation of the limits exacted by the court of Peterfburg would be attended with confequences fatal to the fecurity of the Euxine; and he advifed them refolutely to oppofe that demarcation *.

The Porte, whom the polifh confederates had already petitioned for fuccour, immediately complied with the advice of Vergennes. The turkifh miniftry fent a note to the king of Poland, requefting that the regulation of the

---

* The duke de Choifeul had authorifed M. de Vergennes to employ the moft efficacious meafures for inducing the Turks to declare war againft Ruffia. " If you have any " expectation to fucceed, if you think it poffible," he writes to him, " every neceffary fupply of money fhall be " tranfmitted to you." M. de Vergennes had the merit of wifhing to employ no other means than thofe of perfuafion. They were fufficient with him.

limits

limits might be fufpended till fome explanations fhould be given him of a nature to remove his alarms concerning the ·danger with which the ceffion of the polifh territory threatened the ottoman empire. But Staniflaus Auguftus, who was for ever afraid of giving umbrage to Catharine, and who was defirous, whatever it might coft him, of regaining her friendfhip, anfwered the grand fignor, that there was not the leaft propofal of altering the limits between Ruffia and Poland; and having received this affurance, the divan returned for fome time into its accuftomed apathy.

The court of Peterfburg then * concluded a treaty of alliance and commerce with that of London ; a treaty which extended the privileges of the Englifh, lowered the duties of importation on their merchandize, and granted them great advantages. Her natural inclination for England, as well as the defire of fecuring additional fuccours in the war which fhe was meditating againft the Turks, determined Catharine to feek the alliance of the court of London.

Juft at this time, when Catharine was difplaying her partiality in the moft fignal manner to the britifh nation, an affair of gallantry between

* In the month of December.

tween

tween the minifter of the latter and one of the
maids of honour became fo public, that the emprefs could no longer pretend to be ignorant of
it; fhe therefore difmiffed the guilty lady from
her poft, and forbad, for fome time, the minifter
to appear at court.

The feverity fhewn on this occafion by Catharine formed doubtlefs a ftriking contraft with
fome parts of her own behaviour. It feems
impoffible that fhe could fo ftrangely deceive
herfelf as to imagine that the world was not
aware of the indulgencies fhe permitted herfelf;
but it is neverthelefs certain, that fhe fometimes
put on, in the prefence of thofe who knew her
beft, as great an aufterity of manners as attachment to religion. Two ladies* of her court,
one of whom had formerly been her confidante,
being at a mafquerade, were talking pretty loud
concerning one of their admirers: the emprefs
went up to them, and, with a ftern countenance,
ordered them to leave the ball-room, fince they
knew no better than to pay fo little regard to
decorum.

The diftance Catharine often found it neceffary to affume could neither be fuppofed to gain
her the affection of her courtiers, nor to contri-

* Madame Narifhkin and Madame Goloffkin.

bute

bute to reftore tranquillity to the empire. Princefs Dafhkoff had been, for the fecond time, banifhed to Mofco. That young lady, who feemed to find her greateft pleafure in braving dangers, revenged herfelf for the ingratitude fhe thought fhe experienced, by revealing the crimes of the confpiracy in which fhe had acted a principal part, and in fomenting the difcontents againft the emprefs. Without efteeming princefs Dafhkoff, many perfons partook in her refentments; and the poifon of fedition, artfully mingled by her, was making new progrefs from day to day.

Being informed of the murmurs at Mofco, Catharine·feigned to defpife them, and refolved to fupprefs them by her prefence. But as the feverity of the winter would fcarcely permit her to take a long journey, fhe endeavoured, in the mean time, to divert the difaffected by the tumult of the pleafures fhe contrived for the court. The inhabitants at St. Peterfburg now faw two or three tournaments, at which the ruffian courtiers, arrayed in the habits and the armour of the ancient knights in the days of chivalry, difplayed more magnificence than gallantry, and greater ftrength than dexterity. Thefe fhows, which were continued for feveral days, were beheld with general difapprobation, as frivolous and expenfive.

In

In the amphitheatre erected on purpose for the occasion were two superb boxes, for the empress and the grand duke. In the centre of the arena was raised a throne, whereon sat the grand judge of the exercises, surrounded by forty officers, four heralds at arms, and two trumpets for the purpose of giving signals. Besides these, at four several places, all equally distant from the circus, were kettle-drums and trumpets, making warlike music during the whole time of the carouzel. In short, nothing was neglected that could contribute to the magnificence and effect of the exhibition.

The dames and knights of the tournaments were divided into four quadrilles or troops of horse, representing combatants of four different nations: Sclavonians, Turks, Indians, and Romans; all perfectly observing the customs of those nations, in their dress and ornaments, in their chariots, in their music, and attendants; and were all, ladies and knights, adorned with such a profusion of gold and silver, pearls, and precious stones, on their gorgeous dresses of velvet, silks, feathers, and ermine, that they might truly be said * to

" Shine with the wealth of Ormus and of Ind,
" Or what the gorgeous east, with richest hand,
" Showers on her kings, barbaric pearl and gold."

---

* With a slight alteration from Milton.

But

But that of the Romans, led on by count Gregory
Orloff, was brilliant beyond defcription. The
drefs of his brother count Alexèy Orloff, chief
of the turkifh cohort, was likewife particularly
fplendid.

The four quadrilles rode in great pomp through
the principal ftreets of the city, previous to their
affembling in the circus.

The ladies of the court joufted at thefe tournaments, as well as the chevaliers. Tilting at the
ring, cutting off the heads of ferocious animals
and Saracens, artificially reprefented, then toffing
up the head and catching it on the point of
the fabre, letting off a piftol at a fhield, with a
variety of atchievements of a fimilar nature, all
performed at full gallop and exactly in time with
the mufic, formed the other parts of this magnificent entertainment.

When the carouzel, which had been repeated
with confiderable variations for feveral days, was
ended, and the company were drawn up in their
refpective troops, the famous marfhal count
Munich, who had been appointed grand judge
of the field, previous to decreeing the prizes,
delivered the following fpeech, which fhews
that the veteran foldier was not unacquainted with
the art of flattery :

" Illuftrious

" Illuftrious ladies and chevaliers,

" None of you is ignorant that not a fingle
" day paffes, not a fingle moment, in which we
" do not behold the attention of our moft
" gracious fovereign, towards augmenting the
" fplendour of her empire, towards enlarging the
" fphere of the happinefs of her fubjects in
" general, and towards adding in particular to
" the luftre of her nobility.

" That incomparable fovereign has made
" choice of this grand day, for giving the prime
" nobility of her empire an opportunity for
" fignalizing their addrefs and agility in the
" martial exercifes of a brilliant carouzel, and
" fuch as has never yet been feen in Ruffia.
" Who does not fhare with me the fentiments
" of admiration and gratitude fo juftly due to
" her majefty for this act of goodnefs and
" maternal care ?

" Illuftrious ladies and chevaliers, you have
" acquitted yourfelves, in thefe noble exercifes,
" in a manner worthy of your birth, and adapted
" to give you the affurance of having merited
" the gracious regard of her majefty, the favour
" of monfeigneur the grand duke, and univerfal
" applaufe."

Then,

Then, turning towards countefs Boutturlin *, who had gained the principal prize, and which was valued at 5000 rubles, he faid,

" It is to you, madam, to whom her imperial
" majefty authorizes me to prefent the principal
" prize, the acquifition of an uncommon dexte-
" rity and grace which have won the fuffrages
" of all beholders. Permit me, madam, to be
" the firft to congratulate you on that honourable
" diftinction, which confers on you the right of
" diftributing with your victorious hands, the
" reft of the prizes to the ladies and the
" chevaliers.

" As for me, become hoary under arms during
" a fpace of fixty-five years of fervice †; I, the
" moft aged in years as well as the oldeft general
" in Europe; after having had the glory of
" leading the ruffian armies more than once
" to victory; I regard, as the recompence and
" the crown of all my toils, the honour to have
" been this day, not only the witnefs, but the
" firft umpire of your refplendent exploits."

After this the company, to the amount of fome hundred perfons, fat down to a fplendid

---

* Countefs Boutturlin was fifter to princefs Dafhkoff and countefs Elizabeth Romanovna Vorontzoff, the favourite of Peter III.

† He was at that time 84 years of age.

fupper,

ſupper, the deſſert at the concluſion of which
admirably repreſented the circus wherein the
carouzel had been performed. All the imperial
ſummer-gardens were illuminated throughout,
the walks lighted with numerous arches of lamps
burning with naphtha, temples of one general
radiance, illuminated fountains, and magnificent
fireworks; the whole feſtival terminating with a
maſquerade in theſe gardens, which continued
till day-light the following morning.

But Catharine knew alſo how beſt to employ
more worthy means for eſtabliſhing her authority.
She ſtill buſied herſelf in making reforms and
the erection of uſeful inſtitutions. She corrected
the tribunals, ſhe founded ſchools, ſhe built
hoſpitals, and planted colonies. She endeavoured
to infuſe into her people a love for the laws, and
to ſoften their manners by inſtruction. Jealous
of a power that knew no bounds, greedy of
every ſpecies of glory, ſhe was determined to
be at once both conqueror and legiſlatrix.
Amidſt conſpiracies formed for overturning her
throne, occupied with preparations for war,
which ſeemed ſufficient to arreſt her whole attention, and yet finding time for attachments of
gallantry, ſhe was unmindful of nothing that
could attract the reverence of mankind, and
captivate their admiration,

There

There was at that time no country where the jurifprudence was more perplexed and uncertain than in Ruffia. The intricate code of Alexèy Michailovitch, compiled that it might ferve as the bafis to legiflation, was, if not abrogated, at leaft contradicted by the numerous edicts of his fucceffors, which were always dictated by the intereft or the caprice of the moment. The fenate, the colleges, all the tribunals of the empire, embarraffed by fo many authorities and fuch oppofite laws, protracted caufes without end, or terminated them without juftice. To thefe evils a greater yet was added, the venality of the judges and their unlimited power *.

Catharine refolved to apply a remedy to all thefe diforders. She profecuted what fhe had begun in the fenate and in the colleges by forming them into feparate departments, which, having each but one line of bufinefs, could neceffarily proceed in a more regular courfe, execute their bufinefs with much greater difpatch, and give fewer openings to artifice and chicane. In order then to deprive the judges of all pretext or excufe for either negligence

* The loweft judge, who frequently had never learnt to read, ufed arbitrarily to put culprits to the torture to extort confeffion, and condemn a man to the knoot, or to be banifhed into Siberia.

or

or prevarication, she augmented the emoluments of their offices, a means unhappily insufficient, but which proves that Catharine was well acquainted with the spirit of the nation which she governed. Indeed, if the magistrates had been possessed of any virtue, would it not be rather from the sentiment of reputation, than by pecuniary recompences, that they would have been stimulated to justice? The empress therefore put in motion that spring which she thought would act with the greatest force upon them. She tells them in the ukause she published on the occasion:—" Indigence may perhaps " hitherto have given you a propensity to self-" interest; but now the country itself rewards " your labours, and therefore what might here-" tofore have been pardonable, will hence-" forward be criminal."—

Catharine did more than augment the salaries of the judges; she secured to them an appointment of half-pay for that season of life when age and infirmities should oblige them to retire.

These primary matters being arranged, the empress set herself to work on a new code.

All the provinces of Russia, not excepting the barbarous nations who dwell in the remotest parts of that vast empire, had orders to send deputies to Mosco, to present their ideas on the

laws

laws that were the fitteft for their peculiar exigencies. Catharine herfelf repaired to that antient capital. The opening of the ftates was held with extraordinary pomp. It was furely an interefting and novel tranfaction, to fee deputies of numerous people, different in their manners, their drefs, their languages ; and they themfelves muft have been aftonifhed at being here thus affembled for difcuffing their laws, people who had never thought about law but to obey the arbitrary will of a mafter, whom it often happened that they did not know.

The emprefs, defirous to leave this affembly the appearances of the completeft liberty, had a fort of gallery conftructed in the hall in fuch manner, that, without being perceived, fhe could fee and hear all that paffed. The bufinefs was begun by reading the inftructions tranflated into the ruffian language, the original whereof, in french, almoft entirely in the hand-writing of Catharine, has fince been depofited, enclofed in a magnificent cafe of filver gilt, in an apartment of the imperial academy of fciences at St. Peterfburg.

" The fovereigns of Ruffia poffeffed the moft " extenfive dominions of the world, and every " thing was yet to be done : at laft," fays M. de

Voltaire*, " Peter was born, and Ruffia was " formed ;" that is, doubtlefs, to fay, that at this period it arofe out of chaos. The bare idea of making it was grand, and its execution might juftly excite aftonifhment. Tzar Alexèy Michailovitch, his father, had already fketched out the work, and it muft be confeffed that Peter advanced it to a furprifing degree. To leave his country, that he might return to govern it with greater glory; to go and feek light in all parts where it enlightened mankind; to fubmit for feveral years to be the difciple of other nations, in order to become the mafter and the reformer of his own; to work as a fimple carpenter at Saardam, to prepare himfelf for creating a navy that fhould be formidable to his enemies; to lower himfelf to a common foldier, in order to become a great commander; to form on all hands eftablifhments of great utility, till then unknown to his fubjects; to attack at once all the abufes both in church and ftate, in the manners and cuftoms that had been moft fanctioned by inveterate habit; to extend reformation and care to every particular that was deferving of them; to temper the feverity of his difcipline by the total abolition of the word flave; to mix

* Hiftory of the ruffian empire, vol. i. p. 74.

pomp

pomp with toil, and annex prosperity to triumphs; all together characterised him as the great genius, the great man, and the great monarch.

But if that prince, so justly renowned to all posterity, polished his country in so many respects; if he made regulations, worthy of admiration and praise, with all this he framed no permanent laws, and much less a system of legislation that should embrace all objects. That great work * was left for Catharine II. She alone conceived the grand idea of undertaking it, and she alone had the courage to put it in execution. A code of laws, and especially laws founded on wisdom, is the noblest present that can be made to a people: no woman had yet been a legislatrix; and that part the empress of Russia resolved to act.

The reading of the instructions was frequently interrupted by bursts of applause. All present extolled the sagacity, the wisdom, the humanity of the sovereign. But fear and flattery had a greater share in these exclamations than an admiration proceeding from a just knowledge of the matter. They hoped, perhaps, by that means

---

* This work may be chiefly taken from the writings of Montesquieu, and several others of the french philosophers; but it must always redound to the glory of Catharine that she had the liberality of mind to draw from such sources.

to

to attract the favour of the emprefs, or at leaft to efcape Siberia. The deputies of the Samoyedes alone had the courage to fpeak freely. One of them ftood up in the name of his brethren, and faid,—" We are a fimple and honeft people. " We quietly tend our rein-deer. We are in " no want of a new code : but make laws for the " Ruffians, our neighbours, that may put a ftop " to their depredations."

The following fittings did not pafs fo quietly. Much had been faid about giving liberty to the boors. Some thoufands of this oppreffed clafs of beings were preparing to fupport by force what they expected from equity. The nobility dreaded an infurrection : they dreaded, above all, a defalcation of their revenues; and fome nobles were rafh enough to affert, that they would poignard the firft man who fhould move for the affranchifement of the vaffals *. Notwithftanding this, however, count Scheremetoff, the richeft individual of all Ruffia †, got up, and declared that he would willingly agree to this affranchifement. The debate was carried on

* This fact has been feveral times attefted by Andrew Schuvaloff, known in France by his pretty epiftle to Ninon.

† Potemkin was not as yet favourite. Count Scheremetoff poffeffed an annual income of 170,000 pounds fterling. He had belonging to him 150,000 peafants.

with

with great warmth, which grew to fuch a height that fatal confequences were to be apprehended; and the deputies were difmiffed to their refpective provinces.

However, previous to the diffolution of this affembly, the members were required to figna-lize the meeting by fome confpicuous act of gratitude. It was thought right that, though the benefit that was intended for the fubjects fhould be loft to them, it ought not to be fo to the fovereign, who had conceived the noble idea of it. Accordingly, by a general accla-mation, the titles of Great, Wife, Prudent, and Mother of the Country, were decreed to that princefs; but when fhe was petitioned to accept of thofe titles, fhe anfwered, with an affumed modefty, " That if fhe had rendered herfelf " worthy of the firft, it belonged to pofterity " to confer it upon her; that wifdom and pru-" dence were the gifts of heaven, for which fhe " daily gave thanks, without prefuming to " derive any merit from them herfelf; that, " laftly, the title of mother of the country was " the moft dear of all in her eyes, the only one " that fhe could accept, and which fhe regarded " as the moft benign and glorious recompence " for her labours and folicitudes in behalf of a " people whom fhe loved."

Proud

Proud of the work which had obtained her
such flattering marks of homage, Catharine
eagerly dispatched copies of her instructions to
the sovereigns whose approbation she most coveted: They complimented her on her laborious enterprise, and made no hesitation to pronounce that it would be an eternal monument to
her glory. The king of Prussia, who knew how
sensible she was to praise, and who was always
lavish of it with less delicacy than ease, wrote to
her a long letter, which, among other things,
contained this flattering observation : " No
" woman has hitherto been a legiflatrix. That
" glory was reserved for the empress of Russia,
" who well deserves it."

The empress received this letter at Kasan,
having had a desire to visit her provinces in Asia,
and the famous shores of the Volga. The letter
was couched in the following terms :

" Madam, my sister,
" I must begin by thanking your imperial majesty for
" the favour you have conferred upon me in the com-
" munication of your work on legiflation. Permit me to
" say, that it is a business which has had but few examples
" in the world ; and I may venture to add, madam, that
" your imperial majesty is the first empress who has made
" such a present as that which I have just now received.
" The antient Greeks, who were all appretiators of merit,
" in their deifications of great men, assigned the first place
" to legiflators, whom they deemed the true benefactors of
" the

" the human race. They would have placed your impe-
" rial majefty between Lycurgus and Solon.

" I made it my firft duty, madam, to read the excellent
" work which your majefty has vouchfafed to compofe ;
" and, that I might keep my mind free from all prepoffef-
" fion, I confidered it as coming from a well-known pen.
" I confefs to you, madam, that I was charmed, not only
" with the principle of humanity and gentlenefs that give
" birth to thefe laws, but alfo with the order, with the
" affociation of ideas, with the uncommon clearnefs and
" precifion that reign in this work, and the immenfe
" variety of knowledge diffeminated throughout.

" I put myfelf, madam, in your place, and I immedi-
" ately perceived that every country demands particular
" confiderations, which require the legiflator to comply
" with the genius of the nation, in the fame manner as the
" gardener accommodates himfelf to his foil. There are
" defigns which your imperial majefty is fatisfied with point-
" ing out, and on which your prudence prevents you from
" infifting. In a word, madam, though I am not tho-
" roughly acquainted with the genius of the people whom
" you govern with fo much glory, I fee enough of it to
" perfuade me, that if they govern themfelves by your
" laws, they will be the happieft nation in the world; and
" fince your imperial majefty is defirous of knowing all that
" I think on that matter, I deem it a duty incumbent on
" me to tell it naturally.

" It is, madam, that good laws, formed on the princi-
" ples that you have traced out, will require lawyers for
" their being put in execution in your vaft domains ; and
" I think, madam, that, after the good you have juft been
" doing in legiflation, you have another boon to grant,
" which is the inftitution of an academy of law, for the
" education of perfons defigned for the bar, as well judges

" as

" as advocates. However fimple the feveral laws may be,
" cafes of litigation, cafes complicated and obfcure, will
" arife, in which it will be neceffary to draw up truth from
" the well, which require expert advocates and judges to
" unravel them.

" This, on my honour, is all that I have to fay to your
" imperial majefty, unlefs it be, madam, that this eftimable
" monument of your labour and your activity, with which
" you condefcend to truft me, fhall be preferved as one of
" the choiceft pieces in my library. ..Were there any thing,
" madam, capable of angmenting my admiration, it would
" be the benefit you have herein beftowed upon your
" immenfe people.

" Accept, with your accuftomed goodnefs, the affurances
" of the high confideration with which I am,

" Madam, my fifter,

" Your imperial majefty's good brother and ally,

(Signed)   " FREDERIC."

Count Solms, minifter of the king of Pruffia,
on fending this letter to count Panin, wrote him
a note to the following purport: " I haften to
tranfmit to your excellency the letter which the
king my mafter has had the honour to compofe,
in anfwer to that with which her imperial majefty was gracioufly pleafed to accompany the
prefent of her inftruction for the formation of the
new code in Ruffia, ordering me to caufe it to
be prefented to her imperial majefty. He fub-
joins, with his own hand, in the difpatch which
he has addreffed to me: " I have read with
" admiration the work of the emprefs. I was

" not

" not willing to tell her all that I think of it,
" becaufe fhe might have fufpected me of flat-
" tery ; but I may fay to you, with due defer-
" ence to modefty, that it is a mafculine per-
" formance, nervous, and worthy of a great
" man. We are told by hiftory, that Semi-
" ramis commanded armies. Queen Elizabeth
" has been accounted a good politician. The
" emprefs-queen has fhewn great intrepidity on
" her acceffion to the throne; but no woman
" has ever been a legiflatrix. That glory was
" referved for the emprefs of Ruffia, who
" deferves it."

It certainly redounds much to the praife of
Catharine, that thefe inftructions are founded
on the principles of an enlightened humanity ;
and that, though autocratrix and of unlimited
power, fhe recognizes no legitimate authority
but that which is founded on juftice ; every particular in her laws has a tendency to enervate
defpotifm, and to render a juft authority refpect-
able. Her purpofe is to form a folid, and not
an arbitrary legiflation. Her whole plan is directed to prevent all thofe who govern under her
from exercifing a capricious and cruel authority,
by fubjecting them to invariable laws, which no
authority fhould be able to infringe.

The

The accomplishment of this grand design, however, did not proceed so easily as the first steps gave room to expect. Either it was found that the plan of a convocation of the nation by its deputies was beginning at too high a pitch, and that in an assembly composed of such a diversity of tribes, manners, and tongues, it would be impossible to come to any common conclusions; or the whole apparatus was used only as a machine, and suffered to fall when it had answered the end for which it was contrived.

A few articles in these instructions will suffice to shew the principles on which they are drawn up.

" The spirit of the nation, the nation itself, " ought to be consulted in the framing of " laws.

" These laws should be considered no other- " wise than as a means of conducting mankind " to the greatest happiness.

" It is our duty to mitigate the lot of those " who live in a state of dependence.

" The liberty and the security of the citizens " ought to be the grand and precious objects of " all laws; they should all tend to render life, " honour, and property, as stable and secure " as the constitution of the government itself.

" The

" The liberty of the fubjects ought only to be
" reftricted concerning what it would be dif-
" advantageous to them to do.

" In caufes purely civil, the laws fhould be
" fo clear and precife, that the judgments refult-
" ing from them be always in perfect uniformity
" in the fame cafes; in order to remove that
" jurifprudence of decifions, which is fo often a
" fource of uncertainties, of errors, or acts of
" injuftice, according as a caufe has been well or
" ill defended at one time or at another, gained
" or loft according to influence or circum-
" ftances.''

We read with equal pleafure the inftructions
fhe prefcribes to be followed in the criminal
conftitution :

" It is incomparably better to prevent crimes,
" than to punifh them.

" The life of the meaneft citizen is of confe-
" quence ; and no one fhould be deprived of it,
" except when the country attacks it or requires
" it.

" In like manner his liberty fhould be re-
" fpected, by being difficult about imprifon-
" ment, by carefully diftinguifhing the cafes
" where the laws will difpenfe with it, as alfo
" thofe in which the public fafety requires arreft-
" ation, detention, or formal imprifonment,

" and in this cafe even concerning different
" prifons.

" In the methods of trial, the ufe of torture
" is contrary to found reafon. Humanity cries
" out againſt this practice, and infiſts on its
" being abolished.

" A prifoner is not to be facrificed to the tor-
" rent of opinions. Judgment muſt be nothing
" but the precife text of the law; and the office
" of the judge is only to pronounce whether the
" action is conformable or contrary to it."

Concerning punishments:

" The aim of punishment is not to torment
" fenfible beings.

" All punishment is unjuſt when it is not
" neceffary to the maintenance of the public
" fafety.

" The atrocity of punishments is reprobated
" by the compaffion that is due to human na-
" ture: whenever it is ufelefs, it is a fufficient
" reafon to regard it as unjuſt, and, as fuch, to
" reject it.

" In the ordinary ſtate of fociety, the death
" of a citizen is neither ufeful nor neceffary."

All that follows under this head, touching the
proportion that fhould be obferved between
crimes and punishments; on the rarity of the
cafes where the crime deferves death; on the

rule

rule to be obferved in confifcations, which
the emprefs would not extend beyond acquired
property, and a number of other ideas are fuch
as could only proceed from goodnefs of heart
and profound meditation. The whole amount
of the articles of her inftructions is in number
525; and the very publication and difperfion of
the book throughout the empire has been attended with falutary effects. It was doubtlefs a
great and arduous undertaking, and worthy of an
exalted mind. The laws of this vaft empire
were voluminous to a degree of the greateft
abfurdity, were perplexed, infufficient, in many
cafes contradictory, and fo loaded with pre-
cedents, cafes, and opinions, that they afforded
an eternal fcene of altercation, and were fcarcely
to be reconciled or underftood by the very
profeffors of them. The particular laws of the
different provinces were alfo continually interfer-
ing and clafhing, and caufed fuch confufion that
the whole prefented an endlefs chaos, and
effaced almoft every trace of original fyftem
or defign. This augean ftable the emprefs was
determined to cleanfe; and though the fuccefs of
her patriotic attempt has not as yet been complete,
yet, in confequence of it, a great fimplification has
taken place in the laws, and a milder and more
impartial adminiftration of juftice.

The

The inftruction of the emprefs is not a law-book itfelf. She only fays, " Such regulations " fhould be made.—In the firft place, it fhould " be examined, whether," &c. But what ex-cellent fuggeftions are thus delivered, which certainly have produced, and muft continue to produce, great effects. Thus we find it faid, chap. xi. " Peter I. promulgated a law in 1722, " that perfons who were not of found mind, and " who opprefs their ferfs, fhould be put under " guardians. The former point of this law has " been kept up ; why the latter is not enforced " is not known." Again, chap. xii. " It feems " too, that the new manner in which noblemen " exact their dues from the peafantry is hurtful " to population. There is fcarcely a village " which does not pay certain tributes to its lord " in money. The lord, who never, or but " very rarely, fees his village, impofes on every " head a tax of one, two, and even to five rubles, " without concerning himfelf how the peafant is to pay that fum. It will be abfolutely indif-penfable to prefcribe laws to the nobility, ' obliging them to act more circumfpectly in " the manner of levying their dues, and to " require of the peafant tributes of fuch a nature " as fhall remove him as little as poffible from " his houfe and family. By this means agricul-. " ture

" ture will be better followed, and the popula-
" tion of the empire be increafed.   At prefent,
" a labourer leaves his home at the age of fifteen,
" to go and feek his fubfiftence in diftant towns ;
" roams about the empire, and pays his dues
" annually from what he earns."

    " If, for fome political reafon, it be not prac-
" ticable to free the boors throughout the empire
" from their vaffalage, yet means fhould be
" thought of to enable them to acquire property.
" In purfuance of this idea, fhould not a method
" be devifed for gradually bettering the condition
" of this lower clafs of people ?"   Is not fuch
language, which evinces fo much fagacity and
benevolence, the fitteft for the mouth of a
monarch who is defirous of making improvements, without undertaking the boifterous and
intemperate part of an auftere reformer ?   It is a
great matter, if a prince fhews that he under-
ftands the vices of the country, and knows how
they may be remedied.   Suppofe even that
nothing farther is done, muft not every con-
fiderate fpectator feel himfelf inclined to believe
that this fagacity and this benevolence has met
with difficulties which were abfolutely not to be
overcome ?   But fuch words are never loft:
under Catharine much was effected by what fhe
planned with prudent moderation.   In fome

places, however, fhe expreffes herfelf decifively,
and with command; and wherever this is the
cafe, the inftruction retains the virtual force of
a law.

The whole performance is an excellent com-
pendium of choice obfervations, of juft maxims,
and of generous fentiments; and at the fame
time a beautiful collection of ftriking paffages
from the celebrated philofophers of Greece and
Rome, of apt examples from ancient and modern
hiftory, from the manners of cultivated and
favage nations, and even from fuch nations as
are not fo well known to the reft of Europe, for
inftance, the Chinefe and other Afiatics. Whoever would make himfelf acquainted with the
philofophy of legiflation, might reap confiderable
advantage by taking it as his manual.

In addition to the paffages above cited from
this work, as a fpecimen of the fentiments of
Catharine, it will not be amifs to extract a few
others, if it be only to fhew, that upwards of
thirty years ago a monarch delivered the beft of
thofe which, in the opinion of fome, were firft
difcovered by the republicans of the prefent
day. A lofty philofophical ftation is taken in
the 6th chapter: " Several things rule over
" mankind, the religion, the climate, the laws,
" the maxims of government, the examples of
" things

" things paft, the manners, the cuftoms, from
" which, as the refult, a public mind is formed."
Elucidations of this maxim from the charaċteriftics
of various nations fucceed to this.   Then, " It is
" the bufinefs of the legiflator to follow the tem-
" per of the nation; for we do nothing better than
" what we do voluntarily, and in purfuance of our
" natural difpofition.   For eftablifhing a more
" perfeċt legiflation, it is neceffary that the
" minds of men fhould be previoufly prepared
" for it.   But in order to defeat the pretext
" ufually alleged, that it is not poffible to do
" good, becaufe the minds are not yet difpofed
" to admit it, take the pains to prepare them for
" it; this will be already a great ftep advanced."
" When it is intended to make great changes in a
" nation, that may turn to its benefit, that which
" has been eftablifhed by laws fhould be reformed
" by laws ; and what cuftom has brought into
" praċtice fhould be changed by cuftom ; and it
" is very bad policy to change by laws what ought
" to be changed by cuftom."

Chap. viii. of punifhments.   " Examine with
" attention into the caufe of all relaxations, and
" it will be feen that they arife from the impunity
" of crimes, and not from the moderation of
" punifhments." — " It often happens that a
" legiflator, who intends to correċt an evil, con-

H 4   " fines

" fines his thoughts to that correction : his eyes
" are open to that object, and shut to the incon-
" veniencies attending it."—Chap. ix. " If you
" consider the formalities of justice in regard to
" the trouble a citizen has to obtain his right, or
" to obtain satisfaction for some injury, you will
" doubtless find it too great ; if you regard them
" in the relation they bear to the liberty and
" security of the citizens, you will often find it
" too little, and you will see that the punish-
" ments, the expences, the delays, even the
" danger of the decision, are the price that
" every citizen pays for his liberty." Not to
be farther tedious, we will conclude with the
following : " Would you prevent crimes ? Con-
" trive that the laws favour less the different
" orders of citizens, than each citizen in parti-
" cular. Let men fear the laws, and nothing
" but the laws. Would you prevent crimes ?
" Provide that reason and knowledge be more
" and more diffused among mankind. To con-
" clude, the most sure, but the most difficult
" method of making men better is by rendering
" education more complete." Nothing that
relates to government is left untouched in this
little book. The maxims of politics, of toleration, and of justice, are thus loudly and powerfully delivered from the throne, and have
thereby

thereby received, as it were, one fanction more.

Still proceeding on the fame enlarged and enlightened plan which we have before had occafion to commend, the emprefs continued to cultivate and encourage the arts and fciences; to make her empire an afylum to the learned and ingenious; and to reform the manners and inftruct the minds of the people, through the extent of its moft diftant provinces.

The tranfit of the planet Venus over the fun, which was to happen in the fummer of 1769, added a new opportunity of fhewing as well her munificence, as the attention fhe paid to aftronomy. This great princefs wrote a letter from Mofco with her own hand, to count Vladimir Orloff, director of the academy of fciences at Peterfburg; wherein fhe defires the academy to inform her of the moft proper places in her dominions for the making of thofe obfervations; with an offer to fend workmen and artifts, and to conftruct buildings in all thofe places which the academy may think proper for the purpofe, and to grant every other affiftance to the undertaking which it may require. She alfo defired, if there was not a fufficient number of aftronomers in the academy to make obfervations in all the places required, to give her notice,

that

that she might send a proper number of the officers of her marine, to qualify themselves under the eye of the professors in the academy, for that undertaking. Such is the extent of that vast empire, that the observations which were made, both on the transit and exit of this planet, the one in the frozen regions towards the pole, and the other on the borders of the Caspian, were made within its own limits; to some part of which astronomers from every part of Europe went to behold that remarkable occurrence.

What appears somewhat surprising is, that while Catharine was striving to build her fame upon a solid basis, she made it a matter of much importance to obtain from all the powers of Europe, the title of Imperial majesty, which some of them had refused her. The king of Sweden had long since given it to Catharine; but the swedish diet could not be brought to grant it till the commencement of this year, 1767*.

Lewis XV. pertinaciously delayed to mention her by that style. Knowing that the sovereigns of Russia only began to assume the title of emperor in the time of Peter the great, he con-

* The 6th of February.

sidered

fidered them in fome fort as a new nobility: not confidering that it is the power of princes, and not the antiquity of their race, on which their rights are built. This refufal of the king of France mortified Catharine; but this was not the only reafon fhe had to be irritated againft him. She had no doubt that this monarch was informed of all the fecrets of the confpiracy that had placed her on the throne; and fhe knew, befides, that the ambaffador of France at the Porte, bad been labouring long to make the Turks declare againft Ruffia.

What then would fhe have thought if fhe had read a letter concerning this, written by the duke de Choifeul?—" We know," faid he, " the ill-" judged animofity of the court of Ruffia againft " France. The king fo heartily defpifes at " once the princefs who reigns in that country, " and her fentiments and her conduct, that it is " our intention not to take a fingle ftep towards " inducing her to change them. The king " thinks that the hatred of Catharine II. is " far more honourable than her friendfhip. At " the fame time he is defirous of avoiding " an open rupture."

But the fhuffling tricks of a foreign court and the dangers of war could caufe no great difturbance to Catharine; perhaps they were

even

even as neceſſary to her as the cares ſhe beſtowed on the adminiſtration of the empire, for eluding the bitterneſs of ſuch reflections as might occaſionally ariſe in her mind. She often imagined that in one adverſe moment ſhe might be deſpoiled of the fruit of her labours and ingenuity, and that ſome of her ſubjects might be ardently wiſhing for its arrival. The name of Peter III. was become dear to the Ruſſians. They recollected with pleaſure the good he had done, and the deſire he had of doing more: they forgot his failings and infirmities, expiated by a ſeries of misfortunes. They lamented the deplorable end of that prince; and the multitude of malcontents diſperſed throughout the empire, might ſecretly contain more than one avenger.

Senſibly touched with the deplorable death of the tzar, and incenſed at ſeeing his murderers ſharing his power, a young officer, named Tſchoglokoff, reſolved to avenge it, and even thought himſelf inſpired with the deſign by the ſuggeſtions of heaven. After having long reflected on the means of executing his ſanguinary project, he reſorted to the palace for ſeveral days in ſucceſſion, always lurking in ſome of the dark paſſages leading to the inner apartments, to which the empreſs retired when

ſhe

she wished to be alone. The prefervation of her majefty was on this occafion owing to an accidental circumftance, by preventing her from going, according to cuftom, along the paffage where Tfchoglokoff was waiting her coming. Difconcerted by a delay which he had not forefeen, and impatient to ftrike the blow which he thought beneficial to his country, and glorious to himfelf, this young man had the imprudence to truft his fecret to another officer whom he thought his friend. This officer ran in hafte to betray him. Orloff, thus informed of the meafures that were taken by Tfchoglokoff, and the inftant when he was again to expect the emprefs, caufed him to be arrefted in his ambufcade. He was found armed with a long poignard, and confeffed, without hefitation, the ufe for which he defigned it. Catharine, always fufficiently miftrefs of herfelf for concealing her indignation and her fears, pretended to forgive the rafh attempt of the youth, whom political fanaticifm had deluded from his duty. She even had him brought into her prefence, and fpoke to him with mildnefs. This generofity was only apparent. Catharine wifhed to conceal from the public a wicked defign, which, if it had been known, might foon have been imitated. But, as fhe did

not

not flatter herſelf with the hopes of entirely converting a man who, from an exceſs of humanity,
was about to become an aſſaſſin, ſhe quickly
cauſed Tſchoglokoff to be put into priſon, and
afterwards baniſhed to the heart of Siberia.

Some time before the period of which we are
treating, the deputies of the two ruſſian trading
companies, one eſtabliſhed at Kamtſhatka, and
the other at the mouth of the river Kovima,
gave the court of Peterſburg an account of their
diſcoveries. Thoſe of Kovima, ſetting out
from that river, doubled the cape called Tſchut-
ſki-noſs, in 74 deg. north lat. and falling down
to the ſouth, through the ſtrait which ſeparates
Europe from America, they diſcovered ſome
inhabited iſlands in the 64th degree of latitude,
where they went aſhore, and ſettled a trade with
the inhabitants, for their fineſt furs, ſome of
which they brought to the empreſs, particularly
a parcel of the moſt beautiful black foxes ſkins
that ever were ſeen. They named theſe iſlands
the iſlands of Aleyut; ſome of them are very
near the continent of America *. Thoſe of
Kamtſhatka went to the northward, and met
their companions at the above iſlands; ſo that,

* For a farther proſecution of ſome of theſe diſcoveries
the reader is referred to " Varieties of Literature," vol. ii.
p. 1. printed for Debrett, Piccadilly.

for the convenience of trade, they fixed a factory
at the ifle of Beering. When this report was
made, the court came to a refolution of pufhing
thefe difcoveries; and lieutenant colonel Blenmer
was fent, with feveral able geographers, with
orders to fail from the river Anadyr to the fame
coafts, and even beyond them.

About the middle of the year 1767, the
emprefs conceived the ufeful project of fending
feveral learned men to travel into the interior of
her vaft territories, to enable themfelves to
determine the geographical pofition of the principal places, to mark their temperature, and to
examine into the nature of their foil, their pro-
ductions, their wealth, as well as the manners and
characters of the feveral people by whom they
are inhabited.

A country of fuch a prodigious extent as the
ruffian empire, mufc naturally attract the notice
of every man who wifhes to increafe his knowledge, whether it be confidered in regard to the
aftonifhing number of tribes and nations by
which it is inhabited, the great diverfity of
climates under which they live, or the almoft infinite quantity of natural curiofities with which
it abounds. But the greater part of this country
is ftill immerfed in the profoundeft barbarifm,
and

and almoft inacceffible to the inveftigations of
the ordinary traveller.   Here vagrant hordes of
people, who, entirely addicted to the paftoral
life, roam from place to place, fhunning the
focial manners of towns and villages, negligent of
agriculture, and leaving uncultivated and almoft
in a defert-ftate vaft tracts of land bleffed with the
moft favourable foil and the moft happy temperature of feafons: there, peafants, and even
in many places inhabitants of towns, flaves to a
thoufand prejudices, languifhing in bondage to
the moft ftupid fuperftitions; brought up, befides, in the fevereft fervitude, and, being
accuftomed to obey by no other means than
blows, are forced to fubmit to the harfheft treat-
ment: none of thofe affectionate admonitions,
thofe prudent and impelling motives, which
ufually urge mankind to action, make any impreffion on their degraded minds; they reluct-
antly labour the fields of a hard mafter, and
ftudioufly conceal from his knowledge thofe
riches which fome accident, fo defirable in other
countries, fhould have led them to difcover; as
they would only augment the number of their
toils and the heavinefs of their yoke.   Hence
that carelefs contempt for the treafures prefented
them by nature, and the neglect of thofe bounties

fhe

she lavishes on them. Hence those immense
desarts almost totally destitute of cultivation,
and so many towns that are falling to decay.

Peter the great, of too penetrating a view not
to perceive both the evil and its causes, took all
imaginable pains, and adopted the wisest measures to ameliorate the condition of an empire,
so powerful from numberless other circumstances, to free his subjects by gentle degrees
from the shackles of barbarism, to diffuse on all
sides the benign light of arts and sciences, to
discover the treasures concealed in his dominions,
and to furnish agriculture with the remedies
and assistances adapted to its improvement. His
travels into several countries of Europe for
the acquisition of such kinds of knowledge as
were most applicable to the use of his dominions,
are sufficiently known; as well as that in 1717
he honoured the royal academy of sciences at
Paris with his presence, and expressed his desire
the following year to be admitted a member;
that he kept up a regular correspondence with
that illustrious body, and that he sent to it,
as the first essay of his ingenious and magnificent
enterprises, an accurate chart of the Caspian,
which he caused to be scrupulously taken on
the spot. At the same time he fitted out and
dispatched several men of letters to various

parts of his empire; one of them to make the tour of Ruffia, and two others to proceed to Kafan and Aftrakhan, to gain information of every thing of confequence to be known in thofe countries. In the year 1719, Daniel Amadeus Mefferfchmidt, a phyfician of Dantzic, was fent into Siberia, for the purpofe of making inquiries into the natural hiftory of that immenfe province, from which expedition he only returned at the beginning of 1727. This learned man did honour to the choice that had been made of him, by an indefatigable activity, and by the proofs he gave of his profound knowledge, not only in every department of natural hiftory, but likewife in antiquities, as well as in aftronomy, having carefully determined the elevation of the pole in all the places where he ftopped.

As the northern regions, particularly thofe of Siberia, were as yet but little known, and as it was very uncertain whether the extremity of thefe latter might not touch upon America, Peter I. fent from Archangel two fhips, with orders to proceed, by the white fea and the northern ocean, into the frozen ocean, where they experienced the fame difafters as had befallen the other veffels that had gone before them in this attempt; for one of the two was

caught

caught by the fields of ice, and disabled from proceeding any farther; and as no tidings were ever heard of the other, it, in all probability, perished.

Peter I. was not discouraged by the failure of this undertaking; but he was carried off by death as he was preparing a new expedition; he had given the charge of it to two danish captains, Beering and Spangberg, and a Ruffian named Tschirikoff, with orders to go to Kamtschatka, from whence they were to sail for exploring the northernmost coasts of Siberia. The sorrowful event of the emperor's death made no alteration in these dispositions; and the plan was carried into execution, the same winter, by the empress Catharine, who sent a small company of literati, provided with a paper of instructions, which Peter had framed with his own hand. They returned in 1730, after having penetrated very far towards the north.

The empress Anne was desirous of prosecuting these important researches still farther, and ordered the erection of a new company, in which Beering was to be employed as captain of the ship. Kamtschatka was again the point of departure for making the principal discoveries, with orders to neglect nothing that might shed any light on the knowledge of the globe. One

part of this fociety was to navigate the northern
feas, while the others were to repair by land to
Kamtfhatka over Siberia.   Thefe latter were to
act conformably with the inftructions of the
imperial academy of Peterfburg, and to employ
themfelves particularly in aftronomical obfervations, geometrical operations, and defcriptions
relative to the political and natural hiftory of the
countries through which they were to pafs.

John George Gmelin was one of the chief of
thofe who undertook the journey by land ; almoft
always accompanied by profeffor Muller, who
had the care of the hiftorical part.   They
reached as far as Yakutzk ; where Krafcheni-
nikof, the affiftant Steller, the painter Berkhan,
and the ftudent Gorlanoff, quitted them to go to
Kamtfhatka, of which they collected the political
and natural hiftory, as well as that of the department of Okhotzk.   M. de l'Ifle de la Groyere
likewife went thither with fome land furveyors.
Afterwards M. Fifcher was fent in the department of political hiftory ; he reached very near
to the province of Okhotzk, which he left in the
defign of returning *.

* For more particulars the reader is referred to the
preface of Mr. J. G. Gmelin to the firft volume of his
travels in Siberia, which appeared at Gœttingen 1751. A
french tranflation, or rather abftract of it, was given by
M. de Keralio, Paris 1767.

In

In 1760, M. l'abbé Chappe d'Auteroche was
fent into Ruffia, by order and at the expence of
the king of France, for obferving at Tobolfk
the tranfit of Venus over the fun : his obfervations, publifhed with great oftentation, contain
not near fo much as was expected from that aca-
demician ; and many of thofe which he relates
had been already long fince known.

The emprefs Catharine II. determined to
profecute thefe ufeful inveftigations, and accordingly gave orders to the academy of fciences to
make choice of a company of able and learned
men to travel over different diftricts of the
empire with attention and obfervation. The
felection of the learned travellers, the helps that
were granted them, the excellent inftructions and
advice that were given them, will be a lafting
honour to that academy. The very names of a
Pallas, a Gmelin, and a Guldenftædt, already
promifed much. M. Lepechin had likewife
acquired a reputation by different papers inferted
in the academical collections ; and the refult of
the labours of thefe enlightened men has been
feen in the extenfive utility which they have fince
produced. Very few of the accounts that have
been given by travellers contain fo great a variety of new and important matters. The jour-
nals of thefe celebrated fcholars even furnifh

I 3   fuch

such a great quantity of materials entirely new, for the history of the three kingdoms of nature, for the theory of the earth, for rural œconomy, in short, for so many different objects relative to the arts and sciences, that it would require, according to the judicious remark of M. Bekmann of Gœttingen, whole years and the labour of several literary men only to put these materials in order, and properly to class them.

In order to form an accurate idea of the different objects to which our learned travellers were enjoined to direct their observations, it will be necessary to give an account of the instructions delivered to them by the academy at their departure. By these they were to make accurate examinations into—1. The nature of the soil and that of the waters. 2. The means of putting the desart places into cultivation. 3. The actual state of agriculture. 4. The most common diseases, both of men and cattle; and the methods of healing and preventing them. 5. The breeding of cattle, particularly sheep, and that of bees and silk-worms. 6. The fishery and the chace. 7. Minerals and mineral waters. 8. Arts, trades, and objects of industry. 9. They must also apply to the discovery of interesting plants: and, 10. To rectify the position of places, to make geographical and meteorological observations;

ations; to report all that relates to manners, various cuftoms, languages, traditions, and antiquities; and mark down exactly whatever they fhould find remarkable concerning all thefe points.

All thefe different views were fulfilled in a fuperior manner by thefe gentlemen; and there is no exaggeration in what has been faid, that natural hiftory never at one time obtained fo great an increafe of its treafures, the ineftimable fruit of the labours of thefe truly ufeful men; and their narratives are become a lafting monument of their zeal, their uncommon talents, and their unwearied activity.

Samuel George Gmelin, phyfician of Tubinguen, began the courfe of his travels June 23, 1768, accompanied by four ftudents, James Gliutfharef, Stephen Krafheninikof, Ivan Michailof, and Sergèy Maflof; having with them an apothecary named Joachim Daniel Luther; Ivan Boriffof a draftfman, Michael Kotof, a hunter by profeffion, whofe bufinefs it was to ftuff the animals; and a fufficient efcort of foldiers. He directed his rout, on leaving Peterfburg, through Stararuffa, Valdai, Torjok, and Mofco, towards Voronetch; where he took up his winter-quarters, and whence he afterwards paffed through Oftrogofk, Pavlofk, Kafanka,

Cimlia, and T'fcherkafk to Azoff. From this laft place he fet out, about the middle of Auguft 1769, to proceed by T'zaritzin to Aftrakhan; he paffed the winter in that city, and only quitted it in June 1770; he traverfed, in this laft half year, in the whole courfe of 1771, and part of 1772, the north of Perfia; vifited Derbent, Baku, Schamaky, Entzili, Peribazar, Ghilan, Mafanderan, returned to Entzili, where he paffed the winter, and refumed, in April 1772, the rout to Aftrakhan. The third volume of his journal clofes with the defcription of thefe countries. This able traveller was continually obliged to ftruggle with adverfe events, while traverfing the northern provinces of Perfia; he had efpecially to contend with ficknefſes, and the difficulties thrown in his way by the khans of that kingdom; and he is deferving of the title of a martyr to natural hiftory, with the greater right, as, after having adorned his life with fo many labours, he clofed it under the weight of perfecutions, and in the miferies of captivity *.

The

---

* He was feized upon, at 90 verfts from Derbent, in the diftrict of Ufmey khan, and there actually died in prifon. The emprefs gave a gratification to his widow, after this deplorable event, by granting her one year's pay of the falary fhe had affigned to her hufband during his travels, confifting of 1600 rubles. If the worthy Gmelin had not undertaken his

The greater part of the writings he left behind him were forced, not without great difficulty, from the hands of the barbarians.

Peter Simon Pallas, M. D. and professor of natural history, long famous in that branch of knowledge, took his departure from St. Peterf-burg towards the middle of June 1768. In his progress he visited Novgorod, Valdai, Mosco, Vladimir, Kazimof, Murom, Arsamas, the country extending between the Sura and the Volga, and wintered at Simbirsk, of which he examined all the adjacent parts. The 10th of March 1769, he turned off to Samara, Syzran, Orenburg, crossed the countries watered by the Yaïk, and repaired to Gurief-gorodok, which seemed then to be the general rendezvous of our academical travellers. Here he met, among others, the unfortunate professor Lovitz *, who

had

----

second and unfortunate journey into Persia, rather as a merchant than as a literary man, and if he had not constantly gone by land, he would not easily have fallen into the hands of Ufmey khan.

* M. Lovitz lost his life in a dreadful manner, during the time that the rebels, who produced so much confusion in Russia in the preceding war against the Turks, were ravaging the colonies of the evangelical brethren. Our naturalist

was

had juft eftablifhed his obfervatory, his affiftant Ichonodzof, and lieutenant Euler : M. Lepechin was alfo at that time in the neighbourhood of Gurief. M. Pallas employed himfelf, during the whole of his ftay in this place, in examining the coafts and the ifles of that part of the Cafpian that lay within his reach. Hence he returned by the fame road, in order to go, by the way of Orenburg, to Oufa, where he arrived the 2d of October; and after having fpent there the winter, he fet out, the 10th of March 1770, for the mountains of Oural, and the province of Iffet : the 23d of June he reached Ekatarinenburg, where he made his obfervations on the great number of mines that are worked in that diftrict; he proceeded afterwards to the fortrefs of Tfcheliabinfk, whence, about the middle of December, he took his courfe to Tobolfk. M. Pallas

---

was taken at Dobrinka, where he thought himfelf in the greateft fafety. A band of thefe rebels dragged him as far as the borders of the Slovla, where their chief had his quarters; and, in the month of Auguft 1774, he was there firft impaled alive, and afterwards hanged. The affiftants of Lovitz, Ichonodzof and his fon, having found means of efcaping, faved all his writings and a part of his inftruments. Several farther particulars relating to this learned traveller, may be feen in Bufching's Wochentliche nachrichten, 1775, p. 56 & feq.

had

had fojourned the greater part of the winter at Tfcheliabinfk, and traverfed and examined, partly by himfelf and partly by his affiftant M. Lepechin, and by profeffor Falk, almoft all the government of Orenburg, when this latter alfo came, about the middle of March 1771, followed fhortly after by his affiftant Georgi, to join him in this town of Tfcheliabinfk. Captain Ritfchkof, who had hardly quitted M. Pallas all the winter, now left him, and fet out upon another journey.

M. Pallas finàlly left his winter-quarters at Tfcheliabinfk the 16th of April 1771, directed his courfe by the Omfk, followed the courfe of the Irtyfh, vifited the mines in the environs of Kolyvan, went to the Schlangenberge (or ferpent mountains) and to Barnaul; where he found M. Falk fick, who was come from Omfk by the fteppes or defarts of Barabin. From Barnaul M. Pallas proceeded to Toms, and arrived, the 10th of October 1771 at Krafnoyarfk upon the Yenifey, which he had made choice of for his winter-quarters. It was there that the ftudent Suyef came up to him again, in the month of January 1772; he had made, in the courfe of the laft fummer, a journey the length of the Obe towards the frozen ocean, and was come to communicate his obfervations to

M. Pallas,

M. Pallas, who was again joined, in the month
of February, by M. Georgi, who had hitherto
ferved as affiftant to M. Falk, and afterwards by
the ftudents Bykof, Kafchkaref, and Lebedef,
whom M. Falk, forced by the bad ftate of his
health to return, had fent to M. Pallas.

Our learned traveller left his winter-quarters
the 7th of March 1772, to proceed, with
M. Georgi and two ftudents, by Irkutfk to the
lake Baikal, whither he had already fent M. Sokolof in the month of January. After having
feen the environs of that lake, Selinginfk and
Irkutfk, he regained, the 12th of July, the
route of Krafnoyarfk, where he fet up his winter-
quarters, after having vifited the mountains of
Sayan. In the month of January 1773, they
fet out on their return, in which they took the
way of Tomfk, Tara on the Irtyfh, Kafan, Sara-
pul, Yaitzkoi-gorodok, Aftrakhan, and through
the country that borders the Sarpa to Tzaritzin,
where he met again M. Sokolof, whom he had
fent to vifit the fteppe or defart of Kuman.
After having wintered at Tzaritzin, and made
feveral excurfions from that city towards the
Volga, he returned at length by Mofco to
St. Peterfburg, where he arrived the 30th of
June 1774.

We

We fee, by this fhort fketch of M. Pallas's
travels, that he went over a great part of the fame
countries which the firft, third, and fourth volumes
of the travels of J. George Gmelin had defcribed.
But this ought not to induce us to regard the
labour of M. Pallas as a repetition, which might
eafily have been difpenfed with; the map of
M. Gmelin differed entirely from his, and was
incomparably more contracted, as to the department of natural hiftory. Befides, profeffor
Pallas took quite other courfes than thofe of
M. Gmellin: and Siberia had in the interval
acquired an altogether different face, as well by
the extenfion of its frontiers, as by the eftablifhments that have increafed its population, by the
new and important mines that have been put in
produce, and the founderies that have been
erected there; fo that it cannot fail of gaining
infinitely by any comparifon that might be
made between his accounts and thofe of
Gmelin.

John Amadeus Georgi, member of the
fociety of natural hiftory at Berlin, was at firft
deftined by the imperial academy to relieve profeffor Falk, who was commiffioned with what
was called the expedition of Orenburg, and then
known to be in a bad ftate of health. He fet out,
in confequence, the 1ft of June 1770, took the

route

route by Mofco and Aftrakhan, and met M. Falk
in the fteppe of the Kalmucs, very near to an
armenian caravan.   He followed him acrofs
that fteppe to Ouralfk (at that time Yaitzkoi-
gorodok) and to Orenburg, where they remained till the end of the year.   At the beginning of 1771, they travelled by confent into the
province of Iffet, M. Falk along the lines of
Orenburg, and M. Georgi by the Bafchkie and
the Oural.   He took, during the illnefs that
detained M. Falk, feveral little journies from
Tfchelyœba, capital of the province, towards
feveral places, for obferving a variety of natural
curiofities, and the nations of the country ; finding themfelves at length in a capacity to continue
their courfes, at the latter end of June M. Falk
proceeded by Ifetfkoi to Omfk on the Irtyfh,
and directed M. Georgi to come and join him
at the laft-mentioned place by the new lines of
Siberia, or of Ifchim on the frontiers of the Kirg-
hifes.   They then proceeded in company acrofs
the fteppe of Barabin, to fee the filver mines of
Kolyvan near the Obe.   They went alfo afterwards to vifit Barnaul, and, as much as a ferious
malady, with which M. Falk was attacked anew,
would permit, the mountainous diftrict of the
mines of Altai, and the founderies that depend
on Barnaul.   Towards the end of November
                                    they

they continued their journey, following the firft elevations of mount Kufnetzk, to Tomfk. It was in this city that—M. Falk received from Peterfburg a permiffion to return, on account of his ill ftate of health. M. Pallas, the chief of the expedition, now remaining alone in the vaft regions of Siberia, M. Georgi, as we have already feen, was entered of his company, and travelled, though feparately, under his direction.

We fhall here give a fhort intimation of the places vifited by M. Georgi: from Irkutfk he proceeded to the lake Baikal, of which he drew an excellent chart, and thence into Dauria, for the purpofe of examining the mines of that name, and into the diftrict of the mines of Arguffin ; thence he returned by Irkutfk to Tomfk, Tara, Tobolfk, Ifetfkoi, Ilina, Ekatarinenburg, and Oufa, vifiting all the mines of thofe countries; he returned thence by Perme, on the Oural of the Bafchkirs; once more from Oufa to Tzaritzin and Orenburg; and laftly along the Volga, from Aftrakhan to Peterfburg by Saratof, Bolgari, Kafan, Makarief, Pavlova, Nifhneynovgorod, Yaroflavl, and Tver. On the 10th of September 1774, he arrived in the imperial refidence.

On

On coming to Kafan in March 1774, M. Georgi
found profeffor Falk ftill there, and extremely
ill, which he terminated, together with his life,
by his own hand a few days after. Two or
three particulars of his life* will not be difagreeable to the reader.

M. Falk was born in Weftrogothia, a province in Sweden, about the year 1727. He
ftudied medicine in the univerfity of Upfal, and
went through a courfe of botany under the celebrated Linnæus, to whofe fon he was tutor.
He publicly defended the differtation † which
that famous botanift had compofed on a new
fpecies of plants, which he called Aftromeria.
In the year 1760, when M. Georgi for the firft
time was at Upfal, the latter was already fo
deeply affected with depreffion of fpirits, that
M. de Linné, in the view of obliging him to
take exercife and diffipation, fent him to travel
over the ifland of Gothland, to make a collection
of the plants it produces, and the various kinds
of corals and corallines which the fea leaves
on its fhores. This voyage was attended with
no diminution of his diftemper, which found a

* From the journal of M. Georgi.

† In the collection known under the title of *Linnæi ame-
nitates academicæ.*

continual

continual fupply of aliment in a fanguine melancholy temperament, in a too fedentary way of life, and in the bad ftate of his finances.

Profeffor Forfkael having left Upfal for Copen-hagen in 1760, Falk followed him thither, in the defign of applying, by the advice of M. de Linné, to be appointed affiftant to M. Forfkael in his famous journey through Arabia; but, notwithftanding all the pains that M. Œder and feveral other men of literary reputation at Co-penhagen took in his behalf, his application failed, as the fociety that were to go on that important expedition was already formed. Obliged, with much difcontent, to return, he herborifed as he travelled, and enriched the Flora Suecica with feveral new difcoveries.

A man in office at St. Peterfburg, having written to M. Linné to fend him a director for his cabinet of natural hiftory, M. Falk accepted the poft, which led him to the chair of profeffor of botany at the apothecaries garden at St. Peterfburg, a place that had been vacant from the time that it was quitted by M. Siegefbek. His hypochondriac complaint ftill continued to torment him. When the imperial academy of fciences was preparing in 1768 the plan of its learned expeditions, it took M. Falk into its

fervice,

service, though his health was uncertain. He was recalled in 1771; but, having got only to Kafan in 1773, he there obtained permiffion to go and ufe the baths of Kifliar, from which he returned again to Kafan at the end of the year with his health apparently better.

But his difeafe foon returned with redoubled violence. From the month of December 1773, he had never quitted his bed, nor taken any other nourifhment than bread dried in the fwedifh manner (knækebrœd), of which he fcarcely took once a day fome mouthfuls dipped in tea. At firft he received the vifits of a few friends; but afterwards denied himfelf to them, and was reduced to the ftricteft folitude. When M. Georgi went to fee him, nothing feemed left of him but a fkeleton of a wild and terrifying afpect. The few words he drew from him confifted in complaints occafioned by a hoft of difeafes which kept his body in torture, and threw him into the moft cruel fleepleffnefs. The laft evening M. Georgi kept him company till midnight. He fpoke little, and faid nothing that could give reafon to fufpect the defign he was meditating. His hunter, and at the fame time his trufty fervant, offered to fit up with him the night; but he could not be perfuaded to confent.

M. Georgi

M. Georgi being requefted the next day, March 31, to come to the lodging of the unfortunate gentleman, he found him lying before his bed, covered with blood; befide him lay a razor, with which he had given himfelf a flight wound in the throat, the fatal piftol, and a powder-horn; all together prefenting a tremendous fpectacle. He had put the muzzle of the piftol againft his throat, and, refting the pommel upon his bed, he difcharged the difcontents in fuch manner, that the ball having gone through his head, had ftuck in the cieling. His foldier had feen him ftill fitting up in his bed at four o'clock, at which time he ufually fell into a fhort flumber. In his chamber was found a note written the evening before, betraying throughout the diftracted ftate of his mind, but nothing declaratory of his defign, or that was of any importance.

M. Falk, like all hypochondriac perfons, was not very communicative, and on certain occafions was diftruftful. But at the fame time he was of a fedate temper, complaifant, and upright, which made it a very eafy matter to bear with him, and fecured to him the indulgence of all his acquaintance. His extreme fobriety had enabled him to make fome favings from his pay, though he was very beneficent; it was not

there-

therefore indigence that drove him to this act of violence. He was of a cold conſtitution, preſerring ſolitude and quiet to ſociety, to the company of his friends, and to ordinary amuſements, which yet he did not ſhun, except in the latter period of his life. As to religion, he ſhewed on all occaſions more reſpect for it, than any ſtrong effuſions of zeal. It was ſolely to be aſcribed to the violence of his diſtemper, and the weakneſs of mind which it brought on, that led him to put a period to his days. The fate of this unfortunate ſcholar was generally and juſtly lamented*.

In the number of thoſe who were of the expedition of M. Pallas was alſo captain Nicholas Rytſchkof, ſon of Peter Ivanovitch Rytſchkof, counſellor of ſtate, who made himſelf famous for his topography of Orenburg. Rytſchkof, the ſon, in 1769, went over ſome diſtricts of the

---

* His papers were found in the greateſt diſorder. They contain, however, very uſeful and important relations. He particularly made it his buſineſs to inquire about the Kirguiſes and other tartarian nations; and as he frequently remained for the ſpace of nine months together in the ſame place, he was enabled to procure ſatisfactory notions concerning the objects of his inveſtigations. The imperial academy, in 1774, appointed profeſſor Laxmann to arrange his manuſcripts in order for publication; which was done accordingly.

governments

governments of Kafan and Orenburg; proceeded eaftwards from Simbirfk, and thence northwards beyond the Kama, declining afterwards to the north-eaft along the Oural mountains, which he traverfed in his way to Orenburg. In 1770 he vifited the countries extending the length of the weftern bank of the Bielaya, as far as the Kama, which he courfed as far downwards as Kafan; then croffing the province of Viatki, he paffed on to Glinof, came into Perme, and furveyed the environs of Solikamfk; thence, defcending along the Kama nearly as far as Koungour, he proceeded by Ecatarinenburg ro Tfchelyabinfk. In 1771, on departing from Orfk, he vifited the fteppe of the Kirghiskofaks on this fide the Yaïk, paffed the rivers Irgis and Turgai, came as far as the mountains of Ulu-tau, thence bore away to Uft-wifk and Orenburg, and came at laft, by a part of the province of Oufa, quite to the Dioma.

M. Lepechin, by birth a Ruffian, who, after having gone through his firft ftudies at the imperial academy of fciences at St. Peterfburg, went to purfue a courfe of medical ftudy at Strafburg, where he was admitted M. D. and was received in 1768 as adjunctus, and in 1771, member of the fame imperial academy, was at the head of another of thefe expeditions. He fet

K 3　　　　　　　　　　　　out

out the 8th of June 1768, from Peterfburg,
proceeded ftraight to Mofco; thence by Vladimir,
Murom, Arfamas, Alatyr, confequently by the
government of Nifhney-novgorod, to Simbirfk
in the province of Kafan; from which place he
fet out in the month of Auguft, to vifit the
courfe of the river Tfcheremfchan, which divides
the government of Kafan from the province
of Stavropol, and thence travelled over various
parts of the government of Orenburg. In
autumn he reached Stavropol, paffed the winter
at Simbirfk, and the fpring of 1769 in the
province of that name : the following fummer he
came to Aftrakhan; from which city, in the
month of Auguft, he made an extremely remarkable journey to Gurief, croffing the fteppe
which extends between the Volga and the Yaïk ;
from Gurief he went up along the Yaïk as far as
Orenburg, and reached in the month of October
the little town of Tabynfk fituate, near the centre
of the Oural of Orenburg on the river Bielaya,
where he wintered. In the month of May
following, he purfued upwards the courfe of the
Bielaya, examined the mountains, came in July
to Ecatarinenburg, ftruck forwards into the
Oural, and attained, beyond the Koungour, to
the fummit of the higheft of the Oural of
Orenburg, whence he returned to Ecatarinenburg,

burg, and paſſed the winter at Tiumen in the province of Tobolſk.

In the month of May 1771, he reached the ſummit of the higheſt mountain of the Oural-chain, which runs between Verkoturia and Solikamſk, viſited, during the ſummer, the province of Viatka, proceeded by Ouſtioug to Archangel, where he embarked in order to examine the coaſts of the White Sea. He made Archangel his winter-quarters that year. The following year, 1772, was employed by our learned tra-veller in making a ſecond courſe on the ſea juſt mentioned, along the ſhores and the iſles lying to the left of Archangel, as far as the weſtern and northern coaſts, proceeding thence to the mouth of the White Sea : he afterwards doubled Kanin-noſs, and at length returned by the gulf of Mezen to Archángel, whence he ſet out, towards the cloſe of the year, for St. Peterſburg. During the ſpring and ſummer of 1773, he viſited the environs of Pſcove, Velikiye-Luki, and Toro-petz, with divers other parts of the governments of Pſcove and Mohilef : in the month of Auguſt he went from Polotzk, along the Duna to Riga; whence he proceeded, following the ſea-ſhore, to Pernau, then to Valk, Neuhauſen, and Pſcove : after which he returned in December to St. Peterſburg, and probably thus terminated the travels on which he was ſent.

Dr. J. Guldenſtædt took his departure about the middle of June 1768, from St. Peterſburg, in order to proceed, by Novgorod, along the weſtern coaſt of the lake Ilmen, by Porkof, Staraia-ruſſa, and Toropetz, to Moſco, where he tarried from the 11th of September to the 8th of March 1769; when he ſet out for proceeding by Kolomna, Epiſani, Toula, and Eletz, to Voronetch; thence to Tavrof, to Tambof, to the fortreſs of Novochoperſkaia; and after having courſed along the rivers Chopa, Medvieditza, and the banks of the Don, he arrived the 11th of October at Tzaritzin, where he remained till the 23d of November: he afterwards went to Aſtrakhan, where he arrived the 4th of December, and then proceeded to Kitzliar, a ruſſian frontier town on the river Terek.   This place he quitted in 1770, to viſit the countries watered by that ſtream, by the Kunbalni, the Soontſcha, the Akſai, and the Koiſa, with the north-eaſt parts of mount Caucaſus; being often obliged in this courſe to return to Kitzliar, chiefly becauſe of the little ſafety he found in traverſing thoſe parts.   It was for this reaſon, and on account of an illneſs that

detained

detained him, that he did not reach Georgia that year.

The 10th of February 1771, M. Guldenftædt left Kitzliar, with a detachment of ruffian troops, for Offetia, which is a diftrict of mount Caucafus; and fo foon as the 17th of March he was already returned to Kitzliar, which he quitted for the laft time the 18th of May, in order to go to the hot baths on the borders of the Terek. One of the moft confiderable of the princes of the leffer Kabarda accompanied him, and fhewed him, during the months of July and Auguft, all that country, and the northern part of the caucafian mountains, inhabited by the Dugores. Thence he returned a fecond time to Offetia on the Terek, whence he departed the 11th of September under the efcort of fome hundreds of Offetians, whom the tzar Heraclius had taken into his pay, and happily arrived with them in Georgia. He was, the 25th of September, at Dufchet, a town of Karduelia. The 9th of October he left that country, in order to proceed to the river Kur, at the fame place where tzar Heraclius had appointed his troops to make their general rendezvous, and which was only 15 verfts diftant from Tefflis, its capital. It was there that M. Guldenftædt had an audience in form of the tzar, who embraced him, made him

fit

fit down in his prefence, and promifed to grant
him every affiftance that he fhould want; which
promife he afterwards fulfilled. He made the
campaign with the tzar, who pufhed with the
main body of his army to the diftance of above
120 verfts up the courfe of the Kur; and he
returned to Teffis with that prince the 14th of
November. He left this place again the 21ft of
February 1772, for Kachetia, always in the
fuite of the tzar, and paffed the whole of the
month of March in that province of Georgia.
He traverfed, in the month of May, thofe provinces of Turcomania which are in fubjection to
tzar Heraclius. The 20th of June he went, for
the laft time, to Teffis, in the refolution of
quitting Georgia, after he fhould have made the
tour of the provinces of tzar Solomon, and to
return to Mofdok on the river Terek. On the
18th of July he made his obeifance to that tzar,
who had fet up his fummer-camp on the fouthern
bank of the river Rion, fome verfts below the
fortrefs of Minda. The prince gave our traveller a very gracious reception. The 5th of
Auguft 1772 he quitted the diftrict of Radfcha,
which makes part of the kingdom of Immeretia,
and repaired to Kutatis, the capital of the lower
Immeretia; then made the tour of the frontiers
of Mingrelia and Guria, the eaftern part of

Immeretia

Immeretia and middle Georgia.   Tzar Solomon
had given him an efcort of 300 Immeretians
to attend him on his tour.   As he was preparing
to proceed farther on, he was forced for fome
time to fufpend his march, as the greater part of
his people had fallen fick.   In this interval
he received a fupply of men, horfes, and provifions, from a georgian nobleman whom a little
before he had cured of an ailment.   On the 1ft
of October he reached the laft grufinian or
georgian village, where he was again obliged to
ftop for a month, in confequence of advices that
he received of 300 Affetinians who were waiting
on the fhore of the Terek to attack and to
plunder him.   In the interim the major general
of Medem, being informed of his fituation, fent
a detachment of 600 men with two pieces of
cannon, at the arrival of whom the robbers
difperfed.   By this means Mr. Guldenftædt
happily regained the frontiers of Ruffia, and
returned firft to Mofdok and afterwards to
Kifliar.   In April 1773, he made an excurfion
to Peterfbade [the baths of Peter], whence he
returned the fucceeding month and immediately
fet out for Mofdok, and in the month of June
went upwards along the Malka.   From that
river he turned off towards the eaftern branch of
the Kuma, and proceeded to the five mountains

or

or Befch-tau, which form the higheft part of
the firft elevation of Caucafus : he vifited the
mines of Madfchar, from which he took the
route of Tfcherkafk, where he arrived the 24th
of July.   From this laft town he made a tour
to Azoff; being returned to Tfcherkafk, he
proceeded by Taganrog along the fea-coaft,
croffed the river Kalmius, following at the fame
time the Berda and the new lines of the Dniepr,
and came by the eaftern bank of that river
to Krementfchuk, the capital of the government
of New-Ruffia, where he arrived the 7th of
November, and paffed the reft of the winter.
He had not yet quitted this government, though
already on the way to the Crimea, when he
received orders on the 20th of July 1774, as did
all the other academical travellers, to return to
St. Peterfburg.   Accordingly he turned back,
and came by Krementfchuk, and along the lines
of the Ukraine as far as Bielefskaia-krepoft;
thence bent his courfe over Bachmut, and beyond
towards the fouth-eaft and the eaft, as far as
the rivers Mius and Lugantfchik.   Being returned to Bielefskaia-krepoft, he left it for the
fecond time the 16th of December, and came by
Kief to Serpukof; where, having collected all
the perfons and all the effects belonging to his
expedition, he took his departure the 20th
of

of December for Mofco, and in the courfe of March arrived at St. Peterfburg*.

Such is the general outline of thefe interefting travels from which the learned of Europe have received fo much information, and which could not with propriety have been paffed over with flighter notice in this hiftory; yet for the particulars of them the reader muft be referred to the accounts that have been publifhed by the travellers themfelves. The difcoveries made by the Ruffians at fea at various epochas, and particularly during the reign of Catharine II. have been fo faithfully laid before the public by Mr. Coxe in his well-known work profeffedly written on that fubject, that it would be unneceffarily fwelling the bulk of thefe volumes to fay any more of them here. However it is impoffible to take leave of thefe expenfive and important miffions without teftifying our acknowledgment, with that ingenious and candid writer, of the benefits that have accrued to fcience from thefe learned and laborious inveftigations, and to join with him † and every friend

---

* See Bachmeifter's Ruffifche Bibliothek, tom. i, ii, and iii. where very-circumftantial accounts of all the feveral courfes purfued by thefe travellers are to be found.

† Coxe, Ruffian Difcoveries between Afia and America, preface, p. xi.

EO

to rational inquiry, " in the warmeſt admiration " of that enlarged and liberal ſpirit, which " ſo ſtrikingly marked the character of the late " empreſs of Ruſſia; who, from her acceſſion to " the throne, made the inveſtigation and diſ- " covery of uſeful knowledge the conſtant object " of her generous encouragement. The au- " thentic records of the ruſſian hiſtory were by " her orders properly arranged; and permiſſion " was granted of inſpecting them. The moſt " diſtant parts of her vaſt dominions were at her " expence explored and deſcribed by perſons of " great abilities and extenſive learning; by " which means new and important lights have " been thrown upon the geography and natural " hiſtory of thoſe remote regions. In a word, " this truly great princeſs contributed more " in the compaſs of only a few years, towards " civiliſing and informing the minds of her " ſubjects, than had been effected by all the " ſovereigns her predeceſſors ſince the glorious " æra of Peter the great."

The court of Catharine became now the aſylum of the ſciences, to which ſhe invited learned men from every part of Europe. Among the reſt the celebrated profeſſor Euler from Berlin, on whom her majeſty ſettled a large annual ſtipend, made him a preſent of a houſe,

besides

befides fhewing him many other marks of her imperial favour and protection. Well knowing,
that it is not fo much by the power of arms as by
precedence in the fciences and the arts that
nations obtain a confpicuous place in the annals
of the world, Catharine with a laudable zeal
encouraged artifts and fcholars of all denomina-
tions. She granted new privileges to the
academy of fciences, and exhorted its members
to add the names of feveral celebrated foreigners
to thofe which already conferred a luftre on their
fociety.

Nor was fhe lefs attentive to the academy of
arts, by increafing the number of its pupils, and
adding fuch regulations as tended more than
ever to the attainment of the end of its endow-
ment. Scholars were now not to be taken
in after the age of fix years, that the defects of a
bad education might not yet have had time
to fpoil their temper or corrupt their manners.
Delivered for three years to the care of women,
they are then put into the hands of tutors, and
are devoted to the art to which they fhew
the moft inclination. They may become painters,
fculptors, architects, watchmakers, engravers, or
learn the art of cafting in metals, and of making
mathematical and optical inftruments. During
the whole of the time they are in the academy
they

they are not permitted to receive any thing from their parents. They are clothed, fed, and lodged at the public expence. At the end of 15 years they leave the institution; and, if their behaviour corresponds with the pains that have been bestowed on their education, they are granted patents of nobility. -

Independently of these advantages, such of the pupils as have carried the highest prizes, receive the before-mentioned pension, for travelling three years over Europe.

It is frequently observed, that though this institution has now subsisted upwards of half a century, yet it has produced no great artist; and that it has served no other purpose than to furnish Voltaire with a subject of pompous declamation, and to make annually a paragraph in the newspapers of Germany, ostentatiously describing the ceremony of distributing the prizes in the presence of the empress and the grand duke, with their pathetic speeches on the occasion; and that, answering that purpose, nothing farther was intended. Yet even admitting the love of fame to be the only motive at the time, the institution may hereafter find motives of its own, arising from interest, or a desire of excelling, as a civilized public shall increase, and the approbation of their performances no longer be confidered as a matter of form and confined to the court.

Still farther to encourage the fine arts in her dominions, the emprefs affigned an annual fum of 5000 rubles for the tranflation of foreign literary works into the ruffian language.

At this time, 1768, the fmall-pox was very rife in St. Peterfburg, which occafioned the emprefs and the grand duke her fon to remain at Tzarfko-felo, inftead of coming to town as ufual. The countefs Scheremetoff was carried off by that diftemper a few days before fhe was to have been married to count Panin, for which event great preparations had been made. It was neither poffible, nor was it material, to afcertain how the infection penetrated the receffes of the court; but perfons of rank and fortune were alarmed that neither one nor the other afforded any fecurity againft the ravages of this dreadful difeafe. The danger to which her majefty and the grand duke were expofed, together with her majefty's zeal for the welfare of her fubjects, gave rife to a propofal for introducing the practice of inoculating.

The firft perfonages in the empire determined to fet the example, by fubmitting to the operation; and a refolution was accordingly taken by the emprefs, to invite a phyfician from England, where inoculation had been moſt practiſed, and was generally allowed to have received ſome modern and very conſiderable improvements *.

Accordingly Dr. Thomas Dimſdale, about the beginning of July 1768, received a letter at Hertford from M. Pouſchin, the ruſſian miniſter at the court of London, repreſenting that the empreſs, having a deſire to engage an able phyſician to go to St. Peterſburg, in order to introduce inoculation, he wiſhed to ſee him as ſoon as poſſible. At the interview that enſued, great encouragements were held out ; but the doctor, from domeſtic conſiderations, at firſt ſhewed ſome heſitation ; when a ſecond courier arriving, and ſome circumſtances rendering it apparent that the empreſs and grand duke were immediately intereſted in the application, he prepared for his journey with all expedition, and accordingly ſet out on the 28th of July.

Two days after his arrival, the doctor, in conſequence of a previous notice, waited on count Panin, who, after the uſual ſalutations, ſaid to him, " You are now called, ſir, to the moſt " important employment that perhaps any gen-" tleman was ever entruſted with. To your

---

* See tracts on inoculation, written and publiſhed at St. Peterſburg in the year 1768, by command of the empreſs of Ruſſia, by the hon. baron T. Dimſdale, 1781.

6   " ſkill

" fkill and integrity will probably be fubmitted
" no lefs than the precious lives of two of the
" greateft perfonages in the world, with whofe
" fafety the tranquillity and happinefs of this
" great empire are fo intimately connected, that
" fhould an accident deprive us of either, the
" bleffings we now enjoy might be turned to
" the utmoft ftate of mifery and confufion.
" May God avert fuch unfpeakable calamities !
" But the hazard of the infection of the fmall-
" pox, in the natural way, is fo threatening,
" that we are compelled to have recourfe to the
" expedient of inoculation; which, though fo
" little known in this country, has been adopted
" and practifed in England with the greateft
" fuccefs.   We have phyficians of great learn-
" ing and abilities in their profeffion; but not
" being experienced in this new branch of
" practice, her imperial majefty was pleafed to
" lay her commands upon her minifters, to
" inquire after and engage a perfon of the beft
" abilities in it, and whofe fuccefs had been
" confirmed by long practice.   You come to
" us well recommended in thefe effential points;
" I fhall therefore repofe the utmoft confidence
" in you, and have only to requeft that you
" will act without the leaft referve.

" As

" As to the refolution of the emprefs in this
" particular, with regard to herfelf, I muft
" leave to her majefty to explain her own fen-
" timents ; but with refpect to the grand duke;
" he is already determined on the operation,
" provided you encourage it : it has been fub-
" mitted to his own confideration ; he approves,
" and even wifhes it. I have therefore to
" requeft, that before an affair of fo great con-
" fequence is finally fettled, you would make
" yourfelf well acquainted with his conftitution
" and ftate of health.

" His imperial highnefs knows you are ar-
" rived, expects to fee you, and invites you to
" wait on him to-morrow. I can venture to
" affure you, that he will be eafy of accefs,
" and willing to be acquainted with you. Be
" with him as much as poffible ; fee him at his
" table, and at his amufements ; make your
" obfervations, and, in fhort, ftudy his confti-
" tution. Let us not be too precipitate ; but
" when every circumftance has been duly
" attended to, report your opinion freely, and
" depend on this, that if you fhould deem the
" operation hazardous, and advife againft it,
" we fhall think ourfelves equally obliged to
" you ; nor will the acknowledgments on ac-
" count

" count of this expedition be inferior to what
" it will be upon the utmoft fuccefs."

In anfwer to this, the doctor affured the count,
that he would in every refpect attend to his inti-
mations, and that he might depend on his making
a juft report.

The emprefs came to town that evening, and
the next day, the two Dimfdales were prefented.
On this occafion there were only prefent with
her majefty, count Panin and baron Cherkaffoff,
prefident of the college of medicine, who having been educated at the univerfity of Cam-
bridge, fpoke very good englifh. Catharine
fhewed great perfpicacity in the queftions fhe
put concerning the practice and fuccefs of inoculation. On his retiring, Dr. Dimfdale was
invited to dine with her majefty the fame day;
and as the account of the manners obferved at
the emprefs's table will neither be foreign to our
purpofe, nor unentertaining to the reader, we
fhall give it in the doctor's own words:

" The emprefs fat fingly at the upper end of
a long table, at which about twelve of the nobility were guefts. The entertainment confifted
of a variety of excellent difhes, ferved up after
the french manner, and was concluded by a
deffert of the fineft fruits and fweetmeats, fuch
as I little expected to find in that northern cli-

mate.   Moſt of theſe luxuries were, however, the produce of the empreſs's own dominions. Pine-apples indeed are chiefly imported from England, though thoſe of the growth of Ruſſia; of which we had one that day, are of good flavour, but generally ſmall.   Water-melons and grapes are brought from Aſtrakhan ; great plenty of melons from Moſco, and apples and pears from the Ukraine.

" But what enlivened the whole entertainment was the moſt unaffected eaſe and affability of the empreſs herſelf.   Each of her gueſts had a ſhare of her attention and politeneſs ; the converſation was kept up with a freedom and cheerfulneſs to be expected rather from perſons of the ſame rank, than from ſubjects admitted to the honour of their ſovereign's company."

On the following day another converſation with the empreſs enſued, in which Dr. Dimſdale requeſted the aſſiſtance of the court phyſicians, to whom he deſired to communicate every propoſed regulation and medicine ; but the empreſs would by no means conſent to any ſuch conſultation, and gave her reaſons as follows :

" You are come well recommended to me ;
" the converſation I have had with you on this
" ſubject has been very ſatisfactory ; and my
" confidence in you is increaſed.   I have not
                                    " the

" the leaft doubt of your abilities and knowledge
" in this practice; it is impoffible that my
" phyficians can have much fkill in this opera-
" tion; they want experience; their interpofi-
" tion may tend to embarrafs you, without the
" leaft probability of giving any ufeful affiftance.
" My life is my own; and I fhall with the
" utmoft cheerfulnefs and confidence rely on
" your care alone. With regard to my confti-
" tution, you could receive no information from
" them. I have had, I thank God, fo good a
" fhare of health, that their advice' has never
" been required; and you fhall, from myfelf,
" receive every information that can be necef-
" fary. I have alfo to acquaint you, that it is
" my determination to be inoculated before the
" grand duke, and as foon as you judge it conve-
" nient. At the fame time I defire that this
" may remain a fecret bufinefs; and I enjoin
" you to let it be fuppofed that, for the prefent,
" all thoughts of my own inoculation are laid
" afide. The preparation of this great experi-
" ment on the grand duke will countenance
" your vifits to the palace; and I defire to fee
" you as often as it may feem neceffary, that
" you may become ftill better acquainted with
" what relates to my conftitution, and alfo for

L 4   " adjufting

" adjufting the time, and other circumftances of
" my own inoculation."

He promifed obedience to her majefty's commands; and only propofed that fome experi-
ments might firft be made by inoculating fome
of her own fex and age, and as near as could be
of fimilar habit. The emprefs replied, " that
" if the practice had been novel, or the leaft
" doubt of the general fuccefs had remained,
" that precaution might be neceffary; but, as
" fhe was well fatisfied in both particulars, there
" would be no occafion for delay on any
" account."

The emprefs, on being inoculated privately,
went * the next morning to Tzarfko-felo, a
palace about four and twenty verfts from Peterfburg. At firft no other perfons were there but
the neceffary attendants, it being given out that
her majefty's journey was only to give directions
about fome alterations, and that her ftay would
be fhort. But feveral of the nobility foon
followed, and the emprefs obferving among them
fome whom fhe fufpected not to have had
the fmall-pox, faid to Dr. Dimfdale : " I muft
" rely on you to give me notice when it is
" poffible for me to communicate the difeafe:

* On the 12th of October.

" for,

" for, though I could wifh to keep my inocula-
" tion a fecret, yet far be it from me to conceal
" it a moment, when it may become hazardous
" to others." The emprefs, during this interval, took part in every amufement with her
ufual affability, without fhewing the leaft token
of uneafinefs or concern ; conftantly dined at the
fame table with the nobility, and enlivened
the whole court with thofe peculiar graces of
converfation, for which fhe was ever diftinguifhed *.

The grand duke fhortly after † fubmitted to
the operation ; and, on his recovery, Catharine

---

* Shortly after being inoculated Catharine wrote to
Voltaire :—" I have not kept my bed a fingle inftant, and I
" have received company every day. I am about to have
" my only fon inoculated. The grand mafter of artillery,
" count Orloff, that hero who refembles the antient
" Romans in the beft times of the republic (1), both in
" courage and in generofity, doubting whether he had ever
" had the fmall-pox, has put himfelf under the hands of our
" Englifhman ; and the next day after the operation, went
" to the hunt, in a very deep fall of fnow. A great num-
" ber of courtiers have followed his example, and many
" others are preparing to do fo. Befides this, inoculation
" is now carried on at Peterfburg, in three feminaries of
" education, and in an hofpital eftablifhed under the in-
" fpection of M. Dimfdale."

† On the 1ft of November.

(1) Romans!—the Orloffs!

rewarded

rewarded the fervices of Dr. Dimfdale by creating him a baron of the ruffian empire, and appointing him actual counfellor of ftate, and phyfician to her imperial majefty, with a penfion of 500l. a year, to be paid him in England; befides 10,000l. fterling which he immediately received; and alfo prefented him with a miniature picture of herfelf, and another of the grand duke, as a memorial of his fervices. Her majefty was likewife pleafed to exprefs her approbation of the conduct of his fon, by conferring on him the fame title, and ordering him to be prefented with a fuperb gold fnuff-box, richly fet with diamonds.

The examples of thefe illuftrious perfonages had fuch immediate influence, that moft of the nobility both at St. Peterfburg and Mofco were impatient to have their families inoculated. This bufinefs being happily accomplifhed, baron Dimfdale was preparing to return to England, and indeed was juft fetting out, when a nobleman came to inform him that the emprefs was defirous of feeing him. The baron was much concerned to find her with every fymptom of a pleuretic fever, and therefore at her defire again took up his refidence in the palace. The fymptoms increafed; but, upon being bled, her majefty received immediate relief, and in a fhort
time

time the moft alarming fymptoms abated. So foon as the emprefs was recovered, which was in about three weeks, the baron again prepared for his journey to England. Having taken his leave, and received farther proofs of the munificence of her imperial majefly, the baron was attended to Riga by an officer commiffioned to fee that every neceffary accommodation fhould be provided, in the fame manner as at his firft arrival in the country *.

On the 3d of December 1768, a thankfgiving fervice was performed in the chapel of the palace, on account of her majefty's recovery and that of the grand duke, from the fmall-pox. The ceremony was very folemn and magnificent. On each fide of the imperial chapel, which is a lofty and fpacious room in the winter palace, is a row of guilt ionic columns. The walls are covered with taudry and ill-executed pictures of ruffian faints. On the roof, over the catapetafma and holy doors, is a reprefentation of the fupreme being, in the figure of an old man in white raiment. Within a railing extending acrofs the

* Before baron Dimfdale took his departure from St. Peterfburg, the emprefs purchafed the houfe that had been built by baron Wolff, formerly britifh conful in that city, for the purpofe of converting it into an inoculation hofpital, which fhe accordingly did, and the inftitution is ftill fupported.

room,

room, and contiguous to the pillar neareft to the holy doors, on the fouth fide ftood the emprefs and her fon, for, by the greek ritual, no perfon is allowed to fit in church; accordingly there are no feats, not even for the fovereign, who ftands all the while under a canopy, when not making the ufual proftrations. In the fame area, and on both fides of the fanctuary, were chorifters gaudily apparelled. All the reft of the congregation ftood on the outfide of the baluftrade.

The ceremony opened with folemn vocal mufic, no other being admiffible in the greek church; to this fucceeded the prayers and ejaculations, which conftituted the firft part of the office. Prefently the folding doors of the holieft were opened from within, and difplayed to view the penetralia of the temple. Directly oppofite appeared a large picture of the defcent from the crofs; on each fide a gilt colonnade of the ionic order: in the middle an altar covered with golden tiffue; and on the altar a crucifix, a three armed candleftick with lighted tapers, emblem of the trinity, and chalices, flagons, patens, and other holy veffels. A number of venerable priefts with hoary heads and flowing beards, mitres ftudded with precious ftones of every colour, and coftly robes of filk and damafk, ftood stood in folemn attitudes, among the columns of this gorgeous fanctuary.

From the adytum, or inmoft recefs, with flow and folemn fteps, advanced a prieft, bearing in his hand a two branched candleftick with lighted tapers, emblematic of the hypoftatic union of the two natures of the fon of God. He was followed in like manner by another, reciting prayers as he moved along, and fwinging a cenfer fmoking with fragrant odours. Advancing towards her majefty, he waved the cenfer thrice before her, during which fhe feveral times gracefully bowed, and as often made the fign of the crofs upon her breaft. A third prieft fucceeded him bearing on his arms the volume of the gofpel; out of which having read fome paffages adapted to the occafion, he prefented it to the mprefs, who kiffed it with great devotion.

The priefts then retired: the folding doors of the fanctuary were clofed: the chorifters fung an anthem, and were anfwered by mufical voices from within. The intonations were deep and fublime. In a few minutes the folding doors again flew open; the ceremonies of the tapers and incenfe were repeated. Two priefts advanced, bearing the facred fymbols, the bread and wine of the holy euchariſt, veiled with cloth

of

of gold.   Having adminiftered this *, they
retired.   The doors were clofed, and the choral
harmony refumed.

The doors were opened, and the fame ceremonies a third time repeated.   After this the
metropolitan afcended the pulpit againft a column
oppofite to the emprefs, and delivered a difcourfe; in which he celebrated her refolution
and magnanimity; and in the courfe of his
fermon remarked, "that the Ruffians had bor-
"rowed affiftance from Britain, that ifland
"famed for wifdom, bravery, and virtue."
The fermon ended, feveral priefts came from
the recefs, and concluded the fervice with prayers
and benedictions.

The fenate decreed that the event of the
recovery after inoculation of the fovereign and
his imperial highnefs fhould be folemnized by an
anniverfary feftival, which has been regularly
obferved ever fince.

* In the greek church the bread and wine are mixed up
together, and adminiftered with a fpoon.

CHAP. VI.

The ottoman porte declares war against Ruffia.— *1768*
Prince Henry of Pruffia at Peterfburg.—A
ruffian fquadron, under the command of count
Alexius Orloff, fails to the Archipelago.—Vic- *A. Orloff*
tories of count Romantzoff.—Capture of Bender.
—Count Alexius Orloff returns to Peterfburg.
—His conduct in Italy.—Prince Dolgorouky
enters the Krimea.—Peftilence at Mofco.—
Attempt to affaffinate the king of Poland.—
Congrefs at Fokfhiani.—Vaffilfchikoff becomes
favourite of the emprefs.—Gregory Orloff is
difmiffed from court; with other events from
1768 to 1772.

ON the firft menaces held out by Turkey,
Catharine, who felt herfelf not yet in a condition
to make war with advantage, fufpended the fettle-
ment of the limits between Ruffia and Poland,
without, however, abandoning the hope of
feizing on a part of that kingdom, where her
officers were continually haraffing and dividing
the inhabitants. The flattering and fanguine
expectations which had been formed on the
conclufions of the late diet, and the intervention
of the Ruffians in the affairs of the republic,
were

Poland

were totally overthrown almoſt as ſoon as they were conceived; and that unfortunate country became the theatre of the moſt cruel and complicated of all wars; partly civil, partly religious, and partly foreign. Indeed the meaſures relative to the diet, as well as thoſe which had for ſome time paſt directed all the tranſactions in that country, ſeemed pregnant with ſuch ſeeds of diſcontent, as might well be expected to produce, ſooner or later, ſome very extraordinary conſequences. We have ſeen a foreign army, under colour of friendſhip, take poſſeſſion of a country to which no juſt claim was even pretended; we have ſeen them, for a courſe of years, peremptorily dictate to the members of a once great and free nation the meaſures they ſhould purſue, and the laws they ſhould eſtabliſh for their own internal government; and we have ſeen them ſeize the ſenators of that nation, and ſend them priſoners to a foreign country, for daring to have an opinion in their own national councils. It is not then to be wondered at, that the Poles, a brave and haughty nation, long nurſed in independence, and whoſe nobles had exerciſed in their reſpective diſtricts an almoſt unlimited ſovereignty, ſhould ill brook a ſubmiſſion to ſuch unnatural acts of foreign power.

The

The confequences were accordingly fatal.
The refentment excited by patriotifm from a
fenfe of national injury and difhonour, being
embittered and enflamed by the fpirit of cruelty
and animofity, which is almoft always infeparable
from religious difputes, that unhappy country
exhibited, in the courfe of the year 1768, the
fcenes of horror, calamity, and defolation, which
are the common concomitants of civil war.
Citizen deftroying citizen; foreigners drenching
the vaft plains of a great country in the beft
blood of its inhabitants, and the fields covered
with the unburied bodies of thofe who ufed to
till them, are but a part of the horrors of this
dreadful picture. Some that were moft impatient of the ruffian yoke at feveral times attacked
their armies. Encouraged by Auftria, and particularly by France, they made themfelves
mafters of the city of Cracow, of a part of
Podolia, and united in the fortrefs of Bar, the
name whereof was then given to that confederation, which became fo famous by its enormities
and its misfortunes. The emprefs caufed reinforcements of the troops to enter Poland, giving the command of them to lieutenant-general
Soltikoff. The affrighted confederates made a
fecond application to the Turks. The count
de Vergennes, being informed of this ftep,

renewed his remonftrances to the divan, to determine it to fuccour the Poles, and to oppofe the ambitious defigns of Catharine : in which he fucceeded. The ambaffador of that princefs was fhut up in the prifon of feven towers, and the reis effendi delivered to the foreign minifters a manifefto *, by which the grand fignior declared war againft Ruffia, accufing it of having infringed the treaties, and violated the territory, of the ottoman empire. The Turks, at the fame time, announced that they were about to open the campaign with an army of 500,000 men.

The emprefs dreaded now neither the threats nor the undifciplined multitudes of the ottoman forces. On the contrary, fhe fhewed great dignity and firmnefs. Upon the occafion of the arreft of her minifter † at Conftantinople, fhe loudly juftiffed his conduct, and applauded his fpirit in not making any humiliating conceffions, or fubmitting to conditions that were derogatory to the honour and glory of the empire.

The conduct of the grand fignior, in regard to the tranfactions in Poland, was blamelefs

1768

---

* This manifefto was inclofed in a purfe. See the appendix to this volume.

† The 12th of October 1768.

and

and irreproachable, and entirely confiftent with the character of a good neighbour and faithful ally. The affairs of that country had, for fome years paft, greatly attracted the attention of the Porte; nor could it indeed have been an indifferent fpectator of the meafures there lately purfued. The great and growing power of the ruffian empire, and the fupreme afcendant it had acquired in all the tranfactions of the north, were in themfelves fufficient objects of jealoufy to fo near a neighbour. But the almoft abfolute dominion which it had lately acquired, and the unlimited authority it exercifed, in fo confiderable and extenfive a country, and poffeffed of fuch great natural power, as Poland, was an object of fuch moment, as the fultan could not poffibly have overlooked, without giving up every pretenfion to true policy, and even to common prudence.

In fact, while its kings were elected, its laws paffed, and its ftates governed under the influence of a ruffian army, Poland could be confidered in no other light than as a province to that empire; and the fplendid titles of kingdom and republic were only a mockery and cruel infult on its degradation. The Poles might have urged, and the Turks might have been convinced, that the pretences of fulfilling treaties,

protecting

protecting the diffidents, and guarding the freedom of election, was an useful sort of official language, which made a very good figure on paper, and had a plausible effect in manifestos, to the vulgar, or to those who were but little concerned. But these glosses could bear no political test of examination; as reasons of the same or a similar nature might be everlastingly found for the keeping of an army in any country, under pretence of friendship or protection, and at the same time converting it to all the purposes of a conquered province. In truth, the same reasons would have held, for sending a russian army to Constantinople, to protect the divan, to prevent riots among the janissaries, and to restore the christians in that empire to their ancient rights and privileges.

Catharine, however, had lost no time in preparing for her defence; and her preparations were formidable. Accordingly, she caused a manifesto to be delivered to all the ministers of the powers neutral or allied, and published a declaration of war, with the usual forms, in the public places of Petersburg.

1769. The russian armies began to march, and soon extended from the banks of the Danube to those of the river Kuban. The Tartars of the Krimea, who had embraced the party of the

the Turks, were the firft againſt whom the armies of Catharine diſplayed their prowefs. General Izaakoff drove 12,000 of them out of New Servia, which they had entered under the command of their khan *. Maſters of Azoff and Taganrog, the Ruſſians put theſe two places into a condition of refiſting their ancient poſ-feſſors, and laboured, with unremitted induſtry, in augmenting the little ſquadrons, which have fince given them the dominion of the Euxine.

The kofaks of the Ukraine penetrated into Moldavia. Prince Gallitzin, who commanded the principal body of the ruffian army, paſſed the Dniefter, and attacked 30,000 Turks even under the ramparts of Khotyim; but he was repulſed; and the conquerors purfued him to the other fide of the river.

That general then publiſhed a manifeſto, inviting all the Poles, who were not of the con-federation of Bar, to take arms againſt that confederation. Soltikoff had already folemnly announced to his army, that fuch officers or foldiers as ſhould take a confederate, and grant him his life, ſhould be feverely puniſhed.

Nine poliſh nobles foon after appeared in Warfaw with both hands cut off. For this

* In the month of March 1769.

M 3   mutilation

mutilation they had to accufe the ruffian general Drevitch. The barbarian had acted in the double capacity of their judge and their exe-cutioner.

Catharine recalled from Warfaw prince Rep-nin, whofe arrogance was difgufting to all the Poles, without even excepting the warmeft partizans of Ruffia. That ambaffador was fuc-ceeded by prince Volkonfky, who exerted him-felf·in vain to effect the re-confederation already pŕopofed in the manifefto of prince Gallitzin. The emprefs clearly faw how dangerous it would be for her, if all the Poles fhould unite againft the Ruffians. But the efforts of her generals and the intrigues of her minifters were now of lefs fervice to her than the weaknefs and inattention of the court of Verfailles. If that court had been fo inclined, the confederation of Bar would have been generalized, the Porte powerfully defended, and Poland ftill have been in the number of the powers of Europe *.

Long·

---

* In order to raife all Poland in one confederacy, the very eloquent and very able general Mokronofky requefted of the duke de Choifeul no more than 2,000,000 tournois, as a fubfidy, the acknowledgment of count Vilhcorfky as mi-nifter of the confederation of Bar, and the miffion of an agent to it, commiffioned to fee that the fubfidies were well applied.

Long before the plan for the partition of
Poland was put into execution, the emprefs and
the king of Pruffia equally felt the neceffity o
conferring on that grand defign.   But, thinking
that an interview between them would not fai
of giving umbrage to the other potentates, and
that they might perhaps find means for difcover-
ing the motives of it, they thought it moft advifable to decline it altogether.   Frederic, then
giving his inftruftions to prince Henry, his
brother, charged him with a commiffion to go
to Ruffia.   The better to conceal the objeft of
his journey, prince Henry gave out, that he
intended only to make a vifit to his fifter the
queen of Sweden.   While he was at Stockholm,
he mentioned that he fhould return to Pruffia by
the way of Denmark.   But all at once he feemed
to change his refolution, and yield, from complaifance to Catharine, who, hearing that he
was fo near her dominions, gave him preffing
invitations to come and fee her at Peterfburg.
Thus, though prince Henry had quitted Berlin
in no other defign than to proceed to Ruffia, he

---

applied.   The duke de Choifeul approved of the plan ; but
was diffuaded from it by the court of Vienna, who had
doubtlefs already formed fecret views, as the partition of
Poland afterwards made it appear.

found

found means to make it believed, that he was now going upon an unpremeditated journey.

Prince Henry embarked at Stockholm in a galley *, that conveyed him as far as Abo, the capital of Finland. From thence he repaired to Peterfburg. A chamberlain of the emprefs was difpatched to meet him on the frontiers of Ruffia. General Bibikoff received him at the laft ftation, before the entrance of Peterfburg, and conducted him to the palace that had been prepared for his reception, and where the minifter Panin was waiting for him. The prince entered Peterfburg under a difcharge of cannon, and every where received the fame honours that are paid to fovereigns.

1770. The next day he prefented himfelf at court with a numerous fuite, and dined in public with the emprefs. All that paffed this day was conducted with the moft rigorous attention to ceremony; but afterwards all etiquette was banifhed; and the emprefs and the prince might fee and difcourfe with each other without the fmalleft reftraint.

* The prince royal of Sweden, who reigned afterwards under the name of Guftavus III. and prince Frederic his brother, paffed the firft day in the galley with prince Henry. The duke of Sudermania was at that time in France.

Every

Every day was marked with fome feftivity or fome new entertainment *.   It would be fuper-- fluous

* One of thefe is defcribed in a letter from Mr. Richard-fon, then at Peterfburg: " I faw him [prince Henry] a few nights ago at a mafquerade in the palace, faid to be the moft magnificent thing of the kiud ever feen at the ruffian court.   Fourteen large rooms and galleries were opened for the accommodation of the mafks ; and I was informed that there were prefent feveral thoufand people.   A great part of the company wore dominos, or capuchin dreffes ; though, befides thefe, fome fanciful appearances afforded a good deal of amufement.   A very tall kofac appeared completely arrayed in the " hauberk's twifted mail."   He was indeed very grim and martial.   Perfons in emblematical dreffes, reprefenting Apollo and the Seafons, addreffed the emprefs in fpeeches fuited to their characters.   The emprefs herfelf, at the time I faw her majefty, wore a grecian habit ; though I was afterwards told, that fhe varied her drefs two or three times during the mafquerade.   Prince Henry of Pruffia wore a white domino.   Several perfons appeared in the dreffes of Chinefe, Turks, Perfians, and Armenians.   The moft humorous and fantaftical figure was a Frenchman, who, with wonderful nimblenefs and dexterity, reprefented an overgrown, but very beautiful parrot.   He chattered with a great deal of fpirit ; and his fhoulders, covered with green feathers, performed admirably the part of wings.   He drew the attention of the emprefs : a ring was formed ; he was quite happy ; fluttered his plumage ; made fine fpeeches in rufs, french, and tolerable englifh ; the ladies were exceedingly diverted ; every body laughed but prince Henry, who ftood befide the emprefs, and was fo grave and fo folemn,

fluous to enter into the particulars of any, except the feftival that was given at Tzarfko-felo; the

---

folemn, that he would have performed his part moft admirably in the fhape of an owl. The parrot obferved him; was determined to have revenge ; and, having faid as many good things as he could to her majefty, he was hopping away : but juft as he was going out of the circle, feeming to recollect himfelf, he ftopped, looked over his fhoulder at the formal prince, and quite in the parrot tone and french accent, he addreffed him moft emphatically with Henri! Henri! Henri! and then, diving into the crowd, difappeared. His royal highnefs was difconcerted; he was forced to fmile in his own defence, and the company were not a little amufed. —At midnight a fpacious hall of a circular form, capable of containing a vaft number of people, and illuminated in the moft magnificent manner, was fuddenly opened. Twelve tables were placed in alcoves around the fides of the room, where the emprefs, prince Henry, and 150 of the chief nobility and foreign minifters, fat down to fupper. The reft of the company went up by ftairs on the outfide of the room, into the lofty galleries all round the infide. Such a row of mafked vifages, many of them with grotefque features, and bufhy beards, nodding from the fide of the wall, appeared very ludicrous to thofe below. The entertainment was enlivened by a concert of mufic; and at different intervals perfons in various habits entered the hall, and exhibited kofac, chinefe, polifh, fwedifh, and tartar dances. The whole was fo gorgeous, and at the fame time fo fantaftic, that I could not help thinking myfelf prefent at fome

the magnificence of which is deferving to be remembered.

---

fome of the magnificent feftivals defcribed in the old-fafhioned romances :

——the marfhal'd feaft
Served up in hall with fewers and fenefhals.

The reft of the company, on returning to the rooms adjoining, found prepared for them alfo a fumptuous banquet. The mafquerade began at fix in the evening, and continued till five next morning.—Befides the mafquerade and other. feftivities, in honour and for the diverfion of prince Henry, we had lately a moft magnificent fhow of fire-works. They were exhibited in a wide fpace before the winter palace ; and in truth, " beggared defcription." They difplayed, by a variety of emblematical figures, the reduction of Moldavia, Vallachia, Beffarabia, and the various conquefts and victories atchieved fince the commencement of the prefent war. The various colours, the bright green, and the fnowy white, exhibited in thefe fire-works, were truly aftonifhing. For the fpace of twenty minutes, a tree adorned with the lovelieft and moft verdant foliage, feemed to be waving as with a gentle breeze. It was entirely of fire ; and during the whole of this ftupendous fcene, an arch of fire, by the continued throwing of rockets and fire-balls in one direction, formed as it were a fuitable canopy. On this occafion a prodigious multitude of people was affembled ; and the emprefs, it was furmifed, feemed uneafy. She was afraid, it was apprehended, left any accident, like what happened at Paris at the marriage of the dauphin, fhould befail her beloved people." Anecdotes of the ruffian empire, p. 327.

I I   Tzarfko-

Tzarſko-ſelo, or the ſeat of the tzars, the fixed ſummer-reſidence of Catharine II. lies in an open, pleaſant country, diverſified by gentle elevations and ſpots of foreſt, at the diſtance of 24 verſts from Peterſburg. The ſpace of the whole grounds belonging to the palace compriſes 420,000 ſquare fathoms. This princely ſeat owes its origin to Catharine I. and its extenſion and embelliſhment to the empreſs Elizabeth; but for its elegant completion and the greater part of its preſent magnificence, it is indebted to the creative reign of Catharine II.

The columns that mark the verſts on the road from town to Tzarſko-ſelo, are, like thoſe on the Peterhoff road, of marble, jaſper, and granite. On the two ſides of the way are 1100 globular lamps, which on public occaſions, when the court is at Tzarſko-ſelo, are lighted. Along the road the traveller is delighted with the view of private gardens and country-houſes, though neither in number nor elegance and diverſity to be compared with thoſe on the road to Peterhoff. Between the ſixth and ſeventh verſt-ſtones are ſeen the walls of the palace of Tſcheſme, riſing from a ſwampy plain overgrown with buſhes. This palace, which is in the form of a triangle, is built entirely in the gothic taſte, with old gothic ornaments, lofty

windows,

windows, painted glafs, little turrets. The infide
is remarkable for a very good collection of
portraits of all the princes of Europe, that were
reigning about the year 1775, and their families,
the greater part whereof were prefents from
the feveral princes themfelves. The grounds
about it are laid out in the englifh ftyle.

Five or fix verfts farther on is a village of
german colonifts; after which there is no other
object of confequence, till, at the extremity of a
thick foreft, Tzarfko-felo, the grandeft of all the
imperial palaces, appears. On the left hand is
the wall of the park, and oppofite two lofty
portals, practifed through a fteep and rugged
artificial rock, on the top of the higheft whereof
is a chinefe temple. On paffing through this
entrance, on the right hand is a canal and beyond
it the palace, and on the left a chinefe village,
through which the road lies over a chinefe bridge
into the park. The road extends to the neighbouring town of Sophia, through a coloffal gate
of caft iron. The palace itfelf forms an amphitheatre, with the building oppofite to the principal front. On the eaft fide of the garden
are two rows of large houfes for the people
belonging to the palace, and for the entertainment of travellers.

The

The outfide of the palace is grand from its magnitude, and dazzling by its gilded ornaments. It confifts of three ftories, and has a wing on either fide, one of which is the chapel, and the other the imperial baths. The central part was inhabited by her majefty. Here a marble ftaircafe leads up to the fecond ftory, in which are the ftate apartments to the fide of the court-yard, and the proper dwelling rooms look to the gardens. The generality of the former are fitted up and furnifhed in the richeft and coftlieft manner in materials of every kind, and in fuch elegant magnificence, that travellers, after vifiting other countries, unanimoufly declare, they know nothing of the kind with which it can be compared. A defcription of thefe, with the gardens, will certainly not be expected here; as it would require a peculiar work of feveral volumes for that purpofe. Only this cannot be overlooked, that Catharine, amidft the creations of her capacious mind, had here devoted a little temple of fimple architecture to folitary retirement and calm reflection, in which, furrounded by books and the beautiful fcenery of nature, fhe fometimes forgot her immenfe fphere of action, to indulge in the quiet enjoyments of meditation.

From

From the fouth wing of the palace projeﬅs an
arcade, fifty fathoms in length, over which is
a covered colonnade of marble columns.—The
gardens are laid out in the engliﬆ manner, and
are unufually fpacious. Among the remarkable
works in thefe gardens that are fufceptible of defcription are principally the following objeﬅs:
a fmall temple, containing the choiceﬅ colleﬅion
of antique and modern ﬅatues; a folitude for
a rural repaﬆ; together with a hermitage; a
fuperb bath, which may vie with any thing that
antient Rome could produce; piﬅurefque ruins;
a little town, with its ﬆreets and fquares, &c. in
memory of the taking poﬆeﬂion of Tavrida,
with many others. Two artificial lakes, con-
neﬅed by a rivulet, acrofs which is a marble
bridge copied from that in Stowe-gardens. On
an iﬂand in one of thefe lakes is a turkiﬆ
mofque, on the other a fpacious hall for muﬆcal
entertainments. In a wood appears a pyramid
of granite in the ægyptian form, in the neighbourhood of which are two lofty columns.

Tzarﬂko-felo, the magnificent fanﬅuary of
nature and art, pretends alfo to be the grandeﬅ
temple of merit. Formed of the radical mountains of our earth, monuments of great atchievements here tower aloft, fearlefs of the deﬆruﬅive
revolutions of time. A marble obeliﬆk records
the

the victory near Kagul, and the conqueror Ro-
mantzoff-Sadunaiſkoï. To the day of Tſcheſmè
and the hero Orloff-Tſcheſmenſkoï a marble
pillar on a pedeſtal of granite is dedicated.
A ſuperb triumphal arch proclaims the patriotic
courage of prince Orloff, with which he oppoſed
himſelf to the inſurrection and the peſtilence
that raged in the capital, and overcame them
both. A roſtral column perpetuates the conqueſt of the Morea and the name Feodor Orloff.
The reſt of the gardens are filled with objects
that keep the admiration of the beholder on
its utmoſt ſtretch.

It was at this grand ſeat of magnificence and
taſte, that Catharine gave the famous entertainment to prince Henry of Pruſſia. At the coming
on of the night, the empreſs, the grand duke,
prince Henry, and ſeveral perſons of the court,
to the number of 16, ſeated themſelves in an
immenſe ſledge drawn by 16 horſes, covered
and incloſed by double glaſſes, which reflected
the numberleſs images of the objects both
within and without. The ſledge, followed by
upwards of 2000 others, ſet out from Peterſburg:
every perſon of the whole company being
maſked, and dreſſed either in a fancy-habit or
a domino.

At

At the diftance of two verfts from town, the train of fledges paffed under an immenfe triumphal arch, illuminated with lamps of various colours, and adorned with tranfparent emblems. At every fucceeding verft was fome grand ftrufture, a pyramid of lamps, a magnificent temple, illuminated colonnades, or fire-works in full difplay; and oppofite to thefe at every verft on the other fide of the road was a houfe of public entertainment erefted for the purpofe, where ruftics of both fexes, fhepherds and fhepherdeffes, were dancing and amufing themfelves in various ways as at a country wake: every public-houfe of this fort reprefenting fome different nation, all the people being habited in the drefs of the country the inhabitants of which they perfonated; the mufic and the dances likewife in ftrift conformity with the habits. At other intervals, vaulting, tumbling, interludes, &c. were performing.

At about two verfts from the palace of Tzarfkofelo a high mountain rofe to view, feen through an avenue cut in the wood, reprefenting mount Vefuvius during an eruption, darting torrents of flames, and illuminating the atmofphere to a great diftance. This artificial eruption continued during all the time the fledges paffed in fight of the mountain, till they entered the

VOL. II. N lofty

lofty portal through the rock into the chinefe village, and through it to the palace.

The infide of the palace of Tzarfko-felo was lighted by an infinite number of wax-lights. In various apartments the company danced two hours. All at once a grand difcharge of cannon was heard, on which the ball ceafed, the candles were extinguifhed, and all the people ran to the windows, where they enjoyed the fight of magnificent fireworks the whole length of 'the palace. This having lafted for fome time, a thundering difcharge of artillery was heard again; when all the candles were alight once more as if by enchantment, and a fplendid fupper was already ferved up. After rifing from table, the dances continued till a late hour in the morning.

Catharine, during the whole of her reign, gave frequent entertainments to the public, which though inferior to this, were yet conducted with a magnificence not to be exceeded in any court of Europe.

Prince Henry during his ftay at Peterfburg, paffed all his evenings in company with the emprefs, in the favourite fuite of apartments which that princefs called her hermitage.

We ought not perhaps any longer to delay giving fome account of this fumptuous edifice,

9   for

for fo it fhould be ftyled rather than a fuite
of apartments, which, under the modeft appell-
lation of an hermitage, contains every thing that
the moft exquifite luxury could combine. It
occupies a fpacious building contiguous to the
imperial palace, with which it communicates by
a covered paffage over an arch. This ftructure,
which Catharine devoted to focial recreation and
the pleafures of familiar converfe, is perhaps the
only one of its kind that has ever been built
by queens and empreffes for this purpofe. It
had every property that could render it delight-
ful to the elect circle of her intimates. The
treafures of art and induftry with which it
abounds are not here to be defcribed ; but a fhort
account of fome of the remarkable particulars
of this palace it would be unpardonable to omit.
Here is the private library of the emprefs; the
picture-gallery, in which the famous Houghton-
collection makes but a fmall figure ; Raphael's
gallery, built exactly to the dimenfions of that of
the Vatican, with excellent copies of all the paintings, corner-pieces, and other ornaments of
exactly the fame fize and in the fame fituations ;
a cabinet of medals, and another of coins ; a
collection of copper-plate engravings; a collection of natural hiftory, particularly mineralogy;
a collection of curious pieces of art; a collection

N 2   of

of models of mechanical inventions; a cabinet of antique and modern gems; not to mention the extraordinary works of art which compose the furniture of thefe apartments *. Here and there are placed the bufts of great men. It is in one of thefe rooms that the elegant buft of Mr. Charles James Fox ftands in the middle of a marble chimney-piece between two others. Some chambers are deftined to mufical entertainments, another to billiards, and others to various games. One of them opens into a pleafure-garden upon arches, with furnaces beneath them in winter to keep up a gentle heat; fo that in the moft rigorous feafons, here are gathered the peach and the ananas, the hyacinth and the rofe. The whole of this garden is covered with a fine brafs wire, that the beautiful and rare birds from all countries that fly among the trees and bufhes, or hop about the grafs-plots and gravel-walks, and which the emprefs ufed frequently to feed from her hand, may not efcape. Here, in the midft of winter, Catharine, with thofe whom fhe admitted to her converfation, would walk on lawns and gravel, beneath the branches

---

* A great part of the paintings in the hermitage are from the famous cabinet of Crozat, which the emprefs caufed to be bought at Paris.

of

of verdant trees, and amidft fruits and flowers of every kind.

Above this is a terrace, where is a fecond garden, in the afiatic tafte; but this can only be enjoyed during the fummer feafon. A covered gallery leads from this enchanted palace into the court-theatre, at the performances of which, likewife, only a felect company ever appeared.

The other apartments of the hermitage are two large halls ornamented with great elegance, and a dining-room, in which dinner is ferved by a mechanical apparatus, which renders the attendance of fervants entirely unneceffary, by prefenting the difhes on fmall tables which rife through trap-doors. The company take their feats; and each of them, on wifhing to change his plate, has only to ftrike it in the centre, and it falls through the table, and through the floor, ftarting up again and fettling in its place, having upon it whatever was written on the fcrap of paper that defcended with it. At a certain fignal all the plates and difhes defcend, and others with the fecond courfe prefently appear.

Prince Henry expreffed his defire to fee Mofco. The fledges were immediately prepared; and he was tranfported thither with extraordinary rapidity.   Three weeks afterwadrs he was already back in St. Peterfburg.

Among the various prefents which he received of the emprefs was obferved the ftar of the order of St. Andrew, full of very large brilliants, together with a fingle diamond valued at 40,000 rubles.   The portrait of Catharine was inclofed in this ring *.

However, neither feftivities nor pleafures prevented prince Henry from accomplifhing the fecret objeƈt of his journey.   In the private converfations which he had with the emprefs, the difmemberment of Poland was refolved on †.

Catharine

---

* The emprefs, moreover, prefented him with a colleƈtion of medals in gold, and a variety of rich furs.   She alfo made great prefents to all the perfons of his fuite.   ʼ

† A letter written at the time by Mr. profeffor Richardfon, of Glafgow, at that time in the family of the late lord Cathcart, ambaffador at St. Peterfburg, as tutor to the prefent lord, difcovers fuch acutenefs of perfpicacity, as, fince the event, to have the air of prophecy, that it is impoffible to refift the making the following extraƈt from it. It ftands the xlift in his colleƈtion, and bears date Jan. 4, 1771 :—" This city, fince the beginning of winter, has exhibited a continued fcene of feftivity and amufements: feafts, balls, concerts, plays, operas, fireworks, and mafquerades in conftant fucceffion ; and all in honour of, and to divert, his royal highnefs prince Henry of Pruffia, the famous brother of the prefent king.   Yet his royal highnefs does

Catharine and Frederic were equally defirous of undertaking this difmemberment; but they could

---

does not feem much diverted. He looks at them as an old cat looks at the gambols of a young kitten; or as one who had higher fport going on in his own mind, than the paf-time of fiddling and dancing. He came here about the beginning of November, on pretence of a friendly vifit to the emprefs, to have the happinefs of waiting on fo *magna-nimous* a princefs; and to fee with his own eyes the progrefs of thofe immenfe improvements fo highly celebrated by Voltaire, and thofe french writers who receive gifts from her majefty. As the queen of Sheba had heard of king Solomon's " acts and wifdom," and " came to fee whether " fhe had heard a true report of them in her own land;" fo alfo this royal prince hath come to vifit this mighty princefs. It may be too that, like the queen of Sheba, he is come to prove her majefty with " hard queftions;" if fo, he may depend upon getting anfwers to all his queftions; and if he has any defires which fhe can grant, fhe will " grant him " his heart's defire." I could, with the greateft eafe, make out an exact parallel, in which the precious ftones, the camels, and affes, brought by the fheban potentate to Jerufalem, would, I affure you, make no contemptible figure. But do you ferioufly imagine, that this creature of fkin and bone fhould travel through Sweden, whence he is come at prefent, and Finland and Poland, all for the pleafure of feeing the metropolis and emprefs of Ruffia? Other princes may purfue fuch paftime; but the princes of the houfe of Brandenburg fly at a nobler quarry. Or is the king of Pruffia, as a tame fpectator, to reap no advantage from the troubles of Poland and the turkifh war? What is the

meaning

could not do it without a third ally. If Maria
Therefa had been ftill fole miftrefs of the
empire,

---

meaning of his late conferences with the emperor of Germany? Depend upon it, thefe planetary conjunctions are
the forerunners of great events. Time, and perhaps a few
months, may unfold the fecret. You will recollect the
figns, when you fhall hear after this of changes, ufurp-
pations, and revolutions. Prince Henry of Pruffia is one of
the moft celebrated generals of the prefent age. So great
are his military talents, that his brother, who is not apt to
pay compliments, fays of him, that in commanding an army
he was never known to commit a fault. This, however, is
but a negative kind of praife. He referves to himfelf the
glory of fuperior genius, which, though capable of brilliant achievements, is yet liable to unwary miftakes; and
allows him no other than the praife of correctnefs. To
judge of him by his appearance, I fhould form no high
eftimate of his abilities. But the fcythian ambaffadors
judged in the fame manner of Alexander the great. He is
under the middle fize, very thin, he walks firmly enough,
or rather ftruts, as if he wanted to walk firmly; and has
little dignity in his air or gefture. He is dark-complexioned;
and he wears his hair, which is remarkably thick, clubbed,
and dreffed with a high toupée. His forehead is high; his
eyes large, with a little fquint; and when he fmiles, his
upper lip is drawn up a little in the middle. His look
expreffes fagacity and obfervation; but nothing very amiable: and his manner is grave and ftiff, rather than affable.
He was dreffed, when I firft faw him, in a light blue frock,
with filver frogs; and wore a red waiftcoat and blue
breeches. He is not very popular among the Ruffians; and
accord,

empire, they would not perhaps have fucceeded in making her a fharer in fo unjuft a fpoliation. Jofeph II. was not fo difficult. Turkey, France, England, might alfo have maintained the treaties of which they were the guarantees; but thefe powers were fo eafily deceived, or fo indifferent to the fate of other nations, that Catharine faid to prince Henry, " I will frighten Turkey; I " will flatter England; do you take upon you " to buy over Auftria, that fhe may amufe " France."

Prince Henry knew fo well the difpofitions of Jofeph II. and of his minifter Kaunitz, that he acted as if he had been already in concert with them. He fettled with Catharine the conditions to be obferved in the difmemberment of Poland, and fixed the extent of territory that each of the powers in this copartnerfhip fhould appropriate

---

accordingly their wits are difpofed to amufe themfelves with his appearance, and particularly with his toupée. They fay he refembles Sampfon; that all his ftrength lies in his hair; and that, confcious of this, and recollecting the fate of the fon of Manoah, he fuffers not the nigh approaches of any deceitful Dalilah. They fay he is like the comet, which, about fifteen months ago, appeared fo formidable in the ruffian hemifphere; and which, exhibiting a fmall watery body, but a moft enormous train, difmayed the northern and eaftern potentates " with fear of change."

to itſelf. However, the treaty between them was not ſigned till two years afterwards *.

-The war continued to rage with fury on the frontiers of Turkey ; and while it cheriſhed in the mind of Catharine the ambition of conqueſt, it ſerved alſo as a military ſchool to the Ruſſians. Prince Gallitzin, humiliated at his defeat, made a freſh attempt againſt Khotyim. It was not more ſuccefsful than the former. Sixty thouſand Turks marched to the defence of that place ; they defended it bravely, and purſued the Ruſſians quite into Poland : but being vanquiſhed in their turn, they retreated to Moldavia.

At the beginning of this campaign the Turks fought with great courage and obſtinacy; but the ignorance of their generals, and the diſorder that reigned in their armies, often coſt them a defeat. After ten months of war, their army was almoſt entirely deſtroyed, and the fortreſs of Khotyim, which it had at firſt ſo valiantly defended, was abandoned without reſiſtance to 200 ruſſian grenadiers.

The empreſs, on hearing that when the Turks were purſuing prince Gallitzin, they had entered on the poliſh territory, pretended that

* It was ſigned at Peterſburg in the month of February 1772.

Poland ought not to fuffer with impunity this
infraction of the treaty of Carlovitz.   Staniflaus
Auguftus and the fenate of Warfaw, always
fubmiffive to the good pleafure of Catharine,
declared war againft the Porte.   This procedure, however, added nothing to the forces
of the Ruffians.   What exertions could be
made by a country without an army, without
money, and a prey to all the horrors of
anarchy ?

But Catharine conceived a project more worthy of her genius.   While her armies were
haraffing the Ottomans on the banks of the
Pruth, the Danube, and the Dniefter, and her
fleets were triumphing on the Euxine, fhe refolved to attack them even in the ifles of Greece.
Her minifters were againft this plan, excepting
count Ivan Chernicheff and Gregory Orloff.
Catharine, however, fet about the proper meafures for executing her darling fcheme.   The
dock-yards of Archangel, of Cronftadt, and
Reval, now fwarmed with workmen from all
parts of the country; and the keels of as many
fhips as could be begun at one time were immediately laid; the main timbers of thefe fhips
were of oak, and the other parts of fir.   She
exerted herfelf to keep up the beft underftanding

ing with the two maritime powers, England
and Denmark. For the improvement of her
sea-officers, she had before engaged Englishmen
in her service, the number of whom was now
doubled. Others she sent to Malta, to make
themselves acquainted with the art of managing
the gallies. In order to accustom the lower
classes of the marine, from the captain to the
cabin-boy, to seas as yet unknown to them, she
ordered a new-built frigate, the Nadejeda Blo-
gopolutshik (the Successful Hope) to be got
ready for sea, and invited some merchants of
Petersburg to make ventures in it for a direct
commerce with the ports of the Mediterranean.
The empress undertook to provide the crew,
and in all other respects to be an equal partner in
the trade with the rest. This being settled, the
command was given to captain Pleftscheyef.
This was the first ship which bore the ruffian flag
in the Mediterranean : it was out on the voyage
two years, and in that time visited almost all the
ports of that sea. Able and experienced officers;
especially from the british navy, readily entered
into the imperial service; Elphinston, Greig,
Tate, Dugdale, and many others, not to mention fir Charles Knowles, who acted more as
superintendant and director of the dock-yards
                                        than

than in a ftrictly naval capacity *: even the pilots on board the fleet, befides native Ruffians, confifted of Englishmen, Danes, and Dutch. The emprefs concluded a particular treaty with Denmark, by which that kingdom was to keep in conftant readinefs 800 feamen for the fervice of Ruffia. And laftly, fhe requefted of the maritime powers a friendly reception and affift-ance to her fhips of war. England and Tufcany fully complied with this requeft; Malta con-fented that three ruffian men of war, but no more at one time, fhould enter the port of la Valetta; France, Spain, Venice, and Naples, would admit only merchant-fhips from that country in their ports.

Accordingly, in September 1769, what no one would have believed, two fquadrons of ruffian men of war failed from Archangel and Reval, which were foon followed by others from the Baltic, and fteered their hitherto unattempted courfe for the Mediterranean. The fleet now confifting of 20 fail of the line, 6 frigates, feveral tranfports, a number of bomb-ketches, gallies

---

* To the zeal and abilities of admiral fir Charles Knowles, Ruffia is indebted for the prefent improved ftate of the art of fhip-building in that country. The admiral had much to reform in the admiralty; and what he effected was really furprifing.

and

Straits

Archipelago.

Alexey Orloff

and veſſels with troops for land-ſervice, left the Baltic, croſſed the north ſea, paſſed the ſtraits of Gibraltar, and, after having been diſperſed by a tempeſt, collected again, and diſplayed in the Archipelago its victorious flag. 'This fleet was commanded by admiral Spiridoff: but that admiral himſelf was under the orders of Alexèy Orloff, whoſe ſhare in the revolution had raiſed him all at once from a ſimple ſoldier to the rank of general, and whoſe audacity ſerved him inſtead of experience and talents.

All Europe was aſtoniſhed to ſee a nation, which till the preſent century was hardly known but by the map, now entering its harbours and braving its coaſts. What a change of fortune! Ruſſians landed on Paros, Melos, and other iſlands, and even on the continent of antient Greece. Ruſſians conquered Neſtor's Pylos *, and the famous Sparta †; laid ſiege to Corinth, and captured Lemnos and Mytelene ‡. Ruſſians were

Greece.

---

* At preſent Navarino.　　　† Now Miſtra.

‡ Captain Ployart, who commanded one of the ſhips in this expedition, and is now an admiral in the daniſh fleet, going on ſhore at Naxos, took with him a Homer, an old ſchool-book which he happened to have on board, and ſhewed it to ſome of the natives, who begged it of him with the moſt earneſt importunity. The captain complied with their

were fighting in Syria and Ægypt, where, from *Syria*
1770 to 1773, they supported the enterprising *Ali bey.*
Ali-bey.—But here indeed many errors were
committed, whereby several of the advantages
that had been gained were obliged to be abandoned.   A great part of the fault lay with
the unsteady Greeks, Mainots, and Montenegrins, who at first declared themselves very
warmly against the Turks, but more inclined to
robbery and depredation than regular fighting,
shewed neither discipline, fidelity, nor courage.

A long time before the sailing of this fleet for
the Archipelago, the empress had been preparing the way by settling a good understanding
with the principal isles of Greece.   Her emissaries flattered them with the hopes of exciting a
general revolt in those countries.   Marquis
Maruzzi, banker at Corfou, and attached to
the greek religion, came to St. Petersburg,
where he was decorated with the order of
St. Anne, and the title of minister from Russia to
Venice.   He promised in gratitude, to advance
the sums that were necessary for the expedition of

---

their desires ; and on going again on shore the next day, he
saw an elderly man with his back to a wall, reading the
speeches of the first Iliad with all the fury of declamation, to
an audience of 14 or 15 persons.   •

                                                    Alexéy

Alexèy Orloff, and he actually furnished a capital of 35,000,000 of livres tournois *.

On the event of the war againſt the Turks depended the fate of Poland, and the conſideration in which Ruſſia ſhould henceforth be held in Europe. Catharine was not ignorant of it. Accordingly ſhe employed every effort of her power, and every exertion of her mind, in order to triumph in that war.

New ſquadrons were built, numerous recruits went and joined her camps. Not altogether ſatisfied with prince Gallitziñ, the empreſs recalled him, and gave the command of her army to count Romantzoff, who was ſucceeded in the Ukraine by general Panin †. Prince Dolgorouky had a third army under his command.

* The empreſs procured, beſides, ſeveral conſiderable loans at Leghorn, at Genoa, at Lucca, and at Amſterdam. The merchants of Holland had at firſt ſhewn reluctance at lending their money. Piqued with reſentment that Mr. William Gomm, the banker of the court of Peterſburg, had thought fit to diſpenſe with their aſſiſtance, and to eſtabliſh a courſe of exchange direct between Ruſſia and England, they cauſed bills of exchange of his for 300,000 florins to be proteſted in one day, and occaſioned him to ſtop. But they were offered an eſpecial mortgage on the cuſtom-houſes of Peterſburg and Riga ; and allured by this bait, they lent them all that they deſired.

† Brother of the miniſter.

Neither

Neither were the Turks backward in rein-
forcing their armies, and putting at their head
generals whom they thought the moft capable
of leading them on to battle. The grand vizir
took upon himfelf the general command. They
received alfo powerful fuccours from the Krimea.
The famous Kerim-Gueray was lately dead, and
his nephew had fucceeded him. The new khan
was weak and of a pacific difpofition. The
Turks caufed him to be depofed; and in his
room was elected Kaplan Gueray, a warlike
prince, who prefently put himfelf at the head of
a combined army of Turks and Tartars.

The Ruffians opened the campaign by the
fiege of Bender, a place celebrated for the
retreat and the long fojourn of Charles XII.
But, haraffed by the Tartars, they were obliged
for fome time to relinquifh the hope of capturing
that town. More fuccefsful on another fide,
they got poffeffion of Yaffi and of Ibraïloff.

Thefe advantages were of but fmall importance. Two fignal battles decided the fate of
the campaign, and fecured the glory of Romantzoff. The firft was fought on the borders of
the Pruth. The Turks, to the number of
80,000 men, were commanded by the khan of
the Krimea, who had dexteroufly intrenched
himfelf on a hill, where it was not poffible to

attack them. Romantzoff encamped on an opposite station, and for the space of a month was vainly endeavouring to bring them to a battle. At length they lost all patience. A movement of Romantzoff led them to imagine that he was on the point of retreating; and a body of 20,000 men having gone down to pursue him, they were repulsed with loss into their very camp, which they reached in terror and disorder.

Animated by this success, they lost no time in mounting the hill by escalade; and after a vigorous resistance, their enemies abandoned to them their intrenchments and a considerable part of their baggage and artillery.

After this they retired towards the Danube, where they expected to be reinforced by detachments from the grand ottoman army. Indeed the grand vizir, who commanded it, did' pass, the river, and came to the assistance of the vanquished.

Romantzoff, who, thinking he was in pursuit of an army in confusion, had advanced towards the mouth of the river Pruth *, found himself all at once in the face of 150,000 Turks. His situation was the more dangerous, as he had

* The Pruth flows into the Danube.

been

been forced to detach a corps of his army for the protection of a convoy he was hourly expecting. The khan, who was indulging in the hopes of revenge, spread his forces to the left of the ruffian army, and furrounded it in fuch a manner as to cut off all poffibility of retreat.

Though the ruffian troops were far inferior in numbers to thofe of the Turks, thefe latter took the fame precautions as if they had had to contend with an enemy who amounted to an equal number with themfelves. During the night, they furrounded their camp with a triple intrenchment. The following day the grand vizir gave the fignal of battle; and the Ruffians were attacked on all fides at once. The firing was kept up for five hours, without any decided advantage to either party. But general Romantzoff, judging that the cannon and the mufquetry would complete the deftruction of his army, gave orders to fall upon the enemy with bayonets fixed. The Turks gave way, and retreated within their intrenchments, where they defended themfelves a long time with great bravery; but numbers were at length obliged to yield to difcipline and fkill. The defeat of the Ottomans was complete *. They retreated

---

* In the month of July.

carrying off the vizir in their flight, and leaving almost a third of their army on the field of battle. The greater part of the baggage, and the stores of this army, 143 pieces of brass cannon, and 7000 waggons loaded with provifions, remained in poffeffion of the Ruffians, and fupplied them with the means of obtaining new victories.

Soon after this Romantzoff paffed the Dniefter. Prince Repnin made the conqueft of Ifmaïloff. Panin laid fiege to Bender; and that place, well fortified and defended by a numerous garrifon, but entertaining no longer any hope of being relieved, furrendered* after a refiftance of nearly three months; the capture of this fortrefs brought with it the fubmiffion of the Tartars of Budziak and Otchakoff to the ruffian fceptre.

General Igelftrohm took the important town and fortrefs of Ackerman †, the capital of Beffarabia, by affault; it is fituated on the Euxine, at the mouth of the Dniefter ‡.

The news of fuch great and repeated fucceffes augmented the pride and the fecurity of Catha-

---

* At the beginning of September.
† Towards the end of the fame month.
‡ Ackerman fignifies the white town.

rine.

rine. The difaffected, who furrounded her
throne, dared no longer confpire againft a princefs who was triumphing at fuch a diftance over
her moft formidable enemies. The provinces of
Valachia and Moldavia, fubmitting to the ruffian
arms, fent deputies to Peterfburg, to do homage
to the emprefs. She received them with magnificence, and loaded them with benefits.

At the fame time feveral other foreign officers
came to offer their fervices to Catharine, and
obtained employment in her armies; among
whom were general Lloyd *, major Thomas
Carlton †, and other Englifhmen of tried courage and conduct, together with fome naval
officers from England and Denmark, and captain
Kinfbergen from Holland. Thefe officers, diftinguifhed by their talents and experience, were
incorporated into the ruffian navy.

A little after her acceffion to the throne, Catharine had drawn from the converfations of
marfhal Munich the idea of getting poffeffion of
Conftantinople, and of driving the Turks out of
Europe. The old foldier had even offered to
conduct the enterprife. But too many obftacles
were at that time in the way of the execution of

---

* Author of " Reveries," a work on " the poffibility of
" invading England," &c.

† Now governor of New Brunfwick in America.

fo

so great an attempt. The propitious moment seemed now at last arrived. However, unable to hope to keep under her dominion all the grecian isles, the empress determined at least to ravish them from the ottoman power ; and the most despotic of sovereigns resolved to be the patron of liberty in these fine countries, and to be the founder of a republic there *.

We have already observed, that secret agents had disposed the Greeks to rise up in arms. That people, anciently so proud and now so debased, expected the Russians as their deliverers ; and the instant their squadron had got the height of cape Matapan†, the whole Archipelago thought itself free. The Mainots, descendants of the ancient Lacedemonians, were the first that took arms. Their neighbours soon followed their example ; and the Turks were massacred in several of the islands. But the latter cruelly revenged themselves for the insurrection of the Greeks. Some thousands of these miserable people were exterminated by the sabre of the janissaries.

The squadron of admiral Spiridoff was soon joined by that of Elphinston, a native of England, vice-admiral in the service of Russia, and far

* Afterwards she determined Joseph II. to second this project, which nevertheless was not put in execution.

† Formerly the promontory of Tenaros.

more

more capable of commanding than the officer under whofe orders he ferved.

To this double fquadron was oppofed that of the capudan-pafha*, a man of extraordinary intrepidity, and who, on feveral occafions, only wanted, for gaining the victory, to have been better feconded.

He firft forced the Ruffians to retire from Lemnos. Afterwards the two fleets met † in the channel that feparates the ifle of Scio from Natolia. The turkifh fhips were fuperior in number, and were in a manner intrenched behind fome fmall iflands and rocks on a level with the furface of the water. The Ruffians, however, were not afraid to attack them. The capudan-pafha, whofe flag was flying on board the Sultan, of 90 guns, led the van, and offered battle to admiral Spiridoff. The fhips came alongfide of each other. The efforts of courage were terrible on both fides. Showers of balls and grenades interchangeably croffed, with rapidity, on the decks of the two admirals. The fhip of the capudan-pafha caught fire; that of the ruffian commander could not difengage itfelf from it. They blew up together; and the fea was covered with their fmoking fragments.

* The famous Haffan.   † The 5th of July.

O 4   The

The admirals and some other officers were the only persons that escaped the disaster.

While the ships were burning, the other vessels, struck with terror, abandoned the fight; but soon after renewed the attack with redoubled fury. Night coming on, they were obliged to separate. The Turks had now the imprudence to enter the narrow and slimy bay of Tschesmè, where some of their vessels ran aground, and the others were so pressed for room, that they found it impossible for them to act. The Russians, who had observed their mistake, made every preparation for turning it to their advantage.

The day following *, vice-admiral Elphinston took his station at the entrance of the bay, to prevent the Turks from coming out. The next step he took was to order four fire-ships to be got ready, commanded by the english lieutenant Dugdale, and protected by the vessels of another Englishman, vice-admiral Greig. Towards midnight Greig began the attack with four ships of the line and two frigates. Presently after, Dugdale came up with his fire-ships; and braving the vigorous fire of the enemy, and encouraging by his example the Russians who seconded

Dugdale.

* The 6th of July.

him,

him, he himfelf faftened the grapplings of a
fire-fhip to one of the turkifh veffels; and,
with his hands, his face, and his hair, all burnt,
he threw himfelf into the fea, and fwam to the
ruffian fquadron. The turkifh fhips were fo
clofe together, that they all became a prey to the
flames *. The fun at its rifing faw no more of
their flag.

So far from endeavouring to ftop the progrefs
of the combuftion, the turkifh crews thought of
nothing but their own fafety. Several failors
got off in boats, others threw themfelves into
the fea and took to fwimming, and all of them
who gained the fhore difperfed themfelves about
the countries, and were guilty of fuch depredations and exceffes towards the wretched inhabitants, that even the Ruffians themfelves could
not perhaps have furpaffed them. It was found
neceffary to fend a party of troops to put an end
to their ravages.

After the entire deftruction of the turkifh
fquadron, the Ruffians went to anchor at Paros;
whence they might eafily command all the grecian

* It is certain that this famous conflagration was the
work of three Englifhmen, Elphinfton, Greig, and Dugdale. The emprefs, neverthelefs, thought fit to afcribe the
idea of it to Alexius Orloff. She wrote fo to Voltaire; fhe
repeated it again in 1788 to the ambaffador of France.

feas, and where not a fingle veffel was fuffered to
appear without lowering its top-fails.

The Turks were the more uneafy by the
vicinity of fuch an enemy, as a rebellion had
broke out in feveral parts of their empire.
The pafhas of Caramania, almoft always at
variance with the Porte, took advantage of
its difafters for withdrawing themfelves entirely
from its authority. That part of Syria which is
below Sidon and Tripoli followed their example,
and the old fheik Daher excited all the country
which reaches from Acre to the plains of Efdrae-
lon and to the frontiers of Ægypt.

But of all thofe who fignalized themfelves
by their rebellion againft the grand fignior,
he who undoubtedly fhewed himfelf the moft
formidable, and who was moft in capacity to
be of fervice to Ruffia, was Ali-bey. Raifed
from the rank of a fimple mammeluk to that of
bey, he diftinguifhed himfelf by his courage, and
had experienced, though ftill very young, the
favours and the reverfes of fortune. The rivals
of his power fucceeded fo far as to remove him
from Cairo; but he foon returned thither again
and banifhed them in his turn. He knew that
the Porte had been hoftile to him, and, animated
with an implacable refentment, he defired nothing
better than to be able to contribute to the ruin

of

of the ottoman empire. The arrival of the ruffian fquadrons feemed to offer him a favourable opportunity for fatisfying his vengeance.

Perhaps there never was an enterprife in a diftant country more fuccefsfully carried on than that of the Ruffians on the coafts of Afia Minor. But perhaps alfo never were generals more ignorant, more incapable of appreciating the character of foreign nations, more jealous of a vain oftentation, and more addicted to debauchery than Alexèy Orloff and his principal officers. If they had had the fkill to profit by their victories and the fuperiority of their forces, Syria and Ægypt would for ever have been loft to the ottoman empire.

Syria & Egypt.

Ali-bey ufed every effort to induce them to fupport the rebellion, and to fend him troops to affift him in driving the Turks out of Ægypt. But inftead of feconding his exertions, Alexius Orloff amufed himfelf with infifting on his acknowledging the emprefs for his fovereign.

A young venetian merchant, named Carlo Rofetti, had poffeffed himfelf of the confidence of the bey, and was the firft whom he employed to treat with the Ruffians. No one was more difpofed, nor more fit to bring fuch a negotiation to a happy iffue. Orloff had not the fenfe to take advantage of fuch an opportunity.

portunity. Negligent of the advices which this
artful Italian might have given him, and disgust-
ing him by his arrogance, he took Greeks
and Jews into his pay who cheated and deceived
him. He was mistrustful of Ali-bey, and forced
him, by his artifices, to be mistrustful of him.

It was only a short time before he quitted
the Archipelago, that Alexius Orloff sent Plestscheyef * into Ægypt. Plestscheyef was favour-
ably received by the bey. He flattered himself
with being able to draw from his mission great
advantage to the Russians: but it was too late.
Peace intervened to interrupt his negotiations.

A courier dispatched directy to the empress,
brought her the news of the burning of the
turkish fleet; so that she was the first person
in Petersburg informed of the event. Count
Ivan Chernischeff, whom the empress had long
since recalled from London and put at the head
of the marine department, was then deeply engaged in a quarrel with the college of admiralty,
and that quarrel had occasioned some delay

* Plestscheyef obtained in the sequel the rank of vice-
admiral. He drew up an account of his expedition in
Ægypt; but in it he mentions not a word of the money
that he gave to the Copht Risk, to procure for him the
favour of Ali-bey.—See the whole of this narrative in the
" Varieties of Literature," vol. i. p. 477.

in

in the expedition of an affair of little confequence. Catharine complained of this delay, and thought no more of it. She was well acquainted with the obftinacy and the extreme incapacity of Chernifcheff; but fhe continued him in his place, becaufe fhe had laid it down as a fettled principle, to change as feldom as poffible her minifters and her ambaffadors. When fhe fent for Ivan Chernifcheff to communicate to him the news of the affair of Tfchefmè, the minifter, imagining that fhe meant to fpeak again to him of his quarrel, began, as he entered the apártment:—" I affure you, madam, that it was not " my fault."—" Oh! I know that very well," returned the emprefs, " but it is not the lefs certain." —" Alas! yes, madam, and I am very forry " for it."—" What! you are forry that the " Turks have no longer any fleet?" faid the emprefs, fmiling; and fhe then communicated to him the contents of the difpatches which fhe had juft received.

The joy was extreme at the court of Peterfburg. Magnificent feftivities were given to celebrate the victory of Tfchefmè, and the emprefs afterwards caufed a palace to be built*, and the foundations of a town to be laid, for

---

* See before, p. 172.

confecrating

consecrating to posterity the remembrance of so glorious an event.

1771. Count Alexius Orloff returned in all haste to Petersburg*, to repose upon his laurels, to enjoy his triumphs, and to solicit new means for extending his conquests in the Archipelago. On his appearance the festivities were renewed, and he was decorated by his sovereign with the grand riband of St. George.

He laid before the council a plan by which he proposed to render himself master of all Greece, and to rescue Ægypt from the ottoman empire. He concluded by saying that he would pass the dangerous passage of the Dardanelles, and that for all these important purposes he requested no more than 10,000,000 of rubles.— " I grant you twenty," immediately replied Catharine; " for I am resolved that you shall want " for nothing." At the same time orders were issued for the equipment of a new squadron, to reinforce that which was already in the Archipelago.

During the state of extreme loss and misfortune to which the Turks were reduced by the war, that empire seemed convulsed in all its parts; order, submission, and respect to govern-

* He arrived there the 15th of March 1771.

ment

ment feemed totally at an end; massacre and confufion took place; and, to fill up the meafure of calamity, the plague now made the moft cruel ravages: above a thoufand perfons dying daily in Conftantinople for feveral weeks. The deftruction of their fleet was better known in that metropolis, and was in itfelf more immediately alarming, than any other misfortune that could have happened: and, as if the dangers from without were not fufficiently terrible, the run-away failors filled it with flaughter and confufion, and actually fet fire to the city and fuburbs at feveral times. At length thefe mifcreants were fo ftrengthened, by the acceffion of vagabonds and villains of all forts, particularly by the crowds of deferters from the Danube, who had nothing to fubfift on but plunder, that they came to an open engagement with the janiffaries in the fuburbs of Pera, where fome thoufands of them were cut to pieces, and the reft difperfed.

In the mean time, every immediate meafure was taken for the fecurity of the Dardanelles, and all the remaining fhips and gallies were fitted out with the greateft expedition to affift in defending the paffage. The late vizir, Moldavangi Ali-pafha, was recalled from his exile, and fent at the head of 15,000 men for the fame

9   purpofe;

purpose; where the first enemies he had to
encounter were the rebellious sailors, who landed
in a body in spite of the capudan-pasha, and,
making zeal for their religion a cloak for their
avarice and licentiousness, intended to have
plundered and burnt the city of Gallipoli, and
to have massacred the Greeks. They were
however happily disappointed in this cruel design,
by the vigour and resolution of the late vizir,
who severely chastised their profligacy; and,
after killing a great number of them, reduced
the remainder to order. Baron Tot, a french
nobleman who had been consul in Tartary, and
was an engineer of the first abilities, together
with several others of his countrymen, were
also procured, to erect new batteries on the
straights, and to put the castles into a proper
state of defence. By these means, together with
the uncertainty of the winds and currents necessary to facilitate such an enterprise, all the
attempts of the Russians, to force their passage,
had hitherto proved fruitless.

Nor was the revolution in Ægypt, nor the
interception of the trade from the lesser Asia
and Syria by the Russians, attended with the
fatal consequences to the metropolis that were
expected; as amidst all its calamities it was
constantly and plentifully supplied with provisions:
a felicity

a felicity for which it is principally indebted to the long extent of fea-coaft from the mouth of the Hellefpont to the Euxine. In the mean time the winter feafon having obliged the Ruffians to quit their ftation near the Dardanelles, the trade through the ftraights was of courfe again opened.

While the Porte was thus fatally experiencing all the viciffitudes and havoc of war, the calamities of peftilence, and the precipitate deftructive evils of anarchy, in their european dominions; the fame ruinous fyftem of policy, and weaknefs and relaxation of government, extended their effects into other parts of that great empire, and produced a new and extraordinary revolution in Ægypt. Ali-bey, who had fo long made a *Ali Bey* diftinguifhed figure among the factions that for fome years paft had torn that country to pieces, at length threw off the mafk; and, taking advantage of the prefent ftate of d'ftrefs and danger, boldly mounted the throne of the antient fultans of that kingdom.

The Ottomans had from the beginning made but a lax ufe of their authority in the government of Ægypt. The diftance and climate made it difficult to fupport there any confiderable number of troops; while, from its peculiar fituation, and the number of barbarous nations on

its borders, who would naturally join the natives,
or at leaft afford them fhelter and protection
if overcome, nothing lefs than an army could
enforce a very ftrict obedience. Satisfied with
the very great benefits that refulted from its
being a granary to Conftantinople and other parts
of their dominions, as it had formerly been
to antient Rome, the Turks were content with
a very moderate tribute, not above one third of
which came into the treafury. A garrifon of
janiffaries was kept at Cairo, where a pafha,
with the title of governor, but with little more
power than what the great men of the country
chofe to allow him, conftantly refided.   The
princes and grandees of the country had abfolute
power in their refpective territories, and held a
general affembly or council, every year at Cairo,
where they fettled the payment of the revenues,
and debated upon fuch other national matters as
demanded confideration.   To prevent any reftraint from the governor, or their being over-
awed by the janiffaries, as well as from the
continual quarrels among themfelves, they all
came attended by their armed vaffals.   Such
affemblies, among fo barbarous a people, naturally difpofed to faction and treachery, prefented continual fcenes of bloodfhed and confufion;-
while the governors, by occafionally fupporting

one

one party against the other, endeavoured to derive that power and consequence from their
diffensions which the authority of office was
incapable of procuring.

Ali-bey, a man of strong natural parts and *Ali Bey*
confiderable abilities, improved upon the line of
policy ftruck out by the governors; and, by
dextroufly shifting for a number of years, from
one side to the other, and deftroying by degrees
fuch parties as were obnoxious to him, he at
length formed one great one which fwallowed up
all the others. Not content with the kingdom
of Ægypt, he laid claim to Syria, Paleftine, and
the part of Arabia that had belonged to the
antient fultans. The ufurper accordingly marched
at the head of an army to fupport thofe pretenfions, and actually fubdued fome of the
neighbouring provinces both of Arabia and
Syria.

At the fame time that he was engaged in thofe
ambitious purfuits, he was not lefs attentive
to the eftablifhing of a regular form of government, and of introducing order into a country
that has been fo long the feat of anarchy and
confufion. His views were equally extended to
commerce; for which purpofe he gave great
encouragement to the chriftian traders, and took
off fome fhameful reftraints and indignities,

to which they were fubject in that barbarous
country : he alfo wrote a letter to the republic of
Venice, with the warmeft affurances of his
friendfhip, and that their merchants fhould meet
with every degree of protection and fafety. His
great defign was to make himfelf mafter of the
Red Sea; to open the port of Suez to all nations,
but particularly to the Europeans, and to make
Ægypt once more the great centre of commerce.

Proud of the favour of the emprefs, of
victories of. which he took the honour to himfelf, and of thofe he ftill intended to gain, count
Alexèy Orloff departed from St. Peterfburg, in
order to return to the Archipelago. Having
ftopped fome time at Vienna, he there difplayed
an extravagant luxury, and gave himfelf up
to indifcretions very little worthy of the minifter
of a princefs fo difcreet as Catharine. One
evening being at fupper with the ambaffador of
Ruffia with a numerous company, he fpoke of
the revolution that had coft the throne to
Peter III. No one dared to put the leaft
queftion concerning the death of the unfortunate
tzar. Alexèy Orloff related it of his own
accord; and, perceiving that all who heard him
fhuddered with horror, he thought he cleared
himfelf of the crime which he had committed,
by faying, " That it was a lamentable thing
" for

" for a man of fo much humanity as he poffeffed,
" to be forced to do what he had been com-
" manded." But this repentance could not be
thought fincere. The character of Alexèy Orloff
was too well known; and the whole of his
conduct proved that his confcience was not apt
eafily to take the alarm.

On leaving Vienna, Alexèy Orloff went to
rejoin the ruffian fquadron which lay expecting
him at Leghorn; and, though in a fhattered condition, continued to complete the ruin of the
marine and the commerce of the Turks.

The emprefs had commiffioned Alexèy Orloff
to caufe to be painted in Italy four pictures, reprefenting the engagements of her fquadron and
the burning of the turkifh fleet. Orloff made
application to a painter named Hackert. This
artift having told him that he had never feen
a fhip blow up, the Ruffian made no hefitation of
affording him an opportunity of contemplating
fuch an object, and hazarded the firing of all the
veffels in the road of Leghorn for furnifhing the
painter with the means of exhibiting with greater
truth the difafter of the capudan-pafha and
admiral Spiridoff *.

* The four pictures by Hackert are at prefent hanging in
the hall of audience at Peterhoff.

Acts

Acts of extravagance are not always crimes. But there is no crime which such an extravagant character is not capable of committing. On his departure from Peterſburg he had received orders to ſend thither a young unfortunate lady who had been reſcued from tyranny. This barbarous order was now to be accompliſhed.

It has already been mentioned that the empreſs Elizabeth had three children by her clandeſtine marriage with the grand-veneur Alexèy Gregorievitch Razumoffsky. The youngeſt of theſe children was a girl, brought up under the name of princeſs Tarrakanoff. Prince Radzivil, informed of this ſecret, and irritated at Catharine's trampling under foot the rights of the Poles, conceived that the daughter of Elizabeth would furniſh him with a ſignal means of revenge. He thought that it would not be in vain if he oppoſed to the ſovereign, whoſe armies were ſpreading deſolation over his unhappy country, a rival whoſe mother's name ſhould render dear to the Ruſſians. Perhaps his ambition might ſuggeſt to him yet more lofty hopes. Perhaps he might flatter himſelf with being one day enabled to mount the throne on which he intended to place the young Tarrakanoff. However this be, he gained over the perſons to whom the education of this princeſs was committed,

mitted, carried her off, and conveyed her to
Rome *.

Catharine, having intelligence of this tranfaction, took immediate fteps to fruftrate the
defigns of prince Radzivil. Taking advantage
of the circumftance of his being the chief of the
confederacy of the malcontents, fhe caufed all his
eftates to be feized, and reduced him to the
neceffity of living on the produce of the diamonds
and the other valuable effects he had carried
with him to Italy. Thefe fupplies were foon
exhaufted. Radzivil fet out in order to pick
up what intelligence he could concerning affairs
in Poland, leaving the young Tarrakanoff at
Rome, under the care of a fingle gouvernante, and in circumftances extremely confined.
Scarcely had he reached his own country, when
an offer was made to reftore him his poffeffions,
on condition that he would take his young ward
to Ruffia. He refufed to fubmit to fo difgrace-
ful a propofal; but he had the weaknefs to
promife that he would give himfelf no farther
concern about the daughter of Elizabeth. This
was the price of his pardon.

* In 1767 mademoifelle de Tarrakanoff was about
12 years of age.

P 4   Alexey

Alexèy Orloff, charged with the execution of the will of the emprefs, feized the firft moment on his arrival at Leghorn, of laying a fnare for the princefs Tarrakanoff. One * of thofe intriguers who are fo common in Italy, repaired immediately to Rome; and, after having difcovered the lodgings of the young Ruffian, he introduced himfelf to her in a military drefs and under the name of an officer. He told her that he had been brought thither by the fole defire of paying homage to a princefs whofe fate and fortunes were highly interefting to all her countrymen. He feemed very much affected at the ftate of deftitution in which he found her. He offered her fome affiftance which neceffity forced her to accept; and the traitor foon appeared to this unfortunate lady, as well as to the woman that waited on her, in the light of a faviour whom heaven had fent to her deliverance.

When he thought he had fufficiently gained their confidence, he declared that he was com-

---

* It was a Neapolitan, named Ribas. He afterwards came to Ruffia, where he married mademoifelle Anaftafia, reputed daughter of M. de Betfkoï, and has fince been made knight of Malta, and promoted to the rank of vice-admiral of the Black Sea.

miffioned

miffioned by count Alexius Orloff to offer to the
daughter of Elizabeth the throne that had been
filled by her mother.   He faid that the Ruffians
were difcontented with Catharine; that Orloff
efpecially could never forgive her for her ingratitude and her tyranny; and that, if the young
princefs would accept of the fervices of that
general, and recompenfe him by the grant of
her hand, it would not be long ere fhe faw
the breaking out of that revolution which he had
prepared.

Propofals fo brilliant ought naturally to have
opened the eyes of the princefs Tarrakanoff, and
fhewn her the treachery of him that made them.
But her inexperience and her candour permitted
her not to fufpect any guile.   Befides, the language of the emiffary of Alexius Orloff feemed
analogous with the notions fhe had imbibed
from prince Radzivil.   She imagined herfelf
deftined to the throne; and all the airy dreams
that any way related to that opinion could not
but encourage the deceit.   She accordingly
gave herfelf up to thefe flattering hopes, and
with a grateful heart concurred in the defigns of
him who addreffed her only to her deftruction.

Some time after this Alexius Orloff came to
Rome.   His emiffary had already announced
him.   He was received as a benefactor.   How-

ever,

ever, some persons to whom the princess and her gouvernante communicated the good fortune that was promised them, advised them to be on their guard against the designs of a man whose character for wickedness had been long established, and who doubtless had too much reason to remain faithful to the empress to think of conspiring against her. Far from profiting by this good counsel, the princess was so imprudently frank as to speak of it to Alexius Orloff, who with great ease delivered his justification, and thenceforth threw a deeper shade of dissimulation and address into his speeches and behaviour. Not satisfied with fanning the ambition of the young Russian, he put on the semblance of a passion for her, and succeeded so far as to inspire her with a true one. So soon as he was assured of it, he conjured her to enter into a union with him by the most sacred ties. She unhappily consented; and it was even with joy that the poor unfortunate lady promised to solemnize a marriage which must consummate her ruin. She thought that the title of spouse of count Alexius Orloff would shelter her invincibly from those treacheries which she was taught to apprehend. She entertained not the least suspicion that a man could make religion and the most sacred titles subservient to the destruction

of

of an innocent victim. But, alas, was any religion, was any title facred to the barbarian into
whofe fnares fhe had fallen? He who could
ftrangle the unfortunate Peter III. could he
dread to difhonour the daughter of Elizabeth * ?

Feigning a defire that the marriage ceremony
fhould be performed according to the ritual of
the greek church, he fuborned fubaltern villains
to difguife themfelves as priefts and lawyers.
Thus profanation was combined with impofture
againft the unprotected and too confident Tarrakanoff.

When Alexius Orloff was become the hufband
or rather the ravifher of this unhappy princefs,
he reprefented to her that their ftay at Rome
expofed her to too clofe obfervation, and that it
would be advifable for her to go to fome other
city of Italy, to wait for the breaking out of the
confpiracy that was to call her to the throne.
Believing this advice to be dictated by love
and prudence, fhe anfwered that fhe would
follow him wherever he chofe to conduct her.
He brought her immediately to Pifa, where he
had previoufly hired a magnificent palace. There
he continued to treat her with marks of tender-

* The fate of the young Tarrakanoff may be compared
to that of the daughter of Sejanus: " ...... a carnifice
" laqueum juxtà, compreffam ......" Tacit. Ann. lib. v.

nefs and refpect. But he permitted none to come near her except perfons who were entirely at his devotion ; and when fhe went to the play or to the public promenades, he accompanied her always himfelf.

The divifion of the ruffian fquadron under the command of admiral Greig, had juft entered the port of Leghorn. On relating this news to the princefs, Alexius Orloff told her that his prefence was neceffary at Leghorn for the pur- pofe of giving fome orders, and offered to take her with him. To this fhe the more readily confented, as fhe had heard much talk of the beauty of the port of Leghorn and the magni- ficence of the ruffian fhips. Imprudent lady ! the nearer fhe approached the cataftrophe of the plot, the more fhe trufted to the tendernefs and the fincerity of her faithlefs betrayer.

She departed from Pifa with her cuftomary attendance. On arriving at Leghorn, fhe landed at the houfe of the englifh conful, who had prepared for her a fuitable apartment, and who received her with the marks of the pro- foundeft refpect. Several ladies * were early

* It is a miftake that the lady of admiral Greig was among them. Mrs. Greig did not accompany her hufband on the voyage, but remained the whole time of his abfence at St. Peterfburg.

in

in making their vifits, and feduloufly attended
her on all occafions.   She faw herfelf prefently
furrounded by a numerous court, eager to be
beforehand with all her defires, and feeming to
make it their only ftudy inceffantly to procure
her fome new entertainment.   Whenever fhe
went out, the people ran in her way.   At
the theatre all eyes were directed to her box.
All circumftances confpired to lull her into a
fatal fecurity.   All tended to difpel the idea of
any danger at hand.

It is doubtlefs impoffible to believe that an
englifh conful, an englifh admiral, and ladies of
their family or acquaintance, could be fo bafe,
fo inhuman, as to draw into the fnare, by deceitful refpect and careffes, a victim whofe
youth, whofe beauty, whofe innocence, was
capable of affecting the moft infenfible heart.
It is not to be imagined that they were in any
degree privy to the plot contrived againft her,
and that they ftudioufly infpired her with confidence, only the more infallibly to betray her.

The young Tarrakanoff was fo far from
fufpecting her unfortunate fituation, that, after
having paffed feveral days in a round of amufements and diffipation, fhe afked of herfelf to be
fhewn the ruffian fleet.   The idea was applauded.
The

The neceſſary orders were immediately given; and the next day, on riſing from table, every thing was ready at the water-ſide for receiving the princeſs. On her coming down, ſhe was handed into a boat with magnificent awnings. The conſul, and ſeveral ladies, ſeated themſelves with her. A ſecond boat conveyed vice-admiral Greig and count Alexius Orloff; and a third, filled with ruſſian and engliſh officers, cloſed the proceſſion. The boats put off from ſhore in ſight of an immenſe multitude of people, and were received by the fleet, with a band of muſic, ſalutes of artillery, and repeated huzzas. As the princeſs came alongſide the ſhip of which ſhe was to go on board, a ſplendid chair was let down from the yard, in which being ſeated, ſhe was hoiſted upon deck; and it was obſerved to her, that theſe were particular honours paid to her rank.

But no ſooner was ſhe on board than ſhe was handcuffed. In vain ſhe implored for pity of the cruel betrayer, whom ſhe ſtill called her huſband. In vain ſhe threw herſelf at his feet, and watered them with her tears. No anſwer was even vouchſafed to her lamentations. She was carried down into the hold; and the next day the veſſel ſet ſail for Ruſſia.

On

On arriving at Peterfburg, the young victim *Tarrakan* was fhut up in the fortrefs; and what became of her afterwards was never known*.

In the mean time, the inhabitants of Leghorn, who had feen the princefs embark, heard fhortly after with horror, that inftead of a grand entertainment, which fhe was led to expect, on board the fleet, fhe was put into irons. The grand duke of Tufcany, whofe territory was thus fo fhamefully infulted, wrote immediately to Vienna and to Peterfburg to complain of the outrage. But Alexius Orloff infolently braved both the complaints of Leopold and the public indignation.

An adventure that happened during count Orloff's ftay at Rome, may ferve to throw fome

---

* It was affirmed by fome, that the waters of the Neva, fix years afterwards, put an end to her misfortunes, by drowning her in the prifon, in the inundation of 1777. On the 10th of September of that year, a wind at S. S. W. raifed the waters of the gulph of Finland towards the Neva, with a violence fo extraordinary that it fwelled that river to the height of ten feet above its ufual level, and drove many veffels on fhore. The author of the interefting " Memoires " fecrets fur l'Italie," who fome time fince printed a part of thefe particulars, furmifes that the young Tarranakoff fell in prifon by the hands of the executioner. The truth is, the grounds are but very flight for rendering credible either the one or the other account.

light

light on the brutal character of the man. One
evening that he was at fupper in a houfe * with
a large company, he wifhed to difplay his extraordinary ftrength.   He with great eafe broke in
his hand feveral pieces of criftal and iron.   He
then took between two of his fingers an apple,
which he broke into feveral pieces.   A royal
duke, brother of an illuftrious monarch, was
at table; one of the pieces of apple ftruck
the prince on his face, and hurt him.   Every
one prefent was extremely affected at this accident.   Alexius Orloff alone seemed entirely
unmoved, and even deigned not to make the
flighteft apology to the duke.

Though repeatedly vanquifhed, the ottoman
armies were eafily recruited, and refifted the
efforts of the Ruffians; like a terrible hydra,
whofe heads increafed under the reiterated blows
of Romantzoff and his inferior commanders.
The ruffian general Veiffmann croffed the Danube, and beat the Turks near Ifaccia.   Soon
after this the grand vizir forced him to repafs
that river, and advanced to Bukhareft with an
army of 100,000 men.   There the Turks were
completely victorious.   But no long time was

* At the houfe of the marchionefs Gentili Bocca
Paduli.

allowed

allowed them to rejoice in their fucceffes. In three fucceffive battles the Ruffians regained the upper hand.

The grand vizir retreated into the mountains of the Bulgarians; and Romantzoff, leaving the right bank of the Danube, took up his winter-quarters in Moldavia and Valachia.

The khan of the Krimea fought valiantly for the Turks. Catharine refolved to be revenged on him, and deprive the enemy of this affiftance. She had already for fome time eftablifhed a fort of intelligence in the Krimea. Her emiffaries were fecretly working to fow diffentions among the Tartars, and to draw off from the khan the confidence of his fubjects. They fucceeded in thefe endeavours; and valour completed what had been begun by intrigue.

The famous lines of Perekop had fubmitted, forty years before, to the intrepidity of Munich. Learning prudence by this example, the khans of the Krimea rendered this paffage more diffi-cult than it had hitherto been. Neverthelefs, neither a ditch of 72 feet in width, and 42 in depth, nor 50,000 Tartars, who defended it, were able to check the career of prince Dolgo-rucky. By forcing this barrier that general made himfelf mafter of all the Krimea: and as the reward of his victory, he received of the emprefs the surname of Krimsky *.

The khan, forced to abandon his country, to avoid falling into the power of the conqueror, retired to the dependencies of Turkey. Prince Dolgorucky immediately caused a new khan to be elected; but neither was this such an one as the Ruffians wanted; and he detached himself from their party without delay.

The grand signor, incensed that Abaza-pasha, and some other of the turkish commanders, had basely abandoned the Krimea, sent them the fatal bow-string, and caused their bleeding heads to be exposed on the gates of the seraglio.

The defertion of the Krim by the turkish commanders was not the only act of treachery of which the Porte had at that time to complain. It had just concluded †, with the court of Vienna,

---

* This is an ancient custom in Ruffia. Prince Dolgorucky received the surname of Krimsky, because he conquered the Krim; marshal Romantzoff that of Sadunaisky, because he crossed the Danube; Alexius Orloff that of Tschesmenskoï, because of the victory at Tschesmè; marshal Suvaroff that of Rimnitsky; as the famous duke Alexander had anciently received that of Nevsky or Nefsky, on account of his gaining a victory over the Swedes on the banks of the Neva.

† The 6th of July.

a secret

a secret treaty, by which that court engaged to take up arms offensively in its behalf, on condition that it would defray the expences of the war, and that it would restore at the peace a part of Valachia and some other austrian territories which it had conquered. Faithful to these engagements, the Porte began by paying the court of Vienna five millions of imperial florins *. The court of Vienna made use of it immediately : *Vienna* but, to the shame of the professors of the christian faith, it was in making preparations for turning its arms against the Porte itself, and to unite with Russia.

For some time past a dreadful scourge had been ravaging the interior of Russia. The plague had manifested itself in Mosco; and the ignorance of the physicians, in conjunction with the superstition of the people, increased its fury. The physicians at first mistook the distemper for nothing more than an epidemical fever; and the people, who saw that the physicians were not able to cure it, pursued them on all sides, and forced them into concealment in order to escape their rage. But it will be necessary to

* This sum makes 1,093,750l. sterling. Some persons pretend that the Porte reckoned only 6000 purses, or 787,500l. sterling. But the procedure of the court of Vienna is not at all the less odious.

speak

ſpeak ſomewhat more particularly on this ſubject. It is well known that the turkiſh dominions, whether from a want of due attention to cleanli-neſs, or from whatever other cauſe, are more ſubject to this malady than the countries of Europe. The ruſſian army, after defeating the Turks, on their entering their territories and towns as conquerors, were met by the contagion, and brought it with them to their country; where the folly of ſeveral of their generals con‧tributed to its propagation, as if they thought, by a military word of command, to alter the nature of things. Lieutenant-general Stoffeln, at Yaſſy, where the peſtilence raged in the winter of 1770, iſſued peremptory orders, that its name ſhould not be pronounced: he even obliged the phyſicians and the ſurgeons to draw up a declaration in writing, that it was only a ſpotted fever. One honeſt ſurgeon, of the name of Kluge, refuſed to ſign it. In this manner the ſeaſon of prevention was neglected; the men fell dead upon the road in heaps. Several thouſand ruſſian ſoldiers were by this means carried off: the number of burghers that died was never known, as they had run into the country and into the foreſts. At length the havoc of death reached the general's own people; he remained true to his perſuaſion, left

the

the town, and went into the more perilous camp: but his intrepidity availed him nothing; he died of the plague in July 1771. Affiftance now arrived; but it was too late: almoft all the fick were fent to die in lazarets. The defertion of the place was the only remaining remedy. Two regiments of infantry and one battalion amounted only to 400 men. To the fame fmall number were likewife in September the regiments at Khotyim reduced, alfo from want of precaution. The baggages that had been packed up in the time of the plague were brought out, and opened, that the foldiers who had ferved the campaign in their waiftcoats alone might have their coats againft winter; the clothes were fo infected, that the people who were employed in unfolding them were immediately attacked with mortal ulcers. In Kief no phyfician or furgeon had ever feen the plague; they therefore took it for a putrid fpotted fever. Afterwards, but too late, they were better advifed. The free intercourfe at the markets and in the churches had already univerfally fpread the miafma. Add to this, the foldiers were not reftrained from robbing the infected houfes of the dead; thus infecting themfelves and others. Even the commandant was negligent of his duty, in not taking care, by regu-

Q 3   lations

lations and punifhments, that the houfes were duly cleanfed and ventilated ; nay, he was covetous enough to caufe whole chefts full of linen and other goods to be brought out of thefe houfes, and ftowed in the vaults of his. The governor gave rife to a fhameful and ftupid piece of fuperftition, to which he was perfuaded by a turkifh officer taken prifoner, who pur-chafed his freedom by it. This man wrote tickets, containing thefe words: " O great " Muhammed, have pity for this once on the " chriftians, for the fake of our deliverance " from captivity, and free them foon from " the peftilence !" The governor caufed the writing to be ftuck on poles againft the belfries of the chriftian churches ; the people trufted to the remedy, and were ftill more carelefs of themfelves than before : the peftilence, therefore, naturally fpread farther and wider. Within a few months of the year 1770, one quarter of the town alone loft upwards of 6000 perfons.

With fuch miferable doings, it is no wonder that the dreadful diftemper came by the army from Poland and from the Ukraine, about chriftmas 1770, even to Mofco. Alas ! here too at the beginning, an ukaufe was printed and publifhed, to affure the people, that there was no peftilence, and that a falfe alarm had been

                                    wickedly

wickedly raifed among the burghers.   Befides,
fome phyficians and furgeons maintained the
fame thing much later.   But when the emprefs
was informed of the truth of the matter, fhe
difpatched affiftance with all fpeed to Kief and
to Mofco.   The calamity had already rifen to its
height in this great metropolis.   The principal
families left it betimes, and went into the country, and with them went all that were able : the
former might indeed have gone out of clean
houfes; but who would anfwer for the others ?
Hence the contagion was fpread through the
neighbouring villages and towns, where at leaft
30,000 perfons perifhed.   But it may be computed, that in Mofco only the fourth part of the
ordinary number of its inhabitants were left
alive : however, afterwards, in December 1771,
juft upon the ftopping of the plague, it was
found by calculation, that upwards of 60,000
died there within a year not yet complete.   The
dead lay for three or four days in the ftreets
where they had fallen, or where they had been
thrown out from the houfes; as the police had
neither carts nor people enough to carry them
away.   The worthy general Yerapkin was
making every exertion in his power, when in September the emprefs, who, as it is expreffed in
the patent, preferred the welfare of her fubjects

to every other confideration, in this perilous
time fent her favourite Gregory Orloff with
extraordinary full powers to check the further
incurfions of the malady at that place, and to
put an end to the evil on the fpot. On this
preffing exigency the fum of 100,000 rubles
was immediately iffued. Orloff went daily to
the fenate ; and every week a ukaufe came out.
He appointed a commiffion of health, of which,
befides a general and a ftate-counfellor, the moft
fkilful phyficians were members. In addition
to the two peft-houfes, monafteries and palaces
were turned into lazarets, a building was appropriated to orphan children from the infected
houfes, feveral of the public offices were converted into places for the keeping of quarantine,
and other falutary meafures were adopted. At
thefe eftablifhments the neceffary perfons were
put immediately upon ftipends; and all phyficians and furgeons who were confpicuous for
their diligence and zeal were handfomely rewarded. A new turn was given to the whole
bufinefs; and all the precautions for fafety were
vifibly attended with due effects. But methods
of cure were ftill apparently not to be found :
very few of fuch as once caught the infection
efcaped with their lives ; their being inclofed,
however, prevented its farther progrefs. It was
                                        only

only the fevere winter that put an end to the
calamity in Mofco, as well as in the other infected places. At the beginning of September,
in Mofco, died every day 800 perfons; about
the middle of October 700 to 600; the 21ft of
October only 400. The froft continued to
grow more intenfe: on the 15th of November
the plague carried off 150 perfons; on the 30th
ftill 75; but on the 4th of December only 10
died, and fo continually fewer: two, three, five,
and, on fome intervening days, not even one;
till the 6th of January 1772, the plague entirely
ceafed.—In the night of the 30th of December,
during a violent ftorm of wind, a fire broke out
in the imperial palace, inhabited by the newly-
appointed governor, prince Volkonfky. As the
ftructure was chiefly of timber, the whole of it,
together with the church, was entirely confumed.

A more calamitous hiftory of this unfortunate
time to Mofco ftill remains to be related. It
fhould feem as if the afflictive vifitations to
which the human race is fubject from the courfe
of Nature, and to which Nature herfelf at length
applies the moft effectual remedies, were not
fufficient; the moft horrid diftortion of mind,
fanaticifm, muft be brought in to increafe the
calamity. The fuperftitious populace in this
metropolis

superstition metropolis despised the precautions recommended
by government, and the prescriptions of the
physicians. The latter, especially such as were
foreigners, frequently, as they passed through the
streets, were not sure of their lives. Prayers to
the pictures of the saints were held to be the
only true methods of cure. This, which at first
was no more than an unhappy folly, soon grew
into a criminal fury. In September, a fortnight
before the arrival of Gregory Orloff, a hot-
brained enthusiast of the vulgar class of people,
got together a number of the rabble, and declared to them that the picture of God's mother,
near the Varvarskoï gate (the bridge-gate of
St. Barbara leading to a chapel) had appeared to
him, complaining of neglect in the worship of it,
and promising by a miracle to quell the pestilence if that worship was zealously revived.
At this gate he continued standing, and declared
the same thing to the priests and passengers
as they passed through it. The story was spread
from one to the other, and none of the hearers
thought of raising a doubt whether or not the
man was in his right mind. The faithful from
all parts of the town flocked in great multitudes
to St. Barbara's gate, addressing the picture
in vociferous cries, bringing ornaments of dress
to hang about it, and on that and the following
days

days made many confiderable prefents to it
in gold and jewels. Now began proceffions,
and continued in endlefs fucceffion. The fick
particularly preffed forward on this occafion,
and fuch as were not fick mingled among them.
The dæmon of peftilence could have found
no better a helpmate than the dæmon of fuperftition. The primate of Mofco, the archhierèy
or archbifhop Amvrofi, (Ambrofius,) a virtuous
and enlightened man, wifhed to put an end
to this dreadful rage, and to that end applied for
affiftance to general Yerapkin, who gave him
five foldiers. Thefe he fent in filence late in the
winter-evening to the Varvarfkoï gate, to fetch
away the picture that was now become the caufe
of fuch public affliction. But neither night nor
day was the gate free from a fanatical tumult
before the painted mother of God. The foldiers
were driven off. The mob poured invectives on
the archhierèy, and, one and all crying out that
he was a heretic, ran to the church-belfries and
rang all the bells, to rouze the whole populace
of the city, and bring them together to inform
them of the intended violation of the holy
figure. Every one rofe in hafte, and ran into the
ftreets imagining it to be an alarm of fire; but
upon inquiry were informed of what had happened; the prudent were but few in number,
and

and the reſt made a common cauſe with the inſur-
gents and joined the throng.   The prelate in the
mean time had fled to the Donſkoï monaſtery
without the city.   This was reported abroad
in the morning; the wild multitude tumultuouſly
ran thither, and found the archbiſhop in the
celebration of divine worſhip.   Neither the
place, nor the ſtation, nor the age of the man,
neither his dreſs nor his preſent employment,
made any impreſſion on the enthuſiaſtic barbarians; they fell upon the venerable old man,
threw him to the ground, beat him on the head,
and completed his murder with knives.   The
body remained till the following day lying before
the gate of the monaſtery.   Thus fell this
martyr to illumination, the generous friend of
his ungrateful countrymen.

The furious multitude now ran back into
the city.   A party of them attacked the Danii-
lofskoï monaſtery, now converted into a lazaret,
drove the peſtilent out of it, and ill-treated the
ſurgeons.   The ſame thing they did at the
quarantine houſe.   The archiepiſcopal reſidence
was plundered, the moſt valuable of the goods
were taken away, the reſt deſtroyed : the ſtore-
cellars under it, hired by a merchant for wine
and other liquors, were emptied.   Several officers who attempted to check their exceſſes,

4   turned

turned back with bleeding heads. The madnefs increafed every moment, and the cry was now againft the phyficians and furgeons, whom they imagined to have occafioned the peftilence. An italian dancing-mafter happened to come in their way: he muft certainly be a doctor; they broke both his arms and his legs, and in that condition inhumanly left him lying in the ftreet. The houfe of a phyfician was attacked and plundered. They then proceeded to the great hofpital, from which the director and attendants, and even the foldiers who amounted to 100 men with loaded fire-arms, all ran away. All the phyficians and furgeons had already made their efcape into the country.—But now, towards evening the brave general Yerapkin, at the head of 150 foldiers, carabineers and huffars, with two field pieces, marched up to the turbulent crew; the fight was obftinate and lafted till midnight: 250 rebels were laid dead upon the ftreet, 300 taken prifoners, and of thofe that difperfed many were afterwards found wounded and dead. Early on the following morning, the general rode at the head of his men with drawn fabres through the ftreets of Mofco, and placed picquets in proper places. The day after, a regiment of infantry, from the villages, entered the town. The governor, the deputy-governor, police-mafter, general

general of artillery, and all whose duty it was to
be vigilant in preferving peace and order in
the city, had prudently forfaken Mofco.   Catharine rewarded the brave Yerapkin in a truly
imperial manner.

crapshin

Let us figure to ourfelves the ftate of that
enormous city while thefe tumults lafted; at
a time when the minds of all men were oppreffed
with grief at the dreadful vifitation of the plague,
when every one knew that each day 800 perfons
fell around him.   But during the days of confufion it was impoffible to think of enumerating the
dead or of vifiting the fick.   The number of
thofe who died muft have been very great, as
the peftilence increafed beyond all proportion by
the mixture of the people.   From the 1ft to the
9th of October, the calculation was renewed, and
the dead were computed at 5400; till the
numbers afterwards decreafed in the above-
mentioned ratio, by the counteraction of the
froft.—At the re-appearance of fpring 1772, the
return of the calamity was apprehended; the
care of the government was therefore redoubled.
It was publifhed throughout the city, that whoever kept in concealment any goods or other
things in houfes that had been infected, even
though they were ftolen, he might freely produce
them; and, inftead of punifhment, fhould receive

from

from 10 to 20 rubles ; farther, that such articles
as had been in the poffeffion of infected perfons,
and confequently muft be burnt, fhould be paid
for according to their full value. This had the
defired effect : the people very readily produced
what they had, according to the tenor of the
proclamation, as by fo doing they got money and
loft nothing. The vifiting of the fick, of whatever nature were their complaints, was feduloufly
continued. Travellers underwent a ftrict examination, and were obliged to remain a certain
time in quarantine-houfes, of which, between
Mofco and Peterfburg alone there were no lefs
than feven. However, at the clofe of January
1772 the plague had entirely difappeared, which,
according to fome ftatements, during its continuance, from December 1771 to December
1772, had coft the ruffian empire 133,299
perfons.

Concerning the murder of the archbifhop,
fome accounts pretend, that after having caufed
the facred picture to be removed from its place,
the people became more furious *, and accufing
the

* It is difficult to imagine to what length the Ruffians
carry their fanaticifm for thefe pictures of the faints, which
they call bohgs or gods. The figure of fome faint is
painted in gaudy colours on a piece of board, and the filver,
gold,

the archbifhop of inhumanity and facrilege, they
broke open the doors of a monaftery in which
the prelate had fought an afylum : the archbifhop
then thought to efcape the rage of the multitude
by hiding himfelf in the fanctuary, where, ac-

---

gold, or diamonds about the hands and face of it conftitute
its value.   When a Ruffian enters a room, the firft thing he
does is to falute the god, which is placed againft the wall in
one corner, by bowing and croffing himfelf.   St. Nicholas,
St. John the baptift, St. Sergius, and St. Alexander Nefsky,
are the figures in moft requeft, except the hogoroditza, the
mother of God.   Every one has his particular patron, to
which he applies in cafes of need.   When his neighbours fee
that he fucceeds in the culture of his fields or in trade, they
borrow or hire his god, to which they attribute his profperity.
They then pay the borrowed figure all forts of reverence and
offerings.   There are in fome towns god-markets, and the
fole difference between the chaffering, is, that in this the
word money muft never be pronounced.   Some people will
never go to their daily labour, or fet out on a journey, without taking their god with them ; and if a ftranger call
at their houfe in the mean time, and afks to falute the *bog*,
the wife replies that he is gone into the fields, or on
a journey.   St. George is a protector of horned cattle.
The horfes are looked after by St. Anthony, and the fifh
by St. Jonas ; one cures one difeafe and another another.—
But perhaps it is unjuft to deride any religion for its fuperftitions ; all national eftablifhments have them under
one form or another ;

Facies non omnibus una
Nec diverfa tamen, qualem decet effe fororum.

cording

cording to the greek ritual, the priests alone have
a right to enter. Unfortunately, a child feeing
him pafs by, ran and told where he was. The
rabble rufhed into the church, and feizing on the
old man, dragged him to the gate in order to
kill him. The unfortunate archbifhop, perceiving that his death was inevitable, conjured the
affaffins to let him go up to the altar to communicate once more. To this they confented; and
ftood calmly looking on while the venerable
prelate was performing the pious ceremony;
which he had no fooner finifhed, than they
fprung upon him again, and, hauling him out of
the church, barbaroufly put him to death in
the manner already related. The foldiers of the
police arrived too late to fave the archbifhop's
life; but they arrefted fome of the leaders of
the mob, who were knooted to death.

Great praife was certainly due to count Gregory
Orloff for his conduct while the plague was
raging at Mofco. The emprefs, as we have
feen, had already fent affiftance to ftop the
progrefs of the contagion; but it was attended
with no effect. It was neceffary that fome man
of authority fhould go thither to awe the populace, and make them fubmit to the regulations
prefcribed, and to the obfervance of more clean-
linefs than ufual. Gregory Orloff had the

courage to go and brave both the pestilence and superstition. He repaired to Mosco with extraordinary promptitude; he prohibited and prevented all kinds of assemblies; he himself visited the persons afflicted with the epidemical distemper; he procured them all the assistance they wanted; and he took particular care to order the surgeons and the officers who seconded him, to see to the burning of the cloaths of the sick who fell victims to this terrible scourge; till the malady at last yielded to the unceasing attentions of count Gregory Orloff and the severity of the winter.

On his return to St. Petersburg, Gregory Orloff found in Catharine a grateful sovereign. That princess caused a column to be erected and a medal to be struck, as memorials to posterity of the service he had rendered his country.

The pestilence had not only attacked the interior parts of Russia: the russian and ottoman armies, who were fighting on the banks of the Danube, were infected with it. They spread it in Poland; and this it was that served as a pretence for the invasion which had long been meditating by the king of Prussia.

The empress was adding from day to day to the weight of the yoke which she had lain upon Poland. Her troops pursued on all sides

the

the routed confederates of Bar, and pillaged or
ravaged their poffeffions. That princefs herfelf
did not difdain to partake in the fpoil. They
carried off the famous library of prince Radzivil,
containing an invaluable collection of lithuanian
hiftory, and it was tranfported to Peterfburg,
from whence it undoubtedly will never return.
But at the very time that fo odious a depredation
was carrying on, Cathar e tranfmitted to Warfaw declarations, in whic . fhe fpoke of nothing
but her equity, her beneficence, and the defires fhe was cherifhing for the pacification of
Poland.

The Poles, irritated at the tyranny of the
Ruffians, were inceffantly making new efforts to
free themfelves from it. They believed their
unhappy king was in concert with the emprefs;
and in that perfuafion they attempted to revenge
upon him the miferies which fhe was bringing on
them. The confederates had elected for their
general a polifh nobleman named Pulaufsky,
a man of confummate intrepidity, and fo paffion-
ately devoted to the caufe of liberty, that he
made no hefitation of ferving the moft righteous
of caufes by criminal means.

Pulaufsky refolved to get poffeffion of the
king's perfon, and trufted the execution of

his

his project to three other confederates *, of whose boldnefs and capacity he was well acquainted. After having taken an oath to their general either to deliver to him the king, or to put him to death if they could not bring him off alive, the three chiefs and 40 dragoons, difguifed as peafants, entered Warfaw by different routes. They learnt the following funday † that the king was to pafs the evening at prince Chartorinfky's, his uncle. Some of them then went and pofted themfelves without the city, while the others were lurking about in ambufh in the way which the king was to pafs. At about 10 o'clock at night that prince, accompanied by 14 or 15 perfons, and having one of his aides-de-camp in his carriage, were returning to the palace, when all at once the confpirators advanced, and bade the coachman ftop. At the fame-time piftols were feveral times difcharged at the carriage. One of the heyducque's being ftruck with a ball, fell down ‡. The reft of the king's fuite, without excepting the aid-de-camp, took to flight. One of the affaffins fired a piftol at the king, and pierced his hat. Another

* Lukaufsky, Stravenfky, and Kofinfky.
† The 3d of September.   ‡ He died the day after.

made

made a ftroke at his head, and gave him a
deep wound. After this they took him by
the collar, and dragged him between their horfes
along the darkeft ftreets. Perceiving foon that
he began to breathe hard, and that it was
impoffible for him to keep up with them on
foot, they made him get upon a horfe, and
on their coming to the foffé which furrounds
Warfaw, they forced him to take the leap with
them. The horfe on which the king rode
fell and broke his leg. The king received a
hurt in his foot. They then mounted his majefty
on another horfe. One of the chiefs plucked off
his order of the black eagle of Pruffia, and
the crofs of diamonds that was appendant to the
riband. This done, the greater part of the
confpirators difperfed. Seven of them alone,
under the orders of Kofinfky, remained with the
king, and wandered about with him a long
time in the dark, endeavouring to avoid the
beaten paths. Soon after, they found themfelves
in a foreft only one league diftant from Warfaw.
The voices of fome ruffian patrolls were heard.
The confpirators were frightened, and fled. The
king remained alone with Kofinfky: but, not
daring to call for affiftance, for fear that Kofinfky
might kill him, he tried to perfuade him to let
him efcape. Kofinfky hefitated a confiderable

time. His oath ftood in his way. At length,
however, he yielded to the folicitations of the
king ; and, after having implored his pardon on
his knees, he conducted him to a mill which
ftood at no great diftance. The king, without
making himfelf known, immediately wrote a
billet, which he difpatched by a countryman
to the colonel of his guards.

Warfaw was in the utmoft confternation. The
king's hat had been found all covered with
blood ; this naturally led to the belief that
his majefty was dead. But as foon as it was
heard that he had efcaped from his affaffins, the
people gave themfelves up to tranfports of
joy.

Several of the villains were taken, and perifhed
on the fcaffold. Kofinfky obtained his pardon.
He retired into Italy, where the king fettled on
him a penfion. As to general Pulaufsky *, he
publifhed a manifefto, in which he declared that
he had taken no fhare in the atrocious attempt
againft the polifh monarch. This declaration
was believed by no one.

* Pulaufsky went afterwards to America, where he had
the command of a legion in the fervice of the united ftates ;
and, being on a vifit to M. d'Eftaing at the fiege of
Savannah, in 1779, he was killed by a cannon ball by
the fide of that general.

The

The danger which Staniſlaus Auguſtus had run, furniſhed the Ruſſians with a new pretext for purſuing the confederates of Bar, and for preparing the diſmemberment of Poland. But was Catharine in want of pretexts? It will preſently be ſeen that ſhe had ſo ordered matters as to be able to do without them.

1772. The Ruſſians and the Ottomans were equally in want of peace. Their armies, weakened by numerous battles, by ſucceſſive fatigues, and by the contagious diſtemper, were always recruiting and always diminiſhing in greater proportion. The ſquadron of Alexius Orloff ſtill maintained the dominion of the grecian ſeas; but the long ſojourn of the Ruſſians in a climate ſo different from their own, and the intemperance in which they indulged, had brought on an epidemic diſeaſe which threatened to carry off every ſailor of the fleet. The capudan-paſha, ambitious to retaliate the diſaſters he had ſuffered, was buſily employed in preparing new armaments in Conſtantinople, and was in hopes to bring out againſt his conquerors a ſquadron more formidable than that which had fallen a prey to the flames. Baron Tott, a french officer in the ſervice of the Porte, overcame the ignorance of the Turks, and had introduced into their arſenals ſuch order and activity as was

R 4   dangerous

dangerous to their enemies. The valiant Muf-
foum Oglou had rifen, for the fecond time, to
the poft of grand vizir, and had refumed the
command of the army of the Danube. Notwithftanding this, the two powers entered upon
a negotiation by the intervention of the auftrian
and pruffian minifters. An armiftice was agreed
upon* ; and a congrefs was appointed to meet at
Fokfhiani.

This appeared to be a favourable opportunity
to the fchemes of count Gregory Orloff. He
procured the honour of being fent to treat with
the plenipotentiaries of the divan. He had
long been defirous of fharing the throne which
he had fecured to Catharine. He thought that,
by obtaining peace for Ruffia, he fhould acquire
an everlafting claim upon the gratitude of the
empire, and furmount the difficulties that had
been oppofed to his ambition. But it was this
precifely which gave birth to new ones.

Catharine had been, and was ftill, much
attached to Orloff. Orloff, on the contrary,
had never felt any affeſtion for Catharine, but
what arofe from gratitude and ambition. Proud
of the favour of his fovereign, he fhewed him-

---

* This armiftice was figned by the ruffian minifter Simolin,
and by Seïd Abdukerim effendi Mukabedbadzi, grand
notary of the divan.

self

felf zealous to deferve it: but when once he thought that he had acquired fufficient grounds for his pretenfions, his ardour began to cool; and he even affumed a diftant behaviour. The more Catharine wifhed to bring him back to his ufual attentions, the more he feemed inclined to retreat, and to feek his amufement in the company of other ladies. The emprefs could not but refent this ungrateful conduct, and be fhocked at the infenfibility from whence it proceeded. However, on account of her fondnefs for Bobrinfky, the child of Orloff, fhe did not difcard him at once. This boy fhe privately brought up in one of the fuburbs of the city, often going to fee him under a borrowed name, and in an artful difguife. It was faid that, to remedy his inconftancy, and from affection to the child, a propofal was made him of a clandeftine marriage : that he rejected the offer with difdain, prefuming himfelf not unworthy of fitting befide her on a throne which he at firft procured her, and had hitherto upheld. Catharine, furprifed, diffembled her difpleafure for a time; but conceiving that the pride of her favourite might be attended with confequences fatal to her repofe, fhe refolved, without farther delay, to get the better of an attachment which expofed her to too great humiliation.

Though

Though there was no open mifunderftanding between Panin and count Gregory Orloff, he was not the lefs defirous of the downfall of this favourite. Too fagacious, and certainly too timid, to attack him to his face, he miffed no opportunity for giving him a fide-blow. Orloff was far from imitating the minifter in this procedure. He never hated any one, though he was hated by many. His arrogance had procured him a great number of enemies; his favour had raifed him up many more. All were pleafed at feeing him retire from court; and the emprefs partook in the fatisfaction of her courtiers. She was in hopes that his abfence would completely put an end to the remainder of the attachment fhe had cherifhed for him.

Panin, who attentively watched the inclination of her majefty, was not long in perceiving that fhe often looked with complacency on a fub-lieutenant of the guards, named Vaffiltfchikoff. He immediately thought of ufing this young man to the overthrow of Orloff. Zachar Chernicheff, to whom the arrogance of the favourite was ftill more odious than to Panin, gladly feconded the fcheme of the minifter. Both of them thought that the grand duke, who was not ignorant that Orloff had the prefumption to afpire to the throne, would not fail to behold
with

with fatisfaction whatever had a tendency to keep him from it. Every art was therefore employed to flatter the new inclination of the emprefs. Orloff was at the fame time reprefented to her as a man of unbounded ambition, who had only folicited to be employed in negociating the peace at Fokfhiani, in order to betray the interefts of Ruffia, by artfully procuring for himfelf the fovereignty of Moldavia and Valachia. It was the eafier to raife fufpicions againft him in the mind of Catharine, as fhe found his rival more agreeable to her from day to day.

Vaffiltfchikoff pleafed becaufe he was young and well made : but he was deficient in intellectual improvement, in talents, in experience, and even in boldnefs. Perhaps, if it had depended on himfelf alone, he would never have fucceeded with the emprefs : but he was not left without fupport. Prince Baratinfky, expert in the arts of intrigue, was on this occafion neither fparing of his counfels nor of contrivances *. Vaffiltfchikoff was benefited by his cares; for his docility ferved him inftead of merit. The emprefs was fo fatisfied with him, that fhe appointed him her chamberlain, made him mag-

* Prince Baratinfky took upon him to bring about the firft interview of the emprefs and her new favourite.

nificent

nificent prefents, and treated him often in public
with a familiarity that eafily betrayed the underftanding that fubfifted between them.

When Catharine propofed to the imperious
Orloff to enter into fecret nuptials, that favourite
was pleafed with the thought that his refufal
would only fharpen the defire of the fovereign,
and that the accefs to the throne would be eafier
to him. Accuftomed to an affection of which he
had the tendereft pledges, he imagined it impoffible to lofe the heart of the emprefs. What
was he to think on learning that fhe had taken
advantage of his abfence for accepting the offi-
cioufnefs of a new admirer ? His mind was at
firft divided between aftonifhment and rage : but
his pride foon came to his relief; and he thought
that his prefence would be fufficient to revive a
flame which could not be quite extinct. Full of
this idea, he forgot the negotiations, the peace,
all the concerns of the empire, and left Fokfhiani
without even afking permiffion of the emprefs,
and arrived at the gates of Peterfburg. At the
inftant of his appearance, the officer on guard
advanced towards his carriage, and fhewed him
the order which he had, not to let him enter the
city. Orloff kept a profound filence, and took
the road to one of his country-feats.

Two

Two days previous to the coming of Orloff to Peterſburg, intelligence was received that he had quitted Fokſhiani. This ſudden return had excited much uneaſineſs at court. The empreſs, who was well acquainted with the violence of his temper, and was apprehenſive that he might make his appearance in ſpite of her, gave orders to double the guard of the palace, and to place centinels at the gate of the new favourite. Not yet put completely at eaſe by theſe precautions, ſhe cauſed the locks of his apartments to be changed, of which Orloff had the key. But theſe cares were uſeleſs : there was nothing to fear from Orloff. The moment it was known that he was out of favour, he had not a partizan left, and his enemies ſtepped forward from all parts.

Orloff beheld his ſituation in the full extent of its danger ; but his courage remained unſhaken. When the officers came, in the name of the empreſs, to require the demiſſion of his employments, he haughtily refuſed to comply. Her majeſty could eaſily puniſh the ſubject who reſiſted her will : ſhe rather choſe to tréat with indulgence the man for whom ſhe had long entertained a regard. A compromiſe was entered upon with Orloff ; and, overcome by the bounty which his ſovereign ſtill vouchſafed to ſhew him,

he

he confented to retire from Peterfburg, and fet out upon a journey through various parts of Europe. As a recompence for his fubmiffion, he received 100,000 rubles, the brevet of a penfion of 150,000, a magnificent fervice of plate, and an eftate with 6000 peafants upon it. He had already obtained a patent of prince of the roman empire. Catharine chofe that he fhould take the title, defirous, doubtlefs, that her former favourite fhould appear to the eyes of foreign nations with a fplendor worthy of the fituation which he had enjoyed.

This part of Catharine's conduct feems to indicate a degree of weaknefs. But no: it was not inconfiftent with the firmnefs of her character to yield to circumftances, when a different con- duct muft oblige her to compliance. She knew that, by punifhing prince Orloff, fhe would affright all thofe who had ferved her. She wifhed to perfuade them that her gratitude even furvived her affections.

CHAP. VII.

Rupture of the congress of Fokshiani.—Conferences at Bukhareft.—Partition of Poland.—Peace of Kainardgi.—Emigration of the Kalmouks.—Difmiffal of the favourite Vaffiltfchikoff.—Duke Anthony Ulric refufes his liberty.—Firft marriage of the grand duke.—Journey of Diderot to St. Peterfburg.—Magnificence of Catharine. —Defcription of her perfon.—Her way of life. —Patriotic exertions.—Order of St. George.

1772. THE congrefs of Fokfhiani was opened * in fuch a manner as to afford great hopes

* The congrefs opened the 2d of Auguft. The plenipotentiaries were under tents; and the conferences were held in a kiofk, which the Ruffians had caufed to be conftructed for that purpofe. Fokfhiani is at the diftance of about 16 miles to the north of Bukhareft in Valachia. Nothing could afford a ftronger contraft, than the magnificence of the ruffian minifters, oppofed to the ottoman fimplicity. The former approached in four grand coaches, preceded by huffars, and attended by 160 domeftics fuitably habited. The turkifh minifters were on horfeback, with about 60 fervants, as plainly appareled and accoutred as themfelves. Prince Orloff was all over one blaze of jewels: on his breaft was the emprefs's portrait fet with brilliants, together with the enfigns of the feveral orders with which he had been invefted; all of which, as well as his epaulet and

hopes of an approaching peace. The ottoman minifters prefented the Ruffians with fuperb carpets, very fine ftuffs, and excellent arms: and Ofman effendi, who firft broke filence, faid, " That " the grand fignor his mafter had recommended " him to ferve God, and to love peace."

The Ruffians offered to Ofman and his colleagues diamonds and precious ftones elegantly fet, a variety of trinkets of gold, and a quantity of rich furs; on delivering which they anfwered, that they alfo were lovers of peace and juftice. However, they demanded fuch great facrifices, that the Turks were difgufted with their propofals. After much fruitlefs altercation, the plenipotentiaries feparated.

Some time afterwards, the negotiations were refumed at Bukhareft between marfhal Ro-

---

and buckles, and feveral other parts of his drefs, fhone with diamonds. On the other hand, Ofman effendi was clothed in a robe of green camlet faced with ermine, and had nothing to diftinguifh him but a gold-headed cane. It would appear as if riches and magnificence had difplayed their treafures in the wilds of Scythia; and that ancient fimplicity had retired to the voluptuous nations of Afia. M. Obrefkoff, late minifter at the Porte, attended prince Orloff. The auftrian and pruffian minifters at the fame place, having received a prefent of 50 purfes, amounting to about 25,000 dollars, each, from the grand fignor, befides a fixed daily allowance for their expences, attended alfo at the opening of the congrefs.

mantzoff

mantzoff and the grand vizir' Muffum Oglou. Thefe two warriors, who had fo often fought againft each other, were not ignorant how much their armies were in want of reft ; but their conferences were as unfruitful as thofe of Fokfhiani. The term of the armiftice was expired. The pacificators had no longer any thoughts of war.

During all the time that thefe negotiations had been going on, new preparations had been making for recommencing hoftilities. The Ruffians had concluded, with the new khan of the Krimea, a treaty by which that prince declared himfelf independent on the grand fignor, and threw himfelf under the protection of the emprefs. The Porte, incenfed at the defection of the Tartars, no lefs than at the ceffion they had made to the Ruffians of the forts of Kertfch and Yenicaly, which command the ftreights of Keffa, together with the territories belonging to them, fent into the Euxine a ftrong fquadron of galliots and chebecs. Catharine had already fent thither a confiderable fleet, and had difpatched to it feveral englifh and dutch officers, particularly the captains Dennifon, Perry, and Kinfbergen, under the command of admiral fir Charles Knowles.

But an object of higher importance at that time occupied the mind of Catharine. She faw herself at length on the point of reaping the fruit of the troubles and divisions which she had been sowing among the Poles. For a long time in agreement with the king of Prussia, she left to that prince the care of procuring the consent of the court of Vienna to the dismemberment of Poland. She was, moreover, very sure that she would have but few obstacles to overcome on the part of the other powers. France had then a minister not much endowed with foresight *. England was bound to Russia by its commerce. The states bordering on the Baltic might be jealous at seeing the Russians and the Prussians gaining ports upon that sea; but none of them had either the means or the temerity to make head against them. The Ottomans were scarcely more to be dreaded. How should they be in a condition to send succours to Poland, when they were so badly able to defend themselves, and saw themselves attacked in all parts of their vast empire? Catharine, in short, was only afraid of the refusal of the court of Vienna; but Frederic promised her the accession of that court.

* The duke d'Aiguillon, who had been put at the head of the department of foreign affairs, was more qualified for paying attendance on the intrigues of the boudoir and court cabals, than to balance the interests of Europe, and to support the honour of the french nation.

Frederic,

Frederic, without hazarding any thing, might make her that promife. He had been long acquainted, by the relations of his minifters, with the character of the heir of the houfe of Auftria.

When Jofeph II. in 1769, had an interview with him at Neifs in Silefia, the pruffian monarch, profiting by the afcendant he had acquired from his experience and his fame, propofed to the young emperor the firft partition of Poland. Jofeph II. pleafed with the idea of extending his dominion, beheld with joy the project of the king of Pruffia; but deferred to enter into any engagement to concur in it, till he fhould have conferred upon the fubject with the old prince Kaunitz, by whofe counfels he was guided. Kaunitz applauded the predatory plan. Some time after this * the monarchs had a fecond interview, at Neuftadt in Auftria; and the difmemberment of Poland was finally fettled.

The plague, which had been ravaging the frontiers of Poland fince the foregoing year, furnifhed the king of Pruffia with an occafion for advancing his troops pretty far into polifh Pruffia. The emperor had the fame pretext for marching his into fuch of the provinces as lay moft conveniently for him.

* In 1770.

Joseph II. seemed about to give succours to the confederates of Bar. His last treaty obliged him even to join with the Turks against the Russians; but that prince entertained very different designs; and he was so well practised in the arts of dissimulation, that the confederates, deceived by his promises, regarded for a long time as their defenders the soldiers who were come to make a prey of their country.

The foreign armies extended from one end of Poland to the other, and acted equally against the confederates, who were soon obliged to disperse. The greater part returned to their homes. The rest went to publish abroad among foreign nations their complaints and their misfortunes.

All Europe had its eyes fixed on Poland. It could not be conceived why three formidable powers, in a time of profound peace, should seize upon a country, the independence whereof had been guaranteed by the most solemn treaties. Mankind were likewise at a loss to know what might be the drift of the negociations which continually employed these powers. It was at length discovered. The minister of the emperor was the first who notified the treaty of Petersburg to the king and the senate of Poland. The

ambassador

ambaſſador of Ruſſia and the envoy of Pruſſia preſented to them, almoſt immediately upon it, declarations in ſupport of that treaty.

We ſhall here inſert the declaration of baron Stackelberg, miniſter of Ruſſia, to ſhew what falſe and inſidious language the authors of the deſolations dared to hold :

" The powers in the vicinity of Poland have been ſo " often involved in the troubles which almoſt every vacancy " of the throne has excited in that kingdom, that from the " recollection of the paſt it behoved them to give the moſt " ſerious attention to the affairs of the poliſh nation, as " ſoon as, by the death of the late king, Auguſtus III, " the throne was become vacant.

" Urged by theſe conſiderations, and deſirous of pre- " venting the dreadful effects of thoſe diſſentions, which, " as in former inſtances, might have ariſen at this laſt " vacancy of the throne, the court of St. Peterſburg " haſtened to take all poſſible meaſures to unite the citizens " of Poland in favour of the candidate who ſhould appear " to be moſt worthy of the throne, moſt agreeable to his " fellow-citizens, and moſt acceptable to the neigh- " bouring powers.

" This court applied herſelf at the ſame time, and with " equal zeal, to the rectifying of many abuſes and defects in " the conſtitution, which had been equally prejudicial to " Poland and her neighbours.

" The court of Berlin ſeconded the attempts of her ally. " And the court of Vienna, deſirous, on her part, of contri- " buting to the ſucceſs of ſuch laudable views, but willing, " at the ſame time, to avoid the danger of augmenting the " difficulties and intricacies which might ariſe from multi-

s 3   " plying

" plying the number of thofe who undertook openly and
" directly to fettle the affairs of Poland, thought proper
" to obferve the moft exact neutrality, with regard both to
" the arrangement of the affairs of Poland, and the war
" which was afterwards kindled on this fubject between
" Ruffia and the Porte.

" The immediate confequences of thefe meafures were
" the free and legal election of Staniflaus Auguftus *,
" reigning king of Poland, and the forming of many ufeful
" and falutary eftablifhments. In a word, every thing
" feemed to promife to Poland and her neighbours a firm
" and lafting tranquillity.

" But unhappily, in the midft of thefe promifing appear-
" ances, the fpirit of difcord feized upon one part of the
" nation: citizen armed againft citizen ; the fons of faction
" feized the reins of authority ; and laws, and order, and
" public fafety, and juftice, and police, and commerce, and
" agriculture, all are either gone to ruin, or ftand on the
" brink of deftruction. And the exceffes of every kind,
" natural confequences of fuch an anarchy, will bring on
" the total diffolution of the ftate, if not timely prevented.

" The connections between nations which border on each
" other are fo intimate, that the fubjects of the neighbour-
" ing powers have already felt the moft difagreeable effects
" from thefe diforders. Thefe powers are obliged, at a
" great expence, to take meafures of precaution, in order
" to fecure the tranquillity of their own frontiers ; they are
" expofed to the uncertain but poffible confequences of the
" entire diffolution of Poland ; to the danger of feeing their

---

* And it was to the Poles that the minifter Stackelberg
had the affurance to fay, that the election of Poniatofsky
had been free and legal!

" mutual

" mutual harmony and good friendfhip deftroyed; the
" maintenance of which, at the fame time that it fecures
" their own peace and tranquillity, is a matter of the
" higheft importance to all Europe.

" From this view of things it will appear, that nothing
" can be of a more urgent neceffity than to apply an imme-
" diate remedy to evils from which the neighbouring nations
" have already experienced the moft difagreeable effects;
" and the confequences of which, if not timely prevented,
" muft bring on fuch changes in the political fyftem of
" this part of Europe, as may be fatal to the general
" tranquillity,

" Impelled by reafons fo many and fo weighty, her
" majefty the emprefs of all the Ruffias, her majefty the
" emprefs dowager queen of Hungary and Bohemia, and
" his majefty the king of Pruffia, find themfelves under
" a neceffity of taking a decifive part, in circumftances
" fo very critical. And their faid majefties have determined
" among themfelves, without lofs of time, and with one
" accord, to take the moft effectual and beft-combined
" meafures, for the purpofe of re-eftablifhing tranquillity
" and good order in Poland, to ftop the prefent troubles,
" and to put the ancient conftitution of that kingdom, and
" the liberties of the people, on a fure and folid found-
" ation.

" But whilft they take advantage of that mutual friend-
" fhip and harmony which happily fubfifts between them at
" prefent, in order to prevent the abfolute ruin and arbi-
" trary diffolution of Poland; they cannot but be fenfible
" how little it is in their power to promife themfelves in
" future periods the fame happy concurrence. And as
" they have refpectively very confiderable claims on the
" poffeffions of the republic, which they cannot permit
" themfelves to expofe to the hazard of poffible contin-

s 4   " gencies,

" gencies, they have therefore determined among them-
" felves to aſſert theſe their ancient rights and lawful
" claims, which each of them will be ready to juſtify in time
" and place by authentic records and ſolid reaſons ; but for
" which the ſituation of the republic will never leave them
" hopes of obtaining juſtice in the ordinary courſe of pro-
" ceeding.

" In conſequence hereof her majeſty the empreſs of all
" the Ruſſias, her majeſty the empreſs dowager queen of
" Hungary and Bohemia, and his majeſty the king of
" Pruſſia, having communicated reciprocally their re-
" ſpective rights and claims, and being mutually con-
" vinced of the juſtice thereof, are determined to ſecure
" to themſelves a proportionable equivalent, by taking
" immediate and effectual poſſeſſion of ſuch parts of the
" territories of the republic as may ſerve to fix more natural
" and ſure bounds between her and the three powers : the
" ſaid three powers engaging to give hereafter an exact
" ſpecification of their reſpective quotas ; and renouncing
" from the preſent moment all revival of right, demand, or
" claim, on account of damages ſuſtained, debt, intereſt, or
" any other pretence whatever, which they might other-
" wiſe have or form on the poſſeſſions or ſubjects of the
" republic.

" Their ſaid majeſties have thought it right to notify
" theſe their intentions to the whole poliſh nation in general ;
" inviting, at the ſame time, all orders and ranks thereof to
" baniſh, or at leaſt to ſuſpend, all ſpirit of diſcord and
" deluſion, in order that, a diet being legally aſſembled,
" they may co-operate with their ſaid majeſties in eſtabliſhing,
" on a firm and ſolid foundation, the good order and tran-
" quillity of the nation, and may at the ſame time ratify,
" by public and ſolemn acts, the exchange of the titles,
" pretenſions, and claims of each of their majeſties, againſt
" the

" the equivalents of which they have refpectively taken
" poffeffion.
(Signed)   " STACKELBERG.
" Given at Warfaw, September 2, 1772 *."

It has fince been feen how faithfully thefe three
powers adhered to their renunciation !

The indignant Poles cried out againft the
injuftice. They claimed the intervention of the
potentates guarantees of the treaty of Oliva;
a treaty that had affured to them the integrity of
their territory, and which had long been regarded
as the grand charter of the north. Some of
thefe potentates made remonftrances, not lefs unavailing than the complaints of the Poles. Not
content with having already feized on a part
of the provinces of Poland, the three imperial
and royal fpoliators infifted that a diet fhould
folemnly make to them the ceffion of thefe
provinces. The diet was immediately convoked
and affembled †. Promifes and money were
lavifhed to gain over the deputies. Neverthelefs the majority of the diet for a long time

---

* This manifefto was delivered on the 18th of September
by baron Stackelberg, minifter from the court of Peterfburg ;
and by the fieur de Benoit, minifter from the court of Berlin ;
and on the 26th of September by baron Rjevitch, minifter
from the court of Vienna.

† The 19th of April.

refufed

refufed their confent to the difmemberment.
Provoked at a refiftance which had not been
expected, the minifters of the three courts threatened the diet with the full animadverfion of their
fovereigns. They faid, that they would caufe
the king to be arrefted and depofed; and it was
privily circulated by their emiffaries, that if
the diet refufed its compliance, Warfaw fhould
be delivered up to pillage. By repeated alure-
ments and ftratagems, the confent of the diet
was at length obtained. It iffued at the fame
time a decree to confine to a fmall number
of days. the time of their fittings *, and it
appointed commiffioners to fettle with the minifters of the three courts the conditions of the
partition. It may eafily be imagined that thefe
conditions were dictated by the minifters themfelves. They were figned in the month of September following.

· Some nobles of the ufurped provinces had the
courage to proteft againft the treaty, and to
publifh manifeftos. But of what avail were thefe
folitary exclamations againft numerous armies?

Previous to the convocation of the diet, and
during the whole of its continuance, the king
had loudly declared againft the partition. Not-

---

* It broke up in the month of May.

withftanding

withftanding this, it was pretended that he
fecretly favoured it, and perfons who knew
his former devotednefs to Ruffia, could not perfuade themfelves that he would now give it up.

As foon as the acceffion to the treaty of partition was voted, feveral of the principal members
of the diet repaired to the king, and reproached
him fharply with the ruin of their country.
The monarch at firft anfwered them with gentlenefs. But foon perceiving that his moderation
only ferved to embolden them and to provoke
frefh infults, he rofe up, threw his hat upon the
floor, and faid to them haughtily, " Gentlemen,
" I am weary of hearkening to you. The
" partition of our unhappy country is a con-
" fequence of your ambition, of your diffentions,
" and your eternal difputes. It is to yourfelves
" alone that you ought to attribute your misfor-
" tunes. As for me, if no more territory fhould
" be left me than could be covered by this hat,
" I fhould neverthelefs be ftill, in the eyes of all
" Europe, your lawful, but unhappy king."

By the difmemberment of Poland it loft nearly
5,000,000 of inhabitants. The country that fell
to Ruffia, and which was the moft extenfive,
contained 1,500,000. That which Auftria had,
2,500,000, on a territory far lefs extenfive.
Pruffia

Pruſſia acquired only 860,000 ſouls * : but ſhe was compenſated by the commerce and the vicinity of the Viſtula, and by the city of Dantzik, of which Frederic had already laid the plan of rendering himſelf maſter.

The three courts who thus appropriated to themſelves the ſpoils of Poland, were not unmindful at the ſame time of putting it in a ſtate of impoſſibility ever to regain what they had now been uſurping from it. However dangerous the form of its government might have been, they were determined to render it ſtill more corrupt. They cauſed full powers to be granted to the commiſſioners of the diet, to employ themſelves, in concert with them or their miniſters, in making the changes required by the conſtitution of the republic ; and, under the ſpecious pretext of

---

* Ruſſia acquired 3440 ſquare leagues, Auſtria 2700, and Pruſſia 900. The country uſurped by Ruſſia had for its limits the river Vella, from its ſource to the place where it falls into the Niemen, and the river Bercezina, as far as Rjeſieka, where it empties itſelf into the Dniepr.—Auſtria took the whole of the left bank of the Viſtula, from the ſalt mines as far as the mouth of the Virotz, the palatinate of Beltch, Red-Ruſſia, and the greater part of Volhynia.— Frederic took poſſeſſion of Elbing and the whole of poliſh Pruſſia, excepting the cities of Dantzik and Thorne, which he took afterwards.

correcting

correcting its defects, they aggravated them so as to render them incurable.

After conferences prolonged by repeated delays, a new diet was assembled, in which the ministers of the three courts proposed their plan of reform. The diet was more tumultuous and more untractable than the preceding; and, in spite of the influence of the russian minister, who caused his secretary to read the new project of the constitution, this project was at first rejected. It is too curious for us not to introduce here the bases of it, as well as the preamble of the captious memorial which the ministers of the three courts presented at the same time :

" The courts are so strongly interested in the pacification of " Poland, that while the business is in hand of preparing the " treaties for being signed and ratified, their ministers think " that not an instant should be lost of that inestimable inter- " val, for restoring order and tranquillity to that kingdom. " We shall now therefore communicate to the commission, a " part of those fundamental laws, to the acceptance whereof " our courts will not permit any obstacle or delay.

" 1. The crown of Poland shall be elective for ever, and " all order of succession shall remain prohibited. Any " person who shall attempt to infringe this law, shall be de- " clared an enemy of the country, and prosecuted as " such.

" 2. Foreigners who aspire to the throne, occasioning " most frequently divisions and troubles, shall henceforward " be excluded, and a law shall be passed, that in future none
" but

" but a Pole by parentage, born a gentleman, fhall be
" capable of being elected king of Poland and grand duke
" of Lithuania.   The fon or grandfon of a king fhall not be
" eligible immediately after the death of his father, or of his
" grandfather ; and he fhall not be fo till after the interval
" of two reigns.

" 3. The government of Poland fhall be, and fhall
" continue for ever a free and independent government, and
" of the republican form.

" 4. The true principles of that government confifting in
" an exact obfervance of the laws, and in the equilibrium of
" the three orders, viz. the king, the fenate, and the
" nobility, a permanent council fhall be eftablifhed to which
" fhall be attributed the executive power.   Into this council
" fhall be admitted perfons of the rank of nobility, who have
" been hitherto excluded from the adminiftration of affairs,
" in the interval of the diets," &c.

By thefe laws the houfe of Saxony and other
foreign princes, who might have preferved the
integrity of the remnant of Poland, were excluded from the throne, the liberum veto, with
the other dangerous privileges of the nobility,
confirmed, and all the diforders perpetuated.

Stackelberg was ftill ambaffador from Catharine at Warfaw *.   More pliant than Repnin,
he

* It is well known that of all the Poles, the king was him
for whom Stackelberg had the leaft refpect.   Whenever he
was in company with that prince, he ufed to place himfelf
without ceremony before him, with his back to the fire, and
holding up the fkirts of his coat.—The king one day paid a
vifit

he was neither lefs haughty nor lefs addicted to intrigue. By dexterity and corruption he gained over the majority of the deputies, and the diet approved of the new form of government. It feemed proper now that this pernicious plan of government, eftablifhed by Ruffia, Auftria, and Pruffia, fhould be maintained and upheld by thofe powers: but they delayed not to take advantage of its defects to bring it to total deftruction.

It will be difficult for pofterity to know which moft to admire, the great power of Ruffia, or the magnificence of its emprefs, when they are informed, that in the courfe of fo long, fo expenfive, and fo widely extended a war, her expences, whether in rewards to her generals and officers, in prefents to learned men, in the encouragement of arts, or in the purchafe of libraries, ftatues, pictures, antiques, and jewels, infinitely exceed thofe of any late or prefent european prince except Lewis XIV. Among many inftances of this nature which might be given, a diamond of

---

vifit to Stackelberg. He was dealing the cards at the game of pharao, and without quitting his play, he fat ftill and fhewed the king a chair, making a fign to him to fit down. Every perfon at Warfaw was plainly convinced that the ruffian minifter was the real king in that capital.

an

an enormous fize which fhe purchafed this year may be fufficient. This diamond, which weighs 779 carats, was brought fome years before by a greek gentleman from Ifpahan to Holland, and depofited for fecurity in the bank, till he could meet with a purchafer: the greatnefs of the price would have made this difficult, if the emprefs of Ruffia had not exifted. She paid upwards of 100,000l. fterling for it, befides fettling a penfion for life, of 4000 rubles, upon the gentleman, which amounts to little lefs than 1000l. fterling a year.

While Catharine was acquiring by negotiations a part of the provinces of Poland, her armies continued to ravage the frontiers of Turkey. Fortune however was not always favourable to her. Fourteen thoufand Ruffians, in attempting to pafs the Danube, were furprifed * by Dagheftan-Ali, pafha, and 600 of them remained prifoners with the Turks. Prince Repnin was of that number. He was conveyed to Conftantinople, and fhut up in the caftle of feven towers.

Marfhal Romantzoff croffed the Danube, and marched direct to Siliftria. Fourfcore thoufand Turks were encamped on the adjacent heights.

* At Giurgevo.

General

General Veiffmann attacked them: they fhut themfelves up in the town. Romantzoff marched up to it the following day. The grand vizir had already detached from his army 50,000 men for the purpofe of relieving Siliftria. Romantzoff effected his retreat during the night; but he was haraffed by the Turks, who killed a great number of his people. Obliged to repafs the Danube, that general went and encamped near Yablonitch, in Valachia.

The grand vizir occupied the left bank of the Danube. A detachment of his army defeated a confiderable body of Ruffians at Rofkana. Thefe feparate battles often turned out to the advantage of the Ottomans.

Difcontented at perceiving that her armies had not lately been gaining new victories, Catharine fent difpatches to marfhal Romantzoff, defiring to be informed why he did not give battle. The general returned for anfwer, that it was becaufe the grand vizir had three times more people than he, and might eafily find his advantage in fuch an event.—Catharine wrote immediately in reply, " The Romans " never afked after the number of their enemies, " but where they were, in order to fight " them."

1774. Muſtapha III. now died, and Abdul-Ahmet *, his brother, acceded to the throne of Conſtantinople. The latter years of the reign of Muſtapha had been marked by ſanguinary diſaſters. His ſucceſſor attempted to reſtore

---

* Catharine herſelf has drawn the portrait of theſe two princes and their ſiſters in not very flattering colours.—
" No foreign miniſter ever ſees the ſultan except in public
" audiences. Muſtapha underſtands no language but the
" turkiſh; and it is doubtful whether he can read and write.
" This prince is of a ferocious and ſanguinary diſpoſition.
" It is ſaid that he is born with talents: that may be; but
" I will diſpute with him on the ſcore of prudence; he has
" ſhewn none during this war.—His brother is leſs imprudent
" than him; he is a bigot. He adviſed him againſt the
" war; and I cannot think that he will be ſent any
" where with a command.—But what perhaps will make
" you laugh, is, that theſe two princes had a ſiſter, who
" was the terror of all the paſhas. She was, before the
" war, upwards of 60 years of age. She had been married
" 15 times, and when ſhe was without a huſband, the
" ſultan, who was very fond of her, gave her the choice
" of all the paſhas of his empire. Now, when a paſha
" marries a princeſs of the imperial family, he is obliged
" to diſmiſs his whole harem. This ſultana, beſides her
" age, was malicious, jealous, capricious, and intriguing.
" Her intereſt with her brother was without bounds, and
" frequently the paſhas whom ſhe married were without
" heads; which was a circumſtance not at all entertaining
" to them: but the fact is not the leſs true for that."

the

the ottoman empire to its priſtine ſplendor. He made immenſe preparations for opening the approaching campaign. The turkiſh armies were augmented by freſh levies, to the number of 400,000 fighting men.

Marſhal Romantzoff alſo received great reinforcements. He reſolved again to croſs the Danube, and attack the Turks. The latter diſputed his paſſage with ſignal valour: but their efforts were ineffectual. General Soltikoff* was the firſt who reached the oppoſite ſhore. Souvaroff and Kamenſkoï followed cloſe at his heels. The Turks were repulſed. Romantzoff was ſoon after encamped at the gates of Siliſtria.

Not many days after, the Turks attacked Soltikoff. They were 25,000 ſtrong, and fought a long time with the greateſt intrepidity: but they were at length obliged to ſubmit to the ſuperior ſkill and bravery of the Ruſſians.

The ſame day Kamenſkoï and Souvaroff gained an advantage over the reis effendi, who was at the head of 40,000 Turks, and took away with them his artillery.

All theſe diſaſters were greatly diſtreſſing to the Ottomans; as a ſpirit of inſubordination and revolt is uſually, with them, the conſequence of

---

* Since become field-marſhal.

T 2

2 defeat.

a defeat. The troops of the army of the grand vizir were either engaged in bloody contests among themselves, or deserting by whole detachments. That general was encamped at Shumala, where he was at a great distance from the other bodies of the turkish army. Romantzoff, who remarked the disadvantage of that position, so opportunely surrounded the camp of the vizir, that he cut off his communication not only with the detached corps, but also with his magazines. The vizir, unable therefore to receive any succours, or to retire, or to stand a battle, determined to sue for peace.

The plenipotentiaries met accordingly at Kutshuk-Kainardshi, in Bulgaria. The Russians persisted in the demands they had made at the last congress. The Turks agreed to them; and the preliminaries of the treaty were signed * by marshal Romantzoff, and the kiaya of the grand vizir †. By this treaty Russia obtained the free navigation of the Euxine, and in all the ottoman seas, together with the passage of the Dardanelles; on condition, however, that she

* About the month of July.

† In order to avoid appearing again in the presence of his conqueror, the haughty Muffum-Oglou feigned a sickness.

should

fhould never have more than one armed veffel in the feas of Conftantinople. Retaining Azoff, Taganrog, Kiertfh, and Kinburn, fhe reftored the reft of her conquefts. The independence of the Krimea * was one of the principal claufes of the

---

* The peninfula of the Krimea, or Krim, antiently called the Taurica Cherfonefus, is furrounded on all fides by the Euxine and thé Palus Mæotis, except where it is joined to the continent of the leffer Tartary by a narrow ifthmus, fomething lefs than five englifh miles in breadth, This ifthmus has received its name from the antient city of Perekop, which is built at its entrance on the fide of the peninfula, and has been celebrated for the ftrong lines made for its defence by the Turks, which extend quite acrofs from the Euxine to the Palus Mæotis, and were the labour of 5000 men for a courfe of feveral years. The Tartars confidered thefe lines as inexpugnable, until the famous count Munich convinced them of their error in the year 1736, when he forced them without much difficulty. This muft however in a great meafure be attributed to the badnefs of the defence, as the ditch was 72 feet broad, and 42 deep : the height from the bottom of the ditch to the creft of the parapet was 70 feet, and the parapet of a proportional thicknefs. The lines were alfo at that time, befides the fortifications of the city, ftrengthened with fix towers mounted with cannon, and the whole was defended by an army. The peninfula lies between 33 and 37 degrees of eaftern longitude, and between 44 and 46 degrees of northern latitude ; is naturally fertile, and was, at firft, under the government of the Greeks, and afterwards in the hands of the Genoefe

and

the treaty, and that which was moft feverely felt by the Turks. Certainly they were very far from perceiving the policy of Catharine in its full extent; but they feemed to forefee that fhe was only defirous of obtaining the independance of the Krim, as thereby fhe might be the better enabled to bring it into fubjection. Befides thefe conceffions, Catharine obtained from the Porte, that tract of land lying on the Euxine between the Bog and the Dniepr, a large fum of

---

and other italian nations; a place of great trade, and filled with populous towns and cities. The Tartars of the Krim were a free people, governed by khans of their own election, acknowledging the grand fultan as khalif; only in regard to religion, without any influence on the reft of the government· Europe therefore faw in the lift of her ftates a new fovereign prince, Sahin Gueray, a mohammedan, and a defcendant of the mongole conqueror Tfchinghis khan. He refided at Bachtfheferay. Ruffia would now no longer be neceffitated to defend its borders, by the ufual expenfive lines, againft thefe Tartars, or even to continue the old tribute-like prefents. On the contrary, fhe was now become a friendly and protecting neighbour, (juft as fhe was towards Poland,) and in order the more effectually to do this, fhe altered the form of government, diffolved the relationfhip between the Krim and the Porte, and granted the Tartars the freedom of election, with feveral other privileges to the detriment of their khans.

money

money to defray the expences of the war, and the
title of padifhah, or emprefs, to be no longer
refufed to the ruffian monarch.

Catharine had thus the twofold advantage
of increafing her power and of weakening her
enemy. The commerce of the Euxine and the
mart of the Levant opened to her a fource
of immenfe riches. The protection which fhe
granted the Tartars, furnifhed her with the
means of dividing them, and of conquering their
country. The acquifition of the polifh Ukraine
put her in a capacity of more eafily carrying on a
war in the regions of the Danube, of overawing
the ottoman empire, and of completing the ruin
of Poland. The eftablifhment of difcipline
among the kofaks added to her armies an excellent
cavalry. The good underftanding which fhe
kept up in the iflands of the Archipelago, and
in Valachia and Moldavia, became a never-
ceafing fource of difquiet and annoyance to
the Turks. In a word, the emprefs beheld
her influence and her glory extending throughout
Europe.

But while fhe was in the enjoyment of a condition fo profperous without, deep and cruel
wounds were confuming the interior of her
empire. Her finances were in a dilapidated
ftate. She received no fuccours from England,

but

but by granting immenfe advantages to their commerce. The peftilence had made dreadful ravages at Mofco and in the adjacent countries. That horrible difeafe had long been devouring the ruffian armies; and the fleet of the Archipelago was not exempted from its fury. The provinces of Kafan, Aftrakhan, and Orenburg, were a prey to revolt, which even threatened Mofco; and a remarkable emigration * changed countries that were flourifhing with commerce into wafte and deferted tracts. All thefe calamities at once explain to us likewife how it happened that, during the war againft the Turks, the ruffian forces did not every year difplay equal activity, and were not attended with equal fuccefs.

But this emigration is of confequence fufficient to detain us a while. The afiatic territory of this enormous empire prefents far other fcenes than thofe which the inhabitants of Europe are accuftomed to furvey; and as Ruffia in a manner connects both quarters of the world in the completeft contraft, fo we behold it one while as a political exemplar of civilized human nature,

* This emigration took place towards the clofe of 1770 and the beginning of 1771. Yet the mention of it was deferred, in order that it might not interrupt the account of the progrefs of the war.

but

but at other times involved in fituations which appear quite ftrange to us, and fuch as we only know from the hiftory of the fourth and fifth centuries. Thus, in the year 1771, an emigration took place, by which a very confiderable number of fubjects were loft to the empire.— Of the Kalmuks or Œlœts *, brethren of like race with the Mongoles, feveral branches are in fubjection to the ruffian empire. Their original abode, if we may ufe fuch an expreffion in fpeaking of nomadic hordes, is the Kalmuckia: lying weftward toward the proper Mongolia, and in the north and eaft of the leffer Bukharia. At the latter end of the laft century, two tribes of them, the Torgot and Derbet, drew up in the fteppe on the Volga above Aftrakhan. Till very modern times, they remained however only as protected neighbours, and were tolerably independent on the government. But in 1757 the vice-khan Dondudidafchi, contrary to the eftablifhed cuftom of all the khans to receive their appointment from the dalailama in Tibet, thought fit, though they are of the lama religion, to apply to Ruffia for the nomination of his fon as his fucceffor. At Peterfburg the requeft was granted with great fatisfaction, which perhaps

* Improperly, Eleuts.

would

would not have been the cafe on an application to Tibet: the father was conftituted actual khan; and the fon, only 13 years old, without hefitation declared fucceffor, with an allowance of 500 rubles *per ann.* and inftalled with the ufual folemnities. On the death of the father in 1761, Ruffia thought fhe had a right to meddle in the affairs of the young fovereign: inftead of the accuftomed council of eight faiffans, it was made to confift of a larger number, whom the court eafily retained by paying each of the members a falary of 100 rubles. The friendly protection was thus (as has happened in various other cafes) changed into an actual fovereignty. In confequence of frefh regulations, the khan loft his former unlimited authority, and became nothing more than the prefident of his council; nor had he any longer the right to difmifs this council; he could only complain to the imperial college of Ruffia; and he was taught to efteem it advantage enough that the fovereign tribunal ftood open to his appeal. In all other refpects thefe Kalmuks retained their religion and their manners: they roamed about the fteppe, had an averfion to permanent dwellings, and lived on the produce of their flocks and herds. Thefe confifted in fheep, camels, and principally in horfes; the whole nation was armed and mounted;

and

and their favourite drink, like that of all thefe tartar tribes, was a fpirituous extract of mares milk, called in their language koumifh. The pafture of thefe horfes requires this roving life; as a father of a family may poffefs from 100 to 1000, and fome of them even 4000 heads. Many of them were in good circum-ftances, and very refpectable people; kind, generous, and hofpitable: this laft quality they poffefs in an eminent degree, and fhew it to every one who peaceably enters their tents. But they are quite the reverfe to fuch as attack them as foes, efpecially to nations whom they acknowledge not as brothers. Accordingly, Ruffia employed them in hofts in the pruffian war; and Germany ftill recollects with horror the afiatic favages that were let loofe upon her without regard to morals and the rights of huma-nity. In the turkifh war they likewife fought for Ruffia in the diftrict of the Kuban. Such was the fituation of them till the year 1770.

In the mean time great heart-burnings had long fubfifted among the moft confiderable of them on account of the innovations introduced by the Ruffians. The circumfcription of their primitive liberty, the reducing their khan to a ftate of dependence, the intermeddling of a foreign nation in their conftitution and laws, which

which begot diffentions and difobedience in the horde, the injuries (real or imaginary) which fome princes had received from ruffian officers : all this awakened an irreftible hankering after their former condition ; and as it was not to be hoped for where they were, no choice was left, but they muft feek it in their ancient plains where their anceftors knew of no Europeans. Juft at this time the governor of Aftrakhan appointed a lieutenant named Kifchenfkoï, as infpector of thefe peaceful Kalmuks. Kifchenfkoï, a man of infatiable rapacity, by infenfible degrees got poffeffion of a great part of their cattle, and fold them to his own benefit. His exactions foon procured him an immenfe fortune. But his avarice, far from diminifhing, feemed rather to increafe with the means of its gratification.

One of their princes, a venerable old man, who had fhed his blood in the fervice of Ruffia, in recompence for which the emprefs had given him her miniature portrait fet round with brilliants, and which he wore fufpended to his neck, was one day applied to by Kifchenfkoï for fome prefents in addition to thofe which he had already given him. The old man, irritated at his infolence, could not refrain from breaking out into reproaches on his injuftice and the vexations he employed to the ruin of the unhappy Kalmuks.

Kifchenfkoï,

Kifchenfkoï, offended at the truth of thefe reproaches, had the temerity to ftrike him on the face, and having at the fame time ordered one of the faiffans, the minifter of the khan, who interpofed in his behalf, to be feized by his foldiers, ordered him the punifhment of the battogues *.

The Kalmuks had, if not patiently, at leaft quietly, fuffered the rapacity and peculations of the ruffian officer; but they could not endure the infult that had been put upon this venerable old man, who ftood in great refpect among them. The priefts and the elders of the horde having held a confultation, refolved to abandon the territory of the ruffian empire, and retire to the foot of the mountains of Tibet, the country of their progenitors. The common people were eafily perfuaded; efpecially as they were told that the ruffian regulations were introduced for

---

* Battogues—a fort of punifhment ufed in Ruffia for infe-rior offences. The fufferer is laid on his face upon the ground, ftripped to his waift, and the arms and legs extended. Two men, one of whom fits on his neck, and the other on his legs, beat him alternately on the back with the battogues, which are rods of the thicknefs of the little finger. Perfons having any authority over others may inflict this punifhment upon them without any form of trial or legal procefs. Nobles and peafants are equally liable to it, when it is ordered by fuperiors.

no other purpose than to compel them to the
three things which they most abhorred : christ-
ianity, agriculture, and the raising recruits.   A
little priestcraft was also had recourse to on this
occasion.   The noyons or princes set up a lama,
whom they raised in a moment to be the immortal
archpriest or dalailama, in the following manner :
It was propagated abroad, that a famous kalmuk
priest, who had died three years before, had
now appeared again alive, and had issued a
proclamation to the people, that he was risen
from the dead at Tibet, in the residence of the
great dalailama ; of all which a written testimony
was brought from the immortal high priest ; in
which it was declared, that being now become a
being of a superior order, he foreknew the fates
and fortunes of the nation, and required them, in
the name of their gods, to return, and again
take possession of their ancient territory.   This
happened towards the close of the year 1770,
just when they thought it the proper moment for
the grand rupture ; otherwise they would have
suffered the lama to have slept quietly in his
grave for a longer or a shorter time.

It was an unpardonable neglect in the commanding officer in those parts not to put a stop
to the proceedings of the horde, so as to prevent
the emigration, as their intention was publicly
known

known in thofe parts. He even fuffered himfelf
to be duped by the Kalmuks, to whom, on
their forging fome pretext of apprehenfion from
the Kirguifes, their neighbours, he gave two
pieces of cannon, with ammunition and fome
engineers. Accordingly, in the autumn, they
began their march : a prodigious troop, with
wives, children, and fervants, having their droves,
horfes, flocks, goods, huts, and tents. The
captain ·under the command of the khan was
forced to migrate with them at the head of his
kofaks. The march was conducted regularly
enough, in three troops, who conftantly kept in
fight ; the flanks of each were particularly
covered, and befides this they had a van and a
rear guard. At the beginning they plundered the
fifheries and the trading houfes on the borders of
the Volga and the Cafpian.   But, on their progrefs into the fouthern Siberia, they came upon
the Kofaks of the Yaïk, ·who ftopped and purfued the flying horde, cut thoufands of them to
pieces, and forced thoufands to return.   In the
fpring 1771, they were attacked by the Kirguifes
their inveterate enemies, and, after a bloody engagement, took many of them prifoners.   In
the fummer they proceeded through the antient
Mongolia to the chinefe borders ; where an army
of

of the Mandſhu * received them, and afforded them protection.

The ſecret of their flight was ſo well kept, that it was not known to the Ruſſians till two days after their departure. Three regiments were ſent in purſuit of them to no purpoſe. The Kalmuks were more in haſte than they; and, beſides, they were two days before them. Theſe regiments wandered a long time in the deſarts, and a conſiderable part of the ſoldiers periſhed.

When the news of the emigration was brought to St. Peterſburg, a corps of troops were ordered by the court to go in queſt of them. But, if the former purſuits were too late, it was not likely that theſe ſhould come up with them: the lamentable particulars of this expedition may be read in captain Rytſchkoff's journal; where it may be ſeen what difficulties and hardſhips theſe indefatigable purſuers of the fugitive horde encountered, in their devious marches on this unavailing expedition, and what variety of diſtreſſes they ſuffered in the dreary, inhoſpitable regions and waterleſs deſarts through which they paſſed. At length nothing farther was to be

---

* The preſent emperor of China.

done

done but to make application by a written memorial to China, to demand the reftitution of the runaways. But the fupreme tribunal at Pekin anfwered the refcript of the ruffian fenate abruptly, in a fcornful and derifory manner, and concluded by faying, that " their fovereign " was not a prince fo unjuft as to deliver up his " fubjects to foreigners, nor fo cruel a father as "' to drive away children who returned to the " bofom of their family. That he had no intimation of the defign of the Kalmuks till the " moment of their arrival; and that then without delay he caufed to be reftored to them the " habitations that had belonged to them from " time immemorial. That, in fhort, the emprefs " had no reafon to complain of the Kalmuks, " but certainly of the officer who had dared to " lift his hand againft a fervant of the khans, " and to order their minifters to undergo the " battogues." The letter was thus fubfcribed : " In the 36th year, the 7th month, and the 13th " day of the reign of Kien-Long." On various occafions Catharine frequently received from thefe her neighbours anfwers in a ftyle which muft have ftruck her the more fenfibly, as fhe was accuftomed to hear from all the other monarchs in the world a very different language. On her applying for a frefh treaty for the renewal of the commerce with China by the caravans, which for several years had been interrupted, on account of some differences that had arisen between the subjects of the two potentates, the answer given to her envoy was:—" Let your mistress learn to " keep old treaties; and then it will be time " enough to apply for new ones." Accordingly we see, from her private communications * how sensible she was upon this subject; and she could scarcely endure to hear any praise, even jestingly, bestowed on the emperor of China, who was otherwise known as an author and poet.

Concerning the number of persons lost to Russia by this emigration accounts do not agree. Some state it at 130,000 families; which is certainly exaggerated. More accurate statements say, that the horde in general consisted of not much above 70,000 tents, or hearths, or families. Those who voluntarily returned, (for doubtless many of them, on the fatiguing and painful expedition over the deserts, panted after the more quiet abode on the Volga, and turned back,) and those who were brought in by the Kosaks, are reckoned together at 12,342 tents. Those that escaped therefore, estimating them at

* For example, in her correspondence with Voltaire.

the

the higheft, were 60,000 hearths. But how great the number of the individuals that died upon the road, and of thofe who were carried into captivity by the Kirguifes, can never be known.

A council of war was held to examine into the conduct of lieutenant-colonel Kifchenfkoï, and to pronounce upon it. But the bufinefs was conducted with negligence and every poffible delay. Kifchenfkoï employed a part of the fruit of his rapine in procuring himfelf friends at court, or in corrupting his judges: and to the great fcandal of the majority of the Ruffians, this man, who had occafioned the lofs of fuch a number of fubjects to the country, was recompenfed by the title of colonel.

Amidft the grand concerns by which it was occupied, the court of Peterfburg betrayed no neglect of its little intrigues. Attentive as fhe was to the bufinefs of government, Catharine did not bid adieu to pleafures. She went frequently from the council to the ball-room and the theatre, and from the important fittings of the fenate to the moft frivolous amufements. She gave audience to the ambaffadors of foreign powers, without having need of any other drefs than that fhe wore for receiving her courtiers;

and

and she dictated a law with the same facility as she wrote a billet. Easy in her new attachments, she never spoke of those that had gone before. Panin, Chernicheff, and Baratinsky applauded their own operations.

But what gave them the most satisfaction was the removal of prince Orloff. For nearly five months he had been travelling in foreign parts; and his enemies, pleased themselves with the thought that he was to continue his travels for at least two years. The emissaries who watched his steps wrote them frequent accounts of his proceedings. He was thought to be in Holland: it was imagined that he intended to make the tour of England, France, and Italy. All at once he re-appeared at the court of Petersburg. The empress refused to admit him into her presence. She sent orders to him to repair to Reval. But she at the same time sent him considerable presents, and loaded with honours and caresses the more intimate friends of her discarded favourite.

What then could be the motive to such a singular conduct? Catharine had no longer any regard for Orloff. She no longer stood in awe of him. But she dreaded, she hated a faction she conceived might be forming under the

auspices

aufpices of a name * dear to the empire, and
formidable to Orloff. She was defirous of
oppofing the party of her former favourite to
this faction, and of procuring the fupport of a
man by whom fhe had already been fo well
defended. Triumphant over her enemies, the admiration of Europe, idolized by her courtiers, that
princefs was neverthelefs often a prey to the moft
pungent difquietudes : but fhe concealed them.
She dreaded the thought of being hurled from
the throne; and fhe was forming the project of
aggrandizing her dominions ftill farther. She
was trembling for her life : and fhe difcourfed
with gaiety of the long career fhe was in hopes
to run. One day fhe found a paper in her
cabinet, in which mention was made of a threatened affaffination : never did fhe fhew herfelf
more confident and more fedate.

Ambitious of all kinds of glory, fhe could at
all times put any conftraint on herfelf to obtain
it. Whatever were her fentiments, fhe had
always the appearance of gentlenefs, fincerity,
clemency, and generofity. The blood of the
wretched Ivan was yet reeking from the ground :
Catharine was moved at the unhappy lot of his
family ; and knowing that fhe had no longer
any thing to fear from the duke, Catharine

* That of the grand duke.

U 3   offered

offered him his liberty, with the means of retiring to Germany. The prince refufed. " Why " fhould I go," anfwered he, " out of the ruffian " empire, to publifh the excefs of my miferies, " and to excite a fruitlefs compaffion * ?"

Vaffiltfchikoff had now a long time filled the place of favourite. Never abufing his influence either for accumulating immenfe riches to himfelf, or for hurting his rivals, he excited no envy. The emprefs would frequently praife his moderation; and that quality, fo uncommon in a courtier, feemed to render him more dear to her from day to day. But on a fudden he had loft the art of pleafing; and at the very inftant when he had juft been receiving additional tokens of her tendernefs, an order was brought him to repair to Mofco. He obeyed. Frefh prefents from the fovereign attended him on the road. But it was only a remuneration of form : the heart had no fhare in it whatever †.

* The account of the farther circumftances that attended this family may be feen by turning back to p. 40. of the prefent volume, where the part of the hiftory concerning them was fomewhat anticipated, for the fake of keeping the individuals of the family together in one view.

† Vaffiltfchikoff continued in favour 22 months. It will hereafter be mentioned to what the prefents amounted which Catharine made to him, as well as to her other favourites.

Whether

Whether it was that Orloff had been fecretly recalled from Reval, or whether he found his ftay in that city infupportable, he now came back, and made his appearance at court. The emprefs threw no cenfures on his behaviour. She received him, on the contrary, with an appearance of joy. Proud of this reception and of the remembrance of his paft favour, depending ftill on the fubmiffion of his creatures, who were in great numbers, he thought himfelf able to refume his honours and his influence. While he was in the full enjoyment of them, he often feemed to difdain them. No fooner was he deprived of them than he felt them to be neceffary to him. Orloff, born in obfcurity, and brought up in the licentioufnefs of the barracks, had found himfelf raifed on a fudden to a point of elevation, which, by fwelling his natural pride, had neither altered his tafte, nor polifhed his manners. Eleven years paffed about the perfon of the emprefs, in the refinements of luxury and voluptuoufnefs, withheld him not from braving the inclemency of the feafons, nor from expofing himfelf to the fevereft fatigues, nor from the purfuit of the coarfeft indulgences. Since his difmiffal from the poft of favourite, he remained in poffeffion of an annual revenue of 250,000 rubles, and of valuables to the amount of

300,000;

300,000; inſtead of maintaining a houſehold with grandeur and magnificence, he led the life of an officer in garriſon. In a condition to keep a table delicately ſerved and ſupplied, he ate almoſt always with the commenſals of the court, who kept very ordinary cheer. He was not more choice in his amours. It was indifferent to him, whether he breathed out his flame to an ugly and ſqualid Finn, to a ſavage Kalmuk, or, to the handſomeſt woman of Peterſburg.

Jealous of the authority enjoyed by his rivals, and contemplating with envy the throne on which he had long flattered himſelf with the expeΩation of ſitting, Orloff demanded to be re-eſtabliſhed in the exerciſe of his funΩions, and that he whom he accuſed of being the prime mover of his diſgrace, count Panin, ſhould be ſent into exile. Orloff ſeemed at that moment to have regained his aſcendant over the heart of Catharine. She appeared in his ſight with all the fondneſs that the tendereſt paſſion could in-ſpire, and made not the leaſt heſitation in reſtor-ing him to all his employments. Her majeſty, however, refuſed to conſent to the baniſhment of Panin; and the prince was obliged to be ſatisfied with obtaining her promiſe to remove him from court, as ſoon as the grand duke ſhould be married.

Panin

Panin was deeply chagrined at feeing Orloff reinftated in his employments. But he had no one to blame for it but himfelf, fince he had taken no meafures to prevent it. Happy in the fortune and the confequence which he enjoyed, living in ihdolence in the midft of affairs, and feeking a retreat in the tumult of the court, it was only in fudden fits of refentment that he took any pains to injure his rivals; and, though of greater ability than they, he had often the mortification to fee them victorious.

" Count Panin is a good creature," faid a courtier who had long ftudied his character. " He is fond of nothing but eafe and fullennefs. " Any one may be his friend by pretending to " laugh at his bons mots, and by furnifhing him " with an opportunity for exercifing his talent for " flander. He himfelf, on fuch occafions, will " laugh with all his heart; and he forgets the " affairs of government, the difpatches, the cou- " riers, and the intrigues that are formed againft " him."

Catharine had for fome time been meditating a marriage for the grand duke; but as that prince feemed to be of a weak habit, and a cold conftitution, fhe feared left he might be little difpofed to give heirs to the empire. Her confidants foon found the means for difpelling her fears. They engaged a young polifh lady, a

maid

maid of honour to the emprefs *, to make an attempt with her charms on the heart of the prince. Mademoifelle Sophia confented; and fhe bore him a fon, who received at the font the name of Simeon Velikoï †.

From that time the emprefs bent her thoughts to the choice of a fit confort for the grand duke. In this, however, fhe found herfelf fomewhat embarraffed. She wifhed not for a princefs who might probably become her rival, and who, profiting by her example, was capable of forming attempts on her throne and her life. She was rather in fearch of one who had neither the faculties nor the defire of rendering herfelf formidable. The emprefs at length fixed her views on the daughters of the landgrave of Heffe-Darmftadt. Thefe princeffes were three fifters. Catharine invited their mother to accompany them to her court. How contrary foever to long-eftablifhed cuftom as this propofal might

* This young lady was afterwards married to a noble count, who was living in France in 1788.

† Simeon Velikoï was of a gentle and modeft difpofition, and great care had been taken with his education. Entered, at an early period, in the navy, he ferved during the fwedifh war under that deferving englifh officer, captain Trevenen, in the capacity of lieutenant of a man of war, then being one of the 12 officers fent by the emprefs to learn the art of navigation in England : he acted as a volunteer in the englifh navy, and died in the Weft Indies in 1797.

appear,

appear, the landgravine of Heffe-Darmftadt accepted it without hefitation. That princefs was ambitious; and therefore fhe liftened only to the hope of placing one of her daughters on the throne of Ruffia : fhe fet out for Peterfburg. The emprefs received her with magnificence, and loaded her with prefents *. After having had time to form a judgment of the three young princeffes, Catharine chofe for the fpoufe of the grand duke the princefs Wilhelmina, who embraced the greek orthodox fyftem of faith †, and was joined in wedlock to the heir of the tzars.

Prince Orloff and his party were in hopes that this marriage would be prefently followed by the difgrace of Panin. Orders were fent him to leave the apartments which he occupied in the palace in quality of governor of Paul Petrovitch. His friends took the alarm. The courtiers became fhy of him. He imagined himfelf undone : but his pupil had the generofity to oppofe himfelf to the ftorm; and haftening to his mother, reprefented to her, that Panin had been always a faithful fervant of the empire, and that it would be too cruel an act to difmifs him from the court, at the very moment when

---

* She even infifted that the landgrave fhould permit her to defray the whole expence of her journey thither.

† She took the name of Natalia Alexievna,

he

he had the greatest right to expect substantial rewards. This procedure wrought a change in the mind of the empress. Instead of retaining her resolution of sending an order to Panin to retire from the court, she wrote to him a letter full of testimonies of affection; and, thanking him for the care he had bestowed on the education of the grand duke, she confirmed him in the appointment of minister of foreign affairs.

Those who were unacquainted with the motives by which the empress had been swayed in determining to retain count Panin, found an inexplicable contradiction in her conduct. Orloff had the presumption to reproach her with it: but she did not vouchsafe to inform him better. Unwilling that this favourite should know that a mother had yielded to the solicitations of her son, she told him that it behoved him to sacrifice the satisfaction of removing a minister who failed of pleasing, to the necessity there was for his service. Always ingenious in disguising her sentiments, Catharine made no scruple of deceiving the favourite, who fancied he engrossed the whole of her confidence. Though she seemed to have restored him her former tenderness, yet she secretly cherished in her heart a passion which speedily broke out. She felt some inclination

clination to difmifs Orloff a fecond time: but fhe prudently kept terms with him ftill.

Of the learned and literary men with whom Catharine kept up a regular correfpondence, Voltaire and Diderot were thofe whom fhe moft diftinguifhed. She invited them feveral times to come and vifit her. The philofopher of Ferney had learned by experience the dangers of courts: he would not fubmit to the temptation of feeing that of Ruffia. The philofopher of Paris was more open to perfuafion. He travelled to St. Peterfburg. Catharine lavifhed on him largeffes and encomiums. During the whole time of his ftay at her court, fhe difcourfed with him every day at the conclufion of dinner. Philofophy, legiflation, politics, were commonly the fubject of thefe converfations. Diderot unfolded his principles on the liberty and the rights of nations with his ufual enthufiafm * and eloquence. The emprefs feemed to be delighted with them; but fhe was not at all the more difpofed to put them in practice.

" Monfieur Diderot," faid fhe, " is a hun-
" dred years old in many refpects; but in others
" he is no more than ten."

---

* The emprefs made him fit befide her. In his moments of enthufiafm, Diderot has fometimes hit her knee with the back of his hand: fhe never feemed to take offence at it.

Perhaps

Perhaps her majefty's private opinion was not more in favour of the wifdom of Voltaire; though fhe never fpoke of it but with all the deference that is due to the foremoft difpenfer of fame. The manner in which fhe was wont to write to him is well known. We have already cited feveral fragments of her letters; we fhall, neverthelefs, tranfcribe one of them here, as a further proof of the artful difguife fhe put on before that celebrated author, and how fhe ftrove to obtain thofe flatteries which he fo lavifhly beftowed upon her.

" ...... *Now we are fpeaking of haughti-
" nefs, I have a mind to make my general confef-
" fion to you on that head. I have had great
" fuccefſes during this war : that I am glad of it,
" you will very naturally conclude. I faid, Ruſſia
" will be well known by this war; it will be
" feen how indefatigable a nation it is; that fhe
" poffeffes men of eminent merit, and who have
" all the qualities that go to the forming of
" heroes; it will be feen that fhe is deficient in
" no refources ; but that fhe can defend herfelf,
" and profecute a war with vigour, whenever fhe
" is unjuſtly attacked.

* This letter is dated the 22d of July—the 2d of Auguſt 1771.

" Brimful

" Brimful of thefe ideas, I have never once
" thought of Catharine, who, at the age of
" forty-two, can increafe neither in body nor
" mind, but, in the natural order of things,
" ought to remain, and will remain, as fhe is.
" Do her affairs go on well? She fays, fo
" much the better! If they profpered lefs, fhe
" would employ all her faculties to put them in
" the beft train poffible.

" This is my ambition, and I have none other;
" what I tell you is the truth. I will go farther:
" I will tell you that, for the fparing of human
" blood, I fincerely wifh for peace. But this
" peace is ftill a long way off, though the Turks,
" from different motives, are ardently defirous
" of it. Thofe people know not how to go
" about it.

" I wifh as much for the pacification of the
" unreafonable contentions of Poland. I have
" to do there with brainlefs heads, each of
" which, inftead of contributing to the common
" peace, on the contrary throws impediments in
" the way of it by caprice and levity. My
" ambaffador has publifhed a declaration adapted
" to open their eyes. But it is to be prefumed,
" that they will rather expofe themfelves to the
" laft extremity, than adopt without delay a wife
" and confiftent rule of conduct. The vortices
" of

" of Defcartes never exifted any where but in
" Poland.   There every head is a vortex, turn-
"ing continually round itfelf.   It is ftopped by
" chance alone, and never by reafon or judg-
" ment.

" I have not yet received either your quef-
" tions *, or your watches from Ferney.   I
" have no doubt that the work of your artificers
" is perfect, fince they work under your eyes.

" Do not fcold your ruftics for having fent me
" a furplus of watches : the expence of them
" will not ruin me.   It would be very unfor-
" tunate for me, if I were fo far reduced as not
" to have, for fudden emergencies, fuch fmall
" fums whenever I want them.   Judge not, I
" befeech you, of our finances by thofe of the
" other ruined potentates of Europe.   Though
" we have been engaged in a war for three
" years, we proceed in our buildings ; and every
" thing elfe goes on as in a time of profound
" peace.   It is two years fince any new impoft
" has been levied †.   The war at prefent has its

---

* The " Queftions fur l'Encyclopedie."

† With all due deference for her imperial majefty, this
does not exactly tally with the augmentation of the capi-
tation tax of 80 kopeeks, which fhe was obliged to abolifh
at the peace ; any more than with the extraordinary taxes
laid on feveral manufactures, and on all works in iron.

fixed

" fixed eftablifhment; that once regulated,
" it never difturbs the courfe of other affairs.
" If we capture another Kaffa or two, the war is
" paid for.

" I fhall be fatisfied with myfelf whenever I
" meet with your approbation, monfieur. I
" likewife a few weeks ago read over again my
" inftruions for the code, becaufe I then
" thought peace to be nearer at hand than it is,
" and I found that I was right in compofing
" them. I confefs that this code, for which
" a great quantity of materials are preparing,
" and many others are now ready, will yet give
" me a confiderable deal of trouble before it is
" brought to that degree of perfection at which
" I wifh to fee it. But no matter: it muft be
" completed, though Taganrok has the fea to
" the fouth and mountains to the north.

" However, your defigns upon that place
" cannot be brought to effect till a peace fhall
" have fecured its environs againft all apprehen-
" fion on the fide of the land and the fide of the
" fea; for till the Krimea was taken, it was the
" frontier place againft the Tartars. Perhaps
" in a little time the khan of the Krimea will be
" brought to me in perfon. I learn this moment
" that he did not crofs the fea with the Turks,

" but that he remained in the mountains with a
" very fmall number of followers, nearly as was
" the cafe with the pretender in Scotland after
" the defeat at Culloden. If he comes to me,
" we will ftrive to polifh him this winter ; and,
" to take my revenge of him, I will make him
" dance, and he fhall go to the french co-
" medy.......

    " Juft as I was about to fold up this letter, I
" received yours of the 10th of July, in which
" you inform me of the adventure that happened
" to my " Inftruction " * in France. I knew
" that anecdote, and even the appendix to it, in
" confequence of the order of the duc de Choi-
" feul. I own that I laughed on reading it in
" the news-papers, and I found that I was
" amply revenged.

    " The conflagration that happened at Peterf-
" burg has, according to the report of the police,
" confumed in all 140 houfes, among which
" about 20 were brick buildings ; the reft were
" only barracks conftructed of wood. The
" high wind wafted the flames and the burning
" fplinters on all fides, which occafioned the fire
" to break out again the following day, and gave

---

    * Her majefty's inftruction for a code of laws.

                                                 " it

" it a fupernatural appearance. But there is no
" doubt that the high wind and the exceffive heat
" were the fole caufes of this difafter, which
" will be foon repaired.

" With us buildings are raifed with greater
" celerity than in any other country in Europe.
" In 1762 a fire happened of twice the extent,
" which confumed a large quarter of the town,
" confifting of wooden buildings. The whole
" was rebuilt in brick within lefs than three
" years."

The fucceffes of the turkifh war begot in
the hearts of the nation an enthufiaftic love and
veneration for their fovereign; the fentiments of
joy at the humiliation of the oriental pride were
univerfal; and it muft be confeffed that many
truly heroic atchievements in thefe campaigns,
both by fea and land, might well excite the
ruffian patriots to jubilation. To perpetuate the
memory of them Catharine caufed medals to be
ftruck, and columns to be erected.

In the mean time the buildings and embellifh-
ments of St. Peterfburg proceeded without interruption; and works of really imperial magnificence were brought to effect, which render that
city in many refpects fuperior to any other.
The Neva, the Fontanka, and the Katarina-

canal*, were embanked with granite; and provided with fpacious quays of the fame material,
and elegant baluftrades of iron, fo as to form
agreeable walks through the feveral quarters of
the town. Sumptuous bridges richly ornamented,
of hewn granite, were likewife conftructed in
various parts acrofs the Moika, the Fontanka,
and the feveral canals that unite their ftreams.
Palaces and public offices were erected; among
them a palace of prodigious magnitude, built entirely of marble of divers colours from Siberia†.
If the eye of the ftranger, dazzled with fo much
brilliance and fplendour as this refidence affords,
fees with concern and almoft with difguft, the intervals of wretched huts and dirty lanes; yet the
inhabitant recollecting with real fatisfaction the
former condition of moft of the quarters and
ftreets, feels the more fenfibly the almoft magical

* The beautiful ftream that forms the Neva, branches off
into the little Neva, the Nefka, the river Moika, the river
Fontanka, into all which fall feveral canals, all together forming the large and little iflands (oftrofs) on which Peterfburg
is built.

† The magnificence of this palace is fuch, that it never
fails to remind the beholder who fees it for the firft time, of
what he has read in the "Arabian Nights," fairy and genii
tales, and the like. The emperor Paul has affigned it for the
refidence of the king of Poland, by whom it is now inhabited.

improve-

improvements, and looks forward with complacency at what the whole muſt gradually become. Of the immenſe Ladoga-canal, the banks that were ſupported by timbers are, ſince 1763, faced with ſtone. The many beneficent and public-ſpirited inſtitutions of the emprefs required new buildings, which were conſtantly erected with magnificence and taſte. Nor were her cares confined to the reſidence alone, other cities likewiſe were growing in riches and ſplendour under her forming hand; Moſko, Tver, Toula, Kief, &c. In the neighbourhood of St. Peterſburg aroſe and grew up in 1767, and is ſince in a flouriſhing ſtate, the german colony Saratoſka.

In the midſt of the turkiſh war, Catharine purchaſed in Holland pictures to the amount of 60,000 rubles *; in France for 15,000 rubles, and in Italy a multitude of inimitable curioſities. —That noble act of bounty which ſhe ſhewed to Diderot in 1775, gained her the eſteem of all literary men, in buying his library at a price far above its value, and then appointing him her librarian of it for his life, with a large annual ſtipend.

* The ſhip which had them on board was wrecked on the coaſt of Finland, and the whole collection was loſt.

The

The expenditure on her court-eſtabliſhment at this time was reckoned at 4,000,000 of rubles annually; the numerous and always imperial preſents to her officers, ſtateſmen, and favourites, not included. Her court, the moſt brilliant in all Europe, was the reſort of male and female beauty; young perſons of talents, greyheaded commanders, able politicians, reſpectable matrons, and a multitude of high nobility, who, by their friendlineſs, affability, hoſpitality, and poliſhed manners, rendered their ſociety extremely agreeable.—Prince Gregory Orloff was no niggard of his wealth. He cauſed to be built, at the diſtance of eight or ten miles from Tzarſko-ſelo, the magnificent palace of Gatſhinà; which the empreſs, on his death, purchaſed at a very high price, and made it a preſent to her ſon the grand duke; who, as is well known, always reſided there, and was fond of the place*. About 1774, when Orloff was out of favour, ſome people imagined it was for having preferred his private intereſt to the good of the ſtate: it certainly was not the caſe in that

---

* In 1780 the grand duke built a palace for himſelf at the diſtance of five verſts from Tzarko-ſelo, which he named Pavlofsk, and furniſhed it with greater taſte than magnificence. However he ſtill retained his liking for Gatſhina.

in-

inftance; but it is no lefs true, that fhe made it a conftant rule to, employ no minifter of that defcription. She knew how and when to reward without being fummoned to it; and never would fuffer herfelf to be governed by perfonal regards. Even in Orloff's golden days, when he was in the higheft favour, his influence in ftate affairs was far from decifive: Panin oppofed him; and held his place in defiance of him. Other favourites were of ftill lefs fignificance. If afterwards Potemkin, for a continuance of 30 years, could do every thing with Catharine, and at laft raifed himfelf to an all-directing ftatefman; yet it cannot be denied that he had the head, and the courage and energy, which with the gradual unfolding of his talents as he advanced, fitted him for a prime minifter: though withal, his ambition and love of command were of the rudeft and moft dangerous nature.—The princefs Dafhkoff was not of Orloff's party, but belonged rather to Panin's; after a long abfence in a kind of folitude fhe appeared again at court in 1773, received from the emprefs a prefent of 60,000 rubles, with fubfequent marks of her favour and the poft of director of the academy of fciences. Count Panin united the moft important places with the emprefs and the tzar-

X 4   evitch;

evitch *; and nothing can be said more to his honour than that he gained the esteem and affection of them both. The whole public also ascribed to him perfect integrity united with a too great love of ease. He directed the foreign affairs, and his voice in the council was of very great weight. As preceptor of the grand duke he was beloved by that prince with a truly filial affection. Few princely families can shew an instance of greater tenderness of heart than one which we know of Paul Petrovitch : in count Panin's last illness the tears of the imperial youth incessantly flowed as he knelt by his bed-side, and gratefully kissed the hand of his dying master. After his death the sincerity of the prince's grief was manifest to the few who then had access to him.

An impartial observer who saw the empress in 1772 and 1773, describes her in the following manner: " She is of that stature which is necessarily requisite to perfect elegance of form in a lady. She has fine large blue eyes; her eyebrows and hair are of a brownish colour; her mouth is well-proportioned, the chin round, the nose rather

* Literally the tzar's son; the imperial successor. Formerly this was the only style of the heir apparent. So lately as the time of Peter the great, his son was always called tzarevitch. .

long;

long; the forehead regular and open, her hands and arms round and white, her complection not entirely clear, and her fhape rather plump than meagre; her neck and bofom high, and fhe bears her head with peculiar grace and dignity. She lays on, as is univerfally the cuftom with the fair fex in Ruffia, a pretty ftrong rouge. She has adopted the ufual habit of the ruffian ladies as the model of her drefs, which, by fome flight alterations in it, fhe has fo improved, that it is not only very becoming, but may very properly be deemed an elegant mode of attire. She never puts on rich cloaths except on folemn feftivals; when her head and corfet are entirely fet with brilliants: in grand proceffions fhe wears a crown of diamonds and precious ftones.—Her gait is majeftic; in the whole of her form and manner there is fomething fo dignified and noble, that if fhe were to be feen, without ornament or any outward marks of diftinction, among a great number of ladies of rank, fhe would be immediately efteemed the chief. There is withal in the features of her face and in her looks an uncommon degree of authority and command. In her character there is more of livelinefs than gravity. She is courteous, gentle, beneficent; outwardly devout.

ʺ Her

" Her ordinary method of life, in which she has almost always persevered, was at that time, this: About six o'clock in the morning the empress usually rises. Frequently, and even in the depth of winter, (nay, in the latter years of her life almost commonly,) earlier. She uses, without calling any one, to prepare her own breakfast; as in general she is not fond of being much waited on, and accordingly dispenses with all attendance on her person as much as possible. The business of her toilet lasts not long; during which she signs commissions, orders, and papers of various purport. On days when the council does not meet in her apartments, she is busied alone in the cabinet from eight till eleven of the forenoon; she then usually goes to chapel, where the service continues till twelve. From this time till one, some of the ministers of the several departments have access to her. After the table is removed, to which she sits down at latest at about half after one, she goes to work again for an hour or two, according as business may require; she then walks, rides on horseback, or goes out in a coach or sledge; and at six her majesty appears at the play-house, where the performances are alternately in french and russian. If the empress takes her supper in public, (which happens ex-

tremely

tremely feldom,) it never continues later than half after ten; at other times fhe retires at ten.

" The only court-day in the whole week, holidays excepted, is funday. On this day in the morning, as the emprefs paffes from chapel to her apartments, fhe gives the ambaffadors and foreigners of rank who have been once prefented, her hand to kifs; likewife fuch perfons as have any petition to prefent or defire to return thanks for bounties received, are prefented on this day to the emprefs, and kifs her hand, dropping on one knee.—The court begins not till fix o'clock in the evening. At the fame time a ball or concert is ufually given: the emprefs never dances, but fits down immediately to cards, having previoufly told the chamberlain in waiting whom fhe will have of her party. In autumn 1772, it was commonly the auftrian and pruffian minifters, and of her own minifters count Razumoffsky, prince Gallitzin, and the two counts Chernicheff. The emprefs plays at picquet, or fome other game at which fhe is not obliged to be conftantly filent. A femi-circle is formed round her card-table, which the ladies begin on the left hand, and the privy-counfellors clofe on the right. When the emprefs has finifhed her game, fhe gets up and talks indifcriminately with the ladies, generals, and

minifters

minifters that form the circle. At about ten o'clock, and often earlier, fhe breaks up her party, and then retires unobferved through a fide-door. What has been here mentioned, relates only to the winter months, when the court is at St. Peterfburg. While the emprefs is at Tzarfko-felo there is no court held except on extraordinary feftivals.

" Of civil procefses, criminal and confiftorial caufes, the emprefs allows nothing to be referred to her in the hours of the forenoon allotted to confer with the minifter. Yet no perfon can be condemned to death without previous inform-ation delivered to her: this punifhment is almoft always commuted or mitigated. But all matters relating to the army, the navy, the finances, to foreign affairs, the taxes, and public buildings, muft be reported to her by the chiefs of the feveral departments.—Every one knows that the emprefs is made acquainted with whatever con-cerns the adminiftration of government, and acts from herfelf in all ftate affairs.—As fhe never interferes in private matters and the family con-cerns of her houfehold, fhe has always time enough for bufinefs of a public nature ; efpecially as fhe regularly and uniformly apportions the hours of her day to the accurate interchange of writing, converfation, exercife, and company,

In

In conſtitution ſhe is healthy and robuſt; her mind is tranquil, cheerful, and always diſpoſed to buſineſs."

In order to introduce the practice of inocula-tion into the remoter parts of her empire, Ca-tharine inſtituted hoſpitals for that purpoſe in various places, even to the extremities of Aſia, where the practice is carried on with ſucceſs, not only in cities and towns, but even among the nations of the ſteppes. In the northern regions the ſmall-pox frequently made dreadful havoc: the peninſula of Kamtſhatka alone, from December 1768 to December 1769, loſt by this diſtemper 5638 perſons. But relief was now extended alſo to Siberia: at Irkutzk, the government town on the lake Baikal, a ſmall-pox hoſpital was in-ſtituted in 1772. The number of perſons cured of that diſtemper in this ſame year amounted already to 510; in 1773 the patients that went out in perfect health were 1259; in 1774 the number was 897; and 1775 the perſons cured were 711. On the other hand, in theſe four years, of the inoculated only 28 died from various accidents.

This Irkutzk (to give only one inſtance of the benefit of the inſtitutions which Ca-tharine carried on at the diſtance of near 6000 verſts from her reſidence) is at preſent one

of

of the moft confiderable and largeft towns in all Siberia. This may be eafily known from the travels of the learned profeffor Pallas; fince, as we have feen, the emprefs fpared no expence in caufing the country to be examined by expert furveyors and eminent naturalifts. The furvey of the empire, and the maps made upon it, and fince publifhed, would alone be fufficient to render the name of Catharine immortal. Roads were every where made in conformity with this furvey; and, though they are not all provided with caufeways, but are only levelled and made folid, yet they are all marked out by regularly numbered verft-pofts. Irkutzk, by thefe, lies 2233 verfts from Pekin, 5093 verfts from Mofco, and 5873 from St. Peterfburg. Mr. Pallas found there in 1772 already 1153 dwelling-houfes, and the place in a flourifhing condition; it contains a great number of inhabitants, moftly merchants. The ftreets are broad and ftrait. There is a german congregation, with a place of worfhip and its own paftor. In this town, in 1764 Catharine founded a navigation-fchool, principally in regard to the feas about Japan, and to the ocean between Afia and America. It is fupplied with pilots from the admiralty as teachers of the art of navigation; and native Japanefes were appointed (who were ftill

there

there in 1772) to inftruct the fcholars in the
language of their country.

In 1769 the emprefs inftituted the order
of St. George, for military perfons. A four-
cornered golden ftar, with the initials of
St. George in a black border, and round in
ruffian characters, " For merit and valour,"
is worn, with a riband of black and orange-
coloured ftripes. The knights are divided into
four claffes, and obtain the order on the at-
chievement of fome act of valour, or after having ferved 25 years as fuperior officers without
reproach. A fpecific number of each clafs
enjoy penfions, from 100 to 700 rubles.

CHAP. VIII.

*Difcontents in divers parts of the empire.—
Caufes that determine feveral impoftors to affume
the name of Peter III.—Rebellion of Pugatfheff.—His fucceffes.—His reverfe of fortune.—
His execution.—1774, 1775.*

THE uniform profperity of the emprefs feemed
for a moment to have reached its term. A
terrible ftorm was gathering in the remoteft
provinces

provinces of the empire; the fky of its horizon darkened; the black clouds came on; the thunder growled; the tempeft threatened to overturn the throne of Catharine. Some parts of the conduct of that princefs had excited great difcontents in a confiderable number of her fubjects. Several of the antient nobility took offence at the caprices and arrogant airs of her favourites; while the clergy burnt with the defire of revenge for the lofs of their privileges, and the people murmured at the vexations without number to which they were expofed. The boors, in fhort, were almoft become defperate at feeing their children fuccefiively ravifhed from their families for furnifhing recruits to the armies which the fword of the Turks, and the horrible plague were inceffantly mowing down on the banks of the Danube. The Kofaks of the Don gave the firft fignal of revolt. They had at their head a man, who, knowing their credulity, and feeing the fpirit of difcontent that was fpread among them, quickly fucceeded in caufing feveral provinces to rife, and who, if he had been mafter of more art in taking advantage of his fuccefies, would undoubtedly have given a different turn to the fate of Ruffia.

But it fhould firft be explained what it was that determined this man to take upon him
the

the bold part he played. The popes could not forgive Catharine for not reftoring to them their poffeffions. They had recourfe, therefore, to impofture, as one of the moft fure and eafy means of revenge; having learned, from the ecclefiaftical hiftory of all ages and nations, how feldom it fails of fuccefs. They privately fpread abroad the report that Peter III. was not dead; and that he would foon make his appearance to reclaim his throne of the emprefs.

A falfe Peter III. had indeed prefented himfelf in the province of Voronetch*; but he was taken, declared to be an impoftor, and punifhed with death.

Some years after †, a deferter from the regiment of Orloff, named Chernicheff, appeared in the village of Kopenka, on the frontiers of the Krimea, and alfo gave out that he was the emperor fuppofed to be dead. The popes procured him a great number of partizans; and they were preparing to crown him in a church, when a colonel of the ruffian troops, who had been informed that Chernicheff was inciting the people to a revolt, came and feized on him, and inftantly caufed his head to be ftruck off.

---

* He was a fhoemaker of Voronetch, and appeared in 1767.

† In 1770.

At the beginning of the naval war in the Archipelago, the Montenegrins made head againſt the Turks, refuſed to pay the uſual tribute, and drove the collectors out of their diſtrict. To this they were incited by a foreigner, moſt probably an Illyrian, named Stefano Piccolo, who in the ſeven-years war had ſerved among the auſtrian irregular troops, and afterwards could find no inclination to peace and tranquillity. Count Orloff, in 1769, took advantage of his ſituation in thoſe parts, and ſent to him prince Michael Dolgorouki ; but he would not be perſuaded to agree to the propoſals of theſe commanders, felt himſelf rather uneaſy too under the ruſſian guard that had been ſet over him, and found means, by one artifice or another, to circulate the report that he was really the dethroned emperor, Peter III. The enthuſiaſm inſpired by the ruſſian name among the Greeks of thoſe provinces, led them eaſily to believe that what he pretended was true. Some of their biſhops ſeconded this enthuſiaſm with warmth ; and this ſtratagem occaſioned an inſurrection among the people. But it was not long before the janiſſaries obliged the Illyrian to take to flight : more fortunate than the other falſe Peters, he eſcaped the ſcaffold.

A fourth

A fourth impoſtor appeared afterwards in the government of Oufa. By birth a vaſſal on an eſtate belonging to the family of Vorontzoff, he fled among the koſaks, and followed a detachment which went, at the beginning of 1772, to join the ruſſian army. On coming up to one of the ſtations in the deſart between the Don and the Volga, he aſſembled his comrades, and aſſured them that he was Peter III. This ſtupid and barbarous crew believed him, acknowledged him as emperor, and ſwore to die in his defence. This done, he proceeded to appoint his miniſters, his generals, and prepared himſelf for wearing the crown with as much confidence as if he had been in poſſeſſion of a kingdom and a powerful army. But his reign was not long. At the end of a few hours a ruſſian officer came, and caught hold of his new majeſty by the hair of his head, cauſed him to be bound by his own ſubjects, and ſent him to priſon at Tzaritzin. There the ſoldiers and the inhabitants, excited by the monks, made an attempt to ſet free the impoſtor. But colonel Zipletoff, commandant of the fortreſs, a part of the garriſon having retained their fidelity, ſucceeded, by means of their fire-arms, in diſperſing the ſeditious. The impoſtor was immediately condemned to the knoot, and periſhed under the ſcourge of the hangman.

A pri-

A prifoner at Irkutzk attempted, in 1772, to follow the example of the four delinquents of whom we have juft been fpeaking, and met with no better a fate. All thefe tragical farces were only the prelude to fanguinary fcenes preparing by a more formidable villain.

Catharine now was doomed to fee the third and greateft calamity that befel her during the whole of her reign; an open rebellion and its attendant, a civil war. This calamity alfo took its rife in Afia, and proceeded quite to Mofco. The author of it was Ikhelman* Pugatfheff, the fon of a kofak, and born at Simoveïfk, a village on the borders of the Don. He ferved at firft as a common foldier in the army which the emprefs Elizabeth fent, in 1756, againft the king of Pruffia. He afterwards made the campaign of 1769 againft the Turks, and fought under general Panin at the fiege of Bender. On the furrender of that town he applied for his difmiffion; which was refufed him. Upon this he fled to Poland. Here fome hermits of the greek confeffion, of whom he demanded the rights of hofpitality, kept him concealed for fome time.

---

* Some perfons call him Yemelka, and others Yemelyan Pugatfhef; but he is named Ikhelman in the manifeftos of the emprefs.

With

With thefe hermits he frequently difcourfed of his campaigns and his various adventures. One day he related to them, that while he was in the army of general Panin, a ruffian officer faid to him, after confidering him for a long time, " If the emperor Peter III, my mafter, ". was not dead, I fhould believe that I faw him " once more in thee." The hermits feemed not to pay much attention to this matter; but fome time after, one of their comrades, whom Pugatfheff had not yet feen, exclaimed all at once, " Is not that the emperor Peter III ?" The monks then made attempts to feduce him; and found no great trouble in fucceeding. As foon as he was prepared for being employed as an inftrument in their impofture, he went to the town of Dubranka, where he ftaid fome days. Thence he proceeded to Little Ruffia, and fojourned among the fectaries, who are very numerous in thofe parts, and practife the greek religion as it was taught by the primitive church. Afraid of being detected as a deferter, he ran to the kofaks of the banks of the Yaïk, a river to which Catharine has fince given the name of Oural *. Pugatfheff communicated to feveral

* It was to obliterate the memory of the revolt of thefe kofaks that the emprefs ordered the name of the river Yaïk to be changed into that of Oural, and the name of the mountains of Yaïk into that of the Ouralfkoï mountains.

of

of thefe kofaks the defign he had formed of putting himfelf at the head of a party, and engaged them to accompany him into the mountains of Caucafus, with the affurance that there they would find powerful fuccours. They were ignorant as yet that he had refolved to give himfelf out for Peter III. But, as it was known that he was difpofing the people to fedition, he was feized at Malkoffska, and fent to take his trial at Kafan. The governor here neglected to profecute him. Pugatfheff, while in prifon, was frequently vifited by the popes, who, it is not to be doubted, were in poffeffion of his fecret. They furnifhed him with money, which he employed in corrupting his guards, and made his efcape. He immediately rejoined fome of his old comrades, went down the Volga as far as the mouth of the Irghis, proceeded up that river, and penetrated into the defart. Here he faw his company increafing from day to day ; and when he thought he might fafely reckon on a formidable party, he publicly declared that he was the emperor Peter III. delivered by a miracle from the hand of his affaffins.

It was not at firft known with certainty what could have moved him to this foul revolt, and induced him to act fo dangerous a part. Some imagined it was at the inftigation of the divan : and indeed the Turks could not have wifhed for

a more

a more timely diverſion, and which actually
wrought very powerfully in their behalf in 1773.
Others ſaw in this buſineſs the finger of the
french miniſtry, which, on finding its hopes of
the enervation of Ruſſia by the diſturbances in
Poland and the war with Turkey fruſtrated,
might have recurréd to the artifice of raiſing up
an inteſtine foe. However, of all this no trace
was ever to be diſcovered. Pugatſheff had no
foreigner about him, and at length ſtood in need
of far better counſel than he could obtain from
his own unformed though not very defective
underſtanding. If any european cabinet was
working at a diſtance upon him and through
him, it was neceſſary that he ſhould at leaſt
have begun his rebellion, ere the thought could
have occurred to it of meddling in the matter.
Perhaps therefore, as ſome ſurmiſed, the firſt
movement was in himſelf. What was unde-
niably the cauſe that moved his tribe to join
him was the religious diſcord that ſubſiſted
between that race and the domineering church.
In Ruſſia there is a ſort of ſeparatiſts, who in
the former century ſprung up on the introduction
of ſome alterations in the eccleſiaſtical rites and
ceremonies by the patriarch Nicon. The government encouraged his reformation; while
many of the ſubjects regarded it with abhorrence,

as an innovation, and the patriarch himfelf as
antichrift. For thefe people the party-name,
Rofkolniki, which is tantamount to heretics or
fchifmatics, was invented ; but they call themfelves Starovertzi, or Believers according to the
old faith. They reject all that is done by the
prevailing church as unholy ; becaufe they think
the fucceffion of bifhops interrupted by Nicon,
and therefore refufe to acknowledge his adherents for true priefts. They defpife the public
worfhip which is adminiftered by the clergy
appointed by government, never receive the
communion of them, nor fuffer their children to
be baptized at their hands. On the other hand,
they boaft their bifhops and priefts to have
received genuine confecration from the patriarch
Jofeph, which has been propagated in undif-
turbed fucceffion. They live, however, fo clofe
and retired, that their difcipline and principles are not thoroughly known ; as they have
undergone fome fevere perfecutions, efpecially
in former times, and fo lately as under Peter I.
Catharine II. immediately on her acceffion to
the government, abolifhed feveral regulations
that tended much to the difadvantage of the
Rofkolnicks. In Rúffia proper there are but
few of this fect of faith ; but all Siberia is full
of them ; and all the kofaks of the Don and of

       fouthern

southern Afia are zealoufly attached to it. At firft fight it may appear furprifing, that a rude and half-favage people fhould take part in theological controverfies with fo much zeal. But we learn from the hiftory of Poland, that the horrible wars of that kingdom with its protected relatives the kofaks, in the laft century, had likewife religious coercion for their foundation: a defign was formed to force them to throw off the original form of their primitive religion, and to become of what were called the United. The hordes of kofaks feem to be extremely bigoted to pure orthodoxy, and to hold all attempt at innovation in abhorrence. In fact, it is wonderful that governments fhould think of perfecuting fuch fimple honeft beings for their notions on thefe and fimilar fubjects.

Befides this animofity to the eftablifhed church, and befides the natural inconfiftency of this turbulent people, another circumftance occurred to the kofaks of the Yaïk. They had for feveral years before been engaged in violent differences with their attaman *, concerning the

---

* This word fignifies a commander.—But it differs from hettman, which implies the chief of the kofak ftate collectively. This latter poft, which confers great wealth as well

as

the bounds of their fisheries, and the court was obliged to send, in 1767, general Traubenberg and the captain of the guards Durnoff to quell them. But the kosaks were so dissatisfied with the decisions of these commissioners, that they murdered the general, and cruelly treated the captain. These crimes remained unpunished, because the government was too much employed in foreign concerns : a disadvantage that naturally attends a too great extent of empire, that foreign politics and war take off the attention and energy of government from the interior. The kosaks themselves, however, did not forget what they had done, and apprehended very dangerous consequences from it : they thought the crown was making preparations for revenge, and concluded that the best security on their side against it was a farther resistance by means of rebellion : besides, they fancied that the silence of the court was a mark of its weakness, and that they might therefore take these steps unheeded. In short, their minds in general were bent upon

---

as enormous power, the crown has often suffered to lie dormant. Elizabeth revived it for her favourite, Razumoffsky. Catharine abolished the dignity again in 1764, but afterwards conferred it on prince Potemkin,

violent

violent meafures, when Pugatfheff made his appearance among them, and renewed the tranfactions of the Don-kofak Stenka Razin, which were ftill frefh in the memory of fome, who, in the preceding century, in the time of the reforming patriarch Nicon, had raifed a formidable rebellion, firft among the hordes of the Volga, and then among them of the Yaïk. The kofaks, in general, from the levity natural to a people not tied down to an entirely calm way of life, are not accuftomed to act with con-fummate prudence, and have frequently caufed alarm to the government; but on many occa-fions likewife their bravery and fidelity have been of eminent fervice to the ruffian empire.

Pugatfheff took the moft effectual means of working on the temper of his nation by giving himfelf out for Peter III. who had efcaped by flight from his perfecutors, and in place of whom a foldier very like him had been fubftituted as a victim to their fury.

The kofaks on the borders of the Cafpian, a credulous and ignorant race, and remote from all correfpondence with any principal towns, received in 1773, with honeft joy, the private intelligence of the condition of the man to whom they looked up for deliverance from the oppref-fions of the predominant church; and, ftrange

as

as it may feem, this very circumftance made the
fimple ftory credible to them. In order to
juftify the dethronization of Peter, the people
were at that time told, that he wanted to alter
the drefs and the rites of the clergy, to fhake
the eftablifhed religion to its very foundations,
and unlawfully to diminifh the fplendid revenues
of the church, What idea could the kofaks
entertain of that emperor, according to this
account of him, but as of a genuine rofkolnik *,
who,

* Thefe fectaries are called, by the greek chriftians,
rofkolniki or heretics ; but they defignate themfelves by the
appellation *ftaroverfki*, or people of the ancient faith.—To
give an idea of the fanaticifm and intrepidity of thefe wild
chriftians, we will cite the example of one of their priefts,
named Toma, who lived during the reign of Peter the
great.—Toma thought proper to preach at Mofco againft
the invocation of faints and fome other dogmas of the do-
minant church. The clergy cited him to appear before
them, and exhorted him to make a folemn abjuration of his
erroneous tenets. Inftead of hearkening to their admonitions, Toma armed himfelf with an axe, entered the church
on the day of the feaft of St. Alexius, and hewed to pieces
not only the figure of the faint, but that of the virgin.
This done, he got up into the pulpit, to explain the motives
of his conduct ; but the people would not give him time to
fpeak. He was fentenced to hold his right hand, with the
hatchet in it, over a fire, till it was entirely confumed, and
then to be burnt alive. Toma heard his fentence read with
the utmoft compofure of mind ; nor did his courage forfake
him

Who, for that very reafon, was deprived of his crown ? Thefe rofkolniks now began to look about them, and found it highly natural, that he would throw himfelf into their arms as his brethren in the faith. With hearty attachment, therefore, they joined themfelves to him ; having before them the ravifhing profpect of retaliating on the predominant church all the calamities it had brought upon their fathers, if the emperor fhould re-afcend the throne that of right belonged to him, by their affiftance, and that then the orthodox believers would completely triumph over the execrable innovators, the cruel corruptors of the orthodox faith.

About the middle of September 1773, Pugatfheff's whole retinue confifted of nine perfons : a few days afterwards he was at the head of 300 men. With thefe, on the 17th of September, he boldly prefented himfelf before Yaïtfkoy, and

him at the time of execution. He fedately held his hand extended over the flame ; and when he was laid upon the faggots, he continued to declaim againft the abufes that had been introduced into religion.—Whenever the government has thought fit to oblige the rofkolniks to embrace the ruffian faith, numbers of them have affembled by families in barns, and have fuffered themfelves to be burnt alive. This happened in 1722 in various parts of Ruffia.

fummoned

fummoned that town to furrender, notwithftanding there were in it 5000 kofaks and two field-
regiments.   To thefe troops he fent his manifefto, in which he declared to them, among
other things, " that he was Peter III. who had
" efcaped from Ropfcha at the inftant when his
" affaffins were about to murder him; that the
" traitors who had dethroned him, and dreaded
" his return, had falfely invented and propa-
" gated the report of his death; that he had
" been obliged to put on the difguife of a kofak,
" to bear arms for his perfecutors, and after-
" wards to conceal himfelf among the true and
" faithful believers, to whom he had made him-
" felf known; that having learnt at length that
" the brave kofaks of the Yaïk were refolved
" to free themfelves from the yoke of the ufurp-.
" atrix, he was come to put himfelf into their
" hands, and to offer to march with them to
" victory and to vengeance."   Immediately 500
of the kofaks came over to him, bringing with
them 11 of their officers : the lieutenant-colonel,
who was commander of the place, fearing left
all his people fhould defert him, drew back into
the town.   Pugatfheff followed him, and caufed
that officer to be hanged up; and in this manner
he ever afterwards acted with all the commanders
of the places to which he came.   It would be
impoffible

impoffible to defcribe all the cruelties with which
this barbarian treated the feveral perfons of rank
that fell into his power; as well as to delineate
his marches from place to place, his conquefts
of towns, and his battles, which fhew that he
was not wanting in courage, and frequently not
in regular plans and ftratagems of war: nor
would the attempt be lefs fruitlefs, to recount,
on the other fide, all the miftakes and negli-
gences committed by the ruffian commanders,
and the bafenefs with which numbers of them
fubmitted to him. General Karr was appointed
by the court of Peterfburg to go and reftore
tranquillity. Whether he thought that the bare
news of his arrival would difperfe the rebels, he
travelled poft from Mofco to Orenburg, which
Pugatfheft kept clofe befieged; and by his
imprudence facrificed the whole of a large
detachment; renewed the attack with what
foldiers he had left, was beaten, and returned
by poft to Mofco with as much hafte as he had
left it.

Pugatfheff, attended by his kofaks, as well
thofe who were his firft partizans as the others
who fince attached themfelves to him, attacked
the colonies which the emprefs had newly eftablifhed on the fhores of the Irghis. He wanted
their arms and their horfes: thefe he carried off,

but

but did them no farther harm; for as yet he affected a moderation to which foon fucceeded the moſt atrocious brutality. Having already under his command 14,000 foldiers, he prefented himfelf again before the gates of Yaïtſk. He fent to the governor an order, figned with the name of Peter III. to furrender to him the town. The governor refufed to obey; and Pugatſheff began the affault, but was courageouſly repulfed. Perceiving that it would be impoffible to carry the place by force, he refolved to turn the fiege into a blockade, and oblige it to furrender by famine. This proved alike ineffectual; for the garrifon, though reduced to the neceffity of eating the fleſh of their horfes, and even to live upon boiled leather, obftinately continued to hold out, and repreffed the inhabitants who wanted to open the gates to Pugatſheff. The patience and the zeal of this garrifon were nobly rewarded. A confiderable body of ruffian forces came to its relief juft in time to fave it from the maffacre, to which there is no doubt that it had been devoted by the rebels.

Pugatſheff was not long ere he compenfated himfelf for this difappointment. He furprifed the tribes Œlœets, and took, fword in hand, the two fortreffes by which they were protected. The fort of Tatifcheva, which he afterwards attacked,

made

made a ftouter refiftance : but, the fortifications being only of timber, he configned it to the flames, and forced the garrifon to feek their fafety by flight.

The governor of Orenburg, informed of the progrefs of the rebels, marched againft them a detachment under the orders of colonel Buloff. This officer was deficient both in prudence and fortitude : and, being furprifed in the defiles of the mountains by the troops of Pugatfheff, he was inhumanly put to the fword. Thofe of his foldiers who refufed to enlift among the rebels, remained prifoners. General Chernicheff, who, at the head of a fecond detachment, was to have joined colonel Buloff, fuffered himfelf to be furprifed as the latter had been, and met with no better a fate.

The army of Pugatfheff being now very ftrong by forced recruits and voluntary and more numerous acceffions of Kofaks, that rebel went and laid fiege to Orenburg. The governor of that town had already reduced himfelf by the feveral detachments he had fent againft the rebels. The foldiers that remained to him were not in a condition for making any defence. Orenburg was on the point of being taken, when the garrifon of Krafnogorfk ad-

vanced with fuccours, and valiantly cutting a
paffage through the befiegers, threw themfelves
into the place and faved it.

The noife of the rapid conquefts of Pugatfheff
gained him new adherents. Whole hordes came
and ranked under his ftandards : the Bafchkirs, a
hunting people, who live upon the ruffian territory, and wear its yoke with difcontent, declared
themfelves for the rebels, and furnifhed them
with numerous recruits. The Kirguifes fhortly
after followed the Bafchkirs; they were imitated
by the Budyak Tartars, whom the emprefs had
caufed to be tranfported to the banks of the
Volga, after the capture of Bender, and who
could never forgive that princefs for their tranf-
migration. The revolt fpread itfelf into the
other colonies of thofe countries. The peafants
employed in the copper mines and the founderies
of the mountains of Oural, left their work and
took up arms.

Pugatfheff vigoroufly pufhed the fiege of
Orenburg. While the trenches were occupied
by one part of his troops, the other went and
brought off the copper money which is coined
on the fpot and laid up in ftores. Here he
alfo caft cannon and balls for the fervice of
the operations againft the town. He employed

· fome

fome of the winter months in this fiege, during which time he delivered himfelf up to the excefles of debauchery and cruelty.

The rebels had by this time fo numerous an army, that the regiments fent from Kafan, often narrowly efcaped being forced, in defending the paffage of the mountains which feparate that city from Orenburg. During the winter a body of 10,000 Kalmuks, after having revolted in the environs of Stavropol, and flain the brigadier Véguézac* their commander, joined themfelves to the troops of Pugatfheff. But what contributed perhaps to render his army ftill more formidable, was a great number of the Poles whom Catharine had fent into exile in the defarts of Siberia. Glorying in fo many advantages, Pugatfheff ran over the mountains of the government of Orenburg, committing depredations wherever he came. The petty town of Oufa was the only one that made any refiftance. He committed the fiege of it to one of the chiefs of his army, and marched ftrait to Ekatarinenburg, where he knew that there was a depofit of nearly 1,000,000 of rubles in copper money newly coined. An accident faved the town. At the inftant when Pugatfheff came up

* He was a french refugee.

z 2   to

to it, he received the falfe intelligence, that a ruffian army, fuperior in force to his own, was advancing by a circuitous route. He believed the information : and having flackened his march in order to collect his forces, he left time to the regiments difperfed on the frontiers of Siberia, to come to the defence of Ekatarinenburg.

For fome time after Pugatfheff had taken arms, obfervant of the leffons he had received from the hermits of Podolia, and the priefts of the rofkolniki, he put on the appearance of much moderation and piety. He wore an epif-copal robe, gave the benediction to the people, affuring them that for himfelf he was deftitute of all ambition, and that he had no other defign than to place the grand duke his fon on the throne, and then go and finifh his days among the pious reclufes, who had afforded him fo con-venient an afylum after his efcape from his affaffins. This artful conduct procured him foldiers. Other means obtained him victory ; and then adding courage to activity, he let no opportunity efcape him for fpreading far and wide the terror of his arms. He dextroufly took advantage of the knowledge of the country in which he conducted his warfare, and the im-prudence or the weaknefs of the enemy. He never abandoned the pillage of a canton but in

order

order to fly to a fiege ; and fcarcely had he
obliged a town to fubmit, before he was on
the march to engage in a battle. But this man,
who triumphed with fuch rapidity over all the
feverities of fortune, was incapable of fupporting
its favours. Succefs increafed his arrogance; he
thought it impoffible to meet with obftacles
which he muft not eafily furmount. He threw
afide all conftraint, gave fcope to his fanguinary
temper and to his brutal paffions, fuffered the
enthufiafm of his partizans to cool, gave time to
his adverfaries to prepare to fubdue him, and
foolifhly ftopped in the midft of his career.

The fpirit of rebellion had fpread as far as
Mofco. Marfhal Romantzoff had not dared
to weaken himfelf by fending fuccours to that
capital, which was defended only by a garrifon
of 600 men. Pugatfheff had no more to do
than to prefent himfelf before it, for making
himfelf mafter of the place : he neglected to
go. Thus lofing by his own fault, not only the
fecond city of the empire in point of confequence,
but an army alfo of 100,000 vaffals who expected him there, and only waited his arrival for
running away from bondage.

Pugatfheff neglected even to profit by the advantages he had gained in the provinces which
had fubmitted to his arms. He fpent the greater

part of the winter in the ufelefs fieges of Orenburg and Yaïtfk.   It was before Orenburg that
he exterminated by the fabre all the officers and
gentry of the country round; not fparing even
their wives and their children : determined, as he
faid, to fhed the very laft drop of blood of
the haughty and tyrannical nobility.   But, by a
ftrange inconfiftency, at the fame time that he
was inhumanly butchering the nobles, he conferred on thofe of his partizans, of whom he
thought himfelf moft fure, the names of the
principal families of the empire, and the enfigns
of divers orders of knighthood.

He alienated a number of his countrymen by
braving the religious prejudices in behalf of
which he had at firft performed the part of a
zealot.   Although he had been married for fome
years to Sophia the daughter of a Kofak, and had
three children by this union, he had the effrontery
at Yaïtfk to marry a public woman, and celebrated his nuptials with all the bacchanal licentioufnefs that was worthy of the wife he had
efpoufed.

Catharine, alarmed at the rebellion that me-
naced her throne, ferioufly fet about checking its
progrefs.   She recalled general Bibikoff from
the frontiers of Turkey, gave him the command
of a confiderable army, with orders to march
                                    againft

againft the rebels. At the fame time fhe caufed to be publifhed at St. Peterfburg, and in all the principal towns of the empire, the manifefto which follows:

" By the grace of God, we Catharine II. emprefs and " autocratrix of all the Ruffias, &c. make known to all our " faithful fubjeçts, that we have learnt, with the utmoft in- " dignation and extreme affliçtion, that a certain Kofak, a " deferter and fugitive from the Don, named Ikhelman Pu- " gatfheff, after having traverfed Poland, has been colleçt- " ing for fome time paft, in the diftriçts that border on the " river Irghis in the government of Orenburg, a troop of " vagabonds like himfelf; that he continues to commit in " thofe parts all kinds of exceffes, by inhumanly depriving " the inhabitants of their poffeffions and even of their lives; " and that in order to draw over to his party, hitherto " compofed of robbers, fuch perfons as he meets, and efpe- " cially the unhappy patriots, on whofe credulity he im- " pofes, he has had the infolence to arrogate to himfelf " the name of the late emperor Peter III. It would " be fuperfluous here to prove the abfurdity of fuch an " impofture, which cannot even put on a fhadow of pro- " bability in the eyes of fenfible perfons: for, thanks to the " divine goodnefs, thofe ages are paffed in which the ruffian " empire was plunged in ignorance and barbarifm; when " a Grifka, an Outreper, with their adherents, and feveral " other traitors to their country, made ufe of impoftures as " grofs and deteftable, to arm brother againft brother, and " citizen againft citizen.

" Since thofe æras, which it is grievous to recolleçt, all " true patriots have enjoyed the fruits of public tranquillity, " and fhudder with horror at the very remembrance of " former troubles. In a word, there is not a man deferving

z 4   " of

" of the ruffian name who does not hold in abomination the
" odious and infolent lie by which Pugatfheff fancies himfelf
" able to feduce and to deceive perfons of a fimple and cre-
" dulous difpofition, by promifing to free them from the
" bonds of fubmiffion and obedience to their fovereign, as if
" the creator of the univerfe had eftablifhed human focieties
" in fuch a manner as that they can fubfift without an inter-
" mediate authority between the fovereign and the people.

" Neverthelefs, as the infolence of this vile refufe of the
" human race is attended with confequences pernicious
" to the provinces adjacent to that diftrict ; as the report of
" the flagrant enormities which he has committed may
" affright thofe perfons who are accuftomed to imagine the
" misfortunes of others as ready to fall upon them, and as
" we watch with indefatigable care over the tranquillity of
" our faithful fubjects, we inform them by the prefent mani-
" fefto, that we have taken, without delay, fuch meafures as
" are the beft adapted to ftifle the fedition : and in order to
" annihilate totally the ambitious defigns of Pugatfheff, and
" to exterminate a band of robbers, who have been audacious
" enough to attack the fmall military detachments difperfed
" about thofe countries, and to maffacre the officers, who
" were taken prifoners, we have difpatched thither with a
" competent number of troops, general Alexander Bibikoff,
" general in chief of our armies, and major of our regiment
" of life-guards.

" Accordingly, we have no doubt of the happy fuccefs of
" thefe meafures, and we cherifh the hope that the public
" tranquillity will foon be reftored, and that the profligates
" who are fpreading devaftation over a part of the govern-
" ment of Orenburg will fhortly be difperfed. We are
" moreover perfuaded that our faithful fubjects will juftly
" abhor the impofture of the rebel Pugatfheff, as defti-
" tute of all probability, and will repel the artifices of
" the

" the ill-difpofed, who feek and find their advantage in the
" feduction of the weak and credulous, and who cannot af-
" fuage their avidity but by ravaging their country, and by
" fhedding of innocent blood.

" We truft with equal confidence that every true fon
" of the country will unremittedly fulfil his duty, of contri-
" buting to the maintenance of good order and of the public
" tranquillity, by preferving himfelf from the fnares of feduc-
" tion, and by duly difcharging his obedience to his lawful
" fovereign. All our faithful fubjects therefore may difpel
" their alarms and live in perfect fecurity, fince we employ
" our utmoft care, and make it our peculiar glory, to preferve
" their property and to extend the general felicity.—
" Given at St. Peterfburg, Dec. 23, 1773. O. S."

Three new ukaufes followed clofe upon that which announced the march of Bibikoff. In one the people were admonifhed to obferve hence-forth no laws but fuch as are figned by the emprefs's own hand: in the other all deferters, and efpecially the Kofaks of the Don and the Yaïk, to return to the ftandard of the emprefs, affuring them of an amnefty to be in force till the firft of April in the enfuing year. Laftly, by the third a reward was fet upon the head of Pugatfheff, promifing a recompence of 100,000 rubles to whoever fhould put him to death*.

* It plainly appears that the emprefs was much alarmed at this revolt, and yet fhe had fo much felf-com-mand as to make a jeft of it in fome of her letters. She even called the chief of the rebels, *le marquis Pugatfheff*.

Neither

Neither was Pugatſheff, on his ſide, ſparing of
manifeſtos; and on their publication he always
took care to affix the name of Peter III. By
one of theſe manifeſtos he affranchiſes all the
boors. He alſo cauſed rubles to be ſtruck, with
his effigy and this inſcription: " Peter III. em_
" peror and autocrator of all the Ruſſias." And
on the reverſe, " Redivivus et ultor."

In the mean time general Bibikoff was already
at Kaſan *. Having received advice that the
rebels had made themſelves maſters of Samara,
he detached a part of his army to go and retake
that city. The ſiege was not of long continuance. The rebels abandoned the place with
eight pieces of cannon and 200 priſoners.

The nobleſſe of Kaſan were convoked; and
general Bibikoff invited them to join him in op-
poſing the rebellion. To this the nobleſſe were
already diſpoſed, as it was their own cauſe which
they had to defend. Their example was followed by thoſe of Sinbirſk, of Penza, and
ſeveral other governments; and the regiments
they formed without loſs of time conſiderably
augmented the forces of Bibikoff. Catharine
then wrote to that general, " that not only ſhe ſaw
" with gratitude the zeal which the nobles

* He arrived there the 25th of December 1773.

" had

" had fo generoufly difplayed, in offering to
" facrifice every thing to the public welfare ;
" but that to give on that occafion a fhining
" mark of her benevolence, fhe had refolved to
" become herfelf a member of the nobility'
" of Kafan, and to be regarded as a denizen
" of that city."

Lieutenant-colonel Grineff gained a firft advantage at Alexieff *. After an obftinate refiftance, the rebels left him matter of the field
of battle and three pieces of cannon. A few
days afterwards they fell upon him while on
his march, but they were again difcomfited.
Some other lieutenants of Bibikoff obtained alfo
confiderable fucceffes in engagements with feveral
bodies of Tartars. Notwithftanding which, the
rebels increafed in numbers and infolence from
day to day. They ran from all parts of eaftern
Ruffia, and ravaged an extent of country of upwards of 600 leagues.

General Bibikoff having advanced at the head
of 35,000 men, forced Pugatfheff to raife the
fiege of Orenburg, where a famine was beginning
to rage. The rebels retreated into the environs
. of Tatifcheva. Bibikoff fent in purfuit of them
major-general prince Gallitzin, with a confider-

* The 9th of January.

able

able body of troops. Prince Gallitzin attacked Pugatſheff, and fought him valiantly: but for this firſt time he obtained no decided advantage. On this occaſion he could not help remarking, that the ferocious intrepidity of the rebels was directed by officers who had not acquired the whole of their ſkill in the deſarts of Baſchkiria, or under the tents of the Kalmuks *.

On his retreat from prince Gallitzin, Pugatſheff changed all at once the courſe of his march, and fell upon Bibikoff, who had only kept with him a weak part of his army. The conflict was bloody, and the ruſſian general loſt his life.

Prince Gallitzin burnt with the deſire to revenge the death of Bibikoff. He attacked the rebels again near Kargaula, 12 miles from Orenburg: in this action he killed a great number of them, and diſperſed the reſt. Pugatſheff that day fought ſix hours; but ſeeing himſelf abandoned on all ſides, he took to flight, and eſcaped with difficulty to the mountains of Oural, where he was joined by his partizans with all poſſible ſpeed. But preſently appearing again with a conſiderable army, he made himſelf maſter of

---

* It is affirmed, that among them was a brother of the famous Pulaufsky, general of the confederation of Bar. Beſides, ſome of their leaders, as Antizoff, Uſſeïeff, and Nagai-Baka-Azanoff, were both brave and intelligent men.

ſeveral

feveral places to the eaft of the mountains, fetting fire to fuch as made the leaft refiftance. Here he was attacked by a body of Ruffians, who routed him afrefh, and obliged him to take again to the inacceffible heights: where, perceiving that the only courfe he had to purfue was to attempt at retrieving his fortune by fome fignal advantage, all at once he defcends from the fummits of Oural, and marches with rapidity towards Kafan, leaving marks of his cruelty at every ftep of his way. No fooner had he appeared before Kafan, but he fet the fuburbs in one conflagration. Major-general Paul Potemkin*, governor of the province, might have kept the field againft Pugatfheff, and have oppofed himfelf to the combuftion of Kafan: he chofe rather to fhut himfelf up in the fortrefs, where the rebels befieged him, and would inevitably have taken him, if colonel Mikelfon had not come up to his deliverance. Pugatfheff had not even dared to wait for Mikelfon, but precipitately raifed the fiege, and fled: Mikelfon, however, went after him, came up with him, haraffed him for three days, and at laft gave him a total defeat, after a long and bloody conteft.

* He was a coufin of prince Potemkin.

Pugatfheff

Pugatſheff continued fighting in his defence till he had not above 300 Koſaks left. With this troop, whoſe bravery and fidelity ſupported the hope of the impoſtor, he put ſpurs to his horſe, croſſed the Volga, and gained the deſart.

It might have been reaſonably expected that this defeat would have intimidated all ſuch as had formed the project of joining the rebels; and yet Pugatſheff ſaw daily arriving about him whole ſwarms of Koſaks, of Kalmuks, of Baſhkirs, and boors, whom the very ſound of liberty, and the hope of eſcaping their oppreſſive maſters, had cauſed to abandon their labour, and fly to arms. Proud of the number of his troops, who ſeemed to multiply in proportion as they were deſtroyed by the ruſſian cannon, he reſolved to proceed to the attack of Moſco. His partizans continued ſecretly to fan the flames of rebellion. The people waited for him as for a redeemer; but it was too late. At the inſtant that Pugatſheff was beginning his march, he learnt that the Ruſſians had juſt concluded a peace with the Ottomans. Dreading now that he ſhould have to contend with the greater part of the army of marſhal Romantzoff, he thought of turning his arms to another quarter.

Intelligence.

Intelligence being brought him that some ruffian regiments were encamped on the shores of the Volga, he descended along that river, came upon those regiments by surprise, routed them entirely, and took by assault two or three little forts, of which Saratoff was one. The commander, who knew the cataftrophe to which he was doomed, seized the moment when the conqueror was busied in pillage, and escaped with 50 men alone. The town of Dmitrefsk was basely surrendered by treachery to Pugatsheff, who had the barbarity to cause the governor to be impaled alive.

While he was at Dmitrefsk, he was told that the astronomer Lovitch, member of the imperial academy of sciences at St. Peterfburg, was employed in the neighbourhood in taking levels for a canal projected between the Don and the Volga. He immediately commanded him to be brought before him ; and when the learned and peaceful astronomer was in his presence, he ordered his men to lift him up upon their pikes, " in order," said he, " that he may be nearer " the stars;" and then caused him to be cut in pieces by the Kosaks. But such atrocious acts cannot be of long duration ; and the greater the excesses committed by Pugatsheff, the greater was the security of the emprefs.

That

That princefs, freed from the cares fo long occafioned her by the war with the Turks, gave orders to fend frefh troops againft the rebels, and gave the command of them to general Panin, who had gained great reputation by the taking of Bender. But from the moment that prince Orloff was reinftated in favour, his inve‧ terate hatred to the minifter extended itfelf to his brother alfo; and the emprefs confented, for fome time, to let one of her beft generals remain in a ftate of inaction. The want fhe had of him, or rather the reviving favour of his brother, induced her to employ him again. At length he fet out on his march againft Pugatfheff. The rebel forces were bearing hard upon the town of Tzaritzin, and doubtlefs intending for it a fimilar fate with that of Saratoff; but they were obliged to raife the fiege with precipitation. Panin fent off a detachment to colonel Mikelfon. With this reinforcement Mikelfon cut off the convoys of Pugatfheff, ftarved his army, and attacked him at the very time when, encumbered with many carts loaded with baggage, and a multitude of women who accompanied it, it was engaged in the intricate paffes of the mountains. Notwithftanding the difadvantage of their pofition, the rebels determined not to fubmit. Great numbers of them were killed on the fpot;
and

and many of the reft perifhed in the precipices, and among the fteep and rugged rocks where they fought a refuge.

Pugatfheff kept the field of battle till he had abfolutely no more means of defence. He now again fwam over the Volga; then croffed the vaft defart which extends through the adjacent diftrict, and found himfelf at nearly the fame place where he firft raifed the ftandard of rebellion. Several of his friends had rejoined him on his flight; but hunger, fatigue, and difappointment, determined great numbers to forfake him : notwithftanding which, he might long have caufed difturbance to the empire, if treachery had not ftepped in to the affiftance of the ruffian army.

Antizoff, the intimate confidant of Pugatfheff, and one of the chiefs who had the moft authority with the Kofaks, had been taken prifoner; and his confequence was employed in reducing his nation to obedience. Gifts and promifes were lavifhed upon him ; and he was commiffioned to affure his countrymen that the cuftomary gratifications for the defence of the frontiers fhould be renewed. The expences occafioned by the war againft the Turks had caufed the payment of thefe gratifications to be fufpended; and this was

one of the motives that gave birth to the infurrection of the Kofaks.

But, after all, to the indefatigable exertions of
colonel Mikelfon, Ruffia is peculiarly indebted
for the quelling of this dangerous rebellion.
From January 1774, he purfued the rebels
without intermiffion, how numerous foever their
fwarms, how remote the expedition, and whatever fortune attended his enterprifes. It almoft
exceeds belief with what toilfome perfeverance
Mikelfon purfued his march over the defarts of
tracklefs fnow, without a guide, without fuccours, at times almoft without food; how his
company, always fmall, and often fpent with
fatigue, whenever they met with the great hoft
of the rebels, always attacked and always beat
them; only by the prudence and the bravery of
the colonel, and the confidence he had acquired
from his troops. To upwards of 7000 verfts
did the fpace amount, which this excellent foldier
had travelled over within a few months, in the
moft inclement feafon, with his men.

Pugatfheff had at one time a prodigious concourfe of people. Whole nations, the Bafhkirs,
many of the Votiaks, many Tartars, flocked to
his banners. He conceived the grand idea of conquering the ancient and great capital of the kingdom

dom of Kafan; and it fucceeded. Only the
detached fort which Potemkin had entered held
out againft his attacks. The archbifhop of
Kafan came fubmiffively, with a bag of gold in
his hand, to the conqueror, and only waited for
the fort to furrender, that he might bring him a
fecond bag, and folemnly crown the rebel.
The impreffion this circumftance would have
made on the people is not to be told. In the
regions of Orenburg, Kafan, and Oufa, the
generality of the inhabitants had declared for
the impoftor. When the reftlefs Mikelfon
preffed him hard, when he was in want of provifions, or military operations compelled him to
change his quarters; when, by battles loft, the
number of his effective followers was diminifhed
to 4000 men; he needed only to fhew himfelf in
new diftricts, and the fubjects immediately rofe
up againft their lords, murdered them, or drove
them away, and declared themfelves openly for
Pugatfheff. At length he feemed to have
formed the moft dangerous of his plans: he was
approaching faft to Europe, and had croffed the
Volga. Whole regions went over to him.
With the utmoft confternation it was thought
poffible that he might pufh on to Mofco; for it
is a well-known fact, that the extremely numerous
populace of that capital were difpofed to join

him,

him, and longed for his arrival. If he had attempted this with hafty marches, nothing could have refifted him; and who can calculate the confequences, if Mofco had fallen into his hands? But here Pugatfheff fhewed that, though endowed with talents and great prefence of mind *, yet he was too much of the barbarian for the execution of any great plan as a ftatefman or commander: he neglected Mofco, though it is faid that the general difpofition there was not unknown to him; and loft his time in tempting over the Kofaks of the Don and the Tartars of the Kuban. Now his perfecutor Mikelfon came up, and cut him off from Mofco; the reft of the troops furrounded him, and fhut up his wafted army in a defart 500 verfts in length behind Tzaritzin. Hunger, thirft, and awakening con- fcience, opened the eyes of his followers. As he was prolonging his miferable life by gnawing the bones of a horfe, fome of the principal of

* At the Don his firft wife had been found out, (for at the Yaïk he married a fecond,) and been fent to Kafan before that city was conquered, in order to convince the people of thofe parts of his real condition and origin. On his arrival there he happened quite unexpectedly to fee her, and, knowing her, he faid, without the leaft alteration of countenance, " Clothe that woman well. I knew her huf- " band; he has been of great fervice to me on many " occafions."

them ran up to him, saying, " Come, thou haft
" been long enough emperor." He fired a piftol,
and fhattered the arm of the foremoft ; the reft
of the Kofaks bound him, ran away with their
prifoner over the defart to their feat on the Yaïk,
and fent a meffenger to the commandant of the
place to inform him of what they had done.
General Suvaroff, hearing of the event, put the
rebel under a fufficient guard, and fent him to
prifon at Yaïtzkoï, from which place he brought
him to Sinbirfk, where he delivered him over
to general count Panin (who had formerly taken
his difmiffion, but from real patriotifm had
requefted to be permitted to have a fhare in this
conteft) *. Mikelfon was purfuing the enemy
in the defarts, when he received intelligence of
the fate of the leaders of the infurgents. Upon

---

* It is poffible that, according to one report that was
circulated at the time, thefe Kofaks had been bought over,
though nothing appeared in confirmation of it. It was faid
that, while Antizoff was negotiating his accommodation,
three other Kofaks, who had likewife been bribed, undertook to deliver up Pugatfheff; that, accordingly, they
went to him, and advifed him, as no means were now left
him of fafety, to make a voluntary furrender ; that, incenfed
at this bafenefs as he called it, he wanted to punifh one of
them on the fpot ; and that then the three fell upon him
at once, bound him, &c. The fact, as related in the text,
came out on the trial.

this

this he conducted his troops to Saratoff, to rest after the fatigues they had undergone, but proceeded himself to Sinbirsk, where Panin gave him a noble and friendly reception, and whence Catharine recalled him, in order to recompense him according to his desert.—Thus terminated the rebellion, in which 100,000 men were slain.

General Panin caused the traitor Pugatsheff to be conveyed in an iron cage to Mosco *, together with several of his principal accomplices.

When the empress was informed that Pugatsheff was in the prison of Mosco, she appointed a commission, who united with the senate, for the trial of the rebel :- taking care, at the same time, to recommend to them to be satisfied with the confession of his crime, without applying the torture, and without requiring him to name his accomplices. Her majesty was doubtless apprehensive lest the declarations of the culprit might oblige her to multiply punishments, and plunge the empire into new calamities.

The sentence passed on Pugatsheff was, that he should have his two hands and both his feet cut off; that they should be shewn to the people; and that afterwards he should be quar-

---

* Pugatsheff arrived at Mosco in the month of September 1774, and was executed the 21st of January following.

tered

tered alive. But this butchering sentence was not fulfilled. By some persons it is said that a secret order from the empress mitigated it. Others pretend that the executioner was less inhuman * than the judges; and others again affirm, that it was by a mere mistake of the man. However it be, Pugatsheff was first decapitated; after which his body was cut into quarters, which were exposed in as many parts of the town. Five of his principal accomplices were likewise beheaded; three others were hanged; and eighteen more underwent the knoot, and were sent to Siberia. Pugatsheff met his fate with the most undaunted resolution, but was induced to acknowledge the justice of his sentence, the deception he had used, with his true name and condition. It is said, that an observation made several years ago by the celebrated count Totleben of the striking resemblance which he bore to the late emperor Peter III, took such possession of his mind, as to have been the operating cause of that calamity and ruin in which he involved, with himself, a great part of the empire, which cost it the destruction of a great number of towns, and of

---

* What seems to confirm this opinion is, that, after the execution of Pugatsheff, the wretched hangman had his tongue cut out, and was sent into Siberia.

upwards

upwards of 250 villages, the interruption of the
works at the mines of Orenburg, and the whole
trade of Siberia. The Bafhkirs, who in 1770
amounted to 27,000 families, loft, during the
rebellion, great numbers of people, and, after it
was finally quelled, many of their privileges and
immunities. The Meftfheræks, a tartar nation,
who lived amongft them, formerly paid them
a land-tax; this, as a punifhment on the former,
was now abolifhed; for the Meftfheræks had
remained true to the crown: they were immediately declared free people, on the footing of
the Kofaks, and received feveral of the villages
of the flaughtered Bafhkirs, reckoned at 1849
farms.—Laftly, in order to make an awful impreffion on the nations around by a lafting and
fenfible token of difpleafure, the emprefs, by a
ukaufe, abolifhed the name of Yaïk for ever.
That river, which takes its rife from the eaftern
fide of the mounts Oural, and gave name to the
Kofaks that dwell on its borders, is at prefent,
throughout the ruffian empire, called the Oural;
and the town Yaïtzkoï, where Pugatfheff began
and finifhed his rebellion, bears now the name
of Ouralfk.

On recalling to our memory at once the
momentous occurrences that followed one another fo rapidly in fuch a fhort feries of years,
we

we are loft in admiration of that mind which
could calmly and fedately furvey their tumultuous fucceffion, and could, in perfect compofure, provide the fitteft means for affuaging their
violence and correcting their influence, while it
fhewed itfelf firm and great in all other tranfactions of a public nature, both foreign and
domeftic, fo as to gain the reverence of friends,
and extort the refpect of foes. But this is not
all: ever interefted in promoting the glory and
elevation of the country which had fallen under
her guidance, Catharine at the fame time was
promoting its internal welfare, by encouraging
the fciences and the arts of peace ; and wherever
fhe appeared, eafe and cheerfulnefs were in her
train ; and her converfations and letters were
always feafoned with pleafantry and temperate
mirth.

Shortly after the punifhment of Pugatfheff,
the emprefs had a frefh opportunity for difplaying her clemency, by granting a pardon to men
who, though not guilty of crimes of fo heinous
a nature as thofe of that traitor, yet were juftly
deferving of capital punifhment. They were
the treafurers of the empire, who had embezzled
the public money. Catharine would not even
allow them to be brought to trial. She had
overcome what was naturally irafcible and
                                                    violent

violent in her temper, and had learnt patience
and lenity from the leſſons of philoſophy.   She
has alſo been heard to ſay, " What I cannot
" overthrow, I undermine and root up."   The
heavy burden incurred by her foreign and
domeſtic wars did not prevent the empreſs from
taking off moſt of the taxes which were laid for
their ſupport; and, as if the ſtrength and riches
of government in her country increaſed with its
expence, ſhe alſo aboliſhed a number of the
ancient taxes, which were either conſidered as
diſcouraging to agriculture, or burdenſome and
oppreſſive to particular provinces or orders of
the people.   In the ſame ſpirit of beneficence
and good policy, ſhe lent great ſums of money,
intereſt free, and for a ſpecified term of years,
to thoſe provinces which were ruined by the late
rebellion ; and, to crown a general pardon, ſhe
ſtrictly forbad any particulars of that unfortunate
affair to be called up, or any reproaches uſed on
its account, but condemned all matters relative
to it to perpetual ſilence and oblivion.   .

    She alſo eſtabliſhed a number of other regu-
lations, all tending to the ſecurity, advantage,
and happineſs of her ſubjects, to aboliſh pernicious diſtinctions, deſtroy ruinous monopolies,
reſtrain the cruelty of puniſhment, remove
oppreſſive or impolitic reſtrictions or prohi-
                                                bitions,

bitions, and to reſtore mankind to a more equitable degree of equality, in thoſe different ranks
which they fill in ſociety.   A pardon was alſo
granted to thoſe criminals who had already
undergone a long degree of ſuffering for their
crimes ; and an ordinance iſſued to prevent any
future criminal proſecution from being admitted,
unleſs commenced within ten years after the date
of the charge.   Equal humanity was ſhewn with
reſpect to impriſoned debtors, who, under certain limitations, and in certain circumſtances,
were releaſed from confinement.   All the heirs
of the debtors to the crown were diſcharged
from their bonds and obligations.

Thus Ruſſia enjoyed her power, influence,
and glory, with a noble and ſplendid magnificence.   All her affairs were conducted upon a
great and extenſive ſyſtem ; and all her acts
were in a grand ſtyle.   She ſat ſupreme between
Europe and Aſia, and looked like the dictator
of both.   In her was ſeen a great but ſtill growing empire, which not having reached the ſummit of her deſtined power, felt life and vigour
glowing in every part.   The ſucceſſes and conſequences of the war enlarged the ſpirit, extended
the views, and dignified the minds of the people.
In ſuch a ſtate every thing is bold and maſculine.
Even vices and crimes are great.

If

If Catharine was able to do so much for the benefit of her country during such turbulent times, what might not be expected of her in a period of peace?—She would, however, have performed much more, if even this period had been so calm as at first sight it would appear. But it was not. If no war employed the empress to the detriment of her internal administration of government, yet foreign affairs attracted too much of her attention. There was no great transaction in which she would not interfere; and in order to interfere with so much impression, with so significant an influence, as she did, a great force must be kept up, and a ready participation constantly visible in all the occurrences of Europe. She might have looked on with indifference when ambitious princes jostled each other, or feeble governments were hastening to their fall; but the former contended for her countenance, and the latter awakened in her the idea of still adding to the territory of her prodigious empire. Alliances, guarantees, leagues, preparations, measures for attracting more respect, decisive arbitrations, plans for future enterprises; in short, every thing which the lust of dominion can suggest, and in which policy can be employed, was the object of Catharine's mighty mind; which, secure from every power

on

on the earth, could aft in any voluntary direction. And even envy itfelf muft confefs, that
fhe performed her part in the grand drama of
the world with a dignity never feen before :—
here a kingdom was to be treated as a province
of her dominions; there, an independent ftate
to be annihilated by a manifefto: here bounds
were to be fet to the arrogance of a foreign
potentate; there, a gigantic projeft to be con-
dufted and advanced. All muft allow, that fhe
was never forgetful of the interefts of her empire:
new life and improved organization fprung up
beneath her forming hand. But that outward
aftivity diflurbed the fixed and fteady view of the
interior, and kindled at length a war, which
though fhe again triumphantly concluded, yet
unneceffarily emptied her exchequer, and wafted
her army. Among her neighbours arofe jealoufy and the defire to hurt, which acquired the
legitimate appearance of felf-defence. Thus
were brought together from all fides the embers
of a dangerous combuftion, while fmiling fortune
feemed preparing for the empire the bleffings of
peace.—Had Catharine fhewn a generous fcorn
for foreign fame, and never engaged in a war;
or perhaps more properly, had never felf-intereft
in the mafk of flattery encompaffed her throne;
in all probability hiftory would have had but
one

one voice in extolling her as the model for fovereigns.

A politician of great fagacity *, in fpeaking of the commerce and wealth of Ruffia, faid, many years ago, " Nothing can be more preju-
" dicial to this increafe of wealth than foreign
" wars; by which perhaps more hard money
" goes out of the country than its mines and its
" commerce produce. If, on the contrary, this
" yearly national profit were employed on the
" inner cultivation of the country, far greater
" benefit would accrue; even for foreign com-
" merce, than could be obtained by the moft
" brilliant conquefts. Ruffia fhould avoid all
" wars; and as from her fituation as well as by
" her power, fhe is fafe from all attacks from
" without, fhe may eafily avoid them. Ruffia
" fhould, as little as poffible, take any concern
" in the foreign tranfactions and commerce of
" the monarchs of Europe, and direct the whole
" of its attention to the increafe and extenfion of
" its internal improvement. And though in that
" cafe it is probable that not fo much would be
" read in the foreign gazettes and political pub-
" lications about the ruffian empire as at prefent;
" yet, in return, the ruffian fubjects would

* M. von Struenfee, in his " Account of the Commerce of the States of Europe," 1778, part i. p. 505.

" obtain

" obtain a higher degree of profperity and
" happinefs."

But what did not Alexander do, that the idlers
in Athens might have fomething to fay of him ?
In nearly the fame manner Catharine feemed
afraid that Europe might forget her, nay, that
the name of her empire would be expunged from
the catalogue of its ftates. She even thought
it neceffary, in the firft paragraph of the firft
chapter of her fo frequently mentioned " Inftruction," to make the declaration, " Ruffia is
" an european power." Our quarter of the
world had afterwards frequently occafion enough
to remember that fhe was a party concerned
in it.

Germany had particular reafon to know it.
Peter III. as duke of Holftein, was a prince of
the empire. The Gottorp divifion bordered on
the german territories of the king of Denmark :
a renewal of the ancient feuds between thefe two
kindred houfes threatened to break out; and no
plan for an accommodation for the future could
ever be brought properly to fucceed. Catharine
at length removed the difficulty, and for her very
trifling relationfhip in a truly exalted manner.
It likewife appeared to her, perhaps, unfuitable,
that her fon, now arrived at his majority, as heir
to the imperial crown of Ruffia, fhould be at the

fame

same time an actually reigning prince in Germany *. In 1773, she proposed, in her son's name, an exchange with the house of Denmark, to which it readily agreed, whereby it was to receive the ducal portion † in return for the county of Oldenburg and Delmenhorst in the circle of Westphalia. These latter, therefore, fell to the grand duke; who directly ceded them, without compensation, to the younger son of the Gottorp line, Frederic Augustus, bishop of Lubek, by whose imbecil son, Peter Frederic William, they are now inherited. The two counties ‡ are estimated at 45 square geographical miles, containing 85,000 inhabitants, and yielding an annual revenue of 230,000 rixdollars. So disinterestedly did Catharine barter, so magnanimously did she make presents. The elder branch of the house of Holstein-Gottorp therefore had no longer a seat among the princes of the german empire; but Catharine kept an ambassador at the diet of Ratisbon, whose vote was certainly not without consequence. The empress in 1779 ratified the peace of Teschen

* See the genealogical tables, in the foregoing volume, tab. ii. p. 107.

† Comprising the city of Kiel, &c.

‡ Converted into a dukedom by the emperor of Germany and the states of the empire in 1776.

concluded

concluded between Pruffia and Auftria under her guarantee; and more lately infifted on being regarded as guarantee of the peace of Weftphalia; and fpoke in a very high tone in the laft diet againft France.

Nor was the emprefs lefs attentive, at this time, to the public internal fecurity of the refidence, and other parts of the empire. Of all political inftitutions and eftablifliments, nothing has a nearer relation to the comfort and fatisfaction of each individual, than the police. The refpect-able aim of this part of the adminiftration of government, fecurity and conveniency, are affociated in the grand idea of civil happinefs, without which no political happinefs is to be conceived. The relations with foreign powers, the riches of the ftate,. nay, even political liberty, are far more remotely related to the happinefs of the individual, as they rather con-cern the whole body of the nation; while the functions of the police relate exactly to thofe duties which affect a man in his more delicate and tender connections, as a citizen, as a man of bufinefs, hufband, and father. There are countries in which the citizen, notwithftanding the great weaknefs and infignificancy of the body politic to which he belongs, or amid the moft ftriking infringements of political liberty, is

happy,

happy, becaufe his civil fecurity and liberty are
guarded; as there are governments in which the
greateft national force and the completeft political organization cannot compenfate the individual citizen for the defect or the lofs of a well-
regulated police.

Civil fecurity muft prefuppofe civil liberty:
otherwife it would produce tranquillity indeed;
but it would be like the tranquillity of the grave,
the confequences of which are foulnefs and corruption. The former is the refult of combined
and artfully-connected aims; whereas the latter
is the effect of one fimple maxim. In a word,
fecurity is forced from the executive power,
liberty may be granted.

The ftate of civil fecurity in every government is an explained problem; the laws, and
the means of obtaining it, are objects of public
notoriety. The ftate of civil liberty can, in
fuch countries as have not a peculiar conftitution,
only be known from the combination of a great
many particular facts, from the fpirit of the
government, from the temper of the people.

In a country which has not the leaft fhadow
of a conftitution, in which all the complicate
relations of a great civil fociety are afcertained
by particular, explicable, frequently contradictory ordinances, and thefe left to the arbi-

trary

trary interpretation of particular courts ; in such
a country, personal and civil security can neither
be enjoyed as a matter lawfully or assuredly
established. In this situation was Ruffia, previous to the reign of Peter the great. The
variety of the ordinances of this monarch, far
superior to his contemporaries, shew that he was
sensible of the want of a civil constitution, and
the necessity of a personal security, settled and
fixed by law. Much however as he did towards
the attainment of this grand object, much still
remained for him to do. " A premature death
" obliged him to abandon this salutary institute,
" while yet in its commencement. The fre-
" quent revolutions which succeeded, the diver-
" sity of principles and opinions, the numerous
" wars that happened, though they by no
" means weakened the power and authority of
" the empire, yet subjected the regulations of
" this great emperor either to alterations, or to
" a difference in the prosecution of the idea
" of the work he had begun, or to the intro-
" duction of other rules, which partly took their
" direction by particular notions of the matter,
" partly by the alteration of circumstances and
" the natural course of things*."

* The words of Catharine II. See the ukause of the
12th of November 1775, which serves as an introduction
to the regulation of the administration of government.

At

At length the genius of Ruffia threw the fate of this great empire into the hands of Catharine II. The comprehenfive mind of this monarch, which had already been occupied in the extenfion and eftablifhment of its external force, in laying the foundations of a philofophical fyftem of legiflation, in the improvement of education, in the diffufion of illumination and tafte, and in the reformation of numberlefs abufes, and which had not yet exhaufted its energy on thefe grand objects, now formed a conftitution for Ruffia *.

The collection of ordinances out of which this conftitution arofe, breathe throughout that liberal philofophical fpirit, that reverence for mankind and their rights, and that mild, benign temper, equally removed from feverity and compliance, which mark the character of the lawgiver, and is its moft venerable fanction.

* The fucceffive conftitutions by which Ruffia obtained an equal and regular diftribution into vice-royalties, a like civil form, like courts and tribunals, a police, a municipality, fpecific rights and relations of the middle rank and the nobility; in a word, a conftitution, are the following:—Ordinances for the adminiftration of government throughout the ruffian empire.—Imperial regulation for the mercantile navigation on rivers, lakes, and feas.—Of nobility.—Municipality.— Regulations of police. They are tranflated collectively into german by the court-counfellor Arndt.

The

The prefervation and advancement of perfonal fecurity cannot be the laft object in a law-book of this nature. It provides a peculiar tribunal in the court of confcience or the court of equity, which is eftablifhed in every government of the empire, and which has for its aim, according to the proper words of the ordinance, the preferv-ation of perfonal fecurity, the mitigation of the lot of unhappy criminals, and the equitable ter-mination of all civil difputes. The conftitution of this highly remarkable inftitute is too novel, too beneficial, and too little known, to render the omiffion of a brief account of it pardonable in the prefent undertaking.

The court of confcience confifts of a judge, who prefides, and of fix members, of whom, every three years, two are elected from the clafs of burghers, and an equal number from the clafs of boors. Each rank has only to do with the accufer and the accufed of his rank. The court of confcience pronounces, in general, according to the laws; but, as it is ordained to be a guard to particular or perfonal fecurity, the rule pre-fcribed in all cafes is — general philanthropy, refpect for man as fuch, and averfion from all oppreffion and injury of mankind. For thefe reafons the court of confcience muft never add to the burthens of any man, but rather make

it a duty confcientioufly to difcufs, and to decide
with humanity, the caufe before it. It muſt
never meddle, of its own motion, in any matter,
but take it up only from an order of the government, from the communication of another court
of juſtice, or from petition and complaint, The
cafes of fuch criminals as, by fome unhappy
accident, or by the concurrence of various
circumſtances, have fallen into guilt, whofe
fufferings far outweigh their demerit, the crimes
of thoughtleffnefs or early age, and all ſtories of
witchcraft and conjuration, arifing from ftupidity,
impoſture, and ignorance, belong to this tribunal.
The duty of it, in civil caufes, is to adjuſt the
differences of contending parties who appeal to
it for that purpofe. The adjuſtment is to be
made either by the court alone, or in conjunction with arbitrators, chofen by the two parties.
If the arbitrators cannot agree together, then the
court lays before them its opinion how the
accufer and the accufed may be reconciled,
without injury, without procefs, contróverfy,
reciprocal reproach, and chicane. If the arbitrators cannot yet be brought to agreement, then
the court orders the accufer and accufed to appear, and lays before them the means of accommodation. If they admit them, the court con-
firms their agreement with its feal of office : in
                                                    the

the contrary cafe, it informs them that it has nothing farther to do with their difpute, and that they may apply to the court appointed by law for that purpofe.

The moft important behoof of the court of confcience, and by which it is in fome meafure the moft venerable tribunal of the nation, and, in the ftri&teft fenfe, the palladium of perfonal fecurity, confifts in this: When any one delivers a petition to the court of confcience, fpecifying that he has been detained in prifon upwards of three days, and that in thefe three days it has not been fhewn him why he is thus kept in prifon, or that in thefe three days he has not been interrogated, then the court of con- fcience is bound, on receiving fuch petition, and before the court breaks up, to iffue an order, that the prifoner (if he be not imprifoned for offences againft the perfon of the fovereign, nor for treafon, murder, theft, or robbery) be brought into the court of confcience, and be fhewn, adding the reafons, why he is detained in arreft, or why he has not been interrogated. The order of the court of confcience in this cafe muft be executed in the place at which it arrives, without lofing an hour ; but if the order is not fulfilled within the fpace of 24 hours, the prefi- dent of the court fhall be fined in the penalty of 500 rubles, and each of the affeffors fhall pay a

fine

fine of 100. In regard to local diſtance, 25 verſts are reckoned to a day. — If the court of conſcience finds that the priſoner has not been detained for any of the crimes above ſpecified, it iſſues an order to ſet him at liberty, on the receipt of that voucher, as well for his being brought forth as alſo for his preſentation before that court of the province which he ſhall chooſe, and where his cauſe ſhall be adjudged. No one may pretend to put again in priſon him who has been liberated by authority of the court of con-ſcience, for their deciſion on the ſame matter : but his cauſe ſhall be determined by courſe of law. But in caſe the petitioner is in confinement on account of any of the before-mentioned crimes, or has impoſed upon the court of conſcience; or can bring no proof, the court of conſcience ſhall remand him to priſon, there to be kept more ſtrictly than before *.

Public ſecurity differs from perſonal, in its having a more general aim. The former is properly the object of the police ; the latter is, in moſt countries, committed to the adminiſtra-tion of juſtice.

In proportion to the bulk, extent, and popu-lation of Peterſburg, the public ſecurity is as

* See Gemælde von St. Peterſburg, by the ingenious M. Heinrich Storch, for theſe and ſeveral other parti-culars.

great

great as any where. Robberies and murder are
fo feldom heard of, that all thought of danger is
entirely banifhed. Accordingly, people walk
alone, without any weapon or attendance, at all
hours of the night, along the ftreets, and even
in the remoteft, moft unfrequented, and even
uninhabited parts of the town. This fact, extraordinary in fuch circumftances, is, however, not
fo much the confequence of a well-organized
and vigilant police, as the effect of the good-
tempered national character. The common
Ruffian, if not corrupted by a long ftay in the
refidence, feduced by the propenfion to drink,
or preffed by extreme want, is feldom difpofed
to exceffes of this nature. To this may be added
a certain reverence towards the fuperior ranks,
which, from the fentiment of their vaffalage, and
from the way in which they are brought up, is
peculiar to this people. This is fo well-known,
that it is no uncommon thing to put an officer's
cockade in the hat as a fure means of defence
againft any attack a man might otherwife be
liable to at fuch times as the populace are accuftomed to think they have the privilege of being
intoxicated, and confequently are more prone to
commit acts of extravagance. An authoritative
word, fpoken in a commanding tone, has frequently more effect than the ftouteft oaken ftaff.

In

In order to employ this method with impreffion, it is neceffary indeed to be able to fpeak the language with fluency; but any one who has that advantage, and is familiar with the manners and the character of the nation, may at any time, in cafes of extremity, excite the good nature of the populace, and fave his purfe or his life from any hoftile attack. Among feveral inftances afforded by experience of this, one may fuffice.

A lady fome years ago travelled up the country. Her road led through a village which had lately got an ill name for robberies and murders, and indeed was become formidable to the whole diftrict. By fome unforefeen circum-ftances, her arrival at this place was delayed till the night was fomewhat advanced; and as the poft-boors abfolutely refufed to drive her any further, fhe was obliged to put up at a cottage. A converfation between her driver and fome people of the village, which by favour of the darknefs fhe happened to overhear, juftly filled her with ferious alarm. On entering the cottage, fhe perceived feveral fellows, according to the cuftom of the country, lying on the ftove. An old woman, whofe phyfiognomy was not exactly adapted to infpire confidence, accofted her with the queftion, why fhe had hefitated to pafs the night

night in that village, whether it was becaufe
fhe fufpeded that fhe might not be fafe in her
houfe ? and fwore, at the fame time, that there
was not a man in it. The traveller, from long
experience being well acquainted with the character of the nation, took care not to confute this
lie; on the contrary, fhe difplayed the moft
perfect. confidence, fat down with the utmoft
compofure to take fome refrefhment, brought
out a bottle of brandy from her cafe in the
fledge, called down the fellows that were lying
on the ftove, and divided its contents among
them. This behaviour, the bottle of brandy,
and the friendly looks of the donor, had their
due effect : the flumbering but not ftifled fentiment of humanity awoke; and the good-na-
tured, carelefs, and joyful humour, which is fo
peculiar to the common Ruffians, foon broke
out in noify fongs. The traveller, feeing that
fhe had attained her aim, laid herfelf down to
fleep in an adjacent room, in all appearance
without any diftruft, forbad her fervants to bring
the baggage and arms into the houfe, and even
put out the light. At break of day fhe found a
ruffian breakfaft prepared, and her carriage ready
for her farther progrefs. Her departure from
this band of robbers was a moral caricature of a
moft fingular nature. With the confeffion of
their

their criminal way of life, fhe at the fame time received from thefe people the affurance, that fhe and all paffengers that fhould make ufe of her name, fhould be well received, and be lodged in fafety : a promife which was accompanied with the rude but undifguifed teftimony of a hearty affection.

The police of St. Peterfburg has a very fimple and competent organization. Excepting the governor, whofe office naturally extends to all objects of public welfare, the head police-mafter is the proper chief of the whole fyftem of police. His office takes in the great compafs of this department, but confined to the general objects of public fecurity and order. He is not here, as in fome large towns, the formidable co-partner of family fecrets, and the invifible witnefs of the actions of the private man. Here are no fpies, nor ought there to be, if Montef-quieu be in the right *.

Under the head police-mafter is the police-office, where fit a police-mafter, two prefidents, the one for criminal, the other for civil cafes, and two confulters chofen from the burgher clafs. To this is committed the care to maintain decorum,

---

* " Faut-il des efpions dans la monarchie ? Ce n'eft pas " la pratique des bons princes."—Efprit des Loix, I. xii. chap. 25.

good

good order, and morals: alfo it is its bufinefs to fee to the obfervance of the laws, that the orders iffued by government, and the decifions of the courts of juftice, are put in force. The attainment of thefe purpofes is effected by the following mechanifm :

The refidence is divided into ten departments. Each of thefe has a prefident, appointed to watch over the laws, the fecurity, and the order of his diftrict. The duties and rights of this office are not lefs extenfive than important. A prefident muft have exact knowledge of the inhabitants of his department, over which a fort of parental authority is committed to him ; he is the *cenfor morum* of his department ; his houfe muft not be bolted or barred by night or day, but muft be a place of refuge continually open to all that are in danger or diftrefs ; he himfelf may not quit the town for the fpace of two hours, without committing the difcharge of his office to fome other perfon. The police-commando (conftables), and the watchmen of his department, are under his orders; and he is attended on all affairs of his office by two ferjeants. Complaints againft unjuft behaviour in the prefident may be brought to the police-office.

Each department is again divided into three, four, or five fubdivifions, called quarters, of which,

which, in the whole refidence, are two and forty. Each of thefe has a quarter-infpector, in fubordination to whom is a quarter-lieutenant. The duty of thefe police-officers is in harmony with that of the prefident, only that their activity is confined to a fmaller circle. They fettle low affairs and flight altercations on the fpot, and keep a watchful eye on all that paffes.

The number of the nightly watch in the city amounts to 500. They have their ftations affigned them in watch-houfes at the corners of ftreets; and, befides their proper deftination, are to affift in the taking up of offenders, and in any fervice by day or night, as their commanders fhall require. Befides thefe, for the execution of the police orders, and to act as patroles, there is alfo a commando of 120 men, who, in cafes of emergency, are fupported by a pulk or company of kofaks, or a regiment of huffars.

This machine, confifting of fo many fubordinate parts, preferves in its orderly courfe that fecurity and peace which excite the admiration of all foreigners. The activity of every individual member is unobferved in the operation of the whole; and by fuch a diftribution alone is the attainment of fo complicated an aim practicable.—All the quarter-infpectors of a department repair every morning, at feven o'clock, to

their

their infpector's houfe, to lay before him the
report of all that has happened in their quarters
during the laft four and twenty hours; and at
eight o'clock all the infpectors bring together
thefe feveral reports into the police-office, where-.
upon they firft and immediately take into examination the cafes of perfons taken into cuftody
during the night.   On urgent occafions the
police-office affembles at all hours.

This organization, and the extraordinary vigilance of the police, which is found competent to
the bufinefs of a numerous and reftlefs people,
render all fecret inquifitions unneceffary.   The
police has knowledge of all perfons in the
refidence ; travellers who come and go are
fubject to certain formalities, which render it
extremely difficult to conceal their place of
abode, or their departure from the city.   To
this end, every houfeholder and innkeeper is
obliged to declare to the police who lodges with
him, or what ftrangers have put up at his houfe.
If a ftranger or lodger ftays out all night, the
landlord muft inform the police of it at lateft
on the third day of his abfence from his houfe.
The cautionary rules, in regard to travellers
quitting the town, are ftill more ftrict.   Thefe
muft publifh in the news-paper their name, their
quality, and their place of abode, three feveral
times,

times, and produce the news-papers containing the advertisement, as a credential in the government from which they then receive their pass-port, without which it is next to impossible to get out of the empire. This regulation not only secures the creditor of the person about to depart, but also enables the police to keep a closer inspection over all suspected inhabitants.

The great mixture of foreign inhabitants of all nations renders this inspection at all times, but especially at certain critical periods, highly necessary. There are always, in large populous towns, disorderly people, adventurers and im-postors, who, by bold projects, by an infamous industry, or by criminal stratagems and tricks, seek occasion to disturb the quiet of civil society, or to rifle the purses of the public. The lenity of the government, the hospitable reception every honest stranger here enjoys, the easy and various means of gaining a livelihood, and the unlimited permission, attended with so many difficulties in other countries, of pursuing them in a lawful way, without distinction of nation or religious profession;—all these and other ad-vantages are, however, not always sufficient to restrain such people within the bounds of pro-priety and decorum.

If

If individuals may be fufpected by the government, becaufe their means of fupport, the company they keep, and their whole courfe of
action, are clofely wrapped up in myftery, fo
likewife may whole focieties be lefs indifferent to
it, if they carefully conceal the object of their
connection, or their very exiftence, from the eye
of the public. The police watches here, with
laudable attention, over fecret focieties of all
kinds; and frequently as the fanatical fpirit of
religious or political fectaries, or the enthufiafm
of pretended myftagogues, have attempted to
neftle here, they have never been able to proceed, or only for a very fhort time. Animal
magnetifm, Martinifm, Rofycrutianifm, and
by whatever other name the conceits of diftempered imaginations may be called, have always
been attended with the fame bad fuccefs on
this ftage.

With equal diligence the police ranfacks the
blind purlieus of fuch as have an averfion to
honeft induftry, and are attracted by the thirft
of gain. If the ramparts of civil liberty prevent
the police from having recourfe to extreme meafures for quelling the rage of gaming, yet great
difficulties and obftacles are oppofed to the
propagation and extenfion of this dreadful political evil. By the police regulation only fuch

games are allowed as require bodily exertion and dexterity, or confist of a due proportion of hazard and skill. The nicer explanations on this latter are reserved for the laws. Concerning prohibited games, the police must have regard to the motives of the gamesters. All complaints and demands relative to play-debts, and the payment of them, are declared null. That no lotteries are permitted throughout the whole russian empire is well known.

From this sketch it will be readily imagined, that the number of impostors and disturbers of the public peace can be but small. Quarrels and affrays in the street or in the cabaks but seldom happen. The person attacked calls the nearest watchman; and in a moment both the aggressor and the aggrieved are taken into custody, and led to the next sieja, (police watch-house,) where the cause of their quarrel is inquired into, and the aggressor is punished.—For matters of some descriptions, there is a peculiar tribunal, under the denomination of the oral court, which, on account of its singularity, deserves to be briefly noticed.

In each quarter of the town are one or more judges of the oral court, who are chosen from the class of burghers, and with whom are associated a few jurats. This court sits daily in the
forenoon,

·forenoon, and proceeds orally in all the differences that come before it: it, however, keeps a
day-book, in which are entered all the caufes
and decifions of the court, and which muft be
every week laid before the magiftrate. When
a charge is brought, the court declares it orally
to the prefident of the quarter: whereupon the
accufed muft not delay his appearance before the
police longer than one day after he has received
the fummons. Every caufe muft be determined
in one day, or if the examinations require more
time in collecting, in three days. The oral
court communicates the decifion to the prefident
of the quarter by means of his day-book, in
order to its ratification. If either party is not
fatisfied with the fentence, he may appeal to
the court as appointed in the regulations.

The immenfe circulation occafioned by the
neceffaries and luxuries of the refidence might
provide a greater number of people with the
means of fubfiftence. The growing increafe of
the town, and the great undertakings of the
government, which here unite as in one large
central point, employ as many hands as are to
be had, and would employ more; the facility,
therefore, with which work is to be found, and
the high price of labour, leave idlenefs and
indigence without excufe. And indeed no

beggars

beggars are feen here, unlefs one fhould give that name to a few children who here and there run about, and afk for a polufhka. Old, infirm diftempered people, and fimilar objects of difguft, are abfolutely not permitted to follow begging. For the really poor, and perfons incapable of earning their bread, a poor-houfe is provided, and maintained upon an excellent plan; but for the induftrious who look out for work, and the idlers that are able to work, the following ufeful and falutary regulations are made:

In purfuance of the police ordinance of the year 1782, fervant-brokers (or, as we fhould fay, regifter-offices) are appointed, where every day, at certain hours, people who feek fervice or work, as well as mafters who want fervants, may apply. The broker is bound to enter in his book the name, the time, and the requifites or propofals of the feveral perfons who apply, as alfo the terms of the contract; which book is taken as evidence in cafe difputes fhould afterwards arife. In order to induce the public to benefit by this inftitution of fuch general utility, it is at the fame time ordained, that the oral court and the police-office fhall admit of no complaint between mafter and fervant, if the contract cannot be produced in the broker-book; but fervants and workmen who neglect to apply to

the

the broker, are driven out of the town and the diftrict.

The work-houfe of the refidence takes in not only fuch people as would willingly work, and find no employment, but is chiefly filled with idlers, vagrants, diforderly perfons, fturdy beggars, and thieves who have not ftolen above the value of 20 rubles. As fuch a conjunction of crimes with helplefs induftry is contrary to the maxims of an enlightened police, fo this inftitution, according to its original deftination, was dedicated only to the latter. But becaufe, either from prejudices formed againft the inftitution, or becaufe, as it is moft reafonable to think, there is a fuperfluity of means of livelihood, but very few fuch perfons are found, this inftitution is almoft entirely confined to forced workmen. The fuperintendance of it belongs to the college of general provifion, who, therefore, fettle the mode and meafure of employment according to the fex, the age, and the bodily frame of each. It is likewife permitted to private perfons to fend their fervants hither for punifhment; in this cafe, however, they muft pay three kopeeks a day for each perfon's board, in addition to the profit on their labour, to the inftitution. On an average about 800 perfons are kept here annually. A fmall hofpital connected with this

inftitution

inftitution had, on the 1ft of January 1790, 107 patients of both fexes.

For criminals condemned to labour by the laws, there is a houfe of correction. This is likewife under the management of the college of general provifion, which endeavours to make the penal labour of thefe people, particularly in regard to manufactures, ufeful to the ftate. In purfuance of an ordinance of government the houfe of correction is deftined for the following defcriptions of civil and moral offenders; for children who are difobedient to their parents, or habitually purfue bad courfes; for people who having run out their circumftances, have contracted twice as many debts as they have the means to pay, or are guilty of fcandalous breaches of decorum; for perfons who publicly follow a courfe of life which is contrary to found morals and the regulations of a good police; for worthlefs and lazy rogues and vagabonds; for ftout and obftinate vagrants and beggars; laftly, for women who lead a fcandalous, impudent, and profligate life.—Offenders of thefe kinds are put into the houfe of correction, either in purfuance of the fentence of a court of judicature, or at the requeft of parents, prefidents, or mafters, though not without evidence wherefore. Here alfo private perfons muft pay a flight allowance,

as in the work-houfe. The men are feparated
from the women ; and all the people confined
muft be called only by their chriftian names.
The obftinate and refractory may be chaftifed,
by order of the head overfeer, by beating, or
punifhed by being fhut up and kept on bread
and water. The annual number of perfons
under correction here is between 7 and 900.

Thefe inftitutions, into which the refidence
difcharges all its fluggifh, foul, and infectious
parts, as into a receiver, ftand in fo clofe a connection with the prifons of the courts of judicature, that it would render this account incom-
plete, to omit the mention of them here.

The new town-jail, which, as far as practicable, is conftructed and difpofed upon Mr.
Howard's plan, confifts of a large, ftrong-built,
pentagon edifice, of two ftories. Outwardly it
has no windows, and only one gate, which is of
iron ; each of the five angles is terminated by a
tower, which rifes above the roof, and ferves as
a magazine. Each ftory has only one fuite of
chambers, all opening into a covered gallery.
The rooms are diffimilar in fize; but are fitted
up in exactly the fame manner. The windows
are all placed high ; each cell is provided with a
cubic ftove, a fmall table and feat of mafonry,
an iron outer door, and in the wall a water-

c c 4   clofet,

closet. In the open place which forms the area of the building, is a smaller prison of the same shape with the larger, which, with cells of a like construction with the others, contains a chapel, a comptoir, a guard-house, and a chamber of correction. The remaining space, in breadth about six fathom, is left for indulging the prisoners in the benefit of taking the air. The whole building has hitherto continued quite empty.

Of the other jails, which are only three, that of the police is the most remarkable. This house, which is commonly called the Politzey, because here the chancery of it was formerly held, is at present the principal place of detention for all delinquents that come within the cognizance of the police. Accordingly, here are kept, previous to their trial, fraudulent insolvents and bankrupts, swindlers, gamesters, bullies, cheats, thieves, and fanatics of all christian sects, and of all nations in motley mixture. This strange collection of beings is productive of no less singular effects. The rich purchase accommodations of the poor; the cunning overreach the simple; separated from all human society, a sort of petty republic is formed within these walls, in which the two grand levers of human activity, indigence and passion, play

their

their part as well as without them. Thus, a
few years ago, an inhabitant of this manfion
picked up money by the myfteries of an order
of which he was a member, by admitting, for a
fmall reception-fee, a confiderable number of
worthy profelytes. Another had been favoured
with the permiffion to feparate his fleeping-
place by a fcreen, where he lived in company
with his ferfs, who, by the duties of their vaffalage, were obliged to follow him into this abode.
Here he gave a friendly reception to all comers,
whofe looks and drefs feemed promifing, and
drew from them what money they had, either at
cards or by giving them a goblet or two of ftrong
punch, with fuch artifice that never any got out
of his clutches without leaving behind them, in
his lurking corner, whatever they had, and fometimes even a part of their clothes.—This houfe,
which feems to harbour within its walls only vice
and criminality, at times alfo exhibits fome noble
inftance of human action, as a few fcattered rays
are feen to mingle in the gloomy colours of a
painted night-piece. Not for the purpofe of
relieving the fhades, but as a fmall memorial
of an unknown generous action, the following anecdote may here be permitted to find a
place.

A young

A young german nobleman, who had for a long time indulged himfelf in the ufual follies of his age with the utmoft thoughtleffnefs and extravagance, was put into the politzey by his creditors. In this deplorable fituation, abandoned by all his former acquaintance, a damfel of the common clafs, who had fhared his purfe in better days, remained true to him. She followed him to prifon, waited on him with unwearied care during a violent illnefs with which he was attacked, fupplied him with all kinds of neceffaries, fold, when all her money was gone, what furniture and clothes fhe had, and at length went about begging for her unfortunate friend. At the end of eleven months, when he was releafed by death from this unhappy condition, fhe caufed him to be decently interred with the remainder of the alms fhe had procured, and then—confented to the offer of marriage long ago made her by a man in good circumftances, with whom fhe might have enjoyed the conveniencies and pleafures of life, and which fhe had hitherto refufed only becaufe fhe thought it difhonourable to forfake her firft lover in his diftrefs. This circumftance fhe mentioned to her hufband previous to their marriage.

Great

Great as the fecurity of the city is in regard to acts of open violence, yet it is neceffary for every one to be upon his guard againft artful impoftures and deep-laid ftratagems. The frequent inftances of this kind make every Ruffian wary, and therefore they are not fo eafily made the dupes of their countrymen; but fo much the more do they make up for this at the expence of ftrangers and foreigners, particularly when they are not acquainted with the language of the country. The fhopkeepers and merchants commonly afk three times, and frequently even five times as much as the commodity is worth; the unknowing offer the half, and think they have made a good bargain, till they find, when too late, that they have been miferably cheated. To give damaged goods a fair appearance, to defraud in meafure and weight in an imperceptible manner, to flip bad goods among the better that have been bought and ordered home; all thefe, and a multitude of other tricks, no dealers in the world underftand better than the ruffian. As the Ruffians in general are furprifingly cunning and of quick parts, they are eminently addicted to this fpecies of induftry; and the pickpockets of St. Peterfburg and Mofco may fafely lay wagers on their dexterity with thofe of London and Paris.

Some

. Some time fince the following affair happened at Mofco, which excited great curiofity both there and at the refidence; and, on account of its originality, deferves to be noticed while we are on this fubject. A wealthy nobleman, well known as a fancier of precious ftones, fell accidentally in company with a perfon unknown to him, who wore on his finger a ring of great beauty and value. After a long difcourfe on its real worth, the nobleman offered him a confiderable price for it, which the ftranger at firft refufed, on the reafonable ground that he had no defire to part with it. At length, however, to evade the repeated importunities of the nobleman, he declared that he could not fell it, becaufe — the ftones were not genuine. This declaration filled all the company, among whom were connoiffeurs, with amazement. The nobleman, in order to be fure of the matter, defired to have the ring for a few days againft fufficient fecurity, received it, and ran from one jeweller to another, who all unanimoufly pronounced the ftones to be genuine, and of great value. With this affurance, and the hope of a good bargain, he brought back the ring to its owner, who, on receiving it, put it, with great indifference, into his waiftcoat pocket. The negotiation now began afrefh : the ftranger perfifted

fitted in his refolution, till at length the nobleman offered a fum which was pretty near the
true value of it. " This ring," returned the
ftranger, " is a token of friendfhip ; but I am
" not rich enough to reject fo large a fum as
" you offer for it. Yet this high offer is the
" very reafon of my not complying. How can
" you, if you are thoroughly confcious of what
" you are doing, offer fo much money for a
" ring, which the owner himfelf confeffes to be
" made up of falfe ftones ?" " If your deter-
" mination depends only on that," replied the
buyer, " here take at once the fum," (laying it
in bank-notes upon the table,) " and I call the
" gentlemen here prefent to witnefs, that I vo-
" luntarily, and after due confideration, pay it."
The feller took the money, and gave the nobleman the ring, repeating the declaration, that the
ftones were falfe, and that it was ftill time to
make the bargain void. The latter obftinately
refufed to hearken to his advice, haftened joy-
fully home, and found — what the reader has
already gueffed — that the ftranger had faid what
was too true. Inftead of the genuine ring, he
had a falfe one made exactly like the other. The
affair was brought into a court of juftice ; but, as
the feller proved, that during the whole bufinefs
there was no queftion at all about genuine ftones;

that

that the purchaser exprefsly treated only for a falfe ring, and he on the other hand fold him only a falfe ring; accordingly the judge was obliged to pronounce in favour of the latter.

The arts of cheating in the article of provifions are no where better underftood than here. Ordinary deceptions of this nature happen every where; but when one looks at a fowl, which to all appearance is finely fattened, and finds it only filled with wind; or afparagus, deprived of their eatable part, pointed again and coloured with a tempting verdure; no man will call thefe ordinary tricks.

A lady, who had not been long come out of Germany, and had heard much from her acquaintance at Peterfburg of the many artifices of that nature practifed in that city, took the refolution to ufe the utmoft caution in all her dealings, in order to refute the common opinion, that every ftranger muft buy his wifdom. Several days paffed on: one morning, however, a rafnofchtfchik * entered her apartment, and offered her a pound of tea, the laft remains of what he had to fell. She weighed the parcel, and found it juft : fhe made a trial ; the tea was unadulterated, and well flavoured : fhe fhook it

* Rafnofchtfchiks are venders of fmall articles about the ftreets.

all

all out into a bafin ; no deceit was difcoverable. She inquired the price, and offered a third part of what he afked : the vender was naturally not fatisfied with this offer ; turned his tea back again into the box, wrapped a cloth about it, and crammed it into his bofom. At length the bargain was ftruck, and the commodity deli- vered; however, prudence does no harm; the lady opened the box, and faw the tea fhe had bought. She fhut it up, to the great joy of the feller, who in the mean time had afked her, fmiling, why fhe was fo extremely cautious, and why fhe had fo very bad an opinion of his honefty. The money was paid; the rafnofcht- fchik went his way; and fome days after the box was found full of fand and grains, excepting the furface, which was really good tea.

Matters of this kind are frequent in all great towns, where the numerous population renders every detection more difficult, and the diftance and difference between the circumftances of fortune roufe the paffions, and urge the human intellect to every fpecies of induftry. The height of civilization and refinement, as well as the extreme of immorality and corruption, are only to be looked for in towns of the firft magni- tude. The means to prevent thefe evils are not in the hands of the police; no human inven- tion

tion can hinder an effect where the caufe is natural; and to remove this, we muft follow the plan of the philofophers, who banifh the human race into forefts and mountains, where the greateft integrity refides with the greateft brutality.

The public fecurity is not only brought into jeopardy by human attacks of fraud and violence: Nature alfo feems at times to have confpired againft it. The refults of the grand, eternal, and beneficent laws, by which fhe acts upon the whole, are neverthelefs very frequently deftructive to the parts; and man, by an inexplicable decree, is obliged to arm himfelf, as againft an affaffin, even againft Nature, from whofe hand he receives his being, his fupport, and his enjoyments. The natural and accidental violations of public fecurity are therefore not lefs an important object of police. An accurate detail of all the particular inftitutions to this end would lie beyond the limits of this book. The following inftance, drawn from the whole, will fuffice as a characteriftic of this department of the police of St. Peterfburg.

That city, from its fituation at the mouth of a large navigable river, is very often expofed to inundations. On a continuance of wefterly winds the water rifes to the height of ten feet above

above its ordinary level. At five feet it over-
flows only the weftern parts of the town, in
places where the Neva has no rampart; but on
a fwell of the water to ten feet, only the eaftern-
moft parts efcape a general inundation. In the
year 1777, on Sunday the 10th of September,
at ten o'clock in the forenoon, the water rofe to
the height of ten feet feven inches above its
ufual level; and though in two hours afterwards
it had again retired within its banks, yet this
fhort inundation produced very extraordinary
effects. A fhip from Lubeck was carried into
the wood on Vaffilli-oftroff; the duchefs of
Kingfton's famous yacht, which fhe had quitted
a few days before, was caft upon the bar, and
greatly damaged; many wooden houfes were
wafhed away; and feveral perfons had loft their
lives during the obfcurity of the night.

Since this remarkable inundation proper meafures of prudence and caution have been adopted.
For feveral years the height of the water had been
regularly marked at the caftle. Now, at all rifings
of the river, fignals were appointed at the admiralty, as a warning to the inhabitants. Whenever it rifes above its banks at the mouth of the
great Neva, notice is given to the town by three
diftinct firings of a cannon, which are repeated at
intervals, as the danger increafes. Within the

town, in this cafe, five cannons are fired from
the admiralty-battery, and on the fteeple of it
by day four white flags are difplayed, and by
night four lanterns are hung out; and at the
fame time the church-bells are flowly tolled. In
places moft expofed to the inundation, veffels are
kept in readinefs for faving the people. Thefe
regulations, the increafing buildings, the em-
banking, and the magnificent ftone quay of the
Neva, and the extenfion of the water-furface by
the various canals, render thefe weftern gales
lefs alarming to the inhabitants of St. Peterfburg;
fo that a fwell of five feet above the level now
excites but little or even no attention.

Alfo the danger of depredation by fires is no
longer fo great as formerly, as the number of
wooden houfes vifibly diminifhes; and the regulations for extinguifhing the fires and the faving
of property are better and more complete. For
this purpofe the police keeps in its pay ten fire-
mafters and 1622 men, who are employed folely to
this object. Calamities of this nature are at prefent but feldom heard of; and when they happen,
it is commonly in the out-lying parts of the
town, where the houfes are moftly of timber, and
very old. During the laft feven years, in the
better ftreets, never more than one houfe is
burnt down, and even this is generally of wood.

8   The

The people of the police are become so dexter-
ous, that at one of the laft accidents to which
the author of this account was a witnefs, a fmall
wooden houfe that ftood contiguous to the one
on fire, was fo perfectly preferved, that it
received not the flighteft damage. At the imperial loan bank, is an infurance-office, where one
and a half *per cent.* is paid on three fourths of
the annual rate at which the houfe or fabrick is
taxed.

Though quick driving along the ftreets is
forbidden, yet from various caufes it is impoffible
entirely to prevent it; and, for the following
reafons, it is no where attended with lefs danger
than at St. Peterfburg. All the ftreets are broad
and fpacious: their running in ftraight lines
enables the driver to fee a long way before him;
in many of the ftreets is a raifed footway, which
fecures the pedeftrian from danger. Befides,
the Ruffians are excellent coachmen; and, as
they are anfwerable for every accident occafioned
by their negligence or want of fkill, they not
only call out to the foot-paffengers, while at
fome diftance, but even turn off in cafes of neceffity. The manner of their calling too is almoft
always appropriate: for example, " Old gentleman! Good mother! Soldier! Fifh-cryer!"
&c. Not only here, but throughout all Ruffia,

it is the univerſal cuſtom, in driving, to keep the right ſide of the way; hence the perpetual cry in the ſtreets: "Na prava!" *i. e.* "To the right!" Whoever goes contrary to this cuſtom, is in danger of being chaſtiſed on the ſpot, or at leaſt of receiving a volley of abuſe.

On all occaſions when a great number of people or equipages are collected together, the police-officers muſt be preſent, who, by the aſſiſtance of ſoldiers or koſaks on horſeback, keep ſuch good order, that one ſeldom or never hears of an accident. At the theatres, at court, at the clubs, eſpecially at the entertainments given in the palaces, and at promenades on certain feſtivals, there are frequently ſeveral thouſands of carriages and an immenſe multitude of people on foot: the former obſerve exactly certain rules preſcribed, and the latter may be preſent without the leaſt danger, even from the tumultuous rabble. He muſt indeed be a very partial obſerver, who does not take notice of this extraordinary vigilance and caution, which is always admired by foreigners. At every entertainment, every public dinner in the town, on every occaſion where the number of carriages is ſomewhat conſiderable, the police-officers are immediately there, for the preſervation of order and the prevention of accidents. On the bridges
acroſs

acrofs the Neva fome of them are conftantly prefent, as there the throng of paffengers is uncommonly great. The fame care is taken concerning dangerous fcaffolds at buildings and at the diverfions of the populace. The ice-hills and other national fports would certainly coft many people their lives, were it not for thefe good regulations, by which, however, accidents cannot at all times be prevented; and therefore the government is gradually endeavouring to abolifh them by limiting the period of their duration. The freezing and breaking-up of the ice of the Neva may be dangerous to the public fecurity; therefore, on thefe occafions too, the proper cautionary regulations are not forgotten. As foon as the ice begins to be porous and unfafe, care is taken to break it near the fhores, to prevent paffengers from getting upon it; and notices are ftuck upon pofts for the fame purpofe. Befides thefe precautions, the foldiers of the police are at thefe times continually prefent, who are frequently obliged to reftrain by force the fool-hardy populace from venturing their lives for a trifling wager. The writer of this account was himfelf an eye-witnefs of fuch a man, at the moft imminent hazard of his life, walking over the porous, deep-grey coloured ice of the river, which is as

broad

broad as the Thames at London-bridge, by means of a couple of boards which he took with him, laying the one at the end of the other alternately as he paſſed over them, often ſparing himſelf this trouble, on feeling that a piece of the ice would juſt bear his weight without it. In this manner, in the preſence of hundreds of ſpectators, he was got near the oppoſite ſhore, when a police-officer ſtanding there, ſeeing him coming, held up his ſtick, threatening to give him a hearty welcome with it on his reaching the land. The apprehenſion of this ſlight chaſtiſement outweighed the fear for his life; he forgot the precaution he had before obſerved, his boards and his danger; ran back as faſt as he could, and ſafely arrived on the other ſhore.

The making up and the ſending out of medicines from the ſhops of the apothecaries by careleſs or wicked ſervants may ſo eaſily give occaſion to dreadful misfortunes or crimes, that particular prudential regulations are thought neceſſary in this reſpect here. Every recipè muſt not only be ſigned with the name of the phyſician who preſcribes it, but muſt alſo mention the patient for whom it is preſcribed, with the day of the month and the year. To the medicine a label is affixed, mentioning, beſides

this

this date, the price of the medicine, and the name of the apothecary and his fhop. But the beft regulation is, that each, even the moft fimple medicine, muft be fealed. All phyficians, furgeons, and midwives, who intend to practife in the ruffian empire, muft undergo an examin- ation at the college of medicine, which then grants them a licence ; and this licence muft be publifhed in the gazette.

Her majefty's care for the public fecurity extended alfo to the paffing of laws and regulations for the prevention of dangerous and contagious difeafes, to the infpection of damaged provifions, and a multitude of ordinances of like nature ; but moft of them fo much refemble what are met with in other countries, that it would be needlefs to give a particular account of them. This fubject then may properly be concluded by noticing one of the moft important and interefting of all the regulations that belong to the general fyftem of police.

The reader will recollect, that the publication and enforcement of the decrees of the fovereign, according to the before-mentioned Inftruction, is one of the primary duties of the police-office. For the exercife of it the following remarkable form was prefcribed by Catharine II. Whenever a law, promulgated by the

autocratic

autocratic authority, and fubfcribed by her imperial majefty's own hand, or an ordinance from the places conftituted for that purpofe, is fent to the police-office, it muft be entered in the proper books, when, whence, and how it received this law. If it be fent for publication, then the crown advocate of the police-office is to be called, and his legal opinion taken: if there appear then any doubtful point, it muft be reprefented in the place appointed; but if no doubt arife; then a refolution muft be made concerning its publication. This done, the law muft firft be read in the affembly of the members of the police-office, then with open doors at the prefident of the quarter's houfe, and at the quarter-infpector's; and hereupon the publication is performed.

The foregoing facts will probably be fuffi-cient for giving fome adequate notion of the ftate of the police in the refidence, which, for the form and method, is the fame in all the towns throughout the empire; and, at the fame time, will ferve to fhew the fpirit which actuated the inftitutions for which the empire is indebted to Catharine II.

APPENDIX

TO THE

SECOND VOLUME.

No. I.

SUBSTANCE *of the* TREATY *between the Courts of* PETERS-
BURG *and* BERLIN, *ratified the 15th of April* 1764.

BY articles 1 and 2, a treaty of defensive alliance, and a
mutual guarantee, are agreed to, after referving the liberty
of concluding other treaties not contrary to the prefent.

3—9. In cafe of a foreign attack, 10,000 infantry and
2000 cavalry are promifed, three months after the firft
requifition, to be continued till a ceffation of hoftilities.
If thefe are not fufficient, means to be concerted to employ
additional force. The troops to be paid, and furnifhed
with ammunition, by the party affifting; provifions and
quarters to be furnifhed by the affifted. The troops to
receive orders from their own general, and to have their
own religion and laws.

10. No peace, &c. to be concluded without mutual
confent.

11. In cafe of war on the part of the affifting party, it
fhall be exempted from furnifhing its quota, or fhall be at
liberty to withdraw its forces, after two months notice.

12. A free commerce between the two ftates.

13, 14.

13, 14. The treaty to be in force eight years, and renewable before the expiration, according to circumstances. Ratifications to be exchanged in six weeks.

By a secret article it is engaged to maintain Poland in its right of a free election, and to prevent all hereditary succession.

No. II.

MEMORIAL *of the* PORTE, *delivered in March* 1764, *to the* FOREIGN MINISTERS *at that* COURT, *in relation to the future Election of a King of* POLAND.

AMICABLE MEMORIAL.

NOTICE has been lately given to the ambassadors our friends, that it was the intention of the Sublime Porte, that the ancient liberties of the court of Poland should not be encroached upon by foreign courts ; that the king of Poland, who is to be set up, should be elected and established in the person of a native, as by the concurrence of the republic of Poland ; and that no foreigner should be made king. Yet advices received from divers places import, that there is room to think, that disturbances are raised in Poland in order to get a person set by force on the polish throne, who is supported by certain powers. Though we are not quite persuaded of the reality of these advices, a memorial has been delivered to each of the ministers of Russia, Germany, and Prussia, importing, that as the Sublime Porte takes it to be honourable to maintain and support the ancient liberties of the Poles ; and as the same Sublime Porte does not cramp the election that ought to be made of a king in the person of a native of the country ;

the

the Sublime Porte therefore defires, that the other powers will likewife do honour to the liberties of the Poles, and that they will not oppofe the election of a king in the perfon of fuch Piaft (native) as the Poles may judge eligible. In confequence, this notice is given to the ambaffadors our friends.

No. III.

PROTEST *againft the* POLISH DIET *affembled for the Election of a King, drawn up and figned the* 7th *May* 1764, *by twenty Senators ; to which Proteft forty-five Nuncios afterwards figned an Act of Adherence.*

1. THE diet cannot be held in prefence of the foreign troops that furround the city.

2. The fenators did not engage the Ruffians to come; they gave no thanks for their being fent, and have not any way given occafion for their arrival.

3. The Ruffians have committed an act of violence in Lithuania, by favouring a pernicious confederacy made for difturbing the public tranquillity.

4. It is againft all juftice, that in the memorial of the Ruffian minifters, delivered to the primate the 4th inftant, the troops of the crown are accufed of having meddled in the dietines and other public acts.

5. It is by the unjuft proceedings of the fame foreign troops, that the general dietine of Pruffia has proved abortive ; and this is another motive for protefting againft this diet.

6. All good patriots, who love juftice, are invited to unite for the fupport of liberty.

At the end of this manifefto there is an adhefion to the protefts of the fenators, figned by forty-five nuncios.

No. IV.

A Discourse *addreſſed by his* Polish Majesty *to the* Prince Primate *and the* Marshal *of the* Diet, *in the Cathedral of* Warsaw, *when he received the Diploma of his Election, and took the Oath uſual on that Occaſion.*

IT was not my deſign to ſpeak in public at this time; but, in preſenting me with the diploma of my election, that ſolemn token of the nation's love, you, Mr. Marechal, have exhorted the ſovereign to ſpeak to his people. Theſe words of your diſcourſe oblige me to ſpeak, and to diſcover the feelings that paſſed within me, when the moment approached of taking the oath by which I have now bound myſelf in your preſence. Nay, I am even rejoiced that I have now an occaſion of ſhewing you, Mr. Marechal, together with the ſenators and ſtates of the republic, my real ſentiments, that thus ye may judge whether my views, principles, and actions, will in any wiſe tend to ſatisfy your deſires, and to accompliſh your hopes.

When, by united acclamations, the reſpectable citizens of this vaſt kingdom deigned to confer upon their equal the dignity of monarch, I bowed my head with the moſt profound reſpect in receiving this precious mark of the favour, liberty, and unanimity of this great people.

After my election, the impulſe of gratitude led me to the ſanctuary to pay my homage to the King of kings, becauſe it is there that he is more peculiarly pleaſed with the tribute of mortals. And now that I am again called to the ſame ſanctuary, it appeared to me, while I was approaching to it, that I was called before the throne of him who governs the univerſe, and preſides over the courſe of the revolving ages. At this thought I was filled with awe; my veins alſo trembled when I was obliged to pronounce that irrevocable engagement, in conſequence of which the honour
and

and profperity of the polifh nation, and the fafety and happinefs of the individuals that compofe it, are committed to
the truft of one man ; and I feel fo much the more the weight
of this important truft, in that I have long fhared with you
the calamities that flow from that want of order, union, and
vigour, that has clouded the luftre of this once glorious and
flourifhing kingdom. I acknowledge that, in that folemn
moment, a difcouraging view of the obligations I was going
to contract, and a confcioufnefs of my own infufficiency and
weaknefs, made the deepeft impreffion upon me; I was
feized with a fort of terror; my voice loft its ufual tone,
my tongue faultered, and the words of the regal oath,
though dear to my heart, which acquiefces in them perfectly, could not find an utterance : but when I turned my
eyes to you, Mr. Primate, when I heard you repeat the
words of the oath, I could not behold you in any other
light than as the minifter of the Moft High, and therefore
thought it my duty to fubmit to your guidance. Since the
clamours of difcord and party-hatred have been reduced to
filence by your venerable prefence; fince a multitude of
tongues, which fpoke each a different language, have become
all of a fudden, as it were by a miracle, the unanimous
echoes of your's ; you muft certainly be filled with the
Holy Spirit, that fpirit of power, wifdom, and truth.
Hitherto you have been my guide. Be ftill my kind affiftant
and counfellor. Continue to cherifh and keep alive the
zeal and attachment of thofe loyal hearts which your goodnefs and humanity gained over to my caufe. Let your
wifdom and refolution concur with my beft endeavour to
hold with dignity, and manage with prudence, the helm of
government, at which you been charged by the nation to
place me. As the marfhal of the diet has been joined with
you in this commiffion, both inclination and duty oblige me
to addrefs myfelf to him alfo on this occafion.

You defire me to fpeak, fir, and it is with the utmoft
pleafure that I comply with this defire. I thereby have an
oppor-

opportunity of declaring that I love and honour your
perfon, your virtues, and your talents. This declaration is
not the effect of that warm gratitude that impels me to
fpeak to you at this time ; it is the effect of a long obfervation of thofe qualities which have produced one fruit ;
and may that fruit always prove agreeable to our dear
country ! You, fir, are called to appear before the throne,
as the reprefentative of that fpirited and refpectable nobility,
which commands me to govern the republic according to the
laws ; and it is natural, that I fhould be defirous of employing the good offices of one whofe perfon is fo agreeable, and
whofe teftimony is fo weighty as yours, to affure that nobility of the fincerity of my refolutions and intentions with
refpect to that important object. Tell that nobility, that it
is my fixed purpofe to employ the remainder of my days,
and all the means and opportunities that it fhall pleafe the
Divine Providence to place within the extent of my power,
in anfwering the expectations of my dear countrymen : but
at the fame time exhort them, conjure them, to lend their
zealous fuccours to a fovereign who has their happinefs and
profperity deeply at heart, and who will never aim at any
other object than the public good. Where is the perfon
that does not fee, and alfo feel, the diforders and calamities
under which the nation labours ? A difmal experience
points out too plainly the pernicious fource from whence
thefe calamities flow. Self-intereft and envy have produced
difcord, and thus thrown all things into confufion. A
fpirit of faction has perplexed our councils, and thus rendered impotent the natural inftruments of our fafety and of
our glory ; and thofe treafures that ought to have been
employed in maintaining the vigour and fplendour of this
republic, are become the prey of that fatal luxury, whofe
pernicious effects increafe from day to day. Let our union
then heal thofe calamities, which all other means will be
infufficient to remove ! You know by experience, that a
few tools of faction can deftroy with more facility than the

majority

majority can build.   Let emulation, that ufeful virtue, that feems to border upon envy, from which neverthelefs it differs extremely, animate our efforts.   Let us all run the noble race of patriotifm, and endeavour to furpafs one another, in aiming at true merit, and propofing to ourfelves no other glory but that which is acquired by ferving our country.   But to what will amount the defires and the projeɛts of feeble mortals, if they are not feconded by him whofe word commands nations and empires to rife or fall ? Great God ! whofe hand has raifed me to the high ftation I now fill, thou doeft nothing in vain.   Thou haft given me the crown ; and thou haft given me with it an ardent defire to reftore this kingdom to its former profperity and grandeur.   Finifh, therefore, thy own work !   Let my prayer arife to the throne of thee, by whom kings reign ! Infpire the hearts of this people with that zeal for the public that fills mine !

No. V.

MANIFESTO *publifhed by the Court of* PETERSBURG, *on occafion of the Death of Prince* IVAN.

BY the grace of God, we Catharine the fecond, emprefs and fovereign of all the Ruffias, &c. to all whom thefe prefents may concern.

When, by the divine will, and in compliance with the ardent and unanimous defires of our faithful fubjeɛts, we afcended the throne of Ruffia, we were not ignorant that Ivan, fon of Anthony, prince of Brunfwic-Wolfenbuttle, and the princefs Anne of Mecklenburgh, was ftill alive. This prince, as is well known, was, immediately after his birth, unlawfully declared heir to the imperial crown of
Ruffia ;

Ruſſia; but, by the decrees of Providence, he was ſoon after irrevocably excluded from that high dignity, and the ſceptre placed in the hands of the lawful heireſs, Elizabeth, daughter of Peter the great, our beloved aunt of glorious memory. After we had aſcended the throne, and offered up to heaven our juſt thankſgivings, the firſt object that employed our thoughts, in conſequence of that humanity that is natural to us, was the unhappy ſituation of that prince, who was dethroned by the Divine Providence, and had been unfortunate ever ſince his birth; and we formed the reſolution of alleviating his misfortunes, as far as was poſſible. We immediately made a viſit to him, in order to judge of his underſtanding and talents, and, in conſequence thereof, to procure him an agreeable and quiet ſituation, ſuitable to his character, and the education he had received. But how great was our ſurpriſe, when, beſides a defect in his utterance, that was uneaſy to himſelf, and rendered his diſcourſe almoſt unintelligible to others, we obſerved in him a total privation of ſenſe and reaſon! Thoſe who accompanied us during this interview ſaw how much our heart ſuffered at the view of an object ſo fitted to excite compaſſion; they were alſo convinced that the only meaſure we could take to ſuccour the unfortunate prince, was to leave him where we found him, and to procure him all the comforts and conveniences that his ſituation would admit of. We accordingly gave our orders for this purpoſe, though the ſtate he was in prevented his perceiving the marks of our humanity, or being ſenſible of our attention and care; for he knew nobody, could not diſtinguiſh between good and evil, nor did he know the uſe that might be made of reading, to paſs the time with leſs wearineſs and diſguſt: on the contrary, he ſought after pleaſure in objects that diſcovered, with ſufficient evidence, the diſorder of his imagination.

To prevent, therefore, ill-intentioned perſons from giving him any trouble, or from making uſe of his name or orders to diſturb the public tranquillity, we gave him a guard, and placed about his perſon two officers of the garriſon, in whoſe

fidelity

fidelity and integrity we could confide. Thefe officers were captain Vlaffieff and lieutenant Tfchekin, who, by their long military fervices, which had confiderably impaired their health, deferved a fuitable recompence, and a ftation in which they might pafs quietly the reft of their days; they were accordingly charged with the care of the prince, and were ftrictly enjoined to let none approach him. Yet all thefe precautions were not fufficient to prevent an abanboned profligate from committing at Schluffelburg, with unparalleled wickednefs, and at the rifk of his own life, an outrage, whofe enormity infpires horror. A fecond lieutenant of the regiment of Smolenfko, a native of the Ukraine, named Bafil Mirovitch, grandfon of the firft rebel that followed Mazeppa, and a man in whom the perjury of his anceftors feems to have been infufed with their blood; this profligate, having paffed his days in debauchery and diffipation, and being thus deprived of all honourable means of advancing his fortune; having alfo loft fight of what he owed to the law of God, and of the oath of allegiance he had taken to us; and knowing prince Ivan only by name, without any knowledge either of his bodily or mental qualities; took it into his head to make ufe of this prince to advance his fortune at all events, without being reftrained by the confideration of the bloody fcene that fuch an attempt was adapted to occafion. In order to execute this deteftable, dangerous, and defperate project, he defired, during our abfence in Livonia, to be upon guard, out of his turn, in the fortrefs of Schluffelburg, where the guard is relieved every eight days; and the 15th of laft month, about two o'clock in the morning, he all of a fudden called up the main guard, formed it into a line, and ordered the foldiers to load with ball. Berednikoff, governor of the fortrefs, having heard a noife, came out of his apartment, and afked Mirovitch the reafon of this difturbance, but received no other anfwer from this rebel than a blow on the head with the butt-end of his mufket. Mirovitch, having wounded and arrefted the governor, led on his troop with fury, and attacked with fire-arms the handful of foldiers that guarded prince Ivan.   But he was fo warmly received by thofe foldiers under the command of the two officers mentioned above, that he was obliged to retire.   By a particular direction of that Providence that watches over the life of man, there was that night a thick mift, which, together with the inward form and fituation of the fortrefs, had this happy effect, that not one individual was either killed or wounded.   The bad fuccefs of this firft attempt could not engage this enemy of the public peace to defift from his rebellious purpofe.   Driven on by rage and defpair, he ordered a piece of cannon to be brought from one of the baftions, which order was immediately executed.   Captain Vlaffieff and his lieutenant Tfchekin, feeing that it was impoffible to refift fuch a fuperior force, and confidering the unhappy confequences that muft enfue from the deliverance of a perfon that was committed to their care, and the effufion of innocent blood that muft follow from the tumults it was adapted to excite, took, after deliberating together, the only ftep that they thought proper to maintain the public tranquillity, which was to cut fhort the days of the unfortunate prince.   Confidering alfo, that if they fet at liberty a prifoner, whom this defperate party endeavoured to force with fuch violence out of their hands, they ran the rifk of being punifhed according to the rigour of the laws, they affaffinated the prince, without being reftrained by the apprehenfion of being put to death by a villain reduced to defpair. The monfter (Mirovitch), feeing the dead body of the prince, was fo confounded and ftruck at a fight he fo little expected, that he acknowledged, that very inftant, his temerity and his guilt, and difcovered his repentance to the troop which about an hour before he had feduced from their duty, and rendered the accomplices of his crime.

Then it was, that the two officers, who had nipped this rebellion in the bud, joined with the governor of the fortrefs,

in

in fecuring the perfon of this rebel, and in bringing back the foldiers to their duty. They alfo fent to our privy counfellor Panin, under whofe orders they acted, a relation of this event, which, though unhappy, has neverthelefs, under the protection of Heaven, been the occafion of preventing ftill greater calamities. This fenator difpatched immediately lieutenant-colonel Kafchkin, with fufficient inftructions to maintain the public tranquillity, to prevent diforder on the fpot, (*i. e.* where the affaffination was committed,) and fent us, at the fame time, a courier with a circumftantial account of the whole affair. In confequence of this, we ordered lieutenant general Weymarn, of the divifion of St. Peterfburg, to take the neceffary informations upon the fpot; this he has done, and has fent us accordingly the interrogatories, depofitions, and the confeffion of the villain himfelf, who has acknowledged his guilt.

Senfible of the enormity of his crime, and of its confequences with regard to the peace of our country, we have referred the whole affair to the confideration of our fenate, which we have ordered, jointly with the fynod, to invite the three firft claffes, and the prefidents of all the colleges, to hear the verbal relation of general Weymarn, who has taken the proper informations; to pronounce fentence in confequence thereof; and, after that fentence has been figned, to prefent it to us for our confirmation of the fame.

The original is figned by her imperial majefty's own hand. CATHARINE,

COPY *of a* DECLARATION *delivered on the 4th of November* 1766, *to the* KING *and* REPUBLIC *of* POLAND, *by Mr.* WROUGHTON, *the* BRITISH MINISTER *at* WARSAW, *in behalf of the* DISSIDENTS *of that Kingdom.*

HIS britannic majefty, ever excited by reafonable defires of protecting by all methods the chriftian proteftants, efpe-

cially

cially thofe who, by virtue of particular conventions, have
a right to expect his affiftance, finds himfelf obliged to
repeat his preffing reprefentations in favour of that oppreffed
part of the polifh nation, known by the name of Diffidents;
wherefore the underfigned, in conformity to frefh orders
from the king, his moft gracious fovereign, has the honour
to reprefent to you, fir, and to the republic of Poland,
that his britannic majefty, befides the many folid motives
of juftice and humanity, which give him reafon to hope
for a happy fuccefs of the prefent negotiations relative to
this affair, finding himfelf compelled, by a ftrict alliance
with the courts of Peterfburg, Berlin, and Copenhagen, to
intereft himfelf in behalf of the Diffidents, in all the forms
of law, and in quality of guarantee of the treaty of peace of
Oliva, wifhes that, in the prefent diet, this virtuous but
unhappy part of the polifh fubjects may be re-eftablifhed, as
members of the ftate, in the poffeffion of their rights and
privileges, as well as in the peaceable enjoyment of their
mode of worfhip, which every one knows belonged to them
before the figning of the faid treaty of Oliva. At the fame
time his britannic majefty confiders how great is the connection between the interefts even of the republic and the
juftice of this affair, as well as the fundamental laws of the
kingdom; laws which were not only obferved for two
centuries, but renewed by treaties with the northern powers,
fo folemn, that they do not permit the leaft alteration to be
undertaken, unlefs with the general confent of the contract-
ing parties. For thefe caufes his britannic majefty, filled
with confidence of the equity and penetration of his polifh
majefty, who, from the beginning of his reign, has given fo
many teftimonies of zeal for the happinefs of mankind, and
of love towards the adminiftration of juftice in the republic,
has not the leaft doubt that his juft defires will no longer be
oppofed by references to inefficacious conftitutions, eftablifhed in the midft of inteftine troubles, contradicted by the
formal proteftations and exprefs declarations on the part of
foreign powers.

                                        Although

Although the rights and privileges of the Diffidents are founded on a doctrine, whofe principles of charity and benevolence make it characteriftical of chriftianity; and the divinity of its inftitutor, who firft preached it, renders it ftill lefs a matter of doubt; yet it is this religion, of which the exercife is difturbed, and of which its profeffors are excluded from all honourable employments, and deprived of all means of ferving their country. Neverthelefs, their rights and privileges have been confirmed to them by many ordinances of the kingdom, fettled by fo many treaties, fupported on foundations fo facred and fo evident to the eyes of all nations, that the underfigned minifter of a monarch who preferves towards the republic the fincereft fentiments of friendfhip, and of inclination to give proofs of them on every occafion, flatters himfelf, that the mediation of the king his mafter will produce the effects which he may naturally promife himfelf; that the wifdom of the nation affembled will afford a remedy to the evils which rend the ftate, and opprefs the Diffidents; and that, with regard to things ecclefiaftical and civil, they may be re-eftablifhed in the fituation they were in before the treaty of Oliva. As to the reft, the fincere wifhes of his britannic majefty for the glory of the king of Poland, and for the profperity of the republic, are fo notorious, that it would be ufelefs to give frefh affurances of them. In the meanwhile, the underfigned cannot avoid reiterating them, as an inconteftable proof of their reality.

(Signed)   WROUGHTON.

No. VI.

COPY *of a* LETTER *of her* IMPERIAL MAJESTY *of all the* RUSSIAS, *to his Excellency Count* VLADIMIR ORLOFF, *Director of the Academy of Sciences at* PETERSBURG.

MONS. COUNT ORLOFF,

HAVING been informed, that in the summer of the year 1769, the planet Venus will pass over the sun, I write you this letter, that you may acquaint the academy of sciences on my part, 1. That it is my pleasure that the academy should procure the observations to be made with the utmost care; and that I desire, in consequence, to know, 2. which are the most advantageously situated places of the empire that the academy has destined for this observation; to the end that, in case it should be necessary to erect any buildings, workmen, &c. may be sent, and proper measures be taken. 3. That if there be not a sufficient number of astronomers in the academy for completing the observations in the places pitched upon by the academy, I propose, and take upon me to find out, among my marine subjects, such as, during the interval between the present time and the transit of Venus, may be perfected in the habit of observing under the eyes of the professors, so as to be employed to advantage in this expedition, and to the satisfaction of the academy. You will, Mr. Count, transmit me the answer of the academy, with its full opinion about every thing above, that I may give orders for the whole without loss of time.

CATHARINE.

Mosco, 3 *March* 1767.

COPY

Copy of a Letter from M. Ramoffsky of the Imperial Academy of Sciences at Petersburg, to Mr. Short of the Royal Society of London.

Sir,

I expected your letter impatiently, and received it the 1ʃth of October. We were ſomewhat in doubt as to our anſwering the views of our ſovereign, till the arrival of your letter, which diſſipated our uneaſineſs in reſpect of the inſtruments. Judge yourſelf, ſir, how ſatisfactory it was to us to underſtand that you would take upon you to procure us the neceſſary inſtruments, and, moreover, to give us your advice how to proceed ſuccefsfully in this important obſervation.

I thank you, ſir, in the name of the academy, and on my account eſpecially, hoping a more favourable occaſion of teſtifying my obligations. At preſent, I refer to your judgment the meaſures the academy has taken with relation to the tranſit of Venus.

Purſuant to her imperial majeſty's orders, in a letter to his excellency count Vladimir Orloff, director of the academy, the copy whereof I herewith ſend you ; the academy having repreſented, that the propereſt places in the ruſſian empire for the obſervation of the duration of the tranſit, are Kola, and the parts near it, and for the exit, the borders of the caſpian ſea, has beſeeched her majeſty to be pleaſed to ſend two obſervers to the north, and two to the Caſpian. The ſtations named by the academy are Kola, Solowetſkoi monaſtir, Aſtrakhan, and Orenburg. The empreſs, in accordance to the repreſentations of the academy, apprehenſive of the precarious ſtate of the weather, at the end of May, at Kola and thereabouts, has been pleaſed to diſtribute four other obſervers among thoſe quarters. The academy, availing itſelf of the high protection her imperial majeſty has deigned to extend to this enterpriſe, has deter-

mined

mined one to Yakoutík, where the duration will not be
$2\frac{1}{2}$ lefs than at Kola, Torneao, and Cajaneburg.

Mr. Wargentin has informed me, that Mr. Mallet of
Upfal is preparing for Torneao, and Mr. Planmann for his
former Cajaneburg ; fo that this country will be fo fecure in
fuch a multiplicity of obfervers, that it may be well hoped
that fome ftation or other will not fail of affording a complete
obfervation of this phænomenon.

St. Peterfburg, 23 *October* 1767.

No. VII.

MANIFESTO *of the* GRAND SIGNIOR, *conceruing the War
declared by his* HIGHNESS *againft the* EMPRESS *of* RUSSIA,
delivered the 30th *of* October 1767, *to the* FOREIGN
MINISTERS *refiding at* CONSTANTINOPLE.

IT may clearly be feen by what follows, that the Sublime
Porte has ftrictly obferved the articles of the peace eftablifhed between this empire and the court of Ruffia,
who, on the contrary, has infringed them in many
inftances.

The court of Ruffia, againft the faith of treaties, has
not defifted from building various fortreffes on the frontiers
of the two ftates, and has provided them with troops and
ammunition.

In the year 1177 (or 1763), on the death of Auguftus
the third, king of Poland, the republic of Poland, intending, according to the fyftem of the polifh liberty, to proceed to the election of a king, the court of Ruffia fet up
for a king a private polifh officer, in whofe family there had
never been any king, and to whom loyalty was not becoming ; and has, by fiding with this king, intruded on and
                                                    traverfed,

traverfed, againft the will of the republic, all the affairs of
the Poles. The Porte having given notice of this to the
ruffian refident, he declared that the republic of Poland
having required a certain number of troops to protect its own
liberty, 6000 horfe and 1000 kofaks were granted for that
purpofe, who had neither cannon nor ammunition with them,
and were to be under the command of the republic, and
that there was not a fingle ruffian foldier above that number
in Poland. Yet, when he was afked, fome time after, why
the court of Ruffia had fent more troops into Poland, and
why violence had been ufed on the election of Poniatofsky,
fon of one of the grandees of Poland, the faid refident
affured, by a writing figned with his hand, that his court
had not declared for any perfon, nor had ever made ufe of
violent means for the election of any one whatfoever. Notwithftanding this affurance and declaration, the court of
Ruffia has been continually fending troops, cannon, and
ammunition, under the command of its own generals, who
continued to attack the polifh liberty, and put to death
thofe who refufed to fubmit to the perfon that themfelves
had not elected for their king, and who was not the fon of
a king; ftripping them, with clamour and violence, of their
goods and eftates. Such a conduct being productive of
confufion in the good order of the Sublime Porte, he was
given to underftand that, according to the tenor of the
articles of the old and new imperial capitulations, the court
of Ruffia muft order her troops to evacuate Poland; this
the faid refident promifed by feveral memorials figned; but
this promife has not been fulfilled. In the mean time, the
Sublime Porte received advice, that fome ruffian troops had
been fent to Balta, (one of the muffulman frontiers,) with
fome artillery, and had unexpectedly attacked the mufful-
mans, and maffacred upwards of a thoufand perfons, men,
women, and children.

The Sublime Porte, having again demanded fatisfaction
from the court of Ruffia for this outrage, which, againft
the tenor of treaties, had been committed with artillery;
and

and the khan of Krimea having alſo demanded ſatiſfaction
for the ſame, the ſaid court denied the fact, alleging that
the Haydamacks had done ſome damage, but that care
would be taken to puniſh them ; although it is notorious
that the Haydamacks never make uſe of cannon nor bombs
in their irruptions. The Sublime Porte, notwithſtanding,
ſtill perſiſted in requiring ſatisfaction for ſuch a conduct, and
ſtill demanded the reaſon why the court of Ruſſia would
not, theſe three years paſt, withdraw its troops from
Poland, ſince the articles of the treaty, concluded in 1133
(1719), and that of 1152 (1738), ſtipulate, " That as
often as any event ſhall happen, capable of diſturbing the
perpetual peace of the two empires, they ſhould proceed
ipſo facto to the means of terminating them in an amicable
manner ;" nevertheleſs the outrages and devaſtations at
Balta have been denied, and the puniſhment of thoſe who
had the boldneſs to be guilty of them, has been poſtponed
and even neglected.   The ſilence itſelf of the ruſſian reſident,
who having been invited to come to the Porte to anſwer for
this proceeding, and to declare what his court meant by ſtill
keeping its troops in Poland, proves the infraction of the
treaty.   At laſt he was aſked definitively, whether, according to the ancient and new treaties, which ſubſiſt between
the two empires, the court of Ruſſia would deſiſt from
meddling with the affairs of Poland, under pretence of
guarantee and promiſe : he replied, that his full power was
limited, and that he could not anſwer thereupon, ſince that
article was known to his court only.   Such a behaviour
plainly demonſtrates that the above-mentioned power thinks
proper to take upon itſelf the infraction of treaties ; therefore it is, that the illuſtrious doctors of the law have given
by *fetras* (or legal ſentences) their anſwers, that, " according to the exigency of juſtice, it was neceſſary to make war
againſt the Muſcovites :" an opinion that has been unani-
mouſly confirmed.   Thus the arreſt of the ſaid reſident
being become neceſſary, we give by theſe preſents notice
to all the powers of Europe, that the ſaid reſident ſhall be

guarded

guarded in the caftle of the Seven Towers; and that, during the whole time that this tranfaction has lafted, the Sublime Porte has done nothing that might break the friendfhip, nor any thing contrary to the articles of the treaties concluded between the two empires, &c.

The DECLARATION *of the* IMPERIAL COURT *of* RUSSIA *to the* COURTS *of* EUROPE, *upon the* Arreft *of its* Minifter refident at CONSTANTINOPLE.

HER imperial majefty, in taking a part in the tranfactions of the republic of Poland, as humanity on one fide, and the obligations of her crown on the other, had prompted her, was no lefs careful to conduct herfelf in fuch a manner as not to give any umbrage to a jealous and powerful neighbour : every part of her conduct was public; and fhe had likewife a particular attention to communicate in confidence to the ottoman Porte her refolutions upon every ftep fhe took, and the conduct fhe intended to obferve, till the peace and tranquillity of that kingdom was entirely re-eftablifhed. But the enemies to the peace of thefe two empires were not wanting to blacken at the Porte all the actions of her imperial majefty, and to fow there the feeds of difcord by the moft falfe imputations. The Porte, reftrained by the upright conduct the court of Ruffia continued to maintain towards them, liftened, but it was with caution, to the calumny that was fpread. Some attention to the affairs of Poland, and an impartial examination of what Ruffia had done, compared with the overtures made by that court at the Porte, had difpelled all fufpicion, and the public tranquillity feemed to be no more threatened. The common enemies, however, repeated their infinuations with more rage and audacity than ever, to impofe upon the credulity of the turkifh nation, and infufed a fpirit of difcontent among them, which called for the notice of government; for it

had .

had forced its way even into the feraglio. The change in the miniftry, brought about by thefe events, foon produced a revolution in the fyftem of peace, equally dear to both nations. The new vizir, upon his advancement, immediately fent for Mr. Obrefkoi, her imperial majefty's refident at the Porte, and, after having caufed to be read in his prefence a declaration full of heavy charges againft his court, part of which have already been invalidated by the moft fair and candid explanations, and others that had never exifted, or were ever thought of, the vizir preffed him to fign immediately, under the guarantee of the allies of his fovereign, fome very offenfive conditions, in regard to which there never had been made the leaft propofal during the whole courfe of the operations in Poland. Thefe conditions, very derogatory to the honour and glory of an emprefs accuftomed to receive no law, propofed in a tone and form repugnant to the freedom of negotiation adopted by every power, were attended with the alternative of an immediate rupture of the perpetual peace between the two empires. The ruffian minifter, confident of the upright intentions of his court, and confcious of the probity of his own conduct, as having fulfilled the duties of a long miniftry, was incapable of unworthily degrading his court and his own character by a humiliating engagement, and which would have exceeded the power and commiffion of any minifter, let them be ever fo extenfive; he gave therefore a pofitive refufal, as became his honour and his duty; and the refolution of the divan, which followed immediately after, was to arreft him, and part of his retinue, and carry him to the caftle of the Seven Towers. It would be needlefs for the imperial court of Ruffia to dwell any longer upon this event, or to enter here into an examination of it. The fact fpeaks for itfelf. The honour and glory of her imperial majefty—the regard to her empire, point out the part it is right for her to take. Confiding in the juftice of her caufe, fhe appeals to all chriftian courts on the

fituation

ituation fhe finds herfelf in with regard to the common enemy of chriftianity, certain as fhe is, that her conduct will meet with equal approbation from each of them, and that fhe fhall have the advantage to join to the divine protection the juft affiftance of her friends, and the good wifhes of all Chriftendom.

No. VIII.

A Letter *from* M. De Voltaire, *to the* Russian Ambassador *at* Paris.

I SEE by the letters which her imperial majefty and your excellency honour me with, how greatly your nation is rifing, while I am afraid that, in fome refpects, ours is beginning to degenerate. The emprefs deigns herfelf to tranflate that chapter of Belifarius, which fome college-fellows traduce at Paris. We fhould be overwhelmed with fhame and fcorn, if all the men of worth, of whom there is a great number in France, did not ftrongly ftand up againft the egregious fcandal of the times. Folly, ignorance, and envy, there will always be in any country; but then there will alfo be in it fcience and good tafte. I dare even aver to you that, in general, our principal military, and, as to what concerns the counfel, our counfellors of ftate, and the mafters of requefts, are more enlightened than they were in the fhining age of Lewis the fourteenth. Great talents are ftill rare; but fcience and reafon are more common than they.

I fee with pleafure that there is forming in Europe an immenfe republic of cultivated underftandings. The light diffufes and communicates itfelf on all fides. I have things come to me from the north that aftonifh me. Within thefe

laft

laſt fifteen years there has been operated a revolution in the human underſtanding, that will form a great epoch. The outcries of the pedants proclaim the approach of this great change, as the croaking of the crows forebodes fair weather.

I know nothing of the book of M. de la Riviere, which you do me the honour of mentioning to me; but can hardly believe that the author, while avoiding the faults into which M. de Monteſquieu may have fallen, has gone beyond him in thoſe points in which that ſhining genius is in the right. I ſhall ſend for his book; and in the meanwhile congratulate the author on his being ſo near ſuch a ſovereign and empreſs, who patronizes all the talents in foreigners, and whoſe maternal care gives birth to them in her own dominions. But it is you whom I eſpecially congratulate on repreſenting her ſo worthily at Paris.

I have the honour to be, &c.

No. IX.

COUNTER-DECLARATION of the COURT of WARSAW.

THE underwritten miniſters of the king and republic of Poland, having laid before his majeſty the declarations given in on the 18th and 26th of September, by the miniſters from the courts of Vienna, Peterſburg, and Berlin; and his majeſty having taken the advice of his ſenate thereupon, the underwritten are commanded to make the following anſwer thereto:

The diſintereſted and ſucceſsful pains of her majeſty the empreſs of all the Ruſſias, to preſerve tranquillity in Poland during the laſt interregnum, and promote the free election of the reigning king, univerſally recognized; the concurrence

rence of the king of Pruffia in the fame defigns ; and the fyftem of neutrality at that time adopted by the emprefs-queen ; are circumftances which, appreciated as they ought to be by the king, will never be effaced from his memory or heart.

The king is happy in feeing the regulations and internal eftablifhments of the diets, immediately fucceeding the death of Auguftus III. declared " ufeful and falutary" by the three powers : he would ever wifh the emanations of the fovereign power of the republic to be regarded with a favourable eye by all his neighbours.

All Europe is long fince informed of the original and fucceffive caufes of the prefent troubles in Poland : all Europe knows, that the king, and the foundeft part of the nation, exerted their utmoft endeavours to prevent the rife and ftop the progrefs of them ; unfortunately thefe efforts have been unfuccefsful ; and certainly the confequences have been dreadful. The fupreme and legal authority of the ftate has been denied by fome ; anarchy has fpread itfelf over the provinces ; all Poland has been impoverifhed, ravaged, trodden under foot, as well by her own citizens, as by foreign troops : fhe has felt, and all Europe has feen, thofe fufferings proportioned to the length of time thefe troops have been in the country, the orders of their refpect-ive courts, and the manner in which their orders have been put in execution.

In a word, five years of fcourge and defolation have ruined this country, and make the return of peace a matter of urgent and indifpenfable neceffity.

The engagements entered into by the three powers, to co-operate in effectuating this great work, appeared, therefore, full of humanity, and would have been regarded by the king with the livelieft gratitude, if the latter part of their declaration had left room for any fentiment but thofe of the utmoft furprife and the moft profound grief.

Thefe

These courts pretend confiderable claims on the unhappy
Poland: a plan of indemnification, the actual and effectual
feizure of equivalents, are avowed.

The ftrict attention of the king and republic to fulfil all
their engagements with thefe powers; the laws of good
neighbourhood fo religioufly obferved by Poland; the
manner, fo friendly and full of regard, in which the king
has reprefented, on fo many occafions, the different fubjects of
complaint he had unfortunately had againft his neighbours;
the prefent fituation of Poland, fo worthy in all refpects of
the compaffion of generous and fenfible minds; all fhould
have fecured to him the return of mutual good-will, and
protected him for ever from enterprifes fo injurious to his
rights and the legality of his poffeffions.

The rights of the republic to all her provinces have every
poffible mark of folidity and authenticity; an uninterrupted
poffeffion of many ages, avowed and maintained by the moft
folemn treaties, and particularly by thofe of Velaw and
Oliva, guaranteed by the houfe of Auftria, by the crowns
of France, England, Spain, and Sweden; by the treaty of
1686, with Ruffia; by the exprefs and recent declarations
of this laft power; by thofe of Pruffia in 1764; and laftly,
by treaties with the houfe of Auftria, ftill in full force and
vigour; on thefe foundations the rights of the republic are
grounded.

The court of Warfaw contents itfelf with barely point-
ing them out at prefent, referving the right of fupporting
them by proofs more ample and particular in time and
place.

What titles can the three powers oppofe to thefe? If
they are titles dug out of the obfcurity of ancient times,
of thofe times of fudden and momentary revolutions, which
erected and deftroyed, ceded and reftored ftates in the fhort
fpace of a few months or years; thefe titles, if admitted,
would re-unite to the kingdom of Poland many provinces
which formerly belonged to it, but have for many years
been

been occupied by the very powers who now form pretenfions on her.

But as it is undeniable, that not only tranfactions buried in the oblivion of diftant ages, but all tranfactions whatever, are annihilated by fubfequent ftipulations ; as all the latter ftipulations between Poland and her neighbours oppofe directly the partition they now would make, it follows, that the titles on which that partition is founded, cannot be admitted, without undermining the rights of every ftate, without fhaking every throne from its foundation.

The very powers who declare that the fituation of Poland will not permit them to obtain juftice in the ordinary ways of proceedings, cannot be ignorant that its prefent fituation is accidental and momentary ; that it is in their own power to change it. Their confent alone is wanting to reftore the republic to the free and lawful exercife of its independent fovereignty. That would be time to produce and examine their claims. This is the method of proceeding which the king had a right to demand from the equity of the three courts, which he could not but expect to be adopted, rely-ing on the letter written to him by the emprefs-queen of Hungary and Bohemia, on the 28th of January 1771.

But the prefent proceedings of the three courts, giving the moft ferious object of complaint to the king ; and the duties of his crown not permitting him to be filent on this occafion, he declares in the moft folemn manner, that he looks upon the actual feizure of the provinces of Poland by the courts of Vienna, Peterfburg, and Berlin, as unjuft, violent, and contrary to his lawful rights ; he appeals to the treaties and powers guarantees of his kingdom and its appurtenances. And laftly, full of confidence in the juftice of the Almighty, he lays his rights at the feet of the eternal throne, and puts his caufe into the hands of the King of kings, the fupreme judge of nations : and, in the full affurance of his fuccour, he protefts folemnly, and

before the whole univerfe, againſt every ſtep taken, or to
be taken, towards the diſmembering of Poland.

   Given at Warſaw, Oct. 17th, 1772.

            Signed by the great chancellors of Poland and
            Lithuania.

DECLARATION *of the* IMPERIAL MINISTER *at the* COURT *of* WARSAW.

HER majeſty the empreſs-queen of Hungary and Bohemia has ſeen, with unſpeakable aſtoniſhment, the little
impreſſion made by the declaration preſented to his poliſh
majeſty by the underwritten, and the miniſters from Peterſburg and Berlin, in order to accelerate a definitive arrangement between the republic and the three neighbouring
powers, touching the pretenſions formed by the ſaid powers
on Poland ; pretenſions which the eſſential intereſts of their
crowns will not permit them to expoſe to the hazard of
future contingencies, and of thoſe troubles with which
Poland has at all times been agitated.

   The juſtice and dignity of the three courts preſcribe
bounds to their moderation : this truth can neither eſcape
the diſcernment of his poliſh majeſty, nor be indifferent to
his heart, if the cries of his country have preſerved their
influence there.

   Her majeſty the empreſs-queen of Hungary and Bohemia
hopes, therefore, that the king will not expoſe his kingdom
to events which muſt be the conſequences of his delay to
aſſemble a diet, and enter on a negotiation, which alone
can ſave his country, reſtore vigour to the conſtitution of
the republic, which has received ſo many and ſo dangerous
ſhocks ; and terminate the evils to which private intereſt,
ambition, hatred, and diſſentions, have given riſe.

   Done at Warſaw, Dec. 4th, 1772.

            (Signed)   RZEWICKI.

Note.—The miniſters from Peterſburg and Berlin delivered the next day each a declaration in the ſame words.

ANSWER *of the* COURT *of* WARSAW *to the preceding Piece.*

IN anfwer to the declarations of the courts of Vienna, Peterfburg, and Berlin, the underwritten have orders to inform the minifters of the faid courts, that the king, being informed of their defires refpecting the convocation of a diet, and of the inconveniencies which may arife from delays, is determined to comply, as far as it is in his power, not only with the view of taking away all pretext of aggravating the evils which afflict Poland, but under the hopes that this mark of regard will operate on the generofity of the three powers, fo as to induce them to put a fpeedy end to thefe troubles, in a manner the moft equitable and advantageous to the republic.

In confequence hereof, his majefty has iffued circular letters for the convocation of a full council of the fenate, which muft indifpenfably precede the fummoning of a diet ; and has fixed the fame to the 8th of February following ; a term which leaves no more than the time abfolutely neceffary for the arrival of the diftant fenators.

Done at Warfaw, this 14th of December 1772.

Signed by the chancellors of Poland and Lithuania.

No. X.

EXTRACT *of a* LETTER *from* CATHARINE II. *late* EMPRESS *of* RUSSIA, *to* M. DE VOLTAIRE.

SIR,

THE brightnefs of the northern ftar is a mere aurora borealis. It is nothing more than giving to a neighbour

fomething

fomething of our own fuperfluity. But to be the advocate of human kind, the defender of oppreffed innocence ; by this you will be indeed immortalized. The two caufes of Calas and Sirven have procured you the veneration due to fuch miracles. You have combated the united enemies of man-kind, fuperftition, fanaticifm, ignorance, chicane, bad judges, and the power lodged in them all together. To furmount fuch obftacles required both talents and virtue. You have fhewn the world that you poffefs both. You have carried your point. You defire, fir, fome relief for the Sirven family. Can I poffibly refufe it ? Or, fhould you praife me for the action, would there be the leaft foundation for it ? I own to you, that I fhould be much better pleafed if my bill of exchange could pafs unknown. Neverthelefs, if you think my name, unharmonious as it is, may be of any fervice to thofe victims of the fpirit of perfecution, I leave it to your difcretion ; and you may announce me, provided it be no way prejudicial to the parties.

No. XI.

ALPHABETICAL LIST *of the* TOWNS *of the* RUSSIAN EMPIRE, *ſhewing in what Government they lie, and how many Verſts diſtant from the Reſidence, from the Metropolis, and from their reſpective Government Towns, as far as could be collected from the Accounts delivered to* CATHARINE II.

The names of the government towns are diſtinguiſhed by *italics.*

Towns.	In what government.	Verſts from St. Peterſb.	Verſts from Moſco.	Verſts from government-town.
Aktyrka	Kharkoff	1453	723	106
Aklanſk	Irkutſk	10497	9767	4674
Alapayefsk	Perme			510
Alatyr	Simbirſk	1358	618	133
Alexandriya	Ekatarinoſlavl			184
Alexandrof	Vladimir	824	101	117
Alexandrofsk	Caucafus			150
Alexin	Tula	860	130	60
Alexopol	Ekatarinoſlavl			115
Archangel		1145	1236	
Ardatoff	Niſhnè-Novgorod			150
Ardatoff on Alatyr	Simbirſk	1337	597	148
Arenſberg	Riga	626	1356	319
Arſamas	Niſhnè-Novgorod	1120	380	109
Arſk	Kaſan	1463	735	55
Aſoff	Ekatarinoſlavl	1998	1268	625
Aſtrakhan	Caucafus	2142	1412	630
Atkarſk	Saratoff	1630	902	79
Atſchinſk	Tobolſk	4694	3964	1809
Babinovitſchi	Mohileff			111
Bachmut	Ekatarinoſlavl	1490	760	368
Balachna	Niſhnè-Novgorod	1145	415	32
Balaſchoff	Saratoff			244
Baltic port	Reval	394	1122	44
Barguſinſk	Irkutſk	6345	5617	524
Belebey	Ufa			139
Bereſin	Tſchernigoff			36

Bereſoff

Towns.	In what government.	Verſts from St. Peterſb.	Verſts from Moſco.	Verſts from government- town.
Bereſoff	Tobolſk	3814	3084	929
Bieleff	Tula	973	239	120
Bielgorod	Kurſk	1356	626	132
Bielitza	Mohileff			194
Bieloy	Smolenſk	709	410	143
Bielopolye	Kharkoff	1585	857	217
Bieloſerſk	Novgorod	569	540	532
Bielovodſk	Voronetſh	1545	803	307
Biezveſk	Tver	625	287	121
Biiſk	Kolhyvan			260
Biryutſch	Voronetſch	1357	617	150
Birſk	Ufa	1927	1197	105
Bobroff	Voronetſch	1265	535	87
Bogatye	Kuıſk	1330	600	106
Bogodukhoff	Kharkoff	1471	741	60
Bogoroditzk	Tula	957	227	45
Bogorodſk	Moſco			50
Bogutſchar	Voronetſch	1475	735	238
Bolkhoff	Orel	1020	290	54
Boriſoglyebſk	Yaroſlavl	*	†	32
Boriſoglyebſk on the Vorona	Tamboff	1359	629	152
Borovitſchi	Novgorod	360	454	183
Borofsk	Kaluga	893	163	78
Borſna	Tchernigoff	1396	666	90
Brianſk	Orel	1077	347	138
Bronnitzy	Moſco	781	51	
Bugulma	Ufa	1687	957	220
Buguruſlan	Ufa			279
Buï	Koſtroma	932	396	130
Buinſk	Simbirſk	1462	722	70
Buſuluk	Ufa			375
Cronſtadt	St. Peterſburg	47	777	
Dalmatoff	Perme			510
Daniloff	Yaroſlavl	810	316	63
Dankoff	Riazane	950	220	158
Deſchkin	Orel	1060	330	58
St. Dmitri fort	Ekatarinoſlavl	1968	1238	595
Dmitriyef	Kurſk	1241	511	99

* By the way of Uglitſch 814, by the way of Poſchek 797.

† By the way of Yaroſlavl and Roſt. 273, by the way of Poſchek 265.

Towns.	In what government.	Verſts from St. Peterſb.	Verſts from Moſco.	Verſts from government-town.
Dmitroff	Moſco	702	62	
Dmitrofsk	Orel	1181	451	84
Dnieprofsk	Tavrida			300
Donetzk	Ekatarinoſlavl			443
Dorogobuſh	Smolenſk	793	298	86
Doroninſk	Irkutſk	6644	5964	871
Dorpat	Riga	319	1049	230
Driezin	Polotſk	691	697	68
Dukhofshina	Smolenſk	727	363	51
Dynaburg	Polotſk	794	800	173
Ekatarinenburg	Perme	2308	1578	358
Ekatarinoſlaf		1596	868	
Elizabethgrad	Ekatarinoſlavl	1759	1411	211
Epiphan	Tula	962	232	50
Eupatoria	Tavrida			60
Fateſch	Kurſk	1193	463	46
Fellin	Riga			241
Frederikſham	Vyburg	326	1056	186
Gadyatch	Tchernigoff	*	†	254
Galitch	Koſtroma	919	396	117
Gdoff	St. Peterſburg	216	871	
Georgiefsk	Caucaſus	2528	1800	60
Glaſoff	Viatka			214
Glinſk	Tchernigoff			210
Glukhoff	NovgorodSieverſkoi	1280	550	
Goltva	Kief			283
Gordatoff	Niſhnè-Novgorod			70
Gorodetz	Polotzk	698	553	144
Gorodiſchtſche	Penſa			42
Gorodnia	Tchernigoff			50
Gorokovetch	Vladimir	1039	332	157
Gradiſchtſche	Ekatarinoſlavl			136
Griaſovetch	Vologda	709	384	42
Giaſk	Smolenſk	581	160	222
Habſal	Reval	456	1126	95
Inſara	Penſa	1290	560	89
Irbit	Perme	2683	1953	572
Irkutſk		5823	5093	
Iſchim	Tobolſk	2935	2205	344

* Viâ Mtzenſk and Kurſk — — 1450 720
† Viâ Smolenſk and Baturin — — 1712 982

Iſchiginſk

Towns.	In what government.	Verfts from St. Peterfb.	Verfts from Mofco.	Verfts from government-town.
Ifchiginfk	Irkutfk	10307	9577	4484
Ifium	Kharkoff	1550	820	111
Kadnikoff	Vologda	695	468	42
Kadyi	Koftroma	950	427	147
Kaigorod	Viatka	1972	1242	246.
Kainfk	Tobolfk	3788	3058	903
Kaliafin	Tver	734	294	168
Kalitva	Voronetch	1421	681	193
Kaluga		890	160	
Kamyfchin	Saratoff	1806	1076	174
Kamyfchloff	Perme			483
Kanadyei	Simbirfk	1537	797	131
Karatfcheff	Orel	1102	372	84
Kargopol	Olonetz	618	1078	342
Karfun	Simbirfk	1423	683	91
Kafan		1465	735	
Kafchin	Tver	716	312	150
Kafimoff	Riafane	1010	280	140
Kem	Olonetz	885	1479	455
Kerenfk	Penfa	1199	460	135
Kexholm	Viborg	146	876	130
Kharkoff		1421	680	
Kherfon	Ekatarinoflavl	*	†	290
Kholm	Plefkoff	336	592	268
Khoperfk	Saratoff	1419	689	
Khorol	Kief			223
Khotmyfhfk	Kharkoff	1455	725	71
Khvalynfk	Saratoff			197
Kieff		1582	852	
Kinburn fort	Tavrida	2091	1361	
Kinefchma	Koftroma	885	347	83
Kirenfk	Irkutfk	6768	6038	945
Kiriloff	Novgorod	590	495	580
Kirfanoff	Tamboff	1295	565	88
Kirfhatfh	Vladimir	850	123	115
Kifliar	Caucafus	2642	1912	
Klimovitfchi	Mohileff			128
Klin	Mofco	648	82	
Kniaginin	Nifhnè-Novgorod			96

* *Viâ* Mtzenfk, Kurfk, and Krementfhuk　—　1903　1174
† *Viâ* Smolenfk, Baturin, Polt. and Krementfhuk　2141　1411

Kola

Towns.	In what government.	Verſts from St. Peterſb.	Verſts from Moſco.	Verſts from government-town.
Kola	Archangel	1379	2109	1021
Kolmogory	Archangel			
Kologriff	Koſtroma	968	534	254
Kolomna	Moſco	830	100	
Kolyvan		5154	4424	
Konotop	Novgorod Sieverſkoi	1345	615	115
Konſtantinograd	Ekatarinoſlavl	973	864	104
Kopyſs	Mohilef			49
Korop	Novgorod Sieverſkoi		.	70
Korotoyak	Voronetch	1313	573	80
Korotſcha	Kurſk	1359	629	135
Kortſcheva	Tver			82
Koſchira	Tula	900	170	80
Koſeletz	Kieff	1510	780	72
Koſelſk	Kaluga	940	210	57
Koſloff	Tamboff	1155	425	72
Koſtroma		802	280	
Kotelnitſch	Viatka	1811	1081	95
Kotiakoff	Simbirſk	1404	664	110
Kovroff	Vladimir	964	237	62
Kraſnoborſk	Vologda	1100	1006	580
Kraſnoy	Smolenſk	823	430	46
Kraſnoi-Kholm	Tver	586	326	161
Kraſnoi-Yar	Aſtrakhan	2112	1382	30
Kraſnoyarſk	Kolyvan	4839	4109	1981
Kraſnokutſk	Kharkoff	1508	767	86
Kraſnoſlobodſk	Penſa	1564	834	173
Kraſnouſimſk	Perme	2077	1347	188
Kreſtzi	Novgorod	279	451	93
Krolevetch	Novgorod Sieverſkoi	1319	589	64
Kromy	Orel	1133	403	36
Kropivna	Tula	952	222	40
Kungur	Perme	2051	1323	91
Kupenſk	Voronetch	1663	923	283
Kurgan	Toboſk	2875	2145	414
Kurmyſch	Simbirſk	1237	500	257
Kurſk		1224	494	
Kuſmodemyanſk	Kaſan	1294	564	181
Kuſnetzk	Kolyvan	4737	4007	
Kuſnetzk	Saratoff			197
Ladoga	St. Peterſburg	150	744	
Laiſcheff	Kaſan			51

Lalſk

Towns.	In what government.	Verfts from St. Peterfb.	Verfts from Mofco.	Verfts from government-town.
Lalſk	Vologda	1110	981	555
Lebedyan	Tamboff	1104	374	177
Lebedin	Kharkoff	1540	810	147
Levkopol	Tavrida			80
Lgoff	Kurſk	1295	565	71
Lichvin	Kaluga	940	210	45
Lipetzk	Tamboff	1162	432	149
Linbim	Yaroſlavl	826	354	101
Liutzin	Polotzk	593	758	164
Livenſk	Voronetch	1403	654	175
Livny	Orel	1090	360	128
Lochvitza	Tſchernigoff	1462	732	210
Lodeinoë Pole	Olonetz	276	809	215
Lubney	Kieff	1505	775	190
Luch	Koſtroma	913	347	129
Luga	St. Peterſburg	135	614	
Lukoyanoff	Niſhnè-Novgorod			158
Makarief	Niſhnè-Novgorod			80
Makarief	Koſtroma	98	474	195
Malmyſh	Viatka			249
Maloarchangel	Orel	1143	413	70
Maloyaroſlavl	Kaluga	847	113	52
Mamadyſh	Kaſan			146
Mariupol	Ekatarinoſlavl			321
Medynſk	Kaluga	869	135	57
Melenki	Vladimir	1040	313	138
Melitopol	Tavrida			220
Menſelinſk	Ufa	1769	1035	236
Meſchtſchofsk	Kaluga	980	250	69
Meſen	Archangel	1445	1575	511
Mglinſk	Novgorod Sieverſkoi			141
Michailoff	Riazane	910	180	50
Mirgorod	Kieff	1784	1054	233
Miropolie	Kharkoff	1515	785	133
Mohileff		751	534	
Mokſchan	Penſa	1368	638	37
Mologa	Yaroſlavl	740	260	110
Morſchanſk	Tamboff	1156	426	88
Mofalſk	Kaluga	940	210	77
Mofdok	Caucaſus		243	34
Mofhaiſk	Mofco	816	99	
MOSCO	*Metropolis*	728		

Mſtiſlavl

Towns.	In what government.	Verfts from St. Peterfb.	Verfts from Mofco.	Verfts from government-town.
Mſtiſlavl	Mohilef	914	501	94
Murom	Vladimir	1022	295	120
Myſchkin	Yaroſlavl	763	209	92
Mzenſk	Orel	1044	314	53
Nakhitſchevan	Ekatarinoſlavl			
Nagaibak	Orenburg	1733	1003	540
Naroftſchat	Penſa	1356	626	125
Narva	St. Peterſburg	145	875	
Narym	Tobolſk	4644	3934	1759
Nedrigailof	Kharkoff	1574	844	195
Nerechta	Koſtroma	846	236	43
Nertſchinſk	Irkutſk	6784	6054	961
Neyſhlott	Viburg	390	1120	250
Nevel	Polotzk	1338	618	99
Nieſhin	Tſchernigoff	1444	714	74
Nikitſk	Mofco		31	
Nikolſk	Vologda	1164	1061	637
Niſhnaia Dievitza	Voronetch	1284	544	57
Niſhnè Kamtſchatka	Irkutſk	11699	10969	5876
Niſhnè Lomoff	Penſa	1339	609	96
Niſhnè Novgorod		1120	390	
Niſhneudinſk	Irkutſk	5348	4618	475
Nolin	Viatka			112
Novgorod		186	544	
Novgorod Sieverſkoi		*	†	
Novomieſto	NovgorodSieverſkoi			144
Novomirgorod	Ekatarinoſlavl			288
Novomoſkofsk	Ekatarinoſlavl			18
Novorſheff	Pleſkoff	478	853	132
Novoſil	Tula	1292	458	176
Oboian	Kurſk	1283	553	59
Obvinſk	Perme			50
Odoyef	Tula	940	210	70
Okhanſk	Perme			67
Okhotſk	Irkutſk	9259	8529	3436
Olekminſk	Irkutſk	7754	7024	1931
Olenſk	Irkutſk	9309	8579	3496
Olonetz	Olonetz	280	874	150
Omſk	Tobolſk	3286	2556	693

* By Star. and Smolenſk — — 1150 540
† By Tula and Mofco — — — 1328 598

Onega

Towns.	In what government.	Verfts from St. Petersb.	Verfts from Mosco.	Verfts from government-town.
Onega	Archangel	900	1560	232
Opotfcha	Plefkoff	491	727	137
Oranienbaum	St. Petersburg	40	768	
Oranienburg	Riazane	1093	363	170
Orel		1097	367	
Orenburg	Ufa	1984	1254	319
Orloff	Viatka	1663	933	51
Orfcha	Mohileff	685	466	66
Ofa	Perme	2020	1290	113
Ofkol, old	Kurfk	1309	579	130
Ofkol, new	Kurfk	1379	639	191
Oftafchkoff	Tver	426	347	183
Ofter	Kieff	1532	802	89
Oftrogofk	Voronetch	1326	588	95
Oftroff	Plefkoff	425	800	56
Pavlograd	Ekatarinoflavl			202
Pavlofsk	Voronetch	1380	640	150
Penfa		1394	660	
Pereyaflavl	Kieff	1533	823	78
Perekop	Tavrida			140
Peremyfchl	Kaluga	925	195	28
Pereflavl Riaz.		910	180	
Pereflavl Saliefk	Vladimir	750	125	120
Perevolotfchna	Novgorod	2002	1272	50
Perevos	Nifhnè Novgorod			90
Perme		1949	1219	
Pernau	Riga	479	1190	72
Petropavlofskoi	Irkutfk	10648	9918	4620
Petrozavodfk	Olonetz	430	1024	
Petrofsk	Yaroflavl	819	167	76
Petrofsk	Saratoff	1490	760	105
Petfchory	Plefkoff		807	54
Phanagoria	Tavrida			240
Pinega	Archangel	1245	1288	210
Piriatin	Kieff	1480	750	161
Ples	Koftroma	856	295	54
Plefkoff		*	717	
Podol	Mofco	765	35	
Pogar	Novgorod Sieverfkoi	1400	670	64
Pokroff	Vladimir	824	97	78

* By way of Narva — — 346
By way of Luga — — 326

Poloizk

Towns.	In what government.	Verfts from St. Peterfb.	Verfts from Mofco.	Verfts from government-town.
Polotzk		643	1373	
Poltava	Ekatarinoflavl	1535	805	171
Porkhof	Plefkoff	336	694	85
Porietfchy	Smolenfk	752	430	73
Pofchekonia	Yaroflavl	718	314	112
Potfchinki	Nifhnè Novgorod			212
Povienetz	Olonetz	595	1189	765
Priluky	Tfchernigoff	1453	723	
Pronfk	Riazane	950	220	50
Pudafh	Olonetz	516	996	240
Putevl	Kurfk	1404	674	100
Refitza	Polotzk	619	784	190
Reval		340	1070	
Riafhfk	Riazane	1000	270	
Riga		552	1053	
Rogatfheff	Mohileff	1396	636	102
Romanoff	Yaroflavl	796	266	34
Romen	Tfchernigoff	1412	682	194
Rofheftvenfk	St. Peterfburg	79		
Roflavl	Smolenfk	880	443	116
Roftoff	Yaroflavl	806	189	54
Rfheff	Tver	631	300	127
Rufa	Mofco	759	88	
Rybnoi	Yaroflavl	806	252	78
Rylfk	Kurfk	1340	610	116
Sadonfk	Voronetch	1130	400	85
Samara	Simbirfk	1633	893	177
Sт.PETERSBURG	*Refidence*		728	
Sapofhok	Riazane	1030	300	120
Saraifk	Riazane	860	130	56
Saranfk	Penfa	1276	546	123
Sarapul	Viatka	1812	1082	380
Saratoff		1632	902	
Safchiverfk	Irkutfk	9192	8462	3369
Schadrinfk	Perme	2488	1758	556
Schatzk	Tamboff	1090	360	157
Schenkurfk	Archangel	800	848	388
Schefchkeyef	Penfa	1306	576	144
Schluffelburg	St. Peterfburg	60	790	
Schtfchigry	Kurfk	1290	478	50
Schuya	Vladimir	969	239	90
Sebefh	Polotzk	533	718	104

Selenginfk

Towns.	In what government.	Verfts from St. Peterfb.	Verfts from Mofco.	Verfts from government-town.
Selenginſk	Irkutſk	6226	5496	403
Semeonoff	Niſhnè Novgorod			60
Semipalatſk	Kolyvan	2992	2262	
Semlianſk	Voronetch	1204	464	40
Serdob	Saratoff			175
Serdobol	Viburg			238
Sergatſch	Niſhnè Novgorod			138
Sergiefsk	Ufa			350
Serpeiſk	Kaluga	980	250	82
Serpukhof	Mofco	818	88	
Sevaſtopol	Tavrida			
Shiganſk	Irkutſk	9125	8395	3302
Shiſdra	Kaluga	1054	320	156
Sienkof	Tſchernigoff			286
Siennoi	Mohilef			151
Sievſk	Orel	1242	512	145
Simbirſk		1485	745	
Simpheropol	Tavrida	2187	1459	
Singileyef	Simbirſk	1519	779	49
Skopin	Riazane	1026	296	88
Slavianſk	Ekatarinoſlavl	1440	710	200
Slobodſkoy	Viatka	1740	1010	28
Smolenſk		716	384	
Solgalitzkaia	Koſtroma	799	502	223
Solikamſk	Perme	2227	1497	263
Solotonoſcha	Kieff			130
Solotſchef	Kharkoff	1459	718	36
Solvytſchegodſk	Vologda	1086	988	560
Sophia	St. Peterſburg	22	706	
Soſnitza	Novgorod Sieverſkoi			
Spaſk	Kaſan			134
Spaſk	Riazane	966	232	52
Spaſk	Tamboff	1300	570	207
Staraia Ruſſa	Novgorod	306	664	120
Staritza	Tver	595	237	73
Staro Bykhoff	Mohilef	984	569	38
Starodub	Novgorod Sieverſkoi	1083	480	81
Stavropol	Caucaſus			
Stavropol	Simbirſk	1589	849	133
Sterlitamazk	Ufa			111
Strietenſk	Irkutſk	6866	6136	1043
Subtzoff	Tver	628	280	116

Sudogda

Towns.	In what government.	Verfts from St. Peterfb.	Verfts from Mofco.	Verfts from government-town.
Sudogda	Vladimir	939	212	37
Sudfcha	Kurfk	1315	585	91
Sumy	Kharkoff	1383	653	175
Suralh	Polotzk	769	558	149
Surafhfk	Novgorod Sieverfkoi			141
Surgut	Tobolfk	3610	2875	725
Sufdal	Vladimir	936	209	32
Svenigorod	Mofco	718	48	
Sviyabfk	Kafan	1445	715	30
Syfran	Simbirfk	1565	825	123
Sytfchofka	Smolenfk		219	227
Tagai	Simbirfk	1436	696	49
Taganrok	Ekatarinoflavl	2036	1306	460
Tamboff		1207	477	
Tara	Tobolfk	3445	2715	560
Tarufa	Kaluga	848	118	62
Temnikoff	Tamboff	1279	549	291
Tetyufchi	Kafan	1585	855	85
Theodofia	Tavrida			
Tichvin	Novgorod	243	744	210
Tim	Kurfk	1243	513	64
Tiumin	Tobolfk	2631	1901	254
Tobolfk		2885	2155	
Tomfk	Tobolfk	4309	3579	1424
Toropetz	Plefkoff	610	497	347
Torfhok	Tver	503	227	63
Totma	Vologda	889	626	200
Troïtzk	Penfa	1386	656	134
Troïtzk	Ufa			462
Trubtfchevfk	Orel	1166	436	169
Tfchaufy	Mohilef			43
Tfchebokfar	Kafan	1350	620	124
Tfchelyabinfk	Ufa	2488	1758	400
Tfchembar	Penfa			129
Tfcherdyn	Perme	2321	1591	364
Tfcherekoff	Mohilef			82
Tfcherepovetch	Novgorod			476
Tfcherkafk	Ekatarinoflavl	1936	1208	
Tfchernigoff		1124	676	
Tfchern	Tula	970	240	
Tfchernoi Yar	Saratoff	1972	1242	499
Tfchiftopoliye	Kafan			125

7   Tfchuchloma

Towns.	In what government.	Versts from St. Petersb.	Versts from Mosco.	Versts from government-town.
Tschuchloma	Koftroma	920	473	167
Tschuguyef	Kharkoff	1414	684	34
Tula		912	182	
Turinſk	Toboſk	2480	1750	405
Turuchanſk	Toboſk	6190	5460	3305
Tver		568	162	
Tzarevo Kokſhaiſk	Kafan	1354	624	126
Tzarevo Santſchurſk	Viatka	1414	684	253
Tzaritzin	Saratoff	1772	1042	355
Tzyvilſk	Kafan	1390	660	102
Ufa		1913	1183	
Uglitſch	Yaroſlavl	734	180	101
Urſhum	Viatka	1631	901	163
Uſman	Tamboff	1226	496	158
Uſtiugvelikoi	Vologda	1000	899	473
Ultioſhna	Novgorod	450	368	357
Uſtſyſolſk	Vologda	1400	1300	876
Valdai	Novgorod	338	392	152
Valk	Riga			149
Valki	Kharkoff	1466	725	53
Valniki	Voronetch	1376	630	208
Varnavin	Koftroma	1132	666	387
Vaſil	Niſhiè Novgorod	1255	525	144
Veiſſenſtein	Reval			34
Velikiye Luki	Pleſkoff	528	601	259
Veliſk	Polotzk	809	598	189
Velſk	Vologda	870	706	280
Venden	Riga			100
Veneff	Tula	860	130	40
Verchnei Lomoff	Penfa	1339	609	106
Verchoturiye	Perme	2503	1773	540
Verchoudinſk	Irkutſk	6116	5388	295
Verchouralſk	Ufa			309
Vereya	Mofco	831	98	
Verro	Riga			236
Veſenberg	Reval			80
Veſyegonſk	Tver	502	406	241
Vetluga	Koftroma	1084	619	339
Viaſma	Smolenſk	587	221	163
Viaſniki	Vladimir	1022	295	120
Viatka		1815	1085	
Vilmanſtrand	Vyburg	190	920	50

Vitebſk

Towns.	In what government.	Verfts from St. Peterfb.	Verfts from Mofco.	Verfts from government-town.
Vitebfk	Polotzk	729	518	109
Vladimir		902	175	
Volmar	Riga		1171	103
Vologda		689	426	
Voloko Lamfk	Mofco	712	101	
Volfk	Saratoff			110
Voltfchanfk	Kharkoff			60
Voronetch		1220	490	
Vofkrefenfk	Mofco		42	
Vyburg		140	870	
Vyfchnei Volotfchok	Tver	432	298	134
Vytegra	Olonetz	426	876	
Yadrin	Kafan	1250	520	186
Yakutfk	Irkutfk	8309	7579	2486
Yalutorofsk	Tobolfk	2715	1985	254
Yamburg	St. Peterfburg	121	854	
Yaranfk	Viatka	1706	972	202
Yarenfk	Vologda	1721	1147	721
Yaroflavl		830	243	
Yegoriefsk	Riazane	814	80	95
Yelabuga	Viatka			373
Yelatma	Tamboff	1055	325	264
Yeletz	Orel	1094	364	183
Yelna	Smolenfk		326	90
Yenefeifk	Tobolfk	5032	4300	2147
Yenotaiyefsk	Aftrakhan	2084	1354	
Yephremoff	Tula	1024	294	112
Yuknoff	Smolenfk		251	194
Yurieff Polfkoi	Vladimir	820	90	50
Yuryevetz Povolfkoi	Koftroma	974	347	172

No. XII.

LIST *of* TOWNS *in the* EMPIRE *of* RUSSIA *erected during the* REIGN *of* CATHARINE II.

In the government of
NOVGOROD :

1. Borovitſchi.
2. Valdai.
3. Kreſtzy.
4. Kiriloff.
5. Tcherepovctch.

TVER :

6. Vyſchnei Volotſchok.
7. Oſtaſchkoff.
8. Koliaſin.
9. Veſiegonſk.
10. Kraſnoi Kholm.
11. Kortſcheva.

SMOLENSK :

12. Poryetſchiye.
13. Yelnia.
14. Sytſchofka.
15. Kaſplia.
16. Kraſnoi.
17. Rapuſoff.
18. Giatſk.

KALUGA :

19. Schiſdra.

YAROSLAVL :

20. Petrofsk.
21. Rybnoi.
22. Myſchkin.

23. Mologa.
24. Daniloff.
25. Boriſogliebſk.

PLESKOFF :

26. Petſchory.
27. Oſtroff.

TULA :

28. Bogoroditzk.
29. Tſchern.
30. Kropivna.

MOHILEF :

31. Tſchauſy.
32. Staroi Bykhoff.
33. Babinovitſchi.
34. Kopys.
35. Siennoi.
36. Tſcherekoff.
37. Klimovitſchi.
38. Rogatſheff.
39. Bielitza.

POLOTZK :

40. Drieſin.
41. Sebeſh.
42. Nevel.
43. Dunaburg.
44. Rieſitza.
45. Liutzin.
46. Veliſh.

47. Goro-

47. Gorodetch.
48. Surafh.

KOSTROMA:

49. Vetluga.
50. Makarieff on the Unfha.
51. Varnavin.

RIAZANE:

52. Skopin.
53. Spafk.
54. Yegoriefsk.

OREL:

55. Defchkin.
56. Malo-Archangelfk.
57. Dmitrofsk.

VLADIMIR:

58. Alexandroff.
59. Kirfhatfch.
60. Pokroff.
61. Koffroff.
62. Sudogda.
63. Viafniki.
64. Melenki.

KURSK.

65. Fatefh.
66. Bogatoi.
67. Schtfchigry.
68. Tim.
69. Dmitrief.
70. Lgoff.

NISHNE NOVGOROD:

71. Gorbatoff.
72. Lukoyanoff.
73. Perevos.
74. Makarieff.

75. Ardatoff.
76. Kniaginin.
77. Semeonoff.
78. Potfchinki.
79. Sergatfch.

TAMBOFF:

80. Kirfanoff.
81. Morfchanfk.
82. Spafk.
83. Lipetzk.

VORONETCH:

84. Sadonfk.
85. Bobroff.
86. Nifhnaia Dievitza.
87. Biryütfch.
88. Livenfk.
89. Kalitva.
90. Kupenfk.
91. Bogutfchar.
92. Bielovodfk.
93. Semlianfk.

EKATARINOSLAUF:

94. Ekatarinoflauf.
95. Kherfon, fort, haven,
    and admiralty, not
    far from the mouth
    of the Dniepr.
96. Novomofkofsk.
97. Alexopol.
98. Konftantinograd.
99. Slavianfk.
100. Donetzk.
101. Mariupol.
102. Pavlograd.
103. Elizabethgrad.
104. Alexandria.
105. Novomirgorod.
106. Nafchitfchevan.
107. Beriflauf.

VOLOGDA:

VOLOGDA:

108. Vclelk.
109. Griafovetch.
110. Kadnikoff.
111. Lalfk.
112. Nikolfk.
113. Krafnoborfk.
114. Uftfyfolfk.

ARCHANGEL:

115. Pinega.
116. Onega.
117. Kolmogory.
118. Schenkurfk.

KHARKOFF:

119. Voltfchanfk.
120. Solotfcheff.
121. Valki.
122. Krafnokutfk.
123. Bogodukhoff.
124. Miropoliye.
125. Biclopoliye.
126. Lebedin.
127. Nedrigailoff.

In St. PETERSBURG Government.

128. Sophia.
129. Rofheftvenfk.
130. Oranienbaum.
131. Luga.

OLONETZ:

132. Petrozavodfk.
133. Povienetch.
134. Vytegra.
135. Kem.
136. Lodeinoe Pole.
137. Pudoga.

VIATKA.

138. Glafofsk.
139. Yelabuga.
140. Malmyfch.
141. Nolinfk.

PENSA:

142. Tfchembar.
143. Gorodifchtfche.
144. Schefchkeyeff.
145. Mokfchan.
146. Troïtzk.
147. Krafnoflobodfk.

SIMBIRSK:

148. Kanadyei.
149. Tagai.
150. Karfun.
151. Kotyakoff.
152. Buinfk.
153. Singileiyeff.
154. Ardatoff on the Alatyr.

SARATOFF.

155. Kvalynfk.
156. Volfk.
157. Kufnetzk.
158. Balafchoff.
159. Atkar.
160. Serdob.

KIEFF:

161. Ofter.
162. Piriatin.
163. Khorol.
164. Goltva.
165. Gorodifchtfche.
166. Solotonofcha.

167. Go-

TSCHERNIGOFF :

167. Gorodnia.
168. Berefin.
169. Glinfk.
170. Lokvitza.
171. Sienkoff.
172. Borfna.

NOVGOROD SIEVERSKOE :

173. Mglinfk.
174. Krolevetch.
175. Pogar.
176. Korop.
177. Sofnitza.
178. Konotop.
179. Novomiefto.
180. Surafh.

KASAN :

181. Laifcheff.
182. Spafk.
183. Schiftopoliye.
184. Mamadyfch.
185. Arfk.
186. Tetyufchi.

PERME :

187. Perme.
188. Okhanfk.
189. Obvinfk.
190. Dalmatoff.
191. Kamyfchloff.
192. Alapaiyeff.
193. Offa.
- 194. Irbit.

In the Mosco Government :

195. Vofkrefenfk.
196. Bogorodfk.
197. Bronnitzy.
198. Nikitfk.
199. Podol.

UFA :

200. Menfelinfk.
201. Bugulminfk.
202. Buguraflanfk.
203. Belebyei.
204. Sterlitamazk.
205. Verchouralfk.
206. Tfchelyabinfk.
207. Troïtzk.
208. Bufuluk.
209. Sergiefsk.

TOBOLSK :

210. Omfk.
211. Ifchin.
212. Kurgan.
213. Yaluturoff.
214. Atfchinfk.
215. Turukhan.
216. Kainfk.

KOLYVAN :

217. Semipalatfk.
218. Kolyvan.
219. Biifk.

CAUCASUS :

220. Georgiefsk.
221. Alexandrofsk.
222. Yenotaiyefsk.
223. Stavropol.

TAVRIDA :

224. Simpheropol.
225. Eupatoria.
226. Dnieprofsk.
227. Melitopol.
228. Phanagoria.
229. Levkopol.

IRKUTZK :

No. XIII.

NOTE *intended for Inſertion at p. 72, of this Volume, but inadvertently omitted.*

THE ſtruggles of the republicans were of no avail, as they were never unanimous among themſelves. Confederations indeed, in great numbers, ſprung up ; from 1767 to 1772, upwards of twenty were reckoned. The moſt remarkable of them was that which was formed entirely ſeparate from all the reſt, by Kraſinſky, biſhop of Kaminietch, who had withdrawn from Warſaw, even before the termination of the diet in 1768, to Baar in Podolia ; and was actuated by a ſpirit of the wildeſt fanaticiſm. The ruſſian ſuperiority alſo quickly diſſolved this league ; three of its chiefs, Kraſinſky, Pulafsky, and Potocki, fled into the turkiſh territory. The remnant, however, of this confederation continued in Poland; they declared the throne to be vacant ; nay, what would ſcarcely be thought poſſible, they carried off the king from the capital, though ſurrounded by poliſh and ruſſian troops ; but a no leſs won-

derful

derful event preferved his life and liberty, without the neceffity of foreign affiftance.

The confufion was fo great, that nothing but a fignal
battle could bring it to an end.   But in order to this,
foreign nations were induced to take part.   France was in
too nervelefs a condition for being able to do much : however, Choifeul, by cabals and bribes, found the means to
effect fomething.   French foldiers too were fent hither to
fight for the independence of Poland againft the Ruffians.
Dumouriez gathered here his firft, though not very brilliant
laurels.

END OF THE APPENDIX.